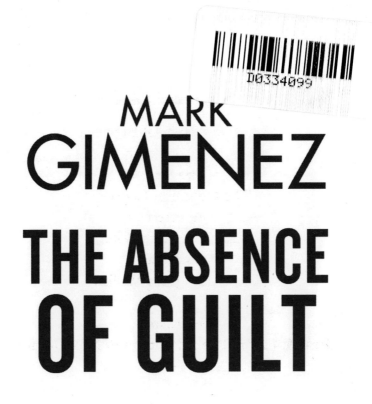

MARK
GIMENEZ

THE ABSENCE
OF GUILT

sphere

SPHERE

First published in 2016 by Navarchus Press LLC
First published in Great Britain in 2016 by Sphere

A CIP catalogue record for this book is available from the British Library.

Hardback ISBN 978-0-7515-6729-8
Trade paperback ISBN 978-0-7515-6730-4

Typeset in Bembo MT by Hewer Text UK Ltd, Edinburgh
Printed and bound in Great Britain by Clays Ltd, St Ives plc

Papers used by Sphere are from well-managed forests and other responsible sources.

MIX
Paper from
responsible sources
FSC
www.fsc.org FSC® C104740

Sphere
An imprint of
Little, Brown Book Group
Carmelite House
50 Victoria Embankment
London EC4Y 0DZ

An Hachette UK Company
www.hachette.co.uk

www.littlebrown.co.uk

For Charlie Rice, may he rest in peace

Author's Note

Back in the late 1980s, while I was a young partner in a large Dallas law firm, I met a terrorist. I didn't know it at the time. At a senior partner's request, I met with a potential client who wanted to invest $100 million in U.S. real estate. He was an older Arab gentleman. When I asked for his contact details, he gave me several locations in London and Europe; and then he said, 'But there are times when I will be unavailable as I will be in the desert of Libya with Muammar Gaddafi.' I asked what he did for Gaddafi. 'Consult.' On what? 'Construction.' Of what? 'Projects.' He declined to be more specific. After escorting him to the elevators, I went to the senior partner and convinced him that the firm didn't need this client. We declined to represent him. End of story.

Or so I thought.

About a year later, I read an article in a national news magazine that reported of his death – and that he was the man who had built Gaddafi's chemical weapons plant. Sarin was reportedly produced at that plant. Twenty-five years later, ISIS captured Libya's cache of sarin.

I met the man who made that possible.

Innocence: The absence of guilt
Black's Law Dictionary, Fifth Ed.

'We will put terror into the hearts of the unbelievers.'
Koran 3:151

Prologue

The Dallas Cowboys don't play in Dallas. They play in Arlington. In Cowboys Stadium – officially known as 'AT&T Stadium' in this age of corporate sponsorship of sports – which sits halfway between Dallas and Fort Worth, seats one hundred thousand spectators, boasts the largest suspended HDTV screen in the world, and cost $1.2 billion to construct. The stadium is domed, but two roof panels retract to reveal a 661,000-square-foot hole that exposes the playing field to the heavens above, supposedly so God can watch His team play. God's team hasn't played so well lately – the Cowboys haven't been to the Super Bowl in twenty years – but Cowboys Stadium would host the next Super Bowl in twenty-four days. The stunning glass-and-steel, three-million-square-foot structure is Texas-sized – almost as long as the Empire State Building is tall and tall enough for the Statue of Liberty to stand inside, raised torch and all – and futuristic in appearance;

1

it rises from the high plains of Texas like something out of a Spielberg movie.

Aabdar Haddad stared at the silver-and-white stadium lit up against the night sky through the front windows of his apartment. It took his breath away, as it did each time he gazed upon it. He lived directly across the street; the stadium loomed large overhead. It was like living in the shadow of the Great Pyramid. He had chosen his apartment for the view. He saw the stadium first thing each morning when he opened the drapes and last thing each night when he closed the drapes. The stadium was his neighbor, his landmark, his dream, and his destiny.

It was his plan for greatness.

His eyes dropped from the stadium to the stadium's architectural plans spread on the desk in front of him. Cowboys Stadium constituted an architectural and engineering feat of genius. Other domed stadiums require strategically placed pillars to support the roof, the same as load-bearing walls in a residence. Proper support of the roof is essential, be it a house or a football stadium. But, just as one cannot sit in a recliner at home and watch television through a load-bearing wall, spectators cannot sit in a stadium and watch the game through a support pillar. The Dallas Cowboys owner was adamant that not a single spectator's view would be blocked by a support pillar. Not in his stadium. The architects would have to find another way to support the roof.

Their answer: arches. Two steel arches – the longest interior structural arches on the planet at 1,290 feet in length – would span the stadium and support the roof and everything attached to the roof. The load the arches would have to bear was not inconsequential: in addition to the roof itself, there would be the two retractable roof panels, each weighing 1.68 million pounds, the seven-story-tall HDTV screen weighing 1.2 million pounds, and the two largest sliding glass doors in the world beyond each end zone. And there was gravity; the constant force of gravity pushing down on the roof would require the arches to transfer eighty million pounds of thrust into the ground. The architects designated 65-grade steel, the strongest steel made by man, and designed ten-story-tall concrete anchors at each end of the arches that would extend seventy feet straight down into the earth and then one hundred seventy feet away from the stadium. The arches would be the load-bearing walls of the stadium. Cowboys Stadium would stand or fall with the arches.

Such thoughts occupied Aabdar Haddad's mind that night.

What would happen if one of the arches suffered a fatal fracture? If both did? Would the stadium still stand? Could it possibly come down? If the World Trade Center could come down, anything could. Three thousand people died on 9/11 when the Twin Towers came down on a workday. How many would die if the stadium came down on a game day? During the Super Bowl. In a terrorist attack.

If the arches failed, and the stadium fell.

Aabdar's eyes again rose to the stadium in the windows. His mind played out a scenario that seemed as real as if he were an eyewitness: a massive bomb exploding at ground level where the arches join the concrete supports . . . the arches buckling . . . the domed roof sagging . . . then collapsing . . . the entire structure imploding . . . the stadium falling . . . a hundred thousand people dying. Their grave had already been dug; the playing field sat five stories below ground level. There they would lie for eternity like the sailors aboard the USS *Arizona* at Pearl Harbor, victims of another surprise attack America had not anticipated. But before his mind could fully comprehend

3

the loss of life such a terrorist attack would bring, the door to his apartment burst from its hinges, and the last two sights Aabdar Haddad saw in this life were Cowboys Stadium still standing and his blood and brains splattered on the architectural plans.

Chapter 1

Friday, 15 January
23 days before the Super Bowl

'I knew the Honorable A. Scott Fenney back when he wasn't so honorable.'

The audience of lawyers chuckled politely.

'Back when we were fraternity brothers at SMU, back when he was still Scotty Fenney, number twenty-two, scoring touchdowns on Saturday afternoons and sorority girls on Saturday nights.'

The lawyers laughed now. The typical introduction of the guest speaker at these continuing legal education luncheons each Friday consisted of a recitation of the speaker's career highlights – top-of-his (or her)-class in law school, editor-in-chief of the law review, partner at a big Dallas law firm, major commercial cases won for corporate clients, that sort of thing. But the man making this introduction, Franklin Turner, famous plaintiffs' lawyer, had never done typical, in or out of a courtroom. Scott braced himself for the worst.

'That twenty years later he would be sitting here as a federal judge was a future I never once entertained. I would've bet on his being a movie star – he had the looks – or maybe an ex-NFL star player turned broadcaster – he had the football ability. But a knee operation took care of that career path.'

Two knee operations.

'So he went to law school. We all went to law school. Hell, we had no choice: none of us were smart enough to get into med school.'

More laughter from other lawyers who were also not smart enough to get into med school. Consequently, in order to maintain their law licenses in good standing, they had to obtain fifteen hours of CLE credit each year, including three hours of ethics, about as enjoyable to lawyers as eating the broccoli that remained untouched on Scott's plate. They would earn one hour of ethics credit that luncheon listening to that day's topic: 'Professionalism in Federal Court.'

'Scotty and I, we graduated together. Well, I graduated. Scotty, he graduated number one in our class. There's a difference, as we all well know. I hired on with the DA's office – I didn't realize at the time there was no money in criminal law; hell, I put two stone-cold killers on death row and all I got was a pat on the back, so I switched to personal injury – and Scotty hired on with Ford Stevens. He became a partner in record time. He represented rich and famous clients, married Miss SMU, lived in a Highland Park mansion, drove a red Ferrari . . .'

Frank smiled and shook his head.

'Used to see Scotty tear-assing around town in that red rocket. That was a hell of a car. Scotty was a hell of a lawyer making a hell of a lot of money . . . not as much as me because by then I had moved on to suing your clients for toxic torts,

6

but he was making a boatload of bucks. Which is to say, he had a perfect life.'

The smile slowly left Frank's face.

'But then Scotty's life changed. That happens, doesn't it? How many lawyers do we know whose lives were changed by bad luck? By disease – a death sentence called cancer or the death of a wife or a child? Or by bad acts? We all know a few lawyers who walked on the wrong side of the law and paid the price. But Scotty's life changed not because he did the wrong thing, but because he did the right thing. Because he defended an innocent person – a black prostitute from South Dallas accused of murdering a white man from North Dallas. And not just any man. But the son of a powerful U.S. senator with White House ambitions. It doesn't get any worse than that for a lawyer.'

The banquet hall fell silent, not an easy feat with two hundred lawyers in attendance. But Franklin Turner could do that; he could command a room. He was lanky and a bit ungainly, but he had a presence. And he had that voice. And something else, some indefinable capacity to connect with people, especially trial juries. Frank Turner could, as they say, sell ice to Eskimos.

'We've all read about that case and Scotty's life in the newspaper. We all know what happened to that prostitute – acquitted only to die of a heroin overdose two months later – and to him – he lost everything. His job, his mansion, his Ferrari . . . and his wife. She ran off with the golf pro at the country club.'

The lawyers stared solemnly at their plates, as if praying this introduction would end soon. But Frank was just warming up.

'No, wait – it gets worse. Two years later, his ex-wife is charged with murdering the golf pro, who just happens to be

Trey Rawlins, the next Tiger on tour. Butcher knife stuck in his chest. Her fingerprints on the knife. His blood all over her. What we call a slam-dunk for the prosecution. But she claims innocence. And whom does she call? Yep. Scotty. Now, I have to be honest . . . well, I'm a plaintiffs' lawyer, so I don't *have* to be honest, but I will be . . . I don't think I could represent my ex-wife who left me for the stud golf pro at the club even if he did cure my slice. But Scotty did. He went down to Galveston and proved her innocent – not to get her back, but to set her free. That's who he is.'

Franklin Turner, famous plaintiffs' lawyer, turned to Scott. Their eyes met. Frank nodded then turned back to his audience.

'I can tell you this about Scotty. He's a better athlete than I ever dreamed of being – hell, I played tuba in the SMU marching band. He's a better lawyer than I ever hoped to be – not richer, just better. And he's a better man than I'll ever be – he adopted the prostitute's daughter. Yes, I'm doing well, damn well. I'm making a hell of a lot more money than he is and I've got a Lear jet . . . but he's doing good – as a lawyer and as a man. And if I ever stray to the wrong side of the law – and get caught – and another man is going to sit in judgment of my life, I pray that that man is Scotty Fenney. Ladies and gentlemen, I am proud to present the very Honorable A. Scott Fenney, United States District Judge.'

Two hours later, United States District Judge A. Scott Fenney sat in judgment of another man's life. Which is not an easy thing, deciding if a man deserves freedom or prison, mercy or misery, two to five or five to ten. He stands before you, his face full of fear if not remorse, his body trembling with the prospect of a long prison sentence, his mother clutching him as if he's dying of cancer.

As if his crimes were all just a big misunderstanding.

They weren't. The government had proven its case against him beyond all reasonable doubt. The evidence against him was overwhelming. He was guilty. After the jury convicted him, he had no choice but to throw himself upon the mercy of the court.

But he didn't.

His mother had pleaded for mercy. 'He's a good boy, Judge,' she had said. 'Please show him mercy. Please don't take my son from me.'

Character witnesses had pleaded for mercy. His MIT professors testified to his genius, his brilliance, his potential to save the world with an invention, a process, or perhaps the cure for cancer. They all said he was a good boy who had lost his way.

But he had not pleaded for mercy.

'My dad gave forty years of his life to that company, and what did he get in return? Fired. They took his pension and his health care and his life. He got sick and died of cancer. They got rich, and he got Obamacare. The CEO took home fifty million dollars last year. Is that right? It's legal, but is it right? I'm going to prison and that asshole is going to the beach, to one of his five mansions. Am I sorry? I'm only sorry I got caught before I destroyed him as well as the company. Another six months, he would've been homeless.'

Denny Macklin was twenty-four years old, the classic geek. Brilliant, arrogant, and as cocky as an NBA star. He looked like the students at SMU Scott had seen loitering outside the mathematics building as he hurried to the football stadium. He had made his name in online video games – not developing them but playing them; he was the best of the best among players, a master of his universe. But when the company fired his father, he turned his genius on them. A Fortune 500 company had destroyed his father's life, so he had destroyed the company. Almost. He hacked the company's computers, he disrupted its sales and shipments, he stole its cash, he ruined its credit ranking. The company plunged from number 378 on the Fortune list to number 8,456. He brought down a public company with a laptop, an Internet connection, and a 187 IQ. And he destroyed the lives of ten thousand employees the company had to lay off. He hadn't thought of that consequence of his actions. In his anger and desire for revenge, he forgot about people just like his father.

The FBI investigated, but he made them look inept. He was always too smart and two steps ahead. They would have never caught him. He could have gotten away with his crimes. Scot-free. But like all seekers of revenge, Denny had to tell his target – the company's CEO – that it was he who was bringing all the misery upon the company, just as the company had brought misery upon his father. The CEO had to know that Denny Macklin had avenged his father.

Once the CEO knew, the FBI soon knew.

Now he stood before Judge A. Scott Fenney and between his lawyers. A top-notch criminal defense lawyer from Houston, famous for winning in Texas courts, and a top-notch corporate lawyer in Dallas, head of one of the richest law firms in Texas.

Dan Ford.

Three and a half years before, Scott had stood where Dan now stood, in front of a federal judge and next to a client about to learn her fate. The case had cost him everything he had held dear, everything except his daughter. When he had refused to betray his client to preserve Senator Mack McCall's White House ambitions, Dan had fired him from the firm. He had shown him no mercy.

Dan had pleaded for mercy for his client that day.

To a federal judge who sat on the bench that day because an older judge had died. Before Sam Buford had succumbed to cancer, he had put Scott's name forward as his replacement. Scott had thought the senator would block his nomination, but the senator had himself died of prostate cancer. Scott had won Senate confirmation by a unanimous and uncontested vote. Federal Judge A. Scott Fenney now sat in judgment of another man's life. The sentencing guidelines called for twenty years, but the guidelines were only advisory, only sentences on a page. Only a judge sentences another human being.

'Mr. Macklin, you have been convicted on one hundred twenty-seven counts, all felonies under federal law. You have expressed no remorse. To the contrary, you have stated that you would have continued your criminal activity until you had put the company and its CEO in bankruptcy. You are proud of your actions because you view your actions as honorable. You think you're innocent. But feeling no guilt is not the same as being innocent. I have nothing but disdain for the way the company treated your father. But that does not justify your actions that destroyed the lives of ten thousand innocent people. Just because you could exact your personal revenge does not mean you should. You've been given a great gift – brainpower that few people possess. You can use that power as a boy might, or you can use that power as a man might. So far, you've used it as a boy. And you stand before this court as a boy. When I walked into this courtroom today, I was still unsure of your sentence. Your statement here today shows me that you need time to think about your power, time to think about your future, time to become a man who will make your father proud. Denny Macklin, you are hereby sentenced to two years in a federal minimum security prison.'

★

11

'His dad was a good man. We went to school together, same fraternity. He went MBA, I went law. We kept up, talked once or twice a year. The company moved him all around the world. He worried about Denny, that he didn't have friends and roots. He was real proud when the boy got into MIT. This would break his heart.'

Dan Ford shook his head. He had requested a meeting in chambers after the sentence. Scott's former senior partner was sixty-four now; he seemed older.

'How are you, Dan?'

'Me?' He shrugged. 'I'm rich.'

'A happy man.'

'Are you? With your salary? What are you making, one-ninety?'

'Two hundred. Plus benefits.'

Dan grimaced. 'Ouch. I make in a month what you make in a year. Plus benefits.'

A federal judge earned a good salary: $201,100. Not for lawyers – Scott had been making $750,000 at Ford Stevens when Dan fired him – but for normal people. And it was guaranteed for life, security normal people did not enjoy. But federal judges were appointed for life so they enjoyed financial security for life. A. Scott Fenney was no longer the poor lawyer on the block, but he was not again a rich lawyer. He was not an upper-class lawyer as he had been at the firm or a lower-class lawyer as he had been after the firm. He was a middle-class lawyer. A federal judge doing good instead of doing well. Living a steady, stable life. A nice life without fame or fortune but with dental. Pajamae had braces. Her teeth would look like pearls.

'You've made your peace?'

'I have.'

'If you ever change your mind, you know my number.'

'Office?'

'Salary. One million a year. Your name on the door.'

'Good to have options.'

That was always a financial option for a lawyer, what most people would call a moral dilemma: To do well instead of good. His appointment as a federal judge was for life, but he could always change his mind. He could always take the money.

'Standing offer. All you have to do is say yes.'

'I'll keep that in mind.'

'You do that.'

Dan Ford gave Scott a fatherly look, a look of concern for the prodigal son. Which reminded Scott.

'Sorry about your son, Dan.'

His son had died of AIDS since the last time Scott had seen Dan.

'You were more of a son to me than he was. But he was my blood. I hope he's in a better place.' His gaze wandered off for a moment, then he said, 'What about Rebecca? Is she in a better place?'

'Better than prison.'

'Where is she?'

'Somewhere with a man.'

Dan grunted. 'Ex-wives are like that. But that was a hell of a trial. Very entertaining.'

'Glad you enjoyed it.'

'I was sure she was guilty.'

'I was, too.'

'You find a replacement for her?'

'As a client?'

'As a wife.'

'No dating sites for federal judges.'

'I guess that would present a problem. Like dating an IRS agent.'

13

Dan smiled as if his heart wasn't in it then reached inside his coat. His hand came out holding tickets with a familiar silver star embossed on them. He held the tickets out to Scott.

'Take the girls to the Cowboys game Sunday.'

Scott took the tickets. He put on his glasses – he was farsighted – and recoiled at the price.

'Dan, these are three-hundred-forty-dollar tickets. And a seventy-five-dollar parking pass. Eight tickets, that's what, almost three thousand dollars? I can't accept these.'

Dan waved off his ethical concerns, as he often had when they had practiced together at the firm.

'The cheap seats. I gave the suite to the governor. Hell, it's not a bribe, you already sentenced my client to prison. This is father to father, Scotty. I should have taken my son to the games. To the movies. To dinner. Anywhere. I should have spent as much time with him as I did with CEOs. Now he's gone, and all I have is regrets. I don't recommend it.' He paused and breathed in and out. 'Take your girls to the game. And find them a mother.'

Dan Ford stared at his former protégé a long moment.

'Scotty, a man can't raise women.'

Chapter 2

The Ford Stevens law firm had a coffee bar that was finer than anything Starbucks could offer, although the firm's barista served Starbucks coffee. Lattes, espressos, cappuccinos, Americanos . . . whatever the lawyers' caffeine addictions craved. Whatever kept their minds alert and billing hours late into the night. The Earle Cabell Federal Building, on the other hand, offered a break room with one Mister Coffee machine and the cheapest bulk coffee available from the same people who brought lunches to public schools, which is to say, a government contractor who had submitted the lowest bid.

It was four that Friday afternoon, and Judge A. Scott Fenney sat with his feet kicked up on his desk in his chambers, drank a cup of the low-bid coffee with a unhealthy dose of non-dairy powder creamer, ate salted butter toffees, and prepped for the next week with his staff. A federal judge needed people he could trust, and he had such people: Bobby Herrin, his magistrate judge, sitting across the desk from him; Karen Douglas, his briefing attorney/court clerk/docket coordinator/surrogate mother to his daughters, sitting next to Bobby; Carlos

Hernandez, thirty-year-old ex-offender (no convictions) who served as his paralegal and Spanish translator, sitting on the couch along the far wall; and Louis Wright, a community college student at age thirty-two and at six-foot-six and three hundred thirty pounds, his bailiff, sitting next to Carlos like baseball fans in the outfield bleachers. Bobby and Karen were married; Louis and Carlos might as well have been the way they argued about everything.

'I'm trading Romo off my fantasy football team after the season,' Carlos said to Louis. 'You want him?'

'For who?' Louis said.

'Whom,' Karen said.

Karen also served as Louis's personal grammar and literature teacher. They were tackling Shakespeare that year.

'What team does he play for?' Carlos said.

'Who?' Louis said.

'Whom. Player Ms. Douglas said.'

'That ain't no—' He peeked at Karen. 'That *isn't* a player. That's a pronoun.'

'That's correct, Louis,' Karen said. 'An objective pronoun. In this case, the object of a preposition, *for* being the preposition, *whom* being the object.'

Carlos glanced from Karen to Louis and back with an expression of utter confusion.

'What the hell is she talking about? You want Romo or not?'

'Not.'

'Who do you want?'

Louis's eyes cut to Karen; his eyebrows arched as if asking, 'Who or whom?' Karen shook her head. Louis turned back to Carlos.

'Whom.'

'Make up your mind. I thought you didn't want whom. Him. Whatever.'

16

'I don't. And why are you trading Romo? He wins the next two games, Cowboys are in the Super Bowl.'

'Then you should want him.'

'I want Joe Namath. When he was young.'

'Who's Joe Namath?'

Bobby turned in his seat to face Carlos. 'You don't know who Joe Namath is? Was?'

'No.'

'Broadway Joe?'

'No.'

'Where the hell have you been all your life?'

'Mexico.'

Bobby grunted. Scott grabbed another toffee out of the bowl Karen kept filled. He was about to pop it in his mouth when he spotted Louis deep. He fired the toffee across the room; Louis snatched it out of the air. Scott threw his hands up as if to signal a touchdown then went back to the bowl. It had been a long week.

'You okay?' Bobby asked.

'A few more toffees, and I will be.'

'After the sentencing?'

'Oh.' Scott regarded the toffee then tossed it back in the bowl. 'Hard to send a man to prison. Harder when the man is just a boy.'

'Maybe he'll become a man in prison, like you said.'

'Maybe.'

The wood-paneled chambers, the lifetime salary, the financial security, the dental plan – it all came with a heavy price. He had to sit in judgment of other people's lives. How would he fare if his life were judged? If his law career were judged? For eleven years of that career, he had been a great lawyer and a lousy man; the last four years he had tried to turn his life around. Unlike Denny Macklin, he got to try outside prison. The room had turned somber, so Bobby changed the subject.

'What did Dan Ford want?'

'Oh, that reminds me.' Scott dug out the tickets. 'Who wants to go to the Cowboys game Sunday?'

Carlos jumped up. 'You got tickets? For the division championship?'

'Dan gave them to me.'

'What did he want in return?' Bobby asked.

'Nothing.'

'That'd be a first.'

'Everyone in for the game?'

Everyone was.

'Game's at three. Let's meet at the house at noon. We'll ride together. Only one parking pass.'

'Shotgun,' Carlos said.

But he looked at Louis and knew he would not be riding shotgun Sunday.

'So how'd the bar luncheon go today?' Bobby said.

'Frank Turner introduced me.'

'Really? What'd he have to say?'

'He gave the lawyers a brief history of my life. Depressed the hell out of me.'

'Did he mention the trials?'

'He did.'

Bobby sighed. 'Those were the days.'

After a moment of silence for the good old days, Scott said, 'So what's on the docket for Monday?'

'Any murder trials?' Carlos said.

'You wish,' Bobby said.

They began each week with a 9:00 A.M. staff meeting Monday morning and ended each week with a 4:00 P.M. staff meeting Friday afternoon. Finishing up old cases, working

18

current cases, assigning responsibilities on new cases. The cases kept coming, relentlessly and mercilessly. Bobby thumbed through the docket sheet.

'A conspiracy nut sued the Feds to release all the Kennedy assassination documents. He's convinced they're covering up a CIA hit.'

'On Kennedy?'

'Yep.'

'CIA didn't kill Kennedy,' Louis said. 'Oswald did.'

'Who's Oswald?' Carlos asked.

This time everyone stared at him.

'You don't know who Lee Harvey Oswald is?' Bobby said.

'Should I?'

'He was alleged to have assassinated President Kennedy.'

'Was he convicted?'

'He was killed.'

'By the real assassin to cover it up?'

'No. By a strip club owner named Jack Ruby.'

'Who really killed Kennedy?'

'No. He was just a nut case.'

'So who killed Kennedy?'

'*That* is the question,' Bobby said.

'*What* is the answer?'

'This nut thinks it's the CIA.'

'Well, that'll be an interesting case,' Carlos said.

'Except it's not ours. Assigned to Judge Jackson. Government filed a Motion to Dismiss.'

'What else?' Scott said.

Bobby thumbed again. 'Black activist group is also suing the Feds, alleges that the federal government used discriminatory crack cocaine sentences to put young black males in prison to keep the black population down. Says it worked. And now the Latino population has overtaken the black

19

population and is enjoying the political power blacks should have.'

'It's true,' Louis said. 'Every homeboy I grew up with is in prison for crack. White boy in North Dallas snorted powder cocaine, he got probation. Black boys in South Dallas smoked crack, they got twenty years. Ain't no . . .' He glanced at Karen and grimaced. 'Aren't many babies in South Dallas.'

Karen gave him an approving smile.

'But the Supreme Court said the sentence disparity between crack and powder cocaine was discriminatory,' Scott said.

'He's suing over the last twenty years,' Bobby said. 'It'll be dismissed.'

'Can I read the brief?' Louis said.

'*May* I read the brief,' Karen said.

Bobby gave her a confused look. 'Why do you want to read the brief?'

'I don't. I was correcting Louis's grammar. He said "can." It should be "may."'

'*May* I read the brief?' Louis said.

Bobby turned back to him. 'No.'

'Why not?'

'Also not our case. Assigned to Judge Porter.'

'What else?' Scott said.

'The president's executive order. He directed Homeland Security to stop deporting Mexicans residing here illegally if they have clean criminal records.'

'Leaves me out,' Carlos said.

'Essentially, he granted amnesty to twelve million illegal immigrants.' Bobby shrugged. 'It's an election year. Twenty-six states sued him. They contend that, A, the EO is unconstitutional, and B, they'll have to incur billions in additional costs for education, health care, and law enforcement. The lead plaintiff is the State of Texas.'

'That's a hot potato case,' Karen said. 'No matter how the judge rules, half the people in America are going to hate her.'

There was only one female federal judge in the district.

'Garza's got the case?'

'She does,' Karen said. 'I talked with her clerk. She's catching some serious heat from Latino activists.'

'I don't envy her,' Scott said. 'Making the tough decisions is hard enough without having your own people putting pressure on you.'

'It's called being a federal judge,' Bobby said.

'So it is.'

'So we don't got none of those cases?' Carlos said.

Carlos had not engaged Karen for grammatical tutoring.

'Nope,' Bobby said.

Carlos groaned. 'Them senior judges grab all the good cases. All we get is motions, motions, motions – I'm so tired of motions.'

'Let me rephrase,' Scott said. 'What *is* on our docket?'

'Motions.'

Now the room groaned. Motions – requests for the court to do something, such as postpone the trial, dismiss a case, force a party to produce evidence – inundated the federal court with paper and rendered judges referees in a boxing match; but instead of throwing punches at each other, the lawyers threw motions. Bobby flipped the pages.

'Motion for Continuance . . . Motion to Dismiss . . . Motion for Injunction . . . Motion for Summary Judgment . . . Response to Motion for Summary Judgment . . . Reply to Response to Motion for Summary Judgment . . . Motion to Compel . . .'

'Not another discovery dispute?'

''Fraid so. Seems the defendant's lawyer – Sid Greenberg, you might remember him – delivered the plaintiff's discovery requests.'

Sid Greenberg had been an associate assigned to Scott at Ford Stevens. Scott had taught Sid everything he knew.

'Three hundred thousand documents.'

'And the one damaging document is hidden in there somewhere, if only the plaintiff can find it?' Scott said.

'Yep.' Bobby turned his eyes down to the docket sheet, but said, 'Wonder who taught Sid that fun little tactic?'

Scott shook his head. 'God, I was a sleazy lawyer.'

'You were a rich lawyer.'

'That's what I said.'

'What did you always tell us?' Karen said. She had also been one of Scott's associates at Ford Stevens. 'If you want odds, go to Vegas. If you want a chance to get filthy rich by the time you're forty, hire on with Ford Stevens.'

Louis and Carlos laughed.

'That's a good line, Judge,' Carlos said.

'You're forty and not rich,' Bobby said. 'Guess you should've gone to Vegas.'

More laughter from the cheap seats.

'Bobby, tell Sid to forget everything I taught him. And then tell him I'll sanction his client for every billable hour it takes the plaintiff's lawyers to go through those documents. So he might want to rethink his discovery response.'

Bobby smiled and thumbed again. 'And we have competing Proposed Scheduling Orders in the Davis case.'

'Tell them it's their case, make their own agreement. They don't need me until trial. Tell them we're not refereeing the case. Tell them they'd better agree.'

'And we've got our weekly Motion for Protective Order in the patent case.'

Another groan from the room.

'Man, I hate patent cases,' Carlos said. 'They're patented boring.'

That brought a chuckle from Louis.

'That one's yours, Bobby,' Scott said.

For $185,012 a year, magistrate judges handled everything district judges didn't want to handle.

'And more Motions for Summary Judgment, in the Robinson and Simpson cases. Both over two hundred pages with appendices.'

'We'll have five hundred civil cases on our docket this year, and the lawyers will file competing Summary Judgment Motions in every case. Is it malpractice if they don't?'

'Must be.'

'It takes so much time to review these motions. Less time just to try the case.'

'Yeah, but the lawyers are being paid a thousand dollars an hour.'

'Okay, Karen, those are ours. You pick one, give me the other.'

'No murder, no mayhem, no nothing?' Carlos said. 'Man, that's gonna be a boring week. Like this week. Tax fraud, bank fraud, securities fraud, patent infringement . . . boring white-collar crimes by boring white guys.'

'You want excitement or financial security?' Scott said.

'Financial security,' Karen said.

'Spoken like a mother.'

'Nice to have a steady paycheck, Judge,' Carlos said. 'But, damn, I need an adrenaline boost.'

'Louis?'

'I concur.'

'With who . . . whom?' He caught Karen smiling. 'Karen or Carlos?'

'Both.'

'Bobby?'

Bobby's eyes went from Louis to Carlos to Karen. Bailiff to paralegal to wife. Wise man that he was, he went with his wife.

'I've never had a regular paycheck before, so it is nice. But my street clients provided a bit more excitement. Like Carlos here.'

Carlos grinned. '*Hombre,* I led an exciting life back then. Sticking up a convenience store with a toy gun, that'll boost your adrenaline.'

'Why a toy gun?' Karen said.

'*Mí madre,* she would not let me have a real gun. She was worried I might shoot myself.'

'As opposed to someone else?' Bobby said.

Scott sighed. As a hotshot partner at Ford Stevens, he had enjoyed an adrenaline-charged albeit ethically challenged legal career. Excitement was never missing from his life; and whenever he felt boredom creeping in, all he had to do was take the Ferrari for a spin on the North Dallas Tollway. It was marvelous. He had become accustomed to marvelous; now all he got was mundane. Sam Buford said he had saved six innocent defendants from wrongful conviction. Six lives in thirty-two years. Now Scott knew what Judge Buford had done the rest of the time: suffered boredom. Scott had not done much good, not in his first year on the bench. He was just moving cases through the machine that is the federal judiciary. He was not saving people's lives; he was sorting corporations' money. It was as if the legal system existed to divvy up billions of dollars among multinational conglomerates. He would sentence a hundred defendants that year. He would make sure they were all guilty. But most of his time would be refereeing lawsuits brought by one corporation against another corporation, legal fictions fighting over real money like lions over a dead carcass. There was a place for that fight in a civilized society, and that place was a courtroom.

But was it his place?

He had settled into an ethical if unexciting life as a federal judge. The ethics of the job made him proud as a lawyer, and the financial security made him grateful as a man and provider for his daughters, but he had to confess: a little excitement would be a nice change of pace. He stood and stuffed a handful of toffees into his pocket.

'Maybe Pajamae will give us a little excitement at the game.'

Pajamae Jones-Fenney stood five feet five inches tall. Her soft brown hair was cut in a bob, which made her look even more like her mother. Her tan skin glowed with sweat, and the braces on her teeth sparkled. She was thirteen years old and in seventh grade. She was the best player on the court and the only black girl. She was the star for the Highland Park Middle School basketball team. She wore number twenty-three, Michael Jordan's number.

'Go, Pajamae!'

Barbara Boo Fenney sat next to her father and cheered for her sister, who was now racing down the court with the ball. A defender fronted her; Pajamae faked left, made a sharp ball move, and broke hard to the right. The defender tried to adjust but could not; she fell to the floor. The crowd 'oohed.'

'Ankle-breaker!' Boo screamed.

Pajamae made an easy layup just as the buzzer sounded to signal halftime. Her teammates high-fived her. Louis and Carlos tried to start a wave through the crowd, but other than their group, no one joined in.

'The hell's wrong with white people?' Carlos said.

The Highland Park girls led 35-16. Pajamae had scored twenty-eight points. She jogged to the bench but glanced up at her family in the stands filled with wealthy white people. She offered a big smile and a wave. Once the braces did their work, she would have teeth like pearls. Just as her father had promised.

'Girl's got game,' Louis said.

25

'A. Scott, can we go for pizza after the game?' Boo asked.

'Sure.'

On weekends they did pizza out and movies in. Or movies out and pizza in. But never both out.

'You guys want anything from the concession stand?'

'I'll go, Judge,' Louis said.

'I got it,' Scott said.

'Then I'll have a root beer.'

'Two,' Carlos said.

'Coffee with cream,' Karen said. 'And see if they have organic baby food, preferably mashed prunes.'

She held their eighteen-month-old son, Scott Carlos Louis Herrin. They called him Little Scotty.

'Mashed prunes?' Carlos said. 'Give that boy some real food, like enchiladas and tacos. *Mí madre*, she fed me that since the day I was born.'

'And she's still feeding you that,' Bobby said.

Carlos lived with his mother. He shrugged it off.

'Hey, Mexican *hombres*, we can't cook, so we live with our mothers until we find a wife who can.'

'You might be living with your mother for a long time,' Louis said.

Bobby gave Louis a fist bump then said to Scott, 'Beer.'

'At a middle school?'

'Root beer.'

Scott did not drink in public, not even a beer. A federal judge could not risk a DUI or a public intoxication charge. And there was the role model thing as well.

'Come on, Boo, I need your help.'

Father and daughter stepped down the stands to the curious glances and whispered voices to which they had become accustomed. That was the way it was if you were a federal judge with a life story like Scott's. It seemed that most of Highland

Park had settled into one of two camps when it came to A. Scott Fenney: either he was a good man who had redeemed his soul when he defended Pajamae's mother against a murder charge and won, or he was a complete fool who gave up the high life in Highland Park to save a black prostitute from the death penalty only to see her die of a heroin overdose two months later. No one knew what to make of his defending his ex-wife accused of murdering the golf pro she had run off with; the consensus seemed to be building that he might be legally insane.

'Hi, Scott. Hi, Boo.'

Just as they had stepped down onto the floor, Kim Dawson stepped up to them. She had been the girls' fourth-grade teacher at the elementary school. They had introduced their father to their teacher several years back.

'Hi, Ms. Dawson,' Boo said.

'How are you, Kim?' Scott said.

'I'm good. I . . . I miss you, Scott. Or do I have to call you judge now?'

They had dated a few times before he had taken the bench. She was smart and sweet, but there had been no sparks for him.

'Scott is fine.'

She smiled and reached out to him but thought better of it.

'Call me, Scott. Anytime.'

Kim walked off. Scott looked after her. She was a very pretty woman. Her tight jeans showed off her round bottom to great effect and brought a stirring in Scott. Perhaps he should give it another try with Kim and . . . but he would only be using her for sex, and he couldn't do that to her. She was a good girl, and he wasn't a college boy. He was a federal judge. He sighed. No drinking, no sex, no fun. The burdens of office. His eyes fell from Kim's bottom to his daughter's face turned up to him. A frown formed around her green eyes. She aimed her thumb at the departing Ms. Dawson.

'And you don't want her for a girlfriend?'

She shook her short red hair at that great mystery then led the way to the concession stand.

'Five root beers, one coffee with cream, and organic mashed prunes.'

They stood at the concession stand in the midst of teenaged girls gossiping and giggling. At forty, Scott didn't have a clue about teenaged girls. Of course, he didn't have a clue about teenaged girls when he was a teenager. The fate of man.

'Hello, Scott.'

Her perfume preceded her. He turned to a young woman with jet black hair, red pouty lips, black yoga tights that appeared painted on her trim lower body, and a tight tube top that left little of her upper body to the imagination and her torso exposed. Penny Birnbaum. After Rebecca had run off with the golf pro, Scott had sold her clothes at a yard sale and the Beverly Drive mansion to Penny and her husband.

'Oh, uh, hi, Penny. Where's, uh . . . ?'

'Jeffrey? We're divorced.'

'So soon?'

She nodded matter-of-factly. 'He couldn't satisfy me. I got alimony and the house. Your old house. You should stop by one morning on your run.' She leaned in and lowered her voice. 'I'll be naked.'

'Penny, I'm a federal judge now.'

'You can handcuff me.'

She got alimony and the house; Jeffrey got away from her. What's known in the law as a win-win. She gave Scott a once-over that made him feel naked.

'You look delicious,' she said. 'It's been almost four years, but I still remember that day in the shower.'

Scott had given Penny and Jeffrey a tour of the mansion. When Jeffrey checked out the Dolby Surround sound in the basement theater, Penny checked out Scott in the master bathroom shower. She had caught him at a weak moment, but he had to confess, he had not forgotten that moment either.

'You know, Scott, we could just be buddies.'

'Buddies?'

She whispered in his ear. 'Fuck buddies.'

She pulled back and gave him a seductive wink. She was young, and she was sexy, and she wanted to be used for sex. He blew out a breath. She was offering sex to him with no strings attached. Friends with benefits. Fuck buddies in the vernacular. For a man who hadn't had sex since – was the shower the last time? – it was a tempting offer. But such an arrangement didn't seem appropriate for a federal judge. Or a father of two teenaged daughters.

'You don't have children, do you?' Scott said. 'Why are you here?'

'Because I knew you'd be here. To watch your daughter.'

'Are you stalking me?'

She gave him a devious look. 'Oh, this isn't stalking, Scott.'

She twirled and sashayed away. Every man she walked past stopped and stared. That was Penny.

'What did you say?'

Boo's voice from behind him. Scott turned to her. But she wasn't talking to him; she was talking to a group of girls who appeared to have stepped out of a glossy fashion magazine. Boo did not; she wore a sweatshirt, non-designer jeans, and retro sneakers. Her fists were embedded in her hips. That usually didn't end well. For the other girl.

'Are you talking about my sister?'

She stepped forward and got in a blonde girl's face.

'Easy, Boo,' Scott said.

29

'She said something about Pajamae.' To the girl: 'What, you don't like black kids at your school?'

The blonde girl's face turned bright red.

'My sister used to score all the points, now your sister does.'

''Cause my sister's way better than your sister.'

''Cause she's blacker than my sister.'

Boo drew her fist back. 'How would you like a knuckle sandwich, you little stuck-up bitch?'

'Sticks and stones, Boo,' Scott said.

'Fists and elbows, A. Scott.'

'Go ahead, hit me,' the blonde said. 'You'll get suspended again.'

This wasn't Boo's first rodeo. She had been suspended a half dozen times for defending her sister.

'Boo, let's take our drinks up to the seats.'

'Yeah, Boo,' the blonde said, 'go back to your seats with your loser dad.'

Loser dad?

'You talking about my dad now?'

'My dad says your dad is a liberal in love with the president.'

'A. Scott, can I hit her?'

'Yes . . . I mean, no.'

But it was too late. Boo decked her. One punch, right in the nose. The blonde landed hard on her butt. Boo stood over her and pointed a stern face and a stiff finger at her.

'You ever call my dad a liberal again, I'm going to knock your teeth out.'

'A. Scott,' Boo said, 'you'd better go with Ms. Dawson. That Penny girl, she scares the hell out of me.'

'Me, too. And stop cussing.'

Boo frowned without looking up from the book. He had read to them until they were ten; now they read together.

30

'What book are you girls reading?'

They always read in bed each night. They shared one bedroom; Scott had the other bedroom. The house had two bedrooms, two bathrooms, and comprised fifteen hundred square feet. It had been built in 1935 when mansions in Highland Park were reserved for oil tycoons. Not for lawyers and doctors and VPs of IP. And certainly not for judges. Fast forward eighty years and things remained the same for judges.

'*Fifty Shades of Grey*,' Boo said without looking up.

'*What?*'

'*Hunger Games.*'

Scott blew out a breath. 'You're going to give me a heart attack.'

Boo looked up with wet eyes. 'A. Scott, don't joke about that.'

'Oh, sorry, honey. You're going to give me grey hair.'

'Blond hair doesn't turn grey.'

'You're going to make me go bald.'

Pajamae burst out laughing.

'What's so funny?' Scott said.

'You without all that hair. Black boys, they shave their heads, looks good, like Michael. But white boys, they don't look right without hair.'

'I'll keep that in mind.'

'Whereas, Judge Fenney,' Pajamae said.

'Judge Fenney?'

'I like the sound of that. My dad the judge.'

'Dad would sound even better.'

Scott's nightly routine still included tucking the girls into bed. At thirteen, they were probably too old for that sort of thing, but at forty, he wasn't. He leaned down and kissed her forehead. She smelled of strawberries; she must have switched shampoos.

'You had another great game, girl.'

She shrugged. 'Competition level isn't very high. I mean, seriously, the Hockadaisies?'

Highland Park's team had played the team from Hockaday, an elite all-girls private school in Dallas. They were the Daisies.

'Well, you still played great. You were the best player on the court. You always are.'

'Because the other players are white girls. I need to play against black girls if I'm going to get good enough to play college ball and then go pro.'

'You're only thirteen. You have time.'

'I'm just the designated black kid at the school.'

'Designated black kid?'

'Like a designated driver.'

'Are you still getting bullied?'

Pajamae looked down, so Boo answered for her.

'The mean girls – like the blonde, her name is Bitzy – they post mean tweets about her on Twitter.'

'How do you know?'

The girls had no Facebook page, no Twitter account, no Snapchat, no Instagram, no pierced ears, no cable TV, and no tattoos. They had books.

'Other girls showed me.'

'And what do they say?'

'No, Boo,' Pajamae said.

'He needs to know.'

'I do, Pajamae.'

'They say she's ugly because she's black. And they posted, "Your mother was a hooker so you'll be a hooker, too." And "If my mother was a hooker, I'd kill myself. Why don't you?"'

Pajamae cried. Boo hugged her.

'Pajamae,' she said, 'I'm going to kick their asses.'

Scott sat back. He had been bullied in middle school, but

back then bullying was being shoved in the hall by the older boys. It wasn't mean tweets on Twitter. They had dealt with the bullying since Pajamae had started school in Highland Park. Scott had gone to the principal several times; he thought it had gotten better. But it had only gotten worse.

'Honey, you're beautiful just like your mother. She took care of you the only way she knew how. Because she loved you so much.'

'I know, Judge Fenney.'

'And your teammates like you. They gave you high-fives.'

'They like me on the court because I win the games for us. But off the court, they ignore me, act like I'm not even there. Like I'm invisible. In the hallway, I'll say "hi" but they don't say "hi" back.'

She looked so small. She frowned, and her wet brown eyes turned up to him.

'Judge Fenney, what's wrong with me?'

She needed consolation, but how did he console her? What was a father supposed to say in such a moment? He felt utterly helpless. So he said the only words he knew to say.

'Nothing is wrong with you. Everything is right. I love you, doll.'

'I know.'

Then he remembered. He dug into his pocket.

'Toffee?'

That brought smiles to both faces. They were also addicted.

'Honey, we can move out of Highland Park.'

'No, sir. This is my home. I have you and Boo and basketball. No one can ignore me on a basketball court. Just like they couldn't ignore Jackie Robinson on a baseball diamond.'

'Good girl. But I'll talk to the principal again.'

'No, please. It'll only get worse. I'll be like Jackie and turn the other cheek.'

'I'll be like Ali and punch them out,' Boo said.

'Boo, you can't go around punching other girls.'

'Of course I can.'

'You'll get suspended again. You'll probably get suspended for tonight.'

'It was worth it.'

That brought a bigger smile from her sister. 'Gosh, I wish I could've seen it, Bitzy on her butt.'

'It was awesome,' Boo said.

Scott had to confess – privately – that it was pretty awesome.

'If I was the star football player,' Pajamae said, 'those white kids would treat me like a god, beg me for my autograph. But I'm just a black girl playing basketball. Judge Fenney, no one's ever asked me for my autograph.'

'And having a federal judge for a dad gets us bullied even more,' Boo said.

The other federal judges were older with grown children and grandchildren. He was the only judge with young children.

'Why?'

'Charlene said her dad said you're a liberal apologist for the president, whatever that means. He hates the president.'

Pajamae jumped in. 'And then I said, "Your daddy hates the president because he's black." But she said, "No, he hates him because he's a liberal Muslim who wasn't even born in America."' Pajamae frowned. 'Is the president Muslim?'

'No.'

'Was he born in America?'

'Yes.'

'What if he wasn't?'

'The Constitution requires that presidents be "natural born citizens," which means a citizen from birth, either born in America or born outside of America to an American parent.'

That tidbit of constitutional law impressed the girls.

'Look, girls, kids hear their parents talking and they just repeat what they heard. They're just trying to get under your skin. Ignore them.'

'But why would they tease us about your job?' Pajamae asked.

'When so many people live together, we have to have rules, like speed limits and laws against stealing. Otherwise, life would be chaotic. But then people disagree about what the rules mean. In some countries, when people disagree, they shoot each other. We think that's a bad way to resolve differences, so we have courts. People who disagree can come to court and ask a judge to decide who's right. But both parties think they're right and they want the judge to say they're right and the other party is wrong, so if he doesn't, they get mad. In America, we don't start a war if a judge rules against us, but people still get mad about it. That just comes with the territory when you're a judge. People are going to be mad at you.'

The girls regarded him with contemplative expressions. He enjoyed these teaching moments when he could share his experiences with the girls and prepare them for life. He was pretty sure other parents didn't talk to their seventh graders about constitutional law and judicial theory. But his seventh graders loved to learn about such matters. And they were so smart. Pajamae raised a finger as if gauging the wind. They often asked insightful questions after a teaching moment, which made Scott proud – and made him feel like a good dad.

'Yes, honey?'

'Do you think I should do my hair in cornrows again?'

Boo's eyes popped wide. 'I will if you will. And we can get tattoos. Right above our butts.'

'I'll do it if you will.'

And the tears were gone. For now. But they would return, as would the bullying.

'No tattoos, above the butt or anywhere else,' Scott said. 'You can do the cornrows, but no tattoos.'

'No tattoos, no pierced ears, no cable TV – we get more Spanish channels than English.'

Pajamae shrugged. 'Our Spanish is better.'

'A. Scott, all the other kids have that stuff.'

'I gave you a cell phone to share. Is this about Facebook?'

'*Facebook?* Kids don't have Facebook, just their moms. This is about our becoming independent young women.'

'With tattoos? Boo, I'm scared to send you off to college. You're going to come back with tattoo sleeves.'

'No, I'll just get a couple where no one can see them.'

'Oh, well then . . .'

His teenaged daughters had no tattoos (yet) and no longer wore their hair in cornrows. When Pajamae had first done Boo's hair in cornrows after she had moved in with the Fenney family, Rebecca had gone ballistic. Her daughter now looked up at her father.

'Mother got a tattoo, after she left.'

'Another good reason not to get one.'

'She said I should never depend on a man. Except you. She said I could always depend on you.'

Scott had last seen his ex-wife a year and a half before in Galveston after her acquittal on murder charges.

'She also said a woman's life is a complicated life. Will Pajamae and I have complicated lives?'

'Only if you get tattoos.'

Pajamae giggled; Boo rolled her eyes.

'A. Scott, did you have a complicated life?'

'I did when I was married to your mother.'

Boo frowned, which meant she was pondering the notion of a complicated life. The frown left her face.

'I think I want a simple life.'

His daughter was a thirteen-year-old girl trapped in a thirty-year-old woman's body. He had said that for years, just updating her biological age.

'I wonder where she's at? Mother.'

Boo could tell from her father's face that A. Scott was thinking of her mother. Again. He would never be free of her, so Boo would never be free of her. Pajamae's mother was dead. Her mother might as well be. They needed to move on, as they say. But they couldn't. A. Scott had told her that he had taken a vow: *Till death do us part.* He had taken it, but they were both living it.

'Find them a mother,' Dan Ford had said that afternoon. 'A man can't raise women.'

This man had a good job with a good salary and great benefits. A home. Two wonderful daughters. Good health. But they had no mother and he had no one. No woman in his life. God created Adam and Eve, not Adam or Eve. A man needs a woman, even if the man is a federal judge. At ten-thirty on a Friday night, A. Scott Fenney lay down in bed. Alone.

He hated to sleep alone.

But he did.

He had.

He would.

Forever?

Chapter 3

'FBI! You're under arrest!'

The SWAT team wore full body armor and carried assault weapons as if they were storming a fortress instead of a mosque. Special Agent Eric Beckeman followed the assault team into the Masjid al Mustafa in Dallas where Aabdar Haddad had prayed to Allah. Haddad hadn't been a lone wolf; he had been part of a larger conspiracy, the leader of which was the imam of this mosque.

Omar al Mustafa was the most dangerous man in Dallas.

The number one job of the FBI post 9/11 is to prevent another terrorist attack in America. The Super Bowl is the biggest media event in America each year. A hundred thousand spectators watch the game in the stadium; a billion people around the world watch the game on television. It is the dream of every practicing Islamic jihadist for a billion people to watch a hundred thousand Americans die on live TV. It was Beckeman's mission in life to kill or capture the jihadists before that happened. Three weeks before the Super Bowl, his Task Force had done exactly that – killed one bad guy and captured the others.

FBI agents led handcuffed males out the door and into the vans for transport to the holding cells at the federal courthouse. Beckeman had staged the raid during evening prayers when he knew the imam and his co-conspirators would be at the mosque. Agent Stryker escorted a small middle-aged man wearing the traditional Muslim attire – a black skullcap and a long white robe buttoned to the neck – and handcuffs over to Beckeman. Grey hair and beard and dark evil eyes, he looked like every other Islamic fanatic Beckeman had killed or captured.

'Look who I found, Captain,' Stryker said.

Beckeman regarded the man with disdain.

'Omar al Mustafa, you're under arrest. You have the right to remain silent. Anything you say can and will be used against you in a court of law. You have the right to an attorney and to have him present with you while you're being questioned. If you cannot afford an attorney, one will be appointed to represent you before you are questioned.'

'Why?'

'Because it's your constitutional right. You live in America, you get a lawyer.'

'No. Why am I under arrest?'

'Domestic terrorism.'

'Can you be more specific?'

'Conspiring to detonate a bomb in Cowboys Stadium during the Super Bowl.'

'Why would I do that?'

Beckeman got in Mustafa's face. 'I don't know. Maybe because you're a fucking Islamic jihadist asshole.' To Stryker: 'Get him out of my sight.'

Beckeman felt as if he had just arrested Osama bin Laden – three weeks before 9/11.

Chapter 4

Saturday, 16 January
22 days before the Super Bowl

Scott woke the next morning at 6:30 A.M. He had slept like a baby: up every two hours. He did not sleep well alone.

And he was still alone.

He sat up. He never lay awake in bed. What was the point? His thoughts always returned to the early days with Rebecca, when morning sex was so good. When she wanted morning sex with him. When she loved him. He missed waking up with a woman who loved him. And whom he loved.

He loved his daughters, but he missed being in love.

He rubbed his face then stumbled the five paces to the bathroom. He took care of his bathroom duties then looked out the French doors leading to the patio to check the thermometer mounted to the exterior wall. Thirty-three degrees and sunny; it would get into the upper fifties that afternoon. In Dallas, you could fry eggs on the sidewalk in summer; but you could play golf on New Year's Eve. That was the Texas tradeoff. He dressed in his black Under Armour Cold Gear shirt, black Nike nylon sweat pants, black Adidas knit cap and running gloves, and red Brooks Cascadia running shoes. He looked like a NASCAR driver on his day off.

He walked down the hall and looked in on the girls – he saw only one big lump under the comforter on their bed – then locked the back door behind him. He didn't worry about leaving them alone for an hour; there was no crime in Highland Park. He inhaled the cold air and felt invigorated. His morning run was his time, time to think of his life, past and present, and plan his future, today and tomorrow. He seldom looked farther out than his docket sheet.

Scott always ran west on Lovers Lane into the heart of Highland Park, never east into Dallas. He ran five miles every morning. Same time, same route, same result. Winter in Dallas was not winter in New York City, but the world was still barren and dull as the concrete. Traffic was nonexistent early on a Saturday morning, so his thoughts turned to things other than his personal safety and—

'*Shit!*'

—a car veered fast around the corner and nearly hit him. And the driver honked at him! Scott's gloved right hand instinctively came up to give the guy the finger, but he thought better of it. His luck, someone would snap a cell phone photo of Federal Judge A. Scott Fenney flipping off a Highland Park driver. That would make the Sunday paper. So he resisted the urge and ran on.

But the near-death experience made him ponder his own mortality again. He had two daughters who depended on him. If he died, who would take care of them? Bobby and Karen were the guardians named in his Last Will and Testament, but they had their own child now. How would they afford three? Scott had a $500,000 life insurance policy that would be paid into a trust for the girls. The house would sell for more than the mortgage, but not a lot more; a fifteen-hundred-square-foot home qualified as a master suite in Highland Park, not a home. There would be death benefits under the Judicial Survivors' Annuities System paid to the girls until they were eighteen. But he had no stocks or bonds or real-estate holdings. No investments. No assets. No nest egg. The estate of A. Scott Fenney consisted entirely of a life insurance policy and federal death benefits.

Which thought depressed the hell out of him.

He was forty, in his prime earning years, but he was earning only a fraction of his potential. His career decisions affected his daughters' lives and futures. In many parts of the world, your parents' class determined your future; in America, your parents' money did. Money determined your health, education, opportunities, careers, socioeconomic status, and longevity of life. Rich people lived longer than poor people. It was democratic but not terribly comforting if your parents had no money. With him, his daughters shared a bed and bedroom and could look forward to sharing a dorm room at a public university; without him, they would share a life insurance policy and a dorm room at an Ivy League college. Their futures were brighter with his money than with him. They were thirteen; he had five years to prove that they were better off with him alive. At the next intersection, he looked both ways for oncoming vehicles.

An hour later, Scott entered the back door to the glorious smell of bacon cooking and Consuelo de la Rosa-Garcia in the kitchen. Esteban, her husband, dropped her off each morning on his way to work; he worked six days a week so she worked six days a week. Fact is, she and her daughter were members of the Fenney family as well. Consuelo was thirty-two, and Maria almost three; she sat in a high chair and Boo at the table with sleepy eyes and a blood pressure cuff. A stethoscope lay draped around her neck. She held out a bottle of yellow water to Scott.

'What's this?' he asked.

Boo shrugged innocently. 'Water.'

'What's in the water?'

'Emergen-C.'

'Which is?'

'A flavored fizzy drink mix containing twenty-four nutrients and seven B vitamins along with antioxidants and electrolytes.'

'You sound like a commercial.'

'Come on, try it.' She gave him a fake smile. 'It's tangerine flavored.'

Scott took the bottle, sniffed it, and then tasted it.

'Not bad.'

'See? Would I steer you wrong?'

Scott drank the Emergen-C then sat and fed Maria with his right hand; he extended his left arm to Boo. She wrapped the cuff around his upper arm and pumped it up. She put the stethoscope over his inside elbow and released the pressure.

'One-ten over seventy. Not bad.'

She removed the cuff then wrote the results in her notebook. She had given him the blood pressure kit for his fortieth birthday. He had hoped for a tie. 'At your age,' she had said, 'you need to check your blood pressure daily.' He hadn't, so she had. Kids could learn anything on the Internet.

'Boo, I'm not going to die on you.'

'Good. Because I'd have to kill you if you did.'

She watched his health like a hypochondriac watched her pill supply. She had prescribed a statin, but his doctor had not. He still weighed in at his playing weight, one-eighty-five, perfect on his six-two frame. He was still fit at forty. He didn't smoke, drink, or do drugs. He ate right. He exercised. He did everything a man could do to stay in good health. Except have sex. A course of treatment Boo continued to recommend.

'A. Scott, you need some stress relief. Why don't you call Ms. Dawson, go out tonight? We're thirteen. You can leave us home alone. Nothing bad happens in Highland Park.'

She bounced her eyebrows and gave him a devilish look. The girls knew too much about sex. He knew less each day.

'Go back to bed.'

She stood and gave him a kiss on the cheek. She turned away then turned back. Her expression was serious.

'You know, A. Scott, we're big girls now. You could invite Ms. Dawson for a sleepover if you want. Pajamae and I, we discussed it. We're okay with it.'

'Go to bed.'

She shrugged and padded away in her footed pajamas. Scott finished off the water and stood. He could not go back to bed. What's the point of sleeping in if you're sleeping alone? He stood, grabbed a piece of bacon, and headed to the shower. One piece of bacon wouldn't kill him.

'Six months ago, the FBI uncovered a plot to detonate a bomb in Cowboys Stadium during the Super Bowl. Our investigation led us to a twenty-two-year-old American citizen named Aabdar Haddad. Mr. Haddad lived in Arlington in the shadow of the stadium. Our investigation culminated in a raid on Mr. Haddad's apartment Thursday night to execute an arrest warrant. Mr. Haddad resisted arrest and was shot and killed.'

Scott sat stunned. He had showered, shaved, and dressed for the day in more Under Armour clothing. He wore a suit six days a week; Saturdays were casual. Even a federal judge needed a break from a necktie. He sat at the kitchen table, ate scrambled eggs (no bacon), wheat toast with peanut butter, and coffee with cream, his only regular dietary vice (other than toffee). He had turned on the morning news to catch the sports but had gotten terrorism instead. A square-jawed, middle-aged white man wearing a whitewall haircut, a dark suit, and a stern expression stood erect at a podium before a clump of microphones and a crowd of reporters. Across the top of the screen in red letters was *Breaking News: ISIS IN DALLAS.* The byline below read: *FBI Special Agent in Charge Eric Beckeman, Joint Terrorism Task Force, FBI Headquarters, Dallas, Texas.*

'Twenty-four male individuals, including Haddad, were charged with conspiracy to detonate a weapon of mass destruction in a sealed indictment handed up by a secret federal grand jury. Last night the FBI raided the Masjid al Mustafa in Dallas and arrested Haddad's co-conspirators, including the imam, Omar al Mustafa. Mr. Mustafa is well known for his radical views supporting the Islamic State of Iraq and Syria, also known as ISIS, which views have attracted many young Muslim males to Dallas. The mosque is essentially an ISIS recruiting center. We believe that at least a dozen young men from the mosque have traveled to Syria to join the ISIS forces. We believe that this plot was funded and coordinated by ISIS. We believe that Mustafa radicalized Haddad, as well as the other co-conspirators. We are convinced that Mustafa was the mastermind behind the stadium plot. If he and his co-conspirators had been successful, tens of thousands of fans might have been killed during the Super Bowl. But the plot was discovered and thwarted thanks to the hard work and determination of dedicated FBI and Homeland Security agents. After nine-eleven, the Joint Terrorism Task Force was created to encourage cooperation instead of competition among law enforcement agencies. It paid off today. The suspects will be arraigned in federal court Monday morning. Questions?'

The reporters' hands shot up; the agent pointed at one reporter.

'ISIS in Dallas?'

'They're everywhere in America.'

45

'Will the Super Bowl be safe?'

'It will be now.'

'Did you capture all of the conspirators?'

'We're confident we apprehended all participants in the plot.'

'Can you assure the American people that they're safe?'

'At the Super Bowl?'

'Every day.'

'Of course I can't.'

'Why not?'

'Because other Islamic jihadists are plotting every day to kill Americans, to do here what they just did in Paris. That's what they do. But we fight every day to keep the American people safe. That's what we do. We won this time. But the war on terror is not yet won.'

Hands punched the air; he nodded at a reporter.

'How far along were they in the plot?' the reporter said. 'Did they have a bomb assembled?'

'We have not found a bomb. But we are still following leads.'

'What evidence was recovered at Haddad's apartment?'

'We're not at liberty to disclose all the evidence at this time, but we did recover architectural plans for the stadium.'

He pointed at another reporter.

'Why are we just now hearing about the Haddad raid and his death?'

'We didn't disclose the Haddad raid until we conducted the raid at the mosque. We didn't want any of the suspects to get word and run.'

Another reporter: 'What put you on to Haddad?'

'An anonymous tip to our terrorism hotline.'

'Were you previously aware of Haddad?'

'No. He wasn't on our radar or in the database. There was nothing on Twitter or Facebook that alerted us to him. If we didn't get this tip, this story might have had a different ending.'

'Do you get a lot of anonymous tips about bombing plots?'
'We do. Hundreds already this year.'
'How many ended with a dead suspect?'
'One.'
'Is Omar al Mustafa the most dangerous man in Dallas?'
'Not as long as he's in that jail cell.'

Scott drank coffee and read the Motion for Summary Judgment in the Robinson case; two corporations claimed the other infringed on patented cell phone app technology that made it easier to order a pizza while driving. It seemed silly after a terrorist plot to kill one hundred thousand people, as if he were being asked to referee a schoolyard dispute. Of course, it wasn't as silly as a federal judge being asked to decide if a quarterback deflated a football in order to get a better grip during a cold game, but still. This was federal court not small claims court. A federal case should be important. It should mean something. He pushed himself out of the chair; he needed another cup of coffee to stay awake. If he could bottle motions filed in federal court, he'd have a sure cure for insomnia. He reached for the coffee pot, but his phone rang. It was Bobby. He was at the courthouse handling weekend intakes.

'You believe that? ISIS in Dallas? Plotting to blow up the Super Bowl? Kind of creepy, knowing they're downstairs in the detention cells.'
'Better than on the streets.'
'Amen.'
'What's up?'
'Garza recused herself from the immigration case.'
'Why?'
'Conflict of interest.'
'Being?'
'Her husband is here illegally.'

'That would constitute a conflict.'

'Now she won't envy you.'

'Why?'

'It's your case.'

'You're kidding?'

'Do I look like I'm kidding?'

'You're on the phone.'

'The answer is no.' Scott could hear Bobby flipping through papers. 'Case status is this: All facts have been stipulated for the record, so no evidentiary hearing is required. The case will be submitted on written briefs and oral arguments. Briefs have already been filed, I'm emailing those to you now. Oral arguments are set for Wednesday.'

'That's fast.'

'Both parties want to fast track the case, the loser is going to appeal all the way to the Supreme Court. So they want a quick decision, make it an election issue in the fall.'

A president would be elected in November. The current Democratic president wanted to be reelected. His executive order would become a hot button campaign issue with the Hispanic vote at stake. Which was why most observers thought the executive order was politically motivated. Of course, what wasn't in America today?

'The constitutionality of the executive order will be irrelevant,' Bobby said.

'Except to the presiding judge.'

Pajamae bounced into the kitchen at nine, perfectly put together as usual in a blue nylon sweat suit, blue socks, and blue sneakers; her hair was brushed and neat. She brought a hint of perfume with her. Boo stumbled in behind her wearing a Willie Nelson sweatshirt, baggy jeans, white socks, and those retro sneakers; she looked as if she had lost her hairbrush. She

48

did not bring a hint of perfume. Scott tapped his cheek; they both dutifully kissed him. It was silly, sure, but he liked it, little girls kissing their father in the morning, even if they were thirteen. He clicked off the TV with the remote. They normally watched the *Today Show* during breakfast, but 'ISIS in Dallas' filled all the non-cable channels, and they didn't have cable. He was determined to allow them to enjoy their innocence for as long as possible, little girls kissing their dad good morning.

'A. Scott, what exactly is oral sex?'

He spit out his coffee. Consuelo shrieked at the stove and covered her face with her apron. Boo and Pajamae looked at him with expressions of complete innocence.

'I mean, is it like talking about sex?'

'Well, uh . . . why do you ask?'

'Some kids at school were talking about it. They said it wasn't really sex, so I figured oral meant just talking and not doing.'

'No, it's doing sex all right.'

'Explain.'

'Do I have to?'

'Is it one of those yukky questions?'

'It is. Particularly at breakfast.'

'Should we ask Karen?'

'You should.'

Girls should ask their mother such questions; but they had no mother so their father had done the only thing he knew to do: he had referred those questions to Karen just has he had referred family law cases to other lawyers when he was at Ford Stevens. He had told the girls that they could talk to him about anything and ask him any question, that he would always tell them the truth and never get mad; but there were some subjects he did not feel professionally competent to handle, divorce and oral sex among them.

'Okay.'

Scott breathed out. He felt relieved and disappointed – in himself. He couldn't run from those questions forever; he was a single father. Which meant he was also their mother. Karen was like their aunt trying to be like their mother. From her they had learned about puberty, menstruation, and how to buy a bra; from him they had learned the definition of pass interference, the steps to changing a flat tire, and how to try a case in federal court. When they were ten, he felt like a father; at thirteen, he felt like a failure. Dan Ford was right: a man can't raise women.

'Let's go,' Boo said.

'To ask Karen about oral sex?'

'No,' Pajamae said. 'To grocery shop.'

In accordance with their Saturday routine, the Fenney family would shop for groceries that morning then grill hamburgers and watch a movie that night. There would be root beer floats or homemade malts or ice cream cones – Saturday movie nights meant ice cream in some form or fashion in the Fenney house – but there would be no date nights for any of them. They were too young to date, and he was too much a judge. The closest any of them would come to romance was watching one of the British classics the girls loved so much: *Jane Eyre. Emma. Sense and Sensibility. Persuasion.*

'*Señor* Judge, Maria, she has the cold, so we will stay home, okay?' Consuelo said. 'But I have made a list.'

She entrusted her shopping list to the girls as if it were a deed to the family estate. Boo frowned.

'It's in Spanish.'

'*Sí.*'

'We watch enough Spanish TV, we can figure it out,' Pajamae said. 'Let's go.'

She loved Saturday shopping. There were no Whole Foods stores in South Dallas where she had lived with her mother in

50

the projects. In fact, there were no grocery stores. Almost four years living in Highland Park, and she still got excited going to the grocery store.

'Let's do it,' Scott said.

They went out back and climbed into the Expedition. Scott had traded in the Jetta when he had won Senate confirmation. They needed more space for road trips, the only vacations they took. He liked the feel of a truck; of course, it didn't have the zero-to-sixty acceleration or the handling of the Ferrari, but they could live in it if they had to. The girls rode in the second seat.

'Buckle up.'

Scott drove north out of Highland Park and into Dallas. The nearest Whole Foods was at Preston Road and Forest Lane. Consequently, each Saturday Parkies ventured out of the Bubble – as Highland Park was locally known – and into Dallas. Highland Park was a small town of eight thousand; Dallas was a big city of one million. There was a different feel to Dallas, as there was to each big city in Texas. Each had its own vibe: drive into San Antonio, and you want to eat Mexican food and sing *La Bamba;* drive into Austin, and you want to eat barbecue and dance to live country-western music; drive into Houston, and you want to drive out; drive into Dallas, and you want to make a lot of money fast. Which was a prerequisite to shopping at Whole Foods.

'OMG, look at her tattoos!' Boo said.

The girls had run into the store, but Boo had skidded to a full open-mouthed stop upon entering. A Whole Foods employee stood at the produce section directly in front of them. She was perhaps twenty; her exposed arms and neck suggested a painted body. She had a sweet face with a nose ring. Boo stood in awe of her.

'She's beautiful.'

The only thing that stood between Barbara Boo Fenney and a painted body was her deathly fear of needles. Scott prayed that she never overcame that fear. He had learned that for a single father fear was his co-parent.

'Look!' Pajamae said. 'Free samples!'

She never passed up a free sample at Whole Foods. Cheese, crackers, cookies, fruit, fish – she tried them all. What they call, simple pleasures. She pushed a basket to Scott then grabbed another for them. She tore Consuelo's list in half and handed the bottom half to Scott. Consuelo knew the store layout well; her list went from one side to the other. He headed to the far side of the store; they started at produce. Consuelo had taught them how to pick the best fruit and vegetables. He went for the meat.

'Meet you girls at the checkout,' Scott said. 'And look for the sale items.'

Boo dismissed him with a little wave that said, 'We know how to shop.' They did. He had learned to shop on a budget, and he had taught them in three simple words: *Check the prices.*

Scott put on his glasses and checked Consuelo's list when he arrived at the meat market: *Dos pollo.*

'Two whole chickens,' he said to the butcher.

The store was abuzz with news of the Super Bowl plot. Dallas had recently been named the least fit city in America; that had shocked no one, not with the annual state fair in Fair Park featuring fried butter, fried ice cream, fried Twinkies, and fried pumpkin pie. But Dallas named the target of a major terrorist attack – that had shocked the city to the core.

'Can you believe those damn Muslims?'

Scott turned to see George Delaney standing before him. George was a lawyer of Dan Ford's generation at another large Dallas firm; he wore a red sweater vest over a crisply starched button-down blue shirt, chinos, and loafers. They had met years back, but George had never given Scott the time of day. Upon his taking the bench, they had apparently become BFFs, as the girls say. They shook hands, and George gave his order to another butcher.

'Thank God we got them before they could kill all those people. Hell, I've got Super Bowl tickets. Hope you don't get the case.'

'A senior judge will take it.'

'Not sure I'd want the most dangerous man in Dallas in my courtroom. Rule against him, he's liable to send his cutthroats to do just that to the judge.'

George rubbed his neck.

'How do you cut someone's head off?'

'Because they left you in the Whole Body department and didn't say where they were going.'

Both men turned to George's second . . . no, third wife and regarded her, the same as men had regarded Rebecca. She was a mannequin in yoga tights: fit and firm and blonde, perfect in a too perfect way, as if she had been airbrushed. Standing next to George, she looked young enough to be his daughter. Which is to say, she was a Highland Park trophy wife.

'That's why, not how,' George said.

She rolled her eyes then looked Scott up and down as one might a new pool boy.

'Honey, this is Judge A. Scott Fenney.'

'State court?' she asked.

'Federal.'

'Ohhh.'

As if she were impressed. Also like Rebecca in that regard; she understood the difference between state and federal judges. Big law firms like her husband's owned state court judges, but they feared federal judges. At times like this, Scott really enjoyed being a federal judge. The young Mrs. Delaney frowned without wrinkles.

'*Fenney?* Are you related to Rebecca Fenney?'

'Not anymore. We divorced three years ago.'

'She was so gorgeous and so athletic. I knew her from the club. She loved golf and . . . ohhh, yes, now I remember.'

It had all come back to her.

'She ran off . . . uh, moved away, didn't she?'

George's face turned ashen, a man desperately seeking an escape path.

'Boy, Judge, your girl sure played a heck of a game last night. My granddaughter's a Daisy. Tiffany. What's her name? Pajama?'

'To Galveston, right?' Mrs. Delaney said. 'And there was a murder? Or something like that?'

To George: 'Pajamae.' *Pa-shu-may.* To his wife: 'Something like that. She was innocent.'

'Oh, good.'

As if he had said she won best pie at the school bakeoff.

'*Pajamae?*' George frowned. 'What's that, French?'

'Black.'

'Ah.'

'So where is she now?' Mrs. Delaney said.

'In the produce department.'

'Rebecca's here?'

'No. Pajamae's in produce.'

'Where's Rebecca?'

'Somewhere with a man.'

George's grimace evidenced his internal strife: trophies were for display only; they were not supposed to talk out of turn. Or preferably at all. He grabbed his meat and his trophy and carried them both away. But he waved over his shoulder.

'Good to see you, Judge.'

Scott had once had a trophy. He had put her on display. He had felt proud to be seen with her. He had regarded her with a certain sense of proprietorship. As if he owned her. As if he had bought her. But trophies are much like politicians: they seldom stay bought. His trophy had not.

He put all his chickens in the basket and rolled on.

Scott met the girls at the checkout. His basket was filled with the aforesaid chicken, ground buffalo, milk, cream, yogurt, eggs, Canadian bacon, oatmeal, granola, whole grain bread, peanut butter, ham, cheese, pickles for Pajamae, and makings for Consuelo's enchiladas. Their basket was filled with lettuce and other green produce (which he worried might find its way into his morning smoothies), tomatoes, avocados, bananas, cucumbers, strawberries, blueberries, ice cream, and half the vitamin/supplement department.

'What's all that?'

Boo placed a plastic container on the checkout belt. 'Omega 3 Fish Oil. Oil from cold-water fish like salmon. Proven to protect your heart.'

'And this?'

Another container. 'Resveratrol. The extract from grape skins. You get the health benefits of red wine without getting drunk.'

She piled more containers onto the belt. Scott checked each one.

'Coenzyme Q-10?'

'There are promising studies that it lowers cholesterol. Since you won't take a statin.'

'Vitamin D?'

'Since you don't get much sun in the courthouse.'

'Lysine?'

'Boosts your immune system and reduces stress, since you won't have sex.'

'Is it safe?'

'Not with that Penny girl.'

She and Pajamae laughed and fist-bumped.

'The lysine,' Scott said.

'Unless you're pregnant or breast-feeding.'

Scott grunted and picked up the next container. 'Saw palmetto.'

'Supposed to be good for your prostate, whatever that is.'

Pajamae looked at Scott and offered a 'beats me' shrug. And the last container.

'Melatonin.'

'To help you sleep. I know you struggle.'

'How do you know that?'

'I hear you.'

He grunted again then did a quick calculation.

'Boo, this adds up to over a hundred dollars.'

'Good health is priceless.'

'Not on a judge's salary.'

'You're a judge?' the checker said. She also had tattooed arms and body piercings. 'Maybe you can help me. I got arrested for possession of marijuana.'

'I'm a federal judge. I'll only see you if you're a drug king-pin.'

'Bummer.'

'Sometimes.' He turned to his daughter. 'Take half this stuff back.'

She turned her hands up to her sister. 'It's like pulling teeth with him.'

Pajamae gave her the same shrug. Boo left four bottles on the checkout belt and shuffled off with the other three bottles. She muttered under her breath.

Scott pushed the basket loaded with grocery bags (reusable from recycled products) to the exit. The automatic double doors flew open, and a cool breeze and a familiar face blew in. Sid Greenberg.

56

'Scott! How are you?'

'Sid.'

They shook hands. Sid introduced his wife then said he'd find her in the store. She went inside, and the girls outside. They knew a lawyer when they saw one.

'Bobby told me what you said.'

Everyone else wanted to talk about the Super Bowl plot; Sid wanted to talk about his pending case. Scott had taught the boy how to focus.

'Sid, we can't have an *ex parte* conference in Whole Foods. But I meant it.'

'You did it.'

'I was wrong.'

'You can't sanction me.'

'I can and I will. You can appeal my order, but I can enter it.'

'Scott—'

'If you insist on talking shop, it's judge.'

'Judge, if I don't do this kind of stuff, I'm not zealously representing my client, as our ethical rules require.'

He was right. Sort of. The ethical rules seemed to require such legal maneuvering.

'Federal court holds lawyers to a higher standard of ethical conduct.'

'You taught me everything I know.'

'And you took my office, my secretary, and my car.' Scott gestured to the parking lot. 'Is the Ferrari out there?'

Sid nodded.

'Enjoy it.'

'I do.'

Scott walked outside to find the red Ferrari parked next to the Expedition. All the memories came flooding back, like running into an old flame who had left for a younger man.

★

'How much did that ride cost?' Pajamae asked.

It was almost five. They had spent the rest of the day at the house. Esteban had picked up Consuelo and Maria at one. Pajamae had watched basketball on TV, Boo had read *Hunger Games*, and Scott had read the states' brief in the immigration case. It belonged in federal court.

'That's the longest car I've ever seen,' Boo said.

The girls now stood at the front windows. Scott stepped over to look. Across the street sat a white stretch limousine. A girl in a short party dress and high heels bounced out of the house.

'That's Brittany,' Pajamae said.

'Her dad's rich,' Boo said.

'Really?'

Boo nodded. 'He's a renowned lawyer. He has his own billboard on the highway.'

'Wow.'

'She's going to study abroad next year.'

'Really? Where?'

'New York City.'

'Double wow.'

The girls contemplated the scene a moment. The driver's door opened, and a man dressed in black leather got out.

'Is that Carlos?' Boo asked.

The driver looked their way, grinned, and waved. It was Carlos.

'He must be moonlighting,' Scott said.

'What does the moon got to do with driving a limo?' Pajamae asked. 'And Carlos hates funerals.'

'Funerals?'

Pajamae pointed. 'White limo, must be a funeral.'

'Why?'

'Black funerals in South Dallas always have white limos.'

Boo seemed impressed by that news.

'It's not a funeral. It's the winter formal at Hockaday. Brittany goes there. She's sixteen.'

The mother across the street took photos of three young couples by the limo. The boys wore dark suits; the girls wore short skirts and stiletto heels.

'Her dress barely covers her butt. Mama's skirts were longer than that. When she sits in that limo, those boys are going to see her undies.'

'If she's wearing any,' Boo said.

'No undies? Not even a G-string?'

'G-string?' Scott said.

'All the girls wear G-strings,' Boo said. 'Except us.'

Oral sex and G-strings, as if they went hand in hand. Perhaps they did. A man can't raise women. Scott averted his eyes. He didn't want to think of sixteen-year-old girls wearing G-strings or nothing at all under their short dresses. His daughters were only three years away from sixteen. How do you raise thirteen-year-old girls in the age of *Fifty Shades of Grey*? How do you tell them to be strong, independent women when the world is telling them to be sex objects?

'I bet there's going to be oral sex in that limo,' Pajamae said. 'Talk, talk, talk.'

'She's wobbling around in those heels,' Boo said. 'How's she going to dance?'

Pajamae grabbed her sister. 'Let's dance.'

The girls turned from the window and started jumping up and down. Scott stared at them.

'What are you doing?' he asked.

'We're dancing.'

'That's not dancing.'

'Yes, it is.'

'No, it's not. This is dancing.'

He reached out to Pajamae with both hands. She regarded his hands as alien objects.

'What?'

'Hold my hands.'

'Why?'

'So we can dance.'

'You hold hands when you dance?'

'Yes.'

'You lie!'

'It's country-western swing dancing. The boy and girl actually hold hands.'

She took his hands, and he pulled her in. He two-stepped a few paces then pushed her out and twirled her under his arm. He showed her several swing dance moves.

'Is this how old people dance?'

'It is.'

Boo played country music on their phone then jumped in. Scott showed her all the moves he could recall. The girls giggled with joy. He loved that sound.

'I love it! A. Scott, I never knew you could dance.'

He could.

A. Scott Fenney was a traditionalist when it came to dancing and grilling. Hands on. Charcoal was simple. Old-fashioned. Innocent. Gas was newfangled and fancy. Charcoal was art; gauging the heat from the color of the coals. Gas was science; four hundred degrees as shown on the thermometer. Anyone could do that. No skill was required. Charcoal harked back to the old days. To a simpler time and place. When life was slower. Less expensive. Less complicated. To a time when thirteen-year-old girls didn't wear G-strings and people didn't plot to blow up football stadiums.

He often longed for those times.

60

Which made him feel like his father. Longing for the good old days. Maybe not for the good old days his father's generation had harked back to – the fifties and sixties weren't so good for minorities and women – but for the good old days before being strip-searched to fly on a plane or before metal detectors at the school entrance or certainly before 9/11.

The afternoon temperature had not hit the upper fifties but instead the upper sixties. It had been a glorious Saturday. Scott sat on the back patio drinking his weekly beer, watching the sunset, and waiting for the coals to turn white. In his prior life, he had a back patio with a built-in grill that was something out of a 'homes of the rich and famous' type magazine. He had often sat on the patio drinking a beer and looking out on the custom pool and the expanse of grass manicured by Mexicans; he could run a forty-yard dash from the patio to the back fence. Now his pool was smaller than the master bath at the mansion on Beverly Drive, he mowed his own grass, and he could spit over the back fence from where he sat. He studied the landscape a while and thought that perhaps in the spring he would plant crepe myrtles along the back fence. Yellow crepe myrtles.

'I love the captain,' Boo said.

Scott sat in the middle of the couch, and the girls sat on either side of him. They ate hamburgers and baked beans and sweet potato fries off folding trays. *Persuasion* played on the small-screen television. He and Rebecca had never watched movies with Boo on Saturday night; Saturday night had been a work night for Rebecca, always diligently climbing the social ladder. Scott liked the two little women in his life. He had lost a wife and gained a daughter.

'Do other girls your age watch movies with their dads on Saturday night?'

'No,' Boo said. 'They go to parties.'

'Do you girls want to go to parties?'

'With them? No.'

'Are you happy at home with me?'

'We are.'

Pajamae nodded then said, 'Can we have malts now?'

'We can.'

Boo paused the movie. They took their plates to the kitchen. The girls rinsed the plates and stacked the dishwasher while Scott made malts. He mixed vanilla ice cream, chocolate milk, vanilla extract, and malt in the blender. Chocolate milk rather than chocolate syrup was the key to a great chocolate malt. Pajamae tasted the result with a spoon.

'More ice cream, I think,' she said.

Scott added more ice cream. The malt then met with her approval. He poured the malts, and they returned to the couch. Boo resumed the movie. Unrequited love was soon requited.

'Look at that girl run,' Pajamae said. 'She's not going to lose her man this time.'

' "I am in receipt of your proposal," ' Boo said. 'Gosh, that's romantic.'

Watching a romantic movie and drinking malts – that too was simple and innocent and old-fashioned. Like charcoal grilling and country-western swing dancing. The way life was supposed to be. The movie ended happily ever after.

Would his life?

Maybe it already had, and he just didn't know it. Maybe he had all a man could hope to have and then some. Maybe he had all he needed in life. Scott had tucked in the girls, and he now lay alone in bed. He had taken melatonin.

'God, please help me raise my girls without a mother. They are my life now. Thank you for giving them to me.'

Chapter 5

Sunday, 17 January
21 days before the Super Bowl

'Thank you, God, for the Joint Terrorism Task Force keeping the Super Bowl safe from radical Islamist jihadists. And please help the liberal president understand that letting in Syrian refugees is a serious mistake and endangers the homeland.'

Scott had run and returned home to a blood pressure test conducted by Boo and a green smoothie of kale, cucumbers, spinach, and wheatgrass concocted by Boo. He had then showered, shaved, and taken the girls to church.

Where they now sat.

He glanced around at the congregation. His gaze always seemed to fall on other fathers and their families, and always he felt a twinge of jealousy. He had never been jealous in his life; and why would he have been? The chips had always fallen his way. He had always had everything he wanted.

Now he just wanted to love and be loved.

He always spotted a few single mothers but seldom another

single father. The children went to the mother in a divorce. Most divorced fathers lived without their children. So he felt fortunate that his lived with him. 'You need her more than she needs me,' Rebecca had said of Boo when she left him. He would live with his daughters but never with another woman; he had resigned himself to that harsh fact. What woman wanted to raise another woman's children, or in his case, *two* other women's children, and a black child to boot?

There was no such woman.

Few federal judges are single fathers; most are grandfathers. Their extended families offer them the sanctuary that the court cannot. Life on the federal bench is a lonely legal existence. Other lawyers offer fealty but not friendship. Other dads at school cannot be friends with a federal judge, a fellow dad who could put them in timeout for five to ten. It was like being buddies with an IRS agent, as Dan had said. They no longer ask you to play golf; golf is four hours when a man can let his guard down, talk openly to his buddies, maybe even boast about the latest greatest tax shelter which saved him tens of thousands in taxes – not something he'd want a federal judge to hear. Golfing with a state court judge is a different matter: he has no jurisdiction over income taxes and he needs the lawyer's money for his next campaign. Which is to say, a state court judge will file that information where the sun don't shine. Would a federal judge? Why take the chance? Better to fill out the foursome with a plaintiffs' lawyer. So Scott no longer played golf because Bobby, Louis, and Carlos did not play golf. And they had their own lives. Bobby had Karen and Little Scotty; Louis had William Shakespeare; Carlos had the gym and a commercial driver's license.

Scott had his daughters.

For five more years. Then they would leave him, go off to college and begin their own lives. Where would he be then?

Alone. He would have no one. He would be a forty-five-year-old spinster. Boo's hand grasped his right hand, and Pajamae's his left. They both squeezed tight, as if they had heard his thoughts.

Thank you, God, for giving them to me.

He would take his girls over any woman. He had already made that choice. They were his life; and he would give his life for his daughters. Sitting in church that Sunday morning, he could not know that life would soon give him that opportunity.

'What do you got in leather?'

'Footballs.'

Carlos frowned at the clerk; Scott smiled and looked for the girls. Their first stop upon entering Cowboys Stadium – after being patted down at the door – was the eighteen-thousand-square-foot pro shop. He found Boo and Pajamae trying on jerseys.

'I'm going for Dez,' Pajamae said.

She wore a number eighty-eight jersey with 'Bryant' across the back. Boo wore a number eleven with 'Beasley' across the back.

'Who's Beasley?' Pajamae said.

'I don't know,' Boo said.

'Then why do you want his jersey?'

'If you don't know who he is then no one knows who he is.'

'So?'

'So no one's buying his jersey. That's got to make him feel bad. If I buy one, it'll make him feel better.'

Pajamae blinked hard. 'Are you serious?'

'I think so.'

Scott had given the girls a budget: $100 each. He figured it was their only shot at the pro shop for at least another year. The jerseys cost $100.

★

'On the fifty-yard line, baby,' Carlos said. 'Cowboys versus Giants for the division title.'

He and Louis high-fived. Three hundred forty dollars bought a seat on the fifty-yard line in the section nearest the field. But Ford Stevens had to pay $300,000 for the license for the eight seats, an up-front payment for the right to buy tickets for those seats. Scott had wanted to bring the girls to a game, but the only available tickets were through brokers and sold for $1,500 per seat and up. That price had dissuaded him, but apparently not many other Cowboys fans. The seats around them were filling up fast with fans wearing Cowboys caps and jerseys and toting $8 beers. Scott sat between Carlos and Louis on his left—

'Big man, what'd you do yesterday?'

'Read Shakespeare. What did you do?'

'Drank Coronas and pumped iron at the gym.'

'You mean, pumped iron then drank Coronas?'

'No, man. I drink beer before I work out. It's called carbo-loading.'

Louis grunted. 'Why do you work out so much?'

'I want bigger muscles.'

'You've got big muscles.'

'*Gracias*, big man. But the *señoritas*, they always want bigger.'

—and Bobby on his right; he pointed at the big four-sided screen—

'Technicians sit in a booth in the middle of that thing during the game, nine stories up. That'd be a long fall.'

—and the girls sat on opposite sides of Karen so they could help with the baby. Little Scotty's eyes were wide at his surroundings, as were Big Scotty's. Cheerleaders dancing on the field to loud music, fire shooting from cannons, colorful lights flashing, the big screen pulsating with clips from prior games, bright advertisements for beer and cars, fans whooping

66

and hollering – it was sensory overload. While at SMU, Scott had played several games at Texas Stadium, the Cowboys' old venue. It was utilitarian in design, a steel frame with seats and a field and no frills; it was only about football. But this stadium seemed more spectacle than football, more Barnum & Bailey than Vince Lombardi, more about merchandise and beer than the thrill of victory and the agony of defeat. Jerry Jones, the owner of the Dallas Cowboys, had made football entertainment; the stadium was colloquially known as 'Jerryworld.'

'I need a Corona,' Carlos said.

'I'll go with you,' Louis said.

They stood. Louis wore slacks and a long-sleeve shirt; he looked like an off-duty pro wrestler. Carlos wore black leather boots and pants, a tight black tee shirt stretched tight on his muscular body that revealed his tattoos, and his black hair slicked back. He finished off the look with a wide silver bracelet on each wrist. He looked like a Mexican matador.

'We're going to the concession stand,' Carlos said. 'You guys want anything? Louis is buying.'

Bobby: 'Beer.'

Scott: 'Root beer.'

Karen: 'Coffee with cream.'

Boo: 'Margarita.'

Carlos: 'Funny.'

'We want knowledge,' Boo said.

Pajamae nodded. Carlos laughed.

'At a football game?'

Boo rolled her eyes and turned to the only person on their row who might offer knowledge.

'Karen, what's oral sex?'

Scott and Bobby jumped out of their seats.

'We'll go with you,' Bobby said.

'Absolutely,' Scott said.

Karen shook her head. 'Cowards.'

The men hurried out of the row and up the steps, but once out of danger, Scott turned back to see the girls in their Dallas Cowboys jerseys huddled around Karen; Pajamae suddenly stood upright with an expression of disbelief.

'You lie!'

Boo followed her up. 'I'm gonna throw up.'

Bobby slapped Scott on the shoulder. 'Narrow escape.'

'Man, those girls,' Carlos said, 'they don't give a man no warning. They just throw it out there.'

Tony Romo threw a long touchdown pass to put the Cowboys in the lead over the Giants. The Dallas Cowboys didn't play in Dallas, and the New York Giants didn't play in New York. But that day they both played where people had once lived. Poor people. The City of Arlington had condemned and demolished ninety homes to make room for the stadium. The City of Dallas had a chance to bring the Cowboys home; they hadn't played a game in Dallas since 1971 when they left the Cotton Bowl for Texas Stadium in Irving. The Cotton Bowl would have been demolished, and Cowboys Stadium built in its place. It was a once-in-a-life-time opportunity to redevelop South Dallas, to bring people and money and business south of downtown. But politics got in the way. So Arlington got the Cowboys, and poor people got the boot. It was perfectly legal. Scott knew, because he had once condemned poor people's homes for Tom Dibrell's hotel.

The roof was open. God could see his team play – the Cowboys were way ahead at halftime, so He was happy that day – and Scott could see the blue sky. But the lights were still on. Bobby gestured around.

'I read in the *Wall Street Journal* that the stadium consumes more electricity during a single game than Liberia's entire electrical generation capacity.'

'I'd hate to see the bill.'

'Cowboys win one more game, three weeks from today they'll play in the Super Bowl right here. Be fun to bring the girls and Little Scotty.'

'Ticket prices are way above our pay grade. And I'm not sure I'd want to be anywhere near this place that day.'

'The bad guys are in jail. The Super Bowl is safe.'

In three weeks, the Super Bowl would be played in that stadium, on that field. Scott again took in the massive stadium, from the tall glass entrance doors beyond each end zone to the playing field and then up thirty stories to the hole in the roof. It didn't seem possible to have built this place and less possible to bring this place down with a bomb. But apparently they had meant to try.

'This place will be a zoo.'

'And it's not now?'

Kelly Clarkson sang on a stage set up on the fifty-yard line; her face played on the big screen. Fans danced in the aisles and sang along. Hawkers offered beer and hot dogs and cotton candy and beer; the aroma of popcorn and nachos filled the air. Pajamae bounced in front of her seat. Boo played with Little Scotty. Karen drank her coffee. Carlos and Louis zoomed in on the cheerleaders with binoculars. Bobby smiled like a man at peace with the world – until Karen deposited Little Scotty in his lap.

'Your turn,' she said.

'Shit.'

Scott recoiled at the smell. Bobby took it in stride; he was still accustomed to baby shit.

'You know, Scotty, our lives at the courthouse might be boring, but we've got good lives. Better life than I ever dreamed of living. For two renters in Highland Park, our lives turned out damn good.'

'Damn good, Bobby.'

Now Scott smiled like a man at peace with the world. He fist-bumped Little Scotty just as Bobby's pocket began singing 'Sweet Home Alabama.'

'What's that?'

'My phone.'

He answered. He listened. He disconnected. He sat back.

'Shit.'

'Get the boy a clean diaper.'

'Not Little Scotty. The call.'

'Who was that?'

'Porter's magistrate.'

Judge Porter was the senior judge in the district.

'And?'

Bobby blew out a big breath.

'And the arraignment's at ten.'

'What arraignment?'

'Omar al Mustafa and his twenty-two co-conspirators.'

'He needs your help?'

Bobby shook his head. 'You do.'

'Why?'

He faced Scott.

'Because, Scotty, you're the presiding judge.'

Chapter 6

Monday, 18 January
20 days before the Super Bowl

The sun was just peeking above the horizon when Scott ran north on Preston Road past the walled estates of Tom Dibrell, Scott's former rich client, and Jean McCall, the senator's widow, and Jerry Jones. A black Lincoln Town Car pulled through the gates in front of Scott; the driver was Jerry himself. He smiled at Scott and drove off; he was a happy man that day, and well he should be. According to *Forbes* magazine, his football team was the most valuable sports franchise in the world at $4 billion; and if his team won one more game, they would play in the Super Bowl for the first time in twenty years. Any other time, that would be the biggest news story in Dallas; but this was not any other time.

ISIS had come to Dallas.

Scott had presided over perhaps a hundred criminal cases in the last year; most had ended quickly with plea bargains. Most defendants were guilty. A criminal case in federal court followed a fixed procedure, whether the case was tax fraud or terrorism:

indictment; arrest; arraignment; detention hearing; pretrial matters; trial; verdict; sentencing or release. There was a routine to criminal cases. A terrorism case would not be routine, but that day – arraignment and detention – would be: the lawyers would make appearances or be appointed, constitutional rights and criminal charges would be read, pleas would be entered, and conditions would be set for the defendants' release pending trial; or the government would move for pretrial detention, a detention hearing would be held, and he would decide whether the defendants stayed in jail or were released pending trial. The defendants had been indicted by a federal grand jury for conspiring to use a weapon of mass destruction; no doubt the evidence against them was overwhelming. And he had no doubt that they would reside in jail until the verdict.

Scott continued north on Preston Road then turned east. His daily route took him past his old house. He wasn't sure why. He slowed as he came to the mansion at 4000 Beverly Drive. Two and a half stories, 7,500 square feet, six bedrooms, six baths, four-car garage, pool, spa, and cabana, all on one acre in the heart of Highland Park. And that master bathroom shower. He noticed a movement in a second-story window; it was Penny, standing there naked, as she had promised. Scott almost ran into a tree.

He avoided the tree and averted his eyes and ran faster.

Almost four years before, a federal case had taken the $3.5 million mansion from him. He had gotten a daughter in return. What they call in the real-estate business, a steal. He now found himself faced with another federal case. But this time, he was the judge. In three hours, the most dangerous man in Dallas and twenty-two co-conspirators would appear before him charged with plotting to kill a hundred thousand people during the Super Bowl. This was not a silly case; this was terrorism. This case belonged in federal court.

His judicial life would no longer be boring.

72

He ran through the safe environs of Highland Park, Texas, that bright sunny morning completely unaware that his life was about to change again. That this federal case would change more than just his judicial life. That it would change his life. And his daughters' lives. Just as America had never been the same after 9/11, they would never be the same after this case. He just didn't know it that day.

Scott turned the Expedition onto Commerce Street and stopped. Directly in front of him stood the federal courthouse. Parked in front of the courthouse were a dozen network and cable TV trucks with satellite booms extended high into the blue sky. The world's attention was again tuned to Dallas, Texas, just as it had been on November 22, 1963. The FBI SWAT team wore full combat gear and wielded military-style weapons and stood guard behind temporary barricades; hundreds of protestors and as many of the press stood on the safe side of the barricades. The protestors chanted 'Allahu Akbar, Allahu Akbar, Allahu Akbar . . .' and waved signs that read 'MURDER' with a photo of Aabdar Haddad and 'RELIGIOUS PERSE-CUTION IN THE USA' and 'NOT ALL MUSLIMS ARE TERRORISTS.' The press collected interviews and outrage from the protestors for the evening news. Scott had been through a trial with the press, but never before with the SWAT team. He steered into the parking garage and was met by four members of that SWAT team. He rolled down the window.

'ID please,' the agent said.

Scott held out his official identification card. While the agent examined his ID and compared the photo to his face, the other agents opened the back doors and searched the inside with bomb-sniffing dogs and the underside with mirrors for bombs attached to the frame. The agent handed the ID card back and waved Scott through.

'Good luck, Judge.'

As if he knew something Scott did not.

The most dangerous man in Dallas looked like a grandfather. He was. He had seven children and six grandchildren. He stood with his hands folded in front of him and no taller than five and a half feet. He had coarse grey hair and a neatly trimmed grey beard, dark eyes and complexion, and a steady gaze over wire-rimmed reading glasses. He wore a white federal detention jumpsuit, a black skullcap, and shackles, but he retained a calm, almost spiritual demeanor. He did not seem outraged at his arrest; it was as if he fully expected it, as one just expects bad things to happen in life.

If the U.S. government had its way, bad things would happen to the little man standing before Judge A. Scott Fenney.

The bench sat high, and Scott sat behind the bench; he looked upon the courtroom crowded with G-men and G-women, members of the press and public, and twenty-two co-conspirators standing shackled behind the Imam Omar al Mustafa like soldiers behind their general. And the young men offered the fierce expressions of fighting men or men itching to fight.

Magistrate Judge Robert Herrin sat to Scott's left. Typically, the magistrate judge presided over arraignments; but this case was not typical. Twenty-three co-defendants in a joint trial assured it would not be a typical case. And the nature of the crime – conspiracy to blow up Cowboys Stadium during the Super Bowl – was anything but typical. This crime was not an attempt to distribute two kilos of cocaine or turn a tidy profit from insider trading; this was a conspiracy to commit mass murder. Consequently, every eye in the courtroom was fixed not on the judge but on the alleged mastermind.

Karen and Carlos sat to Scott's right. Louis stood off to the side in his bailiff's uniform poised to quash any outburst in the courtroom. In the well of the courtroom stood a slight – and scared? – young woman next to the Imam. A few feet away stood a middle-aged man; he was not scared.

'Appearances, please,' Scott said.

The not-scared man spoke. 'U.S. Attorney Mike Donahue for the government.'

Donahue had the face and the body of an Irish boxer; he had fought at Boston College. The face he could not hide; the body he tried to hide behind a buttoned-up suit, but his appearance always suggested that his body was trying to punch its way out. He had been a felony prosecutor with the Dallas County District Attorney's office for twenty years. When a Democrat won the White House, Republican U.S. Attorneys around the country were replaced by Democrats. Mike Donahue was a Democrat. U.S. Attorneys were political appointees of the party in power, but most were experienced prosecutors. Public defenders were neither. The scared young woman now spoke in a voice that was almost a whisper.

'Marcy Meyers, Assistant Federal Public Defender, for the defendants.'

She was a sophomore in high school making her first debate appearance.

'All of the defendants qualify for appointed counsel?'

'I don't know, Your Honor. I got into the office this morning and was sent up here for the arraignment. My boss said to just plead them "not guilty." '

'Did he now?'

'Yes, sir.'

'And when did you start working in the Public Defender's Office?'

'Last Monday.'

'A whole week on the job.'

'Yes, sir.'

'Why wasn't a more experienced PD sent up?'

'I was next up for a case.'

'You said your boss talked to you.'

'On the phone. He's out of town. He called in.'

'What have you done during your first week?'

'I've helped defendants prepare financial affidavits to qualify for our office to represent them.'

'Well, Ms. Meyers, why don't you help these defendants with the affidavits after the arraignment?'

'Yes, sir.'

Scott addressed the defendants. 'Gentlemen, each of you has been named in a federal indictment and in the arrest warrant pursuant to which you were taken into custody. If any of you contend that you are not the individual named in the warrant – that is, that the government arrested the wrong person – please step forward now so that your identity can be verified.'

None of the defendants stepped forward.

'Please raise your hand if you speak and understand English.'

All the defendants raised their hands as far as the shackles allowed.

'Good. I need to inform you of your constitutional rights.' He put on his glasses and read their rights. 'You have the right to remain silent. You are not required to make a statement. If you have already made a statement, you are not required to say anything more. If you start to make a statement, you may stop at any time. Any statement you do make may be used against you at trial. You have the right to an attorney. An attorney will be appointed to represent you if you cannot afford to hire your own attorney. Ms. Meyers has been appointed to represent you at this arraignment, but each of you must complete a financial affidavit to qualify for appointed counsel. Ms. Meyers will assist each of you after the hearing. Keep in mind that you are swear-ing to the statements in the affidavits, so false statements may subject you to a charge of perjury. I need each of you to confirm on the record that you understand your rights. Judge Herrin will call roll. Please step forward and answer aloud for the record.'

Bobby called each defendant's name, and each defendant answered yes.

'Gentlemen, you have each been charged with conspiracy to use a weapon of mass destruction – specifically, that you and your co-defendants plotted to detonate a bomb within Cowboys Stadium during the Super Bowl – which offense carries a statutory maximum punishment of life in prison, and lesser charges which carry lesser penalties. These are serious felonies brought by the U.S. government. If found guilty, you could spend the rest of your life in prison. Ms. Meyers, have you been given a copy of the indictment?'

'Yes, sir. I was reading it in the elevator.'

'And has each defendant been given a copy?'

'I'm having copies made.'

Scott turned to the U.S. Attorney. 'Mr. Donahue, you have twenty-three defendants. You should have delivered twenty-three copies to Ms. Meyers.'

'My bad, Your Honor.'

'The defendants haven't had time to read the charges or consult with their attorney, so I won't be taking any guilty pleas this morning. Not that I expect to since Ms. Meyers's boss instructed her to plead them not guilty.'

Ms. Meyers smiled.

'Judge, would you like me to read the indictment?' Mr. Donahue said.

A copy of the indictment sat on the desk in front of Scott. It numbered 203 pages.

'Ms. Meyers,' Scott said, 'do the defendants waive reading of the indictment?'

'Uhh . . . should they?'

'We might be here a while if they don't.'

'Defendants waive reading of the indictment.'

'Very well.'

'The government objects,' Mr. Donahue said.

'Don't.' Scott again addressed the defendants. 'Gentlemen, do you understand the charges brought against you? I will need you to answer aloud for the record. And each of you must enter a plea to the charges. You may enter a plea of guilty, not guilty, or *nolo contendre*, although the only plea I will accept today is not guilty. If, after reading the indictment and consulting with your lawyer, you want to plead guilty, we will reconvene to change your plea. When Judge Herrin reads your name, please step forward, state yes that you understand the charges or no you do not, and then enter a plea.'

Bobby again read each name.

'Moammar Rahaim.'

A defiant-looking young man raised his shackled hands and spoke. Defiantly.

'Yes. I understand the charges the U.S. government has brought against me and against Islam. We both plead not guilty.'

'Syed Aboud.'

'Yes. Not guilty.'

'Adwan Farhat.'

'Yes. Not guilty.'

Nineteen more defendants pleaded not guilty. Then came the last defendant. Scott addressed him.

'Omar al Mustafa, do you understand the charges brought against you by the U.S. government?'

'I do not.'

'What do you not understand?'

'Why I was charged.'

'You were charged because a federal grand jury determined that there is probable cause to believe that you committed the alleged offenses. Whether you are guilty or not will be determined at trial where you will be represented by counsel appointed by the government if you cannot afford to hire a lawyer.'

Mustafa turned to Ms. Meyers and looked her up and down. He turned back to Scott with a bemused expression.

'This cute little girl? She is my lawyer? She should be home having many Muslim babies.'

'I'm not married or Muslim,' Ms. Meyers said.

'You could convert.'

'I'm Jewish.'

'I'm sorry.'

'Mr. Mustafa,' Scott said, 'the question now is whether you understand that you have been charged with serious felonies that may result in your imprisonment for a very long time.'

'I do understand that.'

'Good. How do you plead to such charges?'

'Not guilty.'

'Not guilty pleas will be entered in the record for all defendants. Under the Speedy Trial Act, a defendant in federal court is entitled to a trial within seventy days of the arraignment. So trial is set for . . .'

Scott waited for Karen to consult the court's docket.

'March the seventh,' she said.

'March the seventh at nine A.M.,' Scott said. 'The defense may request a continuance. The case is currently scheduled as a joint trial of all defendants. If any defendant does not wish to proceed jointly with the others, he may file a motion for a separate trial. And each defendant may request separate counsel. That's your right. Defendants who elect to have joint representation will be required to sign a waiver of their right to separate counsel. After the arraignment, the magistrate judge will go through the waiver procedure with each defendant here in court. The magistrate judge will send out a motion schedule to both attorneys in a few days. Last item: the defendants' release pending trial.'

'Your Honor,' Mr. Donahue said, 'the government requests pretrial detention of all defendants and moves for a detention hearing on the grounds that under the Bail Reform Act, section thirty-one-forty-two-f-two, A, the defendants pose a serious risk that they will flee the jurisdiction before trial, B, they will obstruct or attempt to obstruct justice, and threaten, injure, or intimidate, or attempt to threaten, injure, or intimidate, a prospective witness or juror, and C, under section thirty-one-forty-two-f-one of the Act, they have been indicted for an offense listed in eighteen U.S.C. section twenty-three-thirty-two-b, specifically, the use of weapons of mass destruction. And the presumption applies under thirty-one-forty-two-e-three-B.'

'Ms. Meyers?'

She stared open-mouthed and wide-eyed at the U.S. Attorney like an English major listening to a computer geek explaining algorithms.

'Ms. Meyers?'

She turned her wide eyes to Scott. 'Yes, sir?'

Scott sighed. He had once been where she was, in over her head. Drowning in the complexity of the law. Clueless. She was in desperate need of a teaching moment.

'Ms. Meyers, as I'm sure you learned in law school, under the U.S. Constitution the defendants are entitled to release pending trial unless they are flight risks or dangers to the community. They may not be detained pending trial for any other reason. The Bail Reform Act sets forth rules for release and detention in federal court, rules I must follow. The Act states that I must release the defendants on their personal recognizance unless I determine that they are in fact flight risks or dangers to the community. In that event, I must still release the defendants but I must impose the least restrictive conditions to their release that will ensure their appearance at trial and negate their danger to the community. I am not allowed to set bond in an amount the defendants cannot afford simply to effect their detention. If I determine, after a detention hearing, that there are no conditions that will ensure the defendants' appearance at trial and the safety of the community, only then may I order the defendants detained pending trial.'

Ms. Meyers was actually taking notes.

'The Act further provides that if there is probable cause to believe the defendants committed certain prescribed offenses, there is a rebuttable presumption that no such conditions exist; that is, there is a presumption of pretrial detention. One of those offenses is conspiracy to use weapons of mass destruction. In this case, probable cause has been established by the fact of the indictment; an indictment means a grand jury found probable cause to believe the defendants committed the crime. Which, Ms. Meyers, means that the defendants will be detained pending trial unless you, as their duly appointed counsel, rebut the presumption at the detention hearing.'

'And how do I do that?'

'You must present some evidence at the detention hearing that contradicts the government's assertion that the defendants are flight risks or dangers to the community. You don't have to prove the defendants' innocence on the charges; you only have to present evidence that they are neither flight risks nor dangers to the community. You may cross-examine the government's witnesses and you may present your own evidence and witnesses. And since the government invoked the presumption, you may subpoena witnesses whose testimony will relate to the weight of the evidence against the defendants, one of the factors the court must consider at the hearing.'

She threw her hands up. '*Like who?*'

'I don't know.'

'And when is the detention hearing?'

'Your Honor,' Mr. Donahue said, 'the government requests the hearing be held now.'

'*Now?*' Ms. Meyers said.

'Ms. Meyers,' Scott said, 'if you need time to prepare for the detention hearing, you may seek a continuance.'

'I seek.'

'How much time would you like?'

'A year.'

'How about five days? That's all the time I can give you under the Act.'

'I'll take it.'

'I thought you might. Detention hearing is set for . . .'

'Friday at nine,' Karen said.

'Friday at nine.'

'Your Honor,' Mr. Donahue said, 'the government requests that you preside at the detention hearing rather than the magistrate judge.'

'I was planning to but why do you ask?'

'Timing. With the Super Bowl only twenty days away, if the magistrate judge rules on detention the losing party will file an appeal for the district judge – you – to hear the issue *de novo*, and we'll be back at square one. We don't have time for that.'

'Good point. Given the number of defendants, I think Judge Herrin and I will work this case together.'

'A good decision, Your Honor.'

'Thank you.' To the defendants: 'Gentlemen, a Pretrial Services Officer will consult with each of you before the detention hearing to prepare a release report. This officer works for the court. His or her – actually, her . . . Ms. O'Brien – her job is not to obtain a confession or other evidence or information concerning your guilt or innocence of the crimes for which you are charged. Her sole job is to obtain information about you to determine if you are a flight risk – that is, if you will flee the jurisdiction to avoid trial – or if you are a danger to the community. She will ask for information about your family, criminal history, employment, and other background material. Please help the officer help you. Again, the detention hearing is your only opportunity to secure release from jail pending trial.'

Scott sat back and surveyed the courtroom. As the king said in *Lord of the Rings*, 'And so it begins.' The girls loved those movies, so they had watched the trilogy more than once. Good prevailed over evil on the battlefield of Mordor. Would good prevail in a courtroom of the United States of America?

'The defendants will remain in custody pending the detention hearing. The magistrate judge will handle the joint representation matter with the defendants. I'll see counsel in chambers. Court is adjourned.'

'You're a federal judge. Which means someone will always be mad at you. Because all the issues of the day come before you – abortion, gay rights, gun control, Obamacare, immigration – and you have to decide who wins and who loses. You don't want to, but you have to. It's your job.'

The distinguished-looking man with wavy white hair was a Democrat but he looked like a Republican. He sat directly across the desk from Scott as if he had called this meeting. Which was understandable. J. Hamilton McReynolds III was one of the most powerful men in the world. He presided over the Department of Justice, the Federal Bureau of Investigation, the Bureau of Alcohol, Tobacco, Firearms, and Explosives, the

Drug Enforcement Administration, and the Federal Bureau of Prisons. He was the United States Attorney General, the chief law enforcement officer in America; he reported only to the president, the most powerful man in the world. An Assistant AG sat to his left, the U.S. Attorney to his right; they both knew to keep their mouths shut in front of the boss. The FBI agent named Beckeman whom Scott had seen on the news report stood at attention by the windows; he did not seem the type to keep his mouth shut. The public defender sat on the couch like a child at a gathering of grownups. Scott reached for the bowl.

'Toffee?'

'Don't mind if I do.'

Scott flipped a toffee to the AG. The others shook him off, but the FBI agent held up an open hand. Scott fired a strike.

'Amazing what people expect from federal judges, isn't it?' the AG said. 'God didn't choose to make life fair, but somehow we must. If only we could. I couldn't.' He grunted. 'These are good.'

Scott pushed the bowl to the AG's side of the desk. 'Help yourself.' He did. 'You were a federal judge?'

He nodded. 'Up in Philadelphia. Appointed for life to a lifetime of letting people down. So I jumped when the president offered me this post. Attorney general, I don't have to even think about fair.'

'What do you think about?'

'Terrorism.'

The attorney general had flown to Dallas for the arraignment of Omar al Mustafa — and a photo op to assure other prospective jihadists in America that the Joint Terrorism Task Force would hunt them down and bring them to justice. He sighed as if the weight of the world — or at least the safety of America — rested on his shoulders. It did.

'So, Judge, can I count on you?'

'To do what?'

'The right thing.'

'Which is?'

'Detain Mustafa and the other defendants pending the Super Bowl.'

'You mean pending the trial?'

'No, I mean the Super Bowl. That game is the biggest security risk to the homeland we face each year. It's the biggest worldwide sporting event. They would love to attack us then and there, during the celebration of the American way of life.'

'It's a football game.'

'It's America. It's an expression of our freedom. Our patriotism. Our prosperity. Our place in the world.'

Perhaps he was right. The Super Bowl often seemed to be about everything except the game. A hundred thousand people watching in the stadium, a billion more on television around the world, advertisements that sold for $150,000 per second of airtime, Beyoncé or Springsteen as the halftime entertainment – the Super Bowl had transcended football. It was a uniquely American cultural event.

'The detention hearing Friday will answer that question.'

'I need an answer now. And the answer needs to be yes.'

'What evidence is there that he's a danger to the community?'

'I'm going to tell you.'

'When?'

'Right now.' He leaned forward slightly. 'He's a danger to the community. I give you my word.'

'That's your evidence? Mr. McReynolds—'

'Call me Mac.'

'—the Constitution requires more than your word, even if you are the AG.'

The AG leaned back and blew out a breath. He had not gotten the answer he wanted. He took another toffee.

'May I call you Scott?'

'In here. Not out there.'

'Scott, you're not that naïve.'

'Maybe I am.'

'Maybe you want to be. Innocence is for the innocent, Scott. For children, not grownups. Kids can be blissfully ignorant of the real world around them – my grandkids believe in Santa Claus, and they should – but we can't. We can't afford to be ignorant of the real world. Because when we are, bad guys fly planes into skyscrapers. And people die. Men, women, and children. Innocence kills, Scott.'

'What if Mustafa is innocent?'

'What if he's not? What are you going to do Super Bowl Sunday if that stadium comes down?'

'Mr. McReynolds . . . Mac . . . a grand jury indicted Mustafa for conspiring to use weapons of mass destruction. Certainly you have sufficient evidence that he's a danger to the community.'

The AG sighed. 'Off the record?'

Scott glanced over at Ms. Meyers on the couch. Her head was down; she was shuffling through the indictment like a confused student engaged in last-minute cramming before a final exam. She was clueless and oblivious.

Scott nodded at the AG.

The AG leaned forward again; this time he motioned Scott forward as well. The two men's heads almost met over the desk, close enough that Scott could smell the toffee on his breath. The AG whispered.

'We got nothing.'

'What do you mean, nothing?'

Scott was also whispering.

'I mean, we got nothing. No evidence at all.'

'How'd you get the grand jury to indict? Without evidence, there's no probable cause. Without probable cause, there's no indictment.'

The AG shrugged. 'What grand jury wants to no-bill the next nine-eleven hijackers?'

'Who told the grand jury that Mustafa and his co-defendants were the next nine-eleven hijackers?'

'I did.'

The two lawyers sat back. Scott considered the legal and ethical implications of an alleged terrorist sitting in federal detention on his order despite the allegations against him being supported by no evidence whatsoever, and of the United States Attorney General admitting to the presiding judge that an indictment against an American citizen was without any factual basis whatsoever. His armpits felt damp. He grabbed a toffee.

'You searched his home and mosque?'

The AG nodded. 'Nothing.'

The FBI agent named Beckeman snorted. 'You should see his home. Preston Hollow, got six bedrooms and six bathrooms, big-ass pool and guest house out back. Who needs a home like that?'

Scott bit down on the toffee and turned back to the AG. 'Did you tap his phone?'

'Also nothing.'

'No money transfers?'

'Nope.'

'No incriminating emails or texts?'

'Nope.'

'I read that ISIS communicates with their people over the Internet, Twitter and Facebook.'

'They do. They send out press releases on Twitter, but they plot attacks on the "dark Net," the part of the Internet you can't google. That's where the bad guys live – drug traffickers, human traffickers, pedophiles, and Islamic terrorists. And they use software that routes their messages around the world before the actual destination to hide their locations, and end-to-end encryption to evade NSA eavesdropping. Mustafa might be communicating with ISIS daily.'

'Or he might not be.'

'That's correct. We think he is, but we can't prove he is. Not in a court of law. Not yet.'

'A bunch of terrorists in the desert of Syria are more sophisticated with technology than the FBI?'

'No. But ISIS is the richest terrorist organization in the history of the world. We estimate their cash holdings at just under a billion dollars. That kind of money hires the best geeks in the world.'

'Where do they get their money?'

'Ransom, black-market oil, sale of looted antiquities, donations from our friends in Saudi Arabia.'

Now Scott blew out a breath. 'What am I supposed to do?'

'Cooperate.'

'With the prosecution? I thought a federal judge is supposed to protect individual rights and uphold the Constitution?'

'Not since nine-eleven. Everything changed the moment those planes hit those towers. When we saw Americans jumping out of windows to their deaths, when we saw those buildings come down, the world changed. We changed. Before that day, we worried about whack jobs like Koresh in Waco, and our job was to investigate crimes after the fact. After that day, our number one law enforcement priority has been Islamic terrorism – and there is no number two. Our job now is to prevent terrorist attacks in America. We've had to change our tactics since nine-eleven, and even more so since ISIS called for lone wolf attacks in the West. We can no longer

88

wait for a suspect to act; we have to act before they act. We investigate threats, not crimes. Intentions, not actions. Prevention, not reaction, is our job. We have to kill them before they kill us.'

He aimed a thumb at Agent Beckeman by the window.

'Our Joint Terrorism Task Forces run by guys like Beckeman have proven highly successful. Highly trained, locally based, passionately committed investigators, analysts, linguists, SWAT teams, and other specialists from all our law enforcement and intelligence agencies working in cooperation to prevent terrorist attacks.'

'That sounds like a recruiting commercial.'

The AG smiled. 'It is. I wrote that. The Patriot Act gave us the powers we need to negate these threats – we can search emails and capture phone conversations, we can conduct sneak-and-peak searches of homes and businesses—'

A sneak-and-peak search warrant allowed the government to conduct the search without first informing the suspect.

'—and we can employ roving wiretaps so they can't evade our surveillance with cell phones.'

'What else do you need?'

'Cooperative judges.'

'You mean judges looking the other way.'

'I mean judges looking at terrorists like Mustafa the right way.'

'Even if he's innocent of the charges?'

The AG chuckled. 'Innocent? No, no, Scott, innocence is not the issue. Proof is. He's guilty, we just have to prove it. And we will.'

'When?'

'At trial.'

'But you want me to keep him in that jail cell until then?'

'No. Just until after the Super Bowl.'

'You have no evidence of his involvement in this plot, and thus no evidence that he's a danger to the community, but you want me to detain him anyway?'

'Yes.'

'You got the grand jury to find probable cause where none exists to indict, now you want me to detain him on the basis of that faulty indictment?'

'I want you to protect the American people.'

'This isn't Guantanamo Bay.'

'It should be, at least for guys like Mustafa,' Agent Beckeman said. 'Some of the Muslims the president released from Guantanamo, they're the guys beheading Americans on those ISIS videos.'

'The Constitution says we're not supposed to imprison people without evidence,' Scott said.

'And assholes for Allah aren't supposed to fly planes into fucking office buildings!'

The AG gave the agent a disapproving glance then spoke calmly to Scott.

'Scott, in my job – protecting the American homeland – I have to take a broader view of criminal justice when it comes to terrorism. With your run-of-the-mill criminals – murderers, drug lords, and the like – the Constitution works just fine. The defendant commits the crime; we indict him, arrest him, and prove him guilty of that particular crime. His priors are irrelevant. The fact that he may have murdered two other people before doesn't mean he murdered this victim. His priors are relevant only in sentencing once he's been found guilty. Like O.J. He got off on the double murder charge, but ten years later we nabbed him for armed robbery. The judge threw the book at him because we all know he killed those two people ten years before. He'll die in prison now.'

'But O.J. was found guilty of the second offense, the offense for which he was sentenced. That's different than convicting someone of a crime they didn't commit even if they did commit prior crimes.'

'Yes, it is. But what if we could? For example, what if we suspect a drug kingpin of murder, but we can't prove it. But we know he's killed a number of other people and he will kill again. If we can convict him on a murder he might not have committed, should we do it and put him in prison or let him go? Should we wait till he kills again or should we take him off the streets and prevent future killings?'

'The Founding Fathers answered that question when they wrote the Constitution.'

'They did indeed. But back then, there weren't Islamic terrorists who killed thousands of people at a time. So don't we have to look at the Constitution differently when it comes to terrorism? I think we do. I call it "cumulative justice." I look at a terrorist's entire body of work, not just the plot he's charged with. Scott, what if we could have convicted Osama bin Laden before nine-eleven and put him in prison?'

'Three thousand lives would have been saved.'

'Exactly. And all those lives lost in Iraq and Afghanistan chasing the son of a bitch. But what if we had charged him with a crime of terrorism of which he was innocent, or at least we couldn't prove his guilt?'

'Then he wouldn't have been convicted.'

The AG smiled. 'You are naïve. Of course he would've been convicted in an American court by American jurors who are terrified of terrorism in America. He was a bad guy before nine-eleven, we knew that. We just couldn't take him off the streets since he was in Afghanistan. But Mustafa is right here in Dallas. He's downstairs in a jail cell. We took him off the streets before he could commit his act of terrorism – not after the fact, but before the fact. And with the fear of terrorism, a jury will convict him and sentence him to life in prison for this plot.'

'But you have no evidence of his guilt.'

'Doesn't matter. Even if he didn't do this plot – trust me, he did – he's done other bad things or he's going to do other bad things, so let's take him off the streets now while we can. Before he can. Let's prevent the crime. Let's convict him and put him in prison *before* he kills innocent people.'

'You know, like *Minority Report* without the Pre-Cogs,' Beckeman said.

Scott turned to the FBI agent. 'Without the what?'

'Beckeman's a big movie buff,' the AG said.

'Only thing I know better than movies is Islamic jihadists,' Beckeman said.

Scott turned back to the AG. 'How do you know Mustafa wants to kill people?'

'He's been on our radar for years and on YouTube for longer,' the AG said. 'He's put out hundreds of videos and done hundreds of interviews. Whenever a national news outlet needs a' – the AG fashioned quotation marks with his fingers – ' "radical Muslim cleric" to spew jihadist bullshit, they call him. He's charismatic, articulate, and smart – he never takes the bait. He loves the attention. We figured he was all talk, like Republicans saying on Fox News they want to cut the size of the federal government. But six months ago, we received an anonymous tip to our hotline alerting us to this Haddad boy and the plot to blow up the stadium. We put him under round-the-clock surveillance. He was posing as an architectural student at the University of Texas at Arlington. Perfect cover. His apartment faced the stadium. The manager said he specifically requested that view, like the nine-eleven hijackers getting an apartment with a view of the World

Trade Center. Haddad led us to Mustafa. Prayed at his mosque. All his boys are hardcore Islamic radicals. We recovered ISIS videotapes and magazines and their guidebook to terror.'

The AG held out an open hand to the Assistant AG, who slapped a book into his hand like a nurse slapping a scalpel into a surgeon's hand. The AG dropped the book on the desk in front of Scott. He put on his glasses and read the title: *The Management of Savagery.* The AG shook his head.

'We read *Fifty Shades of Grey* to learn how to have better sex through bondage. These people read books to learn how to behead infidels for maximum shock value.' He turned his palms up. 'How will we ever live in peace with savages?'

The AG gazed out the window; his expression was that of a man who had lost all understanding of the world outside the window. After a moment, his eyes returned to the book. He picked it up and stared at it.

'It's an odd culture.'

'Only three letters separate a culture from a cult,' Agent Beckeman said.

The AG handed the book to the Assistant AG and exhaled. 'Mustafa, he's been operating his own little ISIS franchise right here in Dallas.'

'He wasn't exactly flying under the radar,' Scott said.

'Hiding in plain sight.'

'I'd like to waterboard that son of a bitch,' Beckeman said.

The attorney general exhaled as if a father whose young son had spoken out of turn in front of grownups. Without even glancing that way, he said, 'Beckeman, you're an FBI agent in America now, not a Marine in Afghanistan. Try to keep that in mind.'

'But he has no criminal history?' Scott said.

'No.'

'So you have evidence that he's an ISIS sympathizer,' Scott said, 'but no evidence that ties him to the stadium plot. How do you know he wants to kill Americans?'

'His own words. He hates America. He wants America brought down.'

'Where was he born? Iraq? Afghanistan? Syria?'

'Chicago.'

'He's *American?*'

'As apple pie. Omar Mansour, born three May nineteen fifty-nine. Parents were Jordanian immigrants. Father was a doctor, mother a professor of Islamic theology, the mainstream stuff. Omar was a brilliant student, went to the University of Jordan in Amman to follow in his mother's footsteps. Lived there fourteen years, got a doctorate in Sharia law, but he fell in with the jihadi Salafism crowd. We believe he came under the influence of Abu Musab al Zarqawi, the founder of ISIS, and Sheikh Abu Muhammad al Maqdisi, his spiritual mentor, in Jordan. They believe that any government that does not rule by strict Islamic law as practiced by Muhammad himself – which is to say, *not* the mainstream stuff – is an infidel regime and should be violently overthrown. They consider it their holy duty to wage jihad to bring the world under Sharia.' The AG shrugged. 'Not exactly live-and-let-live sort of guys. Anyway, he came back home in ninety-five, set up shop in Dallas, and adopted the *nom de guerre* Omar al Mustafa. He must have seen that movie.'

'What movie?' Scott said.

'*Lion King,*' Beckeman said. 'All these jihadists, they adopt names from places they lived, where they were born, historical figures they admired – like I'd be Eric Abu al Callahan.' The agent chuckled. 'Dirty Harry. His last name was Callahan.'

Scott grunted in response. How else does one respond to that?

'Yeah, I figure Omar fell in love with the *Lion King*, named himself Mustafa.'

He and the others laughed. Scott did not. He was confused. He had seen that movie only a few Saturdays before with the girls.

'You mean M*ufasa*? That was the lion king's name. Not M*ustafa*.'

'Really?'

The AG turned to Agent Beckeman. 'You got the name wrong? It's not funny now.'

Beckeman offered a lame shrug; the AG shook his head and returned to Scott.

'Osama was an educated elitist from a rich Saudi family. ISIS founders were street thugs from Jordan. During the war, they were the al Qaeda franchise in Iraq, but they split off and became so violent that al Qaeda disavowed them in twenty-fourteen. Imagine that. Anyway, being street thugs was okay at first, but now they need religious cover for their barbarism. And that's where Mustafa comes in. He's one of the most prominent Islamic clerics in apocalyptic exegesis.'

'Which is?'

'End of days. That's the religious foundation of ISIS, that the apocalypse is upon us. The messiah – they call him the Mahdi – will soon return to earth and purify the world of the infidels.'

'Who are?'

'Us.'

'They want an apocalyptic confrontation with America,' Beckeman said. 'In the desert of Syria, in a town called Dabiq. They think the prophecies foretell it, the "final battle," as they say, killing the *kuffars*.'

'Seems crazy, I know,' the AG said, 'but most Muslims in the Middle East believe this end of days crap. Who knows how many in the U.S. But it brings a lot of young Muslims to Mustafa's mosque. He's their spiritual father.'

'He's like that old blind monk in *Kung Fu*,' Beckeman said. 'And they're his grasshoppers. He radicalizes them, brainwashes them, and sends them to their deaths in Syria while he sends his own sons to Ivy League schools.'

'The radicalization of young Muslims by old clerics is a big problem,' the AG said. 'And mosques are jihadist factories right here in America.'

'You saw their faces in the courtroom,' Beckeman said. 'They'd just as soon cut your throat as look at you. Like Haddad. Two years ago, he was just a college kid. Today, he's conspiring to blow up a football stadium. Or he was.'

'Maybe he was just a college kid.'

'He was a terrorist.'

'Are you sure?'

'Pretty sure.'

'Now he's dead.'

Agent Beckeman shrugged. 'Better safe than sorry.'

'What was the probable cause?'

'He was Muslim.'

'He was an American citizen.'

'Scott—'

'You can call me judge.'

Agent Beckeman snorted. '*Judge*, with those guys, being a Muslim comes before being an American.'

'Now he's a dead Muslim American.'

Beckeman almost laughed. '*Muslim* American? I don't tell people I'm a *Catholic* American. I'm just an American, and that's damn well good enough for me.'

There was a long awkward moment, which was finally broken by Beckeman's boss.

'You feel better now?'

'Actually, I do.' The agent turned back to Scott. 'The tip said he was heavily armed and his apartment was rigged with explosives. We couldn't take chances. When he went for his gun . . .'

'Did you recover a gun?'

'No. But I saw him go for a gun.'

'*You* shot him?'

Beckeman nodded. 'Three times in the head.'

'You're a tough guy, Agent Beckeman.'

'That's why I run the Task Force. Watch those ISIS videos, those guys hacking civilians' heads off with machetes, they're tough guys, too.'

'Did you recover bomb-making materials from Haddad's apartment?'

'No. But we recovered architectural plans for the stadium. Why else would he be studying those plans? Because Mustafa wants to bring that stadium down on those people. If he does, he'll be the man among Muslims.'

'Not all Muslims are like that.'

'The hell they're not. There are three kinds of Muslims: jihadists, jihadist wannabes, and jihadist sympathizers. Why aren't the so-called mainstream Muslims calling us, ID-ing the bad guys? Did you know the bullies in your neighborhood? They know the jihadists in their mosques. But Muslims won't rat out Muslims because they say the Koran prohibits it. Because they secretly sympathize with them. Because extremist Islam is mainstream Islam today. After the Paris attacks they had a moment of silence for the victims at a national soccer match in Turkey. The fans – Muslims – booed and chanted "Allahu Akbar." Those fifty thousand fans were mainstream Muslims? We don't want to face the truth: we *are* fighting a religious war – because they are. Because they want it to be. The West versus Islam. Because that feeds into their end of days narrative. Every Muslim's allegiance is to Muhammad, not their country – not to America or Britain or France, as we saw in Paris. If they ever have to choose between America or Muhammad, they'll choose Muhammad.'

'Agent! Those are inappropriate comments.'

The Marine-turned-FBI agent took two quick steps toward his boss as if to punch him. Instead, he took a toffee from the bowl. Which he pointed at his boss.

'You're political, Mac, just like the president. He won't even call them "Islamic jihadists," calls them a generic "jihadists" instead. Like there might be some Baptist jihadists out there. He's playing politics. He's afraid of offending Muslims. I'm not. My job is to stop them. And that's what I intend to do.' He turned the toffee on Scott. 'And you, Judge, need to get on board. You need to understand who these people are. Who Mustafa is. Before people die. They hate us, Judge, and they're not through with us yet.'

'When will they be through with us?'

'When we're all dead.'

'Little dramatic, don't you think?'

'The harsh truth, Judge. Look at the Syrian immigrant crisis. One million Muslims walking into Germany, Austria, Slovenia . . . but they'll never be Germans or Austrians or Slovenians. They'll never assimilate. They'll always be Muslims. And one day they'll rise up against the Germans and Austrians and Slovenians. One day, they'll kill them.'

'How do you know that will happen?'

'Paris. France let the Muslims in, now the Muslims kill the French. Why? Because the country they were born in bombed ISIS Muslims in Syria.'

'This is Dallas. The Bible Belt. You probably arrested half the Muslims in town.'

'Hardly. A hundred fifty thousand Muslims live in Dallas.'

'Really?'

'Really.'

'Still, Paris, London, New York City – but Dallas? Not very sexy.'

'For these people, killing is better than sex. Hell, they do suicide bombings so they can have sex with virgins in heaven.'

The AG nodded. 'They do. Seventy-two virgins.'

'What do they want?'

The agent ticked off on his fingers. 'One, Christians and Jews out of the Middle East. Two, the world under strict Islamic law. Three, a return to the glory days of the Ottoman Empire, when Muslims mattered.'

The AG grimaced as if in pain. 'Scott, please don't quote Agent Beckeman. The liberal press would kill us.'

'You're a liberal Democrat.'

'No. I'm not a Republican. There's a difference.'

'We're off the record.'

'Thank you.'

Agent Beckeman regarded his own fingers then pointed his index finger at Scott again.

'One thing more I know, Judge. They're here. Living among us. Plotting against us. Waiting for instructions to activate. Like that other Cruise movie.'

'*Jerry Maguire?*'

'*Jerry Maguire?* No. *War of the Worlds.*'

'You sure you got the right movie this time?' the AG said.

He gave Scott a sly wink; Beckeman ignored the AG. His voice turned somber.

'And that's exactly what this is, Judge. A war of the worlds. Their world or ours. Their way of life or ours. There's no truce, no peace with honor, no cohabiting this planet peaceably. There's no winning their hearts and minds. There's only dead or alive. Them or us.'

Scott leaned back in his chair and noticed the public defender hiding on the couch. He had forgotten about her.

'Ms. Meyers . . .?'

She looked up like a lost child. 'Yes, sir?'

'Do you have anything to add?'

'Uhh . . . no, sir?'

Scott blew out a breath. The Sixth Amendment to the Constitution guaranteed the imam and the other defendants the right to competent defense counsel. Ms. Meyers might be that counsel one day; but not that day.

'Ms. Meyers, I'm considering appointing experienced private counsel to represent the defendants in the detention hearing. How would you feel about that?'

'Relieved.'

He turned back to the G-men. 'Anything else, gentlemen?'

'We need to discuss your security,' Agent Beckeman said.

'We don't kill judges in America.'

'We also don't fly commercial airplanes into office buildings. But they do.'

'I'm not worried about my security.'

'Say the word, and we'll put a detail on you twenty-four/ seven.'

The attorney general grabbed a toffee and stood. He stepped to the door but turned back to Scott with a somber expression.

'We have a chance to save lives, Scott. American lives, here at home. We have to beat them here because we'll never defeat them over there.'

'Why not?'

'Because we can't kill civilians.'

'So, we have a real-life terrorism case playing out right here in Dallas.'

Four miles north of the federal courthouse, Professor Ken Johnson addressed his constitutional law class at the Southern Methodist University School of Law.

'But, according to my friends in the press – I was in the courtroom this morning for the arraignment – who spoke to their sources in the FBI, the only evidence the government has against the imam is his anti-American and pro-ISIS statements. We would assume that there is some evidence directly connecting him to the alleged plot because he was indicted by a federal grand jury. But we all know that grand juries indict and trial juries acquit. So the fact that he was indicted does not mean he's guilty. Or even that there is probable cause that he committed a crime.'

'He's a radical Islamist cleric,' Mr. Edwards on the third row said. 'Have you seen his YouTube videos?'

'I have. All within free speech. He never advocates or incites violence. And who decides who's radical and who's mainstream? The federal government? The Founding Fathers were considered radical when they created this county, at least to the king of England. What if the imam and other Muslims are rebelling against Middle Eastern dictators that we placed in power and kept in power? Maybe they want to live their lives their way?'

'Killing Jews? A guy named Hitler wanted to live his life that way, too.'

'We're getting off topic. At this moment in time, the imam faces the prospect of sitting in a jail cell until trial because he exercised his right of free speech. He said things the government doesn't like to hear, things many of us don't like to hear, things I don't like to hear, frankly. But he has a right to say things we don't like, doesn't he? Did nine-eleven amend the Bill of Rights? The Patriot Act says yes. It's a brave new world of terrorism, so the Constitution has to be read according to the world we now live in, not the world the Founding Fathers lived in. Ironically, that has always been the judicial philosophy of the liberals, myself included, that the Constitution should be read in light of the current world. The conservatives always argued for original intent. Now, roles are reversed. Liberals argue for original intent, and conservatives argue for a modern view – at least when it comes to the rights of privacy and free speech. Ms. Oliver?'

He pointed to a young woman on the front row.

'He has a free speech right to say those things even if we find them disgusting. Free speech is not evidence that he committed a crime. Just because I say I wish you were dead – I don't – doesn't make me guilty of conspiring to murder you.'

'But what if he wanted the stadium to come down?'

'What if I'm hoping you die? Just because I want it to happen doesn't mean that I'm trying to make it happen. The government must present evidence of that fact, that he's involved in the plot, to establish that he is in fact a danger to the community, to prevent his release.'

'Any contrary opinions?'

Mr. Graber, also on the front row, raised his hand. Professor Johnson nodded at him.

'The imam should not be released. This isn't a case of the *New York Times* wanting to print the Pentagon Papers. That's an easy case. This is more akin to shouting "fire" in a crowded theater. The speaker knows people will likely take action and others will be hurt. Here we have a Muslim cleric whose words encourage if not incite violence, whom the FBI believes is the mastermind behind a plot to kill a hundred thousand people at the Super Bowl. What is his right to freedom pending the verdict versus the right of those hundred thousand people to stay alive? What if the FBI is right?'

'What if they're wrong? Does the imam's exercise of his First Amendment rights make him a danger to the community? Does exercising his free speech rights cause him to lose his

Fifth Amendment rights? What about his Sixth Amendment rights? Do we deny him competent counsel because we don't like what he says? Does the judge keep him in custody until after the Super Bowl just in case? Is that right?'

'We did it during World War Two with the Japanese. We thought they were a danger to America so we rounded them up and put them in concentration camps for the duration of the war. And the Supreme Court said that was okay.'

'We did. But they weren't Japanese. They were American citizens of Japanese descent. The imam is also an American citizen. Why don't we just ship him off to Guantanamo Bay?'

'Why don't we? Professor, all this theory of law is neat, but on Super Bowl Sunday there won't be theories in that stadium. There'll be real people. Who might die. I've got a better idea: let's nuke the Middle East. Bomb those Islamic jihadists back to the Stone Age where they want us to live.'

'Mr. Graber, this is a con law class, not the O'Reilly show. I expect civility.'

'Those Muslims behead innocent people. How civil is that? Why should we be civil to them? They're here living among us, plotting against us.'

He cast a menacing glance at two students sitting on the back row with their heads bowed.

Abdul jabaar and Saddam Siddiqui glanced sideways at each other and knew immediately that they shared the same thoughts. The same fears. They were brothers, they were Muslim, and they were nervous. They knew Aabdar Haddad. They prayed at the same mosque. They were shocked when they had heard of his death. They also knew the imam. And he knew them. Would he lead the FBI to them? Would he break in jail and point fingers at other Muslims to save himself? Would he point an accusing finger at the Siddiqui brothers?

They knew all the other young Muslim men who had been arrested with the imam. Would they be next? Would the FBI SWAT team show up at their house in the middle of the night or at the law school during class and arrest them? They had been anxious since the news had broken Saturday. Their anxiety increased exponentially when they had arrived at the law school that morning to suspicious looks from the other students, looks to which they had become accustomed since 9/11. Suspicion came with being a Muslim in America during the age of al Qaeda, al-Shabab, Ansar al-Shariah, Boko Haram, and ISIS. They understood that. So they laid low. They did not call attention to themselves. They made no overt display of their religion at the law school. They dressed like the other law students. They acted like the other law students. They blended in with the other law students. They looked like law students.

They did not look like terrorists.

'The PD representing Mustafa,' Mike Donahue said, 'we'll kick her pretty little ass Friday.'

Mac nodded at Donahue. They rode in a black Suburban with Agent Beckeman back to FBI Headquarters. His second in command, an agent named Stryker, drove. Four G-men in one car, it was a Brut aftershave commercial.

'You'd better. Mustafa stays in that cell until after the Super Bowl. That's straight from the president.'

'Then the president better call the judge,' Beckeman said. He sighed and shook his head in disgust. 'He's like my goddamned sister.'

'She's a judge?'

'Nun. She thinks all men are good. I tell her, you haven't met an Islamic jihadist.'

'Family reunions at your house must be fun,' Donahue said.

'What if the judge appoints private counsel?' Mac said.

'No defense attorney in Dallas will touch the case. Come Friday, that little girl is going to stand up in court for Mustafa.'

'What's your strategy with her?'

'Stand aside and let her lose the hearing.' He laughed. 'We won't need evidence to beat her.'

'Don't bet the ranch on it,' Mac said. 'Not with Fenney.' He pointed a finger at Beckeman. 'Find some evidence by Friday.'

None of the other federal judges wanted to preside over the imam's case. None of the criminal defense lawyers Scott had called wanted to defend the most dangerous man in Dallas. The prospect that your client might be mad at you if he's convicted comes with defending any criminal defendant; the prospect that your client might behead you if he's convicted comes with defending an Islamic terrorist.

'No way, Judge.'

'Not enough money?'

'Too much danger. These people, Judge, they're not like us. They cut people's heads off, put it on YouTube.'

'They have a constitutional right to competent counsel.'

'I've got a God-given right to keep my family safe.'

'I could appoint you.'

'Please don't.'

Scott had been appointed to a federal case by the judge who had previously sat in his chair. The case had changed his life. For the better. From a big-firm lawyer making $750,000 a year and driving a Ferrari to a federal judge making $201,100 and driving a Ford. From doing well to doing good. But he couldn't do that to another lawyer. Each lawyer had to make his or her own choice in that regard. Scott had the power but not the inclination. He hung up the phone.

'He won't take the case?' Bobby asked.

Scott shook his head.

'All the defendants agreed to joint representation. The PD, she can't handle that.'

'I know.'

'So what are you going to do?'

'Find them competent counsel. Or teach Ms. Meyers how to try a case.'

Abdul jabbar stopped the car at the entrance to the Islamic Garden at the Restland Cemetery in Dallas. The brothers had come for the funeral of Aabdar Haddad. Their friend. Their fellow Muslim. Their brother in Allah.

'What is wrong, brother?'

'Look.'

Abdul pointed to the cemetery entrance ten cars in front of them.

'What?'

'The cameras.'

'Yes, the TV news has come to record Aabdar's funeral.'

'So has the FBI.'

At various vantage points around the perimeter of the crowded funeral service, men in suits manned handheld video cameras.

'They want to capture our faces,' Abdul said. 'So they can use facial recognition software to ID us. We cannot go in, little brother. We cannot be in the FBI database. We cannot be on the FBI watch list.'

Abdul did not follow known jihadists on Twitter or friend them on Facebook. The FBI puts friends and followers on watch lists. Those were lists he did not want to be on.

'But Aabdar was our friend.'

'Yes, but he is with Allah now. The Americans killed him just as they killed our father. And what did we get in return? An apology. "We blew up your father. Sorry. Have a nice day."'

'They let us into America. They gave us citizenship. We are Americans, too.'

'But are we truly American? Does the FBI videotape Christian and Jewish funerals? No, only Muslim funerals. Because all Muslims are terrorists.'

'But we—'

'Will never be Americans. We will always be Muslims. That is what haunts us, and that is what sustains us. Our religion. Not our country.'

'What will we do?'

'We will drive to Oklahoma and buy fertilizer.'

Abdul turned the car around and drove away.

Scott had never realized how many Muslims lived in Dallas. He had never before represented a Muslim as a lawyer or presided over a case involving Muslims as a judge or lived among Muslims in Highland Park. He had never really noticed them. But they were here. The reporter said there were seventy-seven mosques and fifteen Islamic schools in Dallas. Texas was the steel buckle of the Bible Belt of America. Home of the brave and land of the Baptists. But apparently the state was more diverse than meets the eye. That or he had never looked closely enough. He watched the funeral live on the TV in his chambers. On the screen, a reporter interviewed a Muslim man.

'This boy did nothing, but the American government murdered him. Because America hates Muslims.'

'When did you immigrate here?' the reporter asked.

'I was born here.'

'You're an American, but you think America hates you?'

'Yes. America hates Islam. Thus, America hates me.' He looked directly into the camera. 'The end of days is upon us. The end of America is upon you.'

The camera panned back to the reporter.

'O – kay.'

The station cut to another reporter interviewing a young white girl.

'He seemed like a nice guy, I can't believe he was a terrorist.'

'An alleged terrorist,' the reporter said.

'Whatever.'

And now the reporter interviewed an older white male.

'You're a professor at the University of Texas at Arlington where Aabdar Haddad attended?'

'Yes. He was in my architecture class. We were studying the stadium. It was a case study, not a plot. Aabdar wanted to build sports stadiums. He loved football and baseball. The FBI killed the wrong guy. And if there is a plot to blow up the stadium on Super Bowl Sunday, the real bad guys are still out there.'

'Bullshit!'

Beckeman pointed the remote at the television as if to shoot it.

'A fucking college professor.'

The attorney general had gone to the airport to fly back to D.C. in his private jet; the U.S. Attorney had gone back to his office; Beckeman had gone back to work. There was no time off in the war against terror. Fact is, he was married to the Bureau, just as he had been married to the Corps. He was forty-seven years old. Soldiering was all he knew, but he knew it well. His father had often shared his philosophy for success with his son: *Do one thing really well. Do it over and over.* Eric Beckeman knew how to kill Muslim terrorists. He had killed them in Iraq and Afghanistan; those wars had defeated al Qaeda and created ISIS. That was a game changer. They were Islamic, they were barbaric, and they were coming to America. We can't kill them in Syria because of bad press over collateral damage – hell, kill two civilians in a drone strike, and The

Hague wants to try you as a war criminal – so we have to kill them at home. The FBI needed someone with the skills, experience, and determination to do just that. The jump from the Marines to the Joint Terrorism Task Force had not been a change in job description, only a change in uniform. The operational objective remained the same: kill or capture every Islamic jihadist in the world. It wasn't a job. It was a mission. His mission in life.

'I do not know about any plot to blow up the stadium. All I know is that Aabdar had nothing to do with it. He was a good boy.'

The television screen had cut to an older woman identified as 'Aabdar Haddad's mother.'

'Mothers are always the last to know,' Beckeman said.

He hit the pause button; the screen froze on the face of Aabdar Haddad's mother. He turned back to his task force assembled in the war room.

'I want every face at that funeral ID'd and investigated,' Beckeman said. 'Haddad was a bad guy. They were friends of Haddad. Therefore, they are bad guys, too. Any questions?'

Three agents raised their hands.

'Walker.'

Agent Walker waved a sheet of paper. 'Do the breakfast tacos have onions? My gut can't handle onions.'

Beckeman stared at Agent Walker a long moment then turned his hands up at Agent Peña.

'No onions,' she said.

'Maxwell.'

'Are the tortillas flour or corn?'

Beckeman dropped his head.

'Your choice,' Peña said.

'Carson,' Beckeman said without looking up.

'Can I get eggs, cheese, *and* beans?'

'Yes,' Agent Peña said.

The last six months since the tip had come in had been intense and round the clock for his Task Force, right up until the raid at the mosque Friday night. Once the suspects had been placed in the jail cells, the team had acted as if the game had been won. They had relaxed. He had given them the weekend off; they had come in that Monday morning like frat boys, joking and laughing and cutting up, more worried about breakfast tacos than terrorists. They had not served in Afghanistan and Iraq; they didn't understand that you could never relax.

'Are there any other questions?' Two more agents raised their hands. 'Not about breakfast tacos.'

They dropped their hands. Agent Peña raised hers.

'Yes?' Beckeman said.

'I thought you said we got all the bad guys?'

Beckeman glared at the young female agent. She had a great body, sure, and her mother sold the best breakfast tacos in Dallas to the Task Force; but any tactical advantage those facts offered her was negated by her mouth. She had a hell of a mouth on her, and she didn't know when to keep it shut. Like now. He had not wanted her on the task force, but she had been forced upon him. For political correctness. So he had her, as well as black, Asian, and even Muslim agents. During World War II, the government put Japanese-Americans in prison camps for fear of espionage in the fight against the Japanese; now the government puts Muslims inside central command in the fight against Muslims. He was fighting terrorists; the Bureau was playing politics.

'We got the bad guys this time. But we'll never get all the bad guys. They're breeding terrorists faster than we can kill them. But these bad guys are in federal detention, and we've got to keep them there.'

'Is the judge going to let Mustafa out?'

'The president said he stays in that cell until after the Super Bowl. And that's exactly what's going to happen. Because we're going to find the evidence to keep him there.' He pointed at the screen. 'Those Muslims might lead us to that evidence. Find them. Find the evidence. We got the bad guys. All we've got to do now is find the evidence to prove it.'

Which was why Beckeman preferred to avoid the proof issue and just shoot the bad guys.

'Shit, Scotty, remember that Dibrell case? Sexual harassment? What was my client's name?'

'I can't remember.'

'What's Tom up to?'

'I don't know.'

Scott had called his last resort, Franklin Turner, famous plaintiffs' lawyer.

'Frank, I need a favor.'

'You want to borrow the jet?'

'Uh, no. More along the lines of a job.'

'You want a job?'

'No. I've got a job for you.'

'What kind of job? Toxic tort?'

'It is toxic.'

'Asbestos, formaldehyde . . .?'

'Muslim.'

'Muslim?'

'I want you to defend Mustafa.'

Frank laughed. 'That's a good one, Scotty.'

Scott did not laugh.

'You got the case?'

'I do.'

'You're serious?'

'I am.'

'Why me? I'm a personal injury lawyer, not a criminal defense lawyer.'

'You were a prosecutor once, and a damn good one, you can handle a high-profile case, you're not afraid of public pressure, you thrive on controversy, you're the best damn trial lawyer I know—'

'And all the defense lawyers in town turned you down?'

'Yep.'

'What's in it for me?'

'The chance to do good.'

'Defending the most dangerous man in Dallas?'

'Defending the Constitution.'

Frank did not respond.

'I'm in a bind, Frank. Detention hearing is Friday at nine. The PD isn't up to it. Frank, I wouldn't forget this.'

Frank breathed into the phone. 'I'd need a staff.'

'There's a PD on the case. Marcy Meyers, just out of school.'

'Young?'

'Very.'

'Pretty?'

Frank had been married and divorced three times. He had an eye for the ladies.

'Quite. You can have her . . . professionally.'

Frank grunted. He was weighing the upside and downside. The downside was steep, the upside small. But there was an upside.

'The press is all over this case, Frank. You'd be the most famous lawyer in America.'

'I wouldn't mind that.'

'I didn't think you would.'

Frank loved the cameras. Conventional wisdom was, the most dangerous place in Dallas was between Frank Turner and a TV camera. There would be a lot of TV cameras for this case. In terms of publicity, this was a once-in-a-lifetime case.

'And it'd be a change of pace,' Frank said.

'Criminal instead of civil?'

'Trying a case before a judge I haven't bought off with campaign contributions.'

Franklin Turner, famous plaintiffs' lawyer, took the case.

Chapter 7

'Who's Frank Turner?'

'Only the best trial lawyer in Dallas,' Mike Donahue said. 'Maybe in the country.'

'I thought you were,' Agent Beckeman said.

'I'm second best.'

'Never heard of him.'

'He's a plaintiffs' lawyer.'

'Why'd he take a criminal case?'

'The publicity, no doubt. He loves the cameras.'

'You can kick his ass.'

'He ain't that pretty little PD. Frank used to be a prosecutor, a damn good one. He knows what he's doing.'

'Which means what?'

'Which means I can't count on him losing. I've got to win the hearing. And I can't win without evidence, not with Fenney presiding. Find me some evidence, Beckeman. I don't want to walk into court Friday morning holding only my balls.'

'We let Mustafa go free Friday, the president is going to castrate both of us.'

Karen tossed the briefs in the immigration case onto Scott's desk.

'I researched the law, made notes in the margins. The parties argue the opposing views quite well, but I think we should get an *amicus* brief from a law professor.'

'You're smarter than any law professor I know.'

Karen Douglas was not yet thirty, but she was the smartest lawyer in the courthouse; on that everyone agreed (just as everyone agreed that Bobby was the luckiest lawyer in the courthouse, to be married to her). She had graduated first in her class at Rice with a degree in literature and first in her class at UT with a degree in law. The other judges kept trying to borrow her, but Scott refused. They also tried to hire her away, but she refused. She was smiling. She knew he spoke the truth.

'We need an objective view from someone without a political agenda,' she said.

'That rules out Harvard professors.'

'True.'

'Who'd you have in mind?'

'Bookman at UT. I took his class. He's the last known practicing Jeffersonian in America. That's what he says, anyway. So he won't feed us either the Democratic view or the Republican view.'

'Just the Jefferson view.'

'Not a bad view. And he's famous. His opinion carries weight . . . and it might give you some cover, whichever way you rule.'

She always had her judge's back. She was like that. Scott had hired her at Ford Stevens out of UT law school and tried to teach her the law business. It didn't take; after Dan Ford fired

115

Scott, she quit and joined the Shawanda Jones defense team. She met Bobby; it was love at first sight. Bobby married way up and had never forgotten it. The voices of the protestors outside rose again. Muslims demanding Mustafa's release had been joined by Mexicans demanding citizenship.

'I don't think there's cover on either case,' Scott said.

Karen's expression turned down; she seemed almost sad. She pulled the local newspaper from her stack of documents and laid it on the table. *ISIS in Dallas!* the headline screamed. And Scott saw himself on the front page. Again.

'Well, at least the terrorism case pushed the immigration case off the front page,' he said.

Any other time, the immigration case would be front-page news in Texas, but the front page had been consumed by the terrorism case. The former case would fly under the radar; the latter case would not. Karen sat down across the desk from him and stared at her hands. She finally spoke in a soft voice.

'Scott, the last year, we've been cloistered in this courthouse, safe from the world out there. Hearing cases the world didn't care about. But these two cases, the world does care. These cases, they're putting us out there again. Putting you out there again. Making you famous again.' She looked up. 'That didn't work out so well the last time.'

'We're famous!' Boo said. 'All the kids at school were talking about you because you're the judge on that case, those terrorists that tried to blow up Cowboys Stadium. A. Scott, they said you're a hero!'

'Whereas, Judge Fenney.'

Last week he was a loony liberal at the middle school; this week he was a hometown hero. The life of a federal judge. He kissed each girl's forehead. He had just walked in the back door at the end of a long day at the courthouse. The girls had walked

116

home from school. Kids could do that in Highland Park. They now sat at the kitchen table doing homework and watching the news. Their innocence – about terrorism if (hopefully) not oral sex – had ended that day at school. To some extent, anyway. They did not seem to grasp the gravity of the matter, an attempt to kill one hundred thousand people. It was the notoriety of his involvement that had captured their attention.

'I'm not a hero. I'm just the judge on the case.'

Consuelo dabbed her eyes with her apron and came to him with her arms outstretched. She buried her head in his chest and wrapped her arms around him. Her round body shook with her sobs.

'*Señor* Judge, you are my hero.'

He patted her soft back and inhaled the scent of dinner: enchiladas.

'They said it's the biggest legal case in Dallas since "Who shot J.R.?"' Boo said.

'Wow, that's so exciting!' Pajamae said. 'Who's J.R.?'

Boo shrugged. 'I don't know.' She pointed at the television. 'A. Scott, you're on TV again!'

He looked at himself looking back from the television. He had had his first taste of fame in college when he had rushed for 193 yards against Texas; SMU had still lost the game, but he had been the star of the game. In the State of Texas, an amazing performance on a football field for or against the University of Texas brought instant fame. And not just fifteen minutes of fame, but fame that lasted years, perhaps a lifetime, fame that a man could build a life on, fame that could bring fortune if a man played his cards right.

Scott Fenney had.

The pros had not called because of the knee operations, so he had gone pro as a lawyer instead. He was smart, but he knew smart wasn't enough in the law business; smart lawyers

117

without rich clients were a dime a dozen. And there were more smart lawyers in the world than rich clients. He had grown up poor but did not want to end up poor; he needed a rich client. So he played the fame card and lured a rich client into his billable-hour account: Thomas J. Dibrell, SMU alum, rabid football booster, and real-estate developer with a knack for getting himself into legal cracks, extrication from which required the expensive legal services of his lawyer. Life was good and getting better for A. Scott Fenney.

Then Judge Buford called.

His call brought fame to Scott once again; but that time fame did not bring fortune. That time, fame cost him his fortune. Judge Buford appointed him to represent Shawanda Jones, mother of Pajamae and accused murderer of Clark McCall, the ne'er-do-well son of U.S. Senator Mack McCall, leading presidential candidate and the most powerful member of the Senate. Scott defended her and won her acquittal; but his rich client and his fortune were soon gone. As was his wife.

Now his face was again on the front page of the Dallas newspaper and his life story played out in the news. It was like watching a rerun on TV; it wasn't any better the third time around. Fame had entered his life again. What would it be this time: a promise or a threat? What would it bring: fortune or misfortune? This time there was no fortune or wife to take; he had nothing fame could take from him. Which gave him a certain peace of mind. He had learned the hard way about fame and fortune; fortune could be a nice change of pace in life, but fame brought nothing good in life.

'Look, you're on the news! Every channel!' Boo pointed the remote and flicked through the channels. 'ABC, CBS, NBC, Fox . . . It's all A. Scott all the time!'

Photos of Scott Fenney, football player, high-profile lawyer, defender of prostitutes and ex-wives, and federal judge played on the national news. The networks and cable outlets had called his office that morning and requested interviews. He had declined them all; it was unprofessional for a sitting federal judge to grant an interview concerning a pending case. So the reporter had pieced together his segment of the story from old newspaper accounts: his glory days in college, his rise and fall as a superstar lawyer, his successful defenses of Shawanda Jones and Rebecca Fenney, his appointment to the federal bench.

'Judge Fenney has proven himself a lawyer committed to justice, a fact that should give comfort to both the American people and the defendants.'

'Wow, that's cool, A. Scott, all this attention.'

'Not really.'

As a general rule, federal judges below the Supreme Court don't get much attention. Which is a good thing. The way it's supposed to be. We don't want our judges to be celebrities or politicians. We want them to be studious and serious, just and judicious, fair and impartial. We don't want our federal judges yakking it up on *The Late Show* like presidential candidates. We don't want them to advocate or legislate; we want them to adjudicate. To judge.

We want them to avoid notoriety.

And they're able to do that most of the time. But every now and then, an intensely emotional case comes along that captures the attention of the people and the press – integration and school busing back in the sixties and seventies, abortion for the last forty years, and now Obamacare and immigration – and a federal judge comes under the harsh lights of the press and even the harsh scorn of the public. In court, someone always loses; thus, someone always leaves court mad. And they take it out on the only person available: the judge. And any judge who has ever entertained thoughts of a political career after the bench quickly realizes the error of his thinking.

119

'We will prove beyond any doubt that Mustafa was the mastermind behind the plot to bomb Cowboys Stadium on Super Bowl Sunday,' Mike Donahue said on the television.

He said it with the confidence of a prosecutor with damning evidence instead of the doubt of a prosecutor with no evidence. But he was not testifying under oath. The byline on the screen read: *ISIS in Dallas*. The story cut to Frank Turner sitting in a high-backed chair in his elegant office, the kind of law office only a wildly successful plaintiffs' lawyer could afford. He looked like a lord. The lord of the law.

'Look, everyone's happy the plot got thwarted and the stadium won't get blown up – hell, I've got a skybox on the fifty-yard line – but we still have to convict the bad guys. If the imam is the bad guy, he should spend the rest of his life in prison. But there appears to be no evidence that he is. I've asked the prosecutor to provide some evidence – any evidence – tying the imam to the stadium plot. So far, he has provided none. Nothing. *Nada.* So at the detention hearing Friday I will ask the government to do what the Constitution requires: put forth credible evidence that the imam plotted to blow up Cowboys Stadium or that he's a flight risk or a danger to the community, and failing that, I will ask the judge to release the imam pending the trial.'

'Have you met with Mustafa?'

'I'm meeting my client right after this interview.' He smiled. 'First things first.'

That, Scott thought, will be an interesting attorney-client conference. He recalled his first meeting with Pajamae's mother at the same detention center. He was more worried she would throw up on his $2,000 suit than whether she was innocent. It takes a while for a lawyer to warm up to a client he's convinced is guilty.

'Okay, you girls wash up for dinner.'

He shooed them down the hall, fearful of what might come next. The story cut to the president in the White House press-room standing before a room of reporters.

'We are celebrating a great victory today. Thanks to the heroic efforts of the Joint Terrorism Task Force, we have averted another terrorist attack on the homeland. We got the bad guys. The Super Bowl is safe. The game will be played. The American people should know that their government is working nonstop – and we will never stop – to discover and thwart terrorist plots.'

And to Cowboys Stadium and the mayors of Dallas, Fort Worth, and Arlington, the NFL Commissioner, and Jerry Jones standing at a makeshift podium on the fifty-yard line bookended by two blonde and buxom Dallas Cowboys cheer-leaders in short-shorts. The Dallas mayor spoke first.

'It's a great day in Dallas, even if we are in Arlington. The shock of learning about this dastardly plot has abated and been replaced by the thrill of victory – we beat the terrorists! Thanks to the FBI, the people of the Dallas–Fort Worth metroplex will enjoy the five-hundred-million-dollar economic impact of hosting the Super Bowl. It will be an economic bonanza.'

The NFL Commissioner stepped forward.

'We are so proud of our law enforcement personnel. They're the real Super Bowl champions. Thanks to them, the game will be played on February the seventh in this great stadium.'

A reporter shouted: 'Commissioner, did you know about the threat?'

'No, but I know the FBI protects the Super Bowl. And we've since been briefed and assured that the game will be safe. Our fans will be happy.'

The scene cut to rowdy fans at a local Hooters. The reporter shouted above the noise.

'Fans are happy at Hooters.'

The cameras panned the crowd of young males drinking beer and young females wearing orange short-shorts and tight low-cut T-shirts. Scott spotted two familiar faces at a table in the back: Carlos and Louis. It was hard to miss Louis.

'We know how to party in Big D,' the reporter said. 'And the Super Bowl now promises to be the biggest party ever!'

And then to the FBI headquarters in Dallas.

'We were all stunned Saturday morning,' the reporter said to the camera, 'when the FBI announced the arrests of the terrorists and their plot to blow up Cowboys Stadium. The entire city seemed in shock the last few days. We were scared. We needed information, our questions answered: Who are these guys? Did the FBI get all the bad guys? Will we be safe at the Super Bowl? But now the shock has worn off and the realization that we won has taken over. The FBI saved the Super Bowl. We defeated the terrorists.'

Scott had a distinct feeling of *deja vu*, like watching George W. on that aircraft carrier declaring 'Mission Accomplished.' The camera panned back to reveal the entire pressroom. The atmosphere was boisterous, like a locker room after a big victory; all that was missing were corks popping on champagne bottles. The victory was won; the bad guys apprehended; the plot thwarted. Good had prevailed, and evil had failed – except for one small problem: there was no evidence against Mustafa and the other defendants. They were innocent until proven guilty, and there was no evidence of guilt. Not yet, anyway. The attorney general and the grand jury had both overlooked that minor fact, and the trial jury – twelve citizens who want to be safe – would as well. Only the trial judge stood in the way.

Would he?

Would he stand in the way?

Would he stand for the Constitution and set the bad guys free?

122

Or was the attorney general right? Was cumulative justice the new standard for terrorists? Should he act today to prevent crimes tomorrow?

'And the hero of the day is FBI Agent Eric Beckeman, head of the Terrorism Task Force here in Dallas,' the reporter said. 'But he apparently didn't get the memo that this is a victory party.'

It was the end of another long day of coming up empty. Mustafa was a bad guy, Beckeman knew it. He just couldn't prove it. He felt down, like Billy Hope in *Southpaw*, a hell of a boxing movie. Billy lost his Bentley, his mansion, and his kid – after they killed his wife. Of course, Beckeman didn't have a Bentley, a kid, or a wife. He had had one once – a wife – for about a year. But she didn't like being his mistress.

'I'll always be married to the Corps,' he had said.

'Then go fuck the Corps Saturday night,' she had said.

She filed for divorce the next week.

'Agent Beckeman,' a reporter sticking a microphone in his face said, 'you got the bad guys. But you don't seem happy.'

'I'm not.'

'Why not?'

'Because they're already plotting the next attack.'

'The Muslims you arrested?'

'Other radical Muslims.'

'How do you know?'

'Because that's what they do. That's all they do. Normal people get up, make the kids' lunches, drop them off at school, and go to work. These people get up and kill someone or plot to kill someone or celebrate because they killed someone. Killing is their job. It's what they do. And they will do it until we kill them. Every one of them. And their children. And their children's children. It will never end.'

Boisterous had been replaced by silence.

'How do you know this?'

'I've seen the future.'

'Where?'

'In the faces of those young Muslims we arrested.'

'And what did you see?'

'Death.'

'Did you conspire to kill a hundred thousand people at the Super Bowl?'

'I did not. As Allah is my witness.'

'Well, in my experience serving God with a trial subpoena is a bit tricky.'

Frank Turner, famous plaintiffs' lawyer smiled; Omar al Mustafa, the most dangerous man in Dallas, did not. They sat in metal chairs in his bare cell at the federal courthouse. It was quiet; it wasn't like at the county jail this time of night with holding cells occupied by drunks and dopers and hookers. These federal cells held only Islamic terrorists. Mustafa held a small book in his lap.

'But you knew Aabdar Haddad?'

'I did.'

'He was your student?'

'He was.'

'Did you know he was plotting to bomb the stadium?'

'He was not.'

'The FBI says he was. Says he went for a gun, so they killed him.'

'And Bush said there were weapons of mass destruction in Iraq so he invaded.'

'Okay, Omar, let's try to focus. This is about getting you your freedom.'

'I will never be free.'

'If we win Friday, you will be. At least till trial.'

'I am Muslim. I will never be free.'

'You live in America. You're free . . . well, you're in jail at the moment, but—'

'My brothers in the Middle East are not free, not when American drones armed with missiles fly overhead. How would Americans feel if Russia flew drones over California?'

'Most Americans would probably be happy if they took out a few of those crazy liberals out there.'

Still no hint of a smile. Frank prided himself on being able to connect with human beings from all walks of life, particularly jurors who could award his client millions in damages. But finding a connection with this guy was proving tough.

'Look, Omar, we can't solve the world's problems today, okay? Let's focus on the detention hearing Friday. The Feds got nothing except your writings and speeches. Give me the study notes version of what you've said and written.'

Mustafa shrugged. 'I am just a teacher of Islam.'

'And what do you teach?'

'The truth.'

'Which is?'

'Muslims are fighting another crusade, an epic battle between good and evil.'

'Let me guess – you're the good?'

'Yes.'

'And we're the evil?'

'I am afraid so.'

'Who decided that?'

'Allah.'

'How do you know?'

Mustafa held up the book. 'It is written in the Koran.'

'And the Koran is—'

'The word of God.' He opened the book and ran his hand across the pages as if they were made of gold. 'These very words are the message of God communicated by God Himself to Muhammad.'

'In an email, text, what?'

'Counselor, you are treading very close to dishonoring the Prophet, the penalty for which is death.'

Frank laughed. 'You're threatening me? Omar, I've won ten *billion* dollars in verdicts against multinational corporations. You don't scare me.'

'Did they carry swords?'

Frank studied the little man. Was this guy for real?

'So how did God communicate to Muhammad?'

'In visions.'

Frank grunted. 'I had visions once. Free advice: stay away from tequila.'

'You really don't want to be an old man, do you?'

That's it. Frank gave up on establishing an attorney-client rapport.

'So you think our war on terror is a war on Islam?'

'It is.'

'Well, if we hate Muslims so damn much, why are we taking in sixty-five thousand Muslim refugees from Syria?'

'Because you are fools.'

'We're fools? Why? Aren't they going to assimilate, become Americans?'

'Why would Muslims become Americans?' He turned the pages in the book and read. 'God said, "The day will surely come when those who disbelieve will wish that they were Muslim." You see, counselor, it is Americans who must become Muslims.'

'And if we don't?'

'Then one day those Muslims will kill you. We have spread out across the planet, and soon the *ummah*, the global Muslim community, will rise up and conquer the unbelievers.'

'How do you know?'

'The Koran says so. God said so.'

'And you'd like that?'

'What I would like is irrelevant. What will happen will happen.'

Frank leaned in to Mustafa, as if they were kids telling secrets in class; he glanced around then spoke in a low voice.

'So, Omar, tell me, buddy, are you one of those terrorists?'

Mustafa leaned in as well. He also spoke in a low voice.

'Are you my lawyer?'

'Yes.'

'Everything I say to you is confidential?'

'Yes.'

'So you cannot tell anyone what I tell you?'

'No. The attorney-client privilege.'

'Even if you are tortured?'

'Is that a joke?'

'No.'

'Even if I'm tortured.'

'If terrorism is standing up for Islam, then I am a terrorist.'

'Have you ever beheaded anyone?'

'Not yet.'

'Why not?'

'I always wanted my first beheading to be of a lawyer.'

Frank leaned back.

'Funny. Why are you a terrorist?'

'I prefer jihadist.'

'Why are you a jihadist?'

'Jihad means to defend Islam.'

'What does "defend Islam" mean?'

'It means to engage in a holy war to bring the entire population on earth under Islamic law.'

'Ah. That sounds reasonable. Problem is, Omar, each country has its own law.'

'We do not recognize national boundaries.'

'Neither did Hitler.'

Frank felt his blood pressure rising and himself being drawn into a debate with his client, never a good thing for a lawyer—

'More particularly, since Christians and Jews desire control over Muslims, Muslim land, and Muslim oil, jihad means armed resistance against the conspiracies of the West and Israel.' He held up the book. 'Allah tells us to defend our homeland just as the U.S. Army is defending your homeland. Of course, we didn't invade you. You invaded us.'

—particularly when his client is a nut. How do you debate a nut? *Why* was he debating a nut? It was the lawyer in him; he wanted to win every interpersonal encounter. He knew he shouldn't, but he pushed onward.

'*We? Us?* You're American.'

'I was born here and I live here, but my heart is with my brothers in Syria.' He turned the pages of the book. 'God said, "The believers are a band of brothers."'

'Maybe so, but you're an American citizen. You live here, work here, pay taxes here.'

'I do not pay taxes here.'

'You don't? Where do you pay?'

'Nowhere.'

'How much do you make?'

'Last calendar year, about seventeen million.'

'That's not bad. I made almost sixty million.'

'How much did you pay in taxes?'

'Thirty million.'

'I paid zero.'

'Tax shelters?'

'Mosque. I run all the money through the mosque, it is a charitable organization. I have not paid taxes since I returned from Jordan.'

128

'Is that when you became radicalized?'

'I became informed. I met al Maqdisi and al Zarqawi there. I traveled to Palestine and personally witnessed the atrocities committed by the Christians and Jews against Muslims. So when I returned, my first act of jihad was to no longer pay taxes. I mean, why should a Muslim in America pay taxes so the U.S. Army can wage war on Islam? Would you pay taxes to your enemy? I am waging financial jihad.'

'*Financial jihad?*' Frank chuckled. 'I've heard a lot of reasons for cheating on your taxes, but that's a new one.'

Frank hated paying half his income in taxes. But now, listening to this guy, he suddenly wanted to pay more taxes – to the U.S. Army.

'And all Muslim immigrants are encouraged to seek welfare and other government benefits to bankrupt the unbelievers. Also financial jihad.'

'Cheating at taxes and freeloading off society – you guys are assimilating better than you think.' Frank sighed. 'Okay, we're way off topic. What were we talking about?'

'Invasions.'

'Oh, yeah. Some regard nine-eleven as an invasion.'

'An attack. Not an invasion. Not an army of Muslims occupying New York City—'

'Have you been to New York recently?'

'—as Christians occupied Baghdad. Your invasion proved our fears, that America wants to control the Muslim homeland.'

'We invaded because you're terrorists.'

'You invaded because you want our oil. Because you want the Jews to occupy our homeland. So we are fighting for our freedom with the means we have available. We do not have drones. But we do have knives.'

'Which you use to behead people. You put heads on pikes, like we're living in the goddamn *Game of Thrones*!'

'The beheadings were meant to inspire fear. They worked. The Iraqi and Syrian armies dropped their weapons and fled when they saw the black ISIS flag because they knew what their fate would be if they fought and lost.'

'Beheadings are barbaric.'

'And drone missiles are not? You invaded Afghanistan and Iraq and killed hundreds of thousands of Muslims with bombs and bullets. Why is that more civilized than beheadings? People are still dead. If you can kill, why can't we? You kill for oil. We kill for Islam. And Americans must remember that: We will kill for Islam. We will die for Islam. As Sheikh Osama so famously said, "We love death as much as you love life."'

'Those are words to live by.'

'Those are words to die by.'

'What do you people hope to achieve with all this terror?'

'To purify the Arabian Peninsula of Christians and Jews.'

'You want us out?'

'Yes.'

'And the Jews, how do they get out of Israel?'

He shrugged. 'Planes, trains, buses . . . we don't care.'

'But they must leave?'

'Yes. They took our land to create their state. They must give the land back.'

'Anything else?'

'The fall of America. Western civilization would be better, but we would settle for the destruction of America.'

'That will never happen.'

'It is happening.'

Frank groaned. 'Oh, yeah, end of days. What's all that nonsense about?'

Mustafa gave him a look over his reading glasses. '*Nonsense*, counselor?'

'Point of view.'

'Better. I have studied the prophecies that tell of the end of days. The Antichrist takes over the world until the messiah returns to earth, kills the Antichrist, and conquers the infidels. The signs are present. The Antichrist is here. The end of days is upon us.'

'The Antichrist is here?'

'Yes.'

'Is it Putin? I've always thought he's one crazy-ass bastard.'

'Ah, in your ignorance, you have stumbled upon the correct question, counselor, much as a blind squirrel finds a nut now and then. But the Antichrist is not a he, it is a what.'

'What?'

'America.'

'*America?* America is the Antichrist?'

'If you want a person, then the president, the most power-ful man on the planet. Did he not say America has the right to kill anyone anywhere anytime? What are those but the words of the Antichrist? And Americans cheered. So yes, counselor, America is the embodiment of the Antichrist. That is why others never saw its arrival. They were looking for a *he* instead of a *what*. Look at American culture – secular and sexual and debase. Look at American politics – selfish and avaricious and megalomaniac. Look at American foreign policy – aggressive and imperialistic and as the only super power on earth, now in control of this world. Is that not the Antichrist?'

'Have you ever been institutionalized in a mental facility? We could go with an insanity plea.'

'Do be careful, counselor.'

'If you think the end of days is upon us, why do you send your sons to Princeton and Harvard?'

'I could be wrong.'

'The government thinks you're a bad guy. I see why.'

'Your government thinks every Muslim is a bad guy because they are waging war against Islam. Thus, all Muslims are bad. When you waged World War Two, were there any good Germans or good Japanese? Americans said, "The only good Jap is a dead Jap" . . . "The only good Kraut is a dead Kraut."'

'They say you're the ISIS cleric. Is that true?'

'I teach Islam. The ISIS freedom fighters desire to know the truth and live pious lives in accordance with the Koran.'

Frank's blood pressure spiked.

'*Freedom fighters?* They're fucking terrorists.'

Frank fought his emotions. He was a lawyer. This asshole was his client. He had had assholes for clients before. But he had never before wanted to strangle an asshole client.

'One man's terrorist is another man's freedom fighter. Was it not terror to Afghans when the U.S. invaded their country to find Osama? To Iraqis when the U.S. invaded to depose Hussein?'

'ISIS targets civilians. We don't.'

'How many civilians died at Hiroshima and Nagasaki when America dropped the atomic bombs? In Vietnam when America dropped napalm? In Iraq with shock and awe? You see, counselor, when America kills civilians, you call it collateral damage. When Muslims do, you call it terrorism. Because you control the media. You control the message Americans hear.'

Frank had given up on establishing a human connection with his client. What he really wanted to do was pound the son of a bitch into the concrete floor. But that might constitute a conflict of interest. So he went with his standard trial strategy: the best defense was offense. He attacked.

'You know what's wrong with you, Omar? Other than the fact that you're a certifiable fucked-up loon?'

'What's that, counselor?'

'You're irrelevant. You're longing for a return to the Muslim glory days when you were relevant in the world. Today, you're one-point-six billion irrelevant fucking people. You live in the Stone Age, and you want us to live there with you. You don't build things, invent things, produce things, or do things. You just destroy things.'

'We were relevant on nine-eleven. We were relevant in Paris and San Bernardino. We are relevant in presidential politics.'

'Only because you kill. If you didn't commit acts of terror, no one would give a fuck about you or your fucking religion. You're like a little kid throwing a temper tantrum to get attention.'

'And the world is attentive, is it not?'

'Yes. The world has to attend to assholes who commit crimes against humanity. The world attended to Hitler. We'll attend to you.'

'In the meantime, counselor, can you get me out of here?'

'So you can execute the stadium plot?'

'No. So I can cheer when the stadium comes down on all those Americans just as I cheered the Paris attacks.'

'You cheered innocent people dying?'

'France attacked us in Syria, so we attacked them in Paris. America attacks us; we will attack America.'

'At the Super Bowl?'

'That would be glorious.'

Frank stood and stared down at him. '*Glorious?* A hundred thousand people dying would be glorious? You're a sick fucking bastard.'

'Careful, counselor. Keep your head about you.'

Frank locked eyes with the imam. 'Is that a threat?'

'Advice.'

'I'm the lawyer. I give advice to you.'

'I am the imam. I give life to you.'

Frank walked to the far side of the cell. He needed distance from this asshole to breathe.

'I must testify.'

Frank turned to Mustafa. 'With what you just told me? No fucking way.'

'The media will be present. I can speak directly to the American people. They will hear our message. It will be on the network news.'

'You think they want to hear your crap?'

'No. But they will listen.'

'Why?'

'Fear.'

'You're not going to testify.'

'I am not asking your permission, counselor. I am informing you.'

'You're going to lie.'

'I am not going to confess.'

'That's perjury.'

'Our little secret.'

'I can't stand by while you commit perjury. I have a duty to inform the court.'

'Attorney-client privilege, counselor. Punishment for violation of which is severe.'

'Disbarment.'

'Decapitation.'

Back when he worked for the DA, Frank had prosecuted a cold-blooded killer named Benjie Boatwright. Benjie worked for the biggest drug lord in South Dallas. You crossed his boss, you died. But Benjie didn't put a bullet in your head. That was too easy of a death. He cut you to pieces, sliced you open, let you bleed out. Slowly. Painfully. Benjie Boatwright enjoyed torturing other human beings. When the jury sentenced him to death, Benjie swore he would escape and kill every juror, the judge, and Frank. Benjie died in prison before the state could execute him. Other inmates stabbed him to death in the exercise yard. When Frank learned of Benjie's death, he said a prayer of thanks. He had never again wished a man dead. Until now.

He wanted this motherfucker dead.

One hundred thousand people would die if a bomb brought Cowboys Stadium down during the Super Bowl.

Was that even possible?

Of course, no one had thought it possible to bring down the World Trade Center; but then, no one had thought it possible that terrorists could hijack four commercial jets simultaneously and fly them into office buildings and the Pentagon and but for the grace of God, the White House or the Capitol. On 9/11, the impossible had become possible.

What if a bomb brought down the stadium?

But bombings didn't happen in the United States. Americans didn't do that sort of thing. Americans were innocent . . . until April 19, 1995. Oklahoma City. Timothy McVeigh and Terry Nichols, two ex-soldiers turned anti-government losers, were outraged at the federal government over the Waco stand-off with David Koresh and his followers that resulted in the deaths of seventy-six Branch Davidians, including children. They decided to exact revenge.

They bought two thousand pounds of ammonium nitrate fertilizer, liquid nitromethane, diesel fuel, and Tovex, an explosive that supplanted dynamite as the blasting material of choice. Total cost of the materials was less than $5,000. They mixed the fertilizer and nitromethane in nine fifty-five-gallon barrels, and the fertilizer and diesel fuel in four barrels. They added acetylene cylinders to enhance the fire from the explosion. The bomb weighed seven thousand pounds.

They placed the barrels in the back of a rental truck. On the second anniversary of Waco, McVeigh drove the truck to the Alfred P. Murrah Federal Building in downtown Oklahoma City. He parked the truck directly in front of the building, started the detonation sequence, and walked away. The bomb exploded and destroyed the nine-story building, damaged three hundred other buildings, killed one hundred sixty-eight people, including nineteen children, and injured eight hundred more.

America lost its innocence that day.

The FBI had always been an inside-the-box organization. It didn't pay to think outside the box. The past was inside the box; the future was outside. The FBI investigated after the fact; it did not prevent the fact. It did not anticipate. It was reactive and not proactive. It was always a step behind. Consequently, the Oklahoma City bombing shocked the country and surprised the FBI. The federal government failed the people. Six years later, on September 11, 2001, it failed the people again.

FBI Special Agent Catalina Peña wasn't going to fail the people this time. She would think outside the box. She would be proactive. She would anticipate. She would be a step ahead and not a step behind. She would work 24/7/365. She would not waste her time reading the newspapers or watching TV, not even *Walking Dead*. She would not be a friend on Facebook or a follower on Twitter. She would eat, sleep, and work, and she would eat and sleep only when necessary. And when she slept, she would sleep alone. She had no one to go home to, so why go home? She had her parents, but no man. Hard to get a man to stick around when you carried a gun and could kick his ass into next week. Men don't like strong women, especially armed women.

So she was burning the midnight oil.

Again.

A seven-thousand-pound fertilizer bomb had brought down a nine-story office building; could it bring down a football stadium? Would a larger bomb be required? Twice as large? Or even larger? But how would such a massive bomb be transported into the stadium?

Was that possible?

But what if the 'bomb' wasn't an explosive bomb but another kind of bomb? A dirty bomb? Or gas? She googled 'nerve gas,' which led her to VX and sarin. She searched sarin. Twenty-eight million results came up. Sarin is a colorless, odorless liquid that quickly evaporates and becomes gaseous upon exposure to the environment. It is heavier than air, so it sinks to the low ground. If the gas is breathed in, death occurs in less than ten minutes, usually from paralysis of the respiratory system. The victim suffocates. Sarin was first developed as a pesticide by German scientists in the 1930s and weaponized by the Nazis. It is five hundred times as deadly as cyanide. The Nazis so feared sarin that they did not deploy it in World War Two. But Saddam Hussein did in 1988; he used sarin to kill five thousand Kurds. Anarchists killed a dozen people with sarin in a Tokyo subway in 1995. In 1997, the United Nations outlawed its production and use, but that did not prevent Syria's use of sarin in 2013 in its civil war, killing hundreds in Damascus. All of this she read. And then she read this: In February, ISIS seized a large cache of sarin in Libya.

'What are you doing, Peña?'

Agent Beckeman stood over her with his hands on his hips. Agent Stryker stood next to him. Stryker was second in command on the Task Force. He was also Beckeman's body double and an ex-Marine. He had served under Beckeman his entire adult life. Beckeman issued orders; Stryker implemented them. He still addressed Beckeman as captain.

'Researching sarin.'

'Why?'

'I've been thinking.'

'Your first mistake.'

She ignored his remark, a survival skill in the FBI.

'Do you know how big the Oklahoma City bomb was?' she said.

'Seven thousand pounds.'

'Then you know they'd need a bomb five times that big to bring down the stadium.'

'Eight times. Almost. Fifty thousand pounds, give or take.'

'How would they smuggle a bomb that size into the stadium?'

'Not very easily.'

'Exactly. So what if the bomb isn't really a bomb? What if it's something else?'

'Like what?'

'Like sarin. ISIS has sarin. What if the bad guys deployed sarin into the ventilation system at the stadium? The roof will be closed for the Super Bowl and the playing field is below ground level. It's a perfect target for a gas attack. They could kill a lot of people.'

Beckeman sighed as if he were a teacher and she a student who couldn't grasp an easy lesson. The student wanted to punch the teacher.

'A, we got the bad guys. They're in jail.

'B, the tip was about a bomb, not about sarin.

'And C, to weaponize sarin requires a state-of-the-art lab and expertise with chemicals. If amateurs tried to mix the chemicals, the only people they'd kill would be themselves.'

'Anything else?' Peña said.

'Put me down for two breakfast tacos. Eggs, cheese, and beans.'

'Same for me,' Stryker said.

They turned and marched off. Peña offered their backs her middle finger. Beckeman yelled over his shoulder.

'And D, it is absolutely impossible to smuggle sarin into this country!'

Four hundred miles due south, Jorge Romero steered the motorized rubber raft across the Rio Grande. The river stunk more than usual that night – or was it the two *gauchos* that accompanied him? Jorge was a lieutenant in the Chihuahua Cartel. His *jefe* was Hector Calderon. The cartel had been founded in Chihuahua but was now based in Nuevo Laredo. Of course, Hector spent most of his time in Cancun, at least for the last year. He had found a woman there, a woman who liked the beach. So while Jorge was working that night on this stinking river, Hector was having sex with a beautiful *senorita* on the white sand beach of Cancun like the *gringos*. But Jorge did not complain. He followed *el jefe's* orders without question or comment. That night, his orders were to bring this shipment across the river to America and then drive it to Dallas. Consequently, Jorge found himself in this fucking raft at eleven-thirty on a cold night in January.

The trip across the river was short; he could throw a small child across the Rio Grande. They made landfall in America, as Jorge had done on more occasions than he could recall. For Mexicans, it was much like going to the corner grocery store for the *gringos*. Ricardo jumped out and tied the raft to a juniper bush. Pedro followed him onto the bank. Jorge found a dry spot to step onto then gestured at the shipment in the raft.

'*Échale!*'

Jorge climbed the steep embankment to the dirt road above. There he found Manny sleeping in the cab of the pickup truck. Jorge rapped his pistol on the driver's door; Manny jumped and banged his head on the roof of the cab. Jorge laughed.

'I hope you have slept well, Manny. You will drive. I will sleep all the way to Dallas.'

Ricardo and Pedro appeared; each carried a two-gallon metal container. Jorge opened the hatch to the bed cover; they placed the containers inside.

'*Cuidado*,' Jorge said.

'And hurry,' Manny said. 'We do not want to attract the Border Patrol.'

Jorge chuckled. If two hundred million pounds of human beings could cross this border each year without impediment by the Border Patrol, getting two hundred pounds of this product across was child's play. Still, he hastened his men.

'*Échale, ganas!*'

The *gauchos* returned five more times. By the last climb, they were noticeably weary. Pedro's footing failed him, and he went tumbling back down the embankment.

Pedro Martinez rolled down the soft dirt all the way to the river; he came to a safe stop. The container he was carrying tumbled down alongside him, but it did not come to a safe stop. It hit a sharp rock and punctured. Clear liquid oozed out of the gash.

'Shit!'

It would be the last word Pedro Martinez spoke in life.

'Hey! Pedro!' Jorge yelled down the embankment. 'Are you dead?'

Jorge laughed, and the others laughed as well. But Pedro did not respond. Jorge gestured to Ricardo to check on Pedro. Ricardo headed back down the embankment without even a grunt of disapproval.

'Manny, give me the cigarette.'

Jorge took the cigarette and scratched a wood match along the rusty side panel of the pickup. They did not transport shipments in late model vehicles as a tricked-out Ford 150 King Ranch Edition driven by two Mexicans might attract unwanted attention from a state trooper. Jorge had smoked half the cigarette and still Ricardo and Pedro had not returned.

'Hey! Ricardo! Pedro! Are you both dead?'

No answer came back from below. Jorge sighed and pulled out his flashlight.

'I will get my new boots muddy.'

Jorge favored cowboy boots handmade by Juan Castillo, the best boot maker in all of Mexico. *Hombres* came from all around to have Juan make their boots. The normal waiting period often exceeded a year. But when Jorge Romero walked into Juan's shop, his order went to the front of the waiting list. And he would be visiting Juan Castillo when he returned from Dallas.

'Shit.'

His new boots now looked like shit.

'Ricardo! Pedro!'

He arrived at the river and shone the light around. When it landed on the two men, Jorge recoiled. They were dead. Their bodies twitched, but their eyes told of their death. Jorge took only one step closer and put the light on Pedro's eyes, open and fixed. His pupils were pinpoints. Jorge checked Ricardo's eyes and found the same condition.

Jorge backed away but not before making the sign of the cross.

Chapter 8

Wednesday, 20 January
18 days before the Super Bowl

The city lay quiet, like the morning after a big party, as if Dallas suffered a hangover. Perhaps it did. Or perhaps it was just the consequence of coming down after the adrenaline rush of a big victory.

Dallas had defeated the terrorists.

The girls couldn't wait to get to school the next morning and enjoy their fifteen minutes of fame. Scott had assured them that all the attention would soon die down and that that was a good thing.

They didn't believe him.

He pulled into the carpool lane and saw the principal standing there, eyeing each car as if searching for truants. When Scott arrived at the drop-off point, Ms. Williams squinted at him then broke into a big smile. She yanked the back door open for the girls; they jumped out to a waiting throng of kids screaming their names – 'Boo! . . . Pajamae!' – as if they were movie stars on the red carpet at the Oscars. Ms. Williams stuck her head inside.

'Judge Fenney, the superintendent asked me to invite you to be the graduation speaker this year.'

'You're inviting me in carpool?'

'Well, I know how busy you must be, fighting terrorists and all.'

'I'm not fighting them. I'm just the judge.'

'Oh, you're too modest. Will you please consider the invitation?'

'I will.'

'You'll make some man a fine wife, Peña,' Agent Baxter said.

'Fuck you.'

'You wish.'

Upon her arrival, the male agents had deluged Peña; it wasn't her pleasing personality. It was her mom's breakfast tacos. Being teased by the male agents was part of the job description for a female agent. She had been a competitive athlete in college, so she arrived at the Bureau hardened to foul language; it was part of the cop culture just as it was part of the athlete culture. She responded in kind. She shot Baxter the finger with her right hand and snatched his cash with her left. But she did worry that she was becoming too coarse. Too much a man.

'Uh-oh,' Agent Carson said with a dumb-ass grin. 'She's got IBS.'

'Irritable Bowel Syndrome?'

'Irritable Bitch Syndrome.'

The other agents laughed at her through mouthfuls of her mother's breakfast tacos. She felt her brown face flush red. And mad. She grabbed his tacos like a purse-snatcher and tossed his cash in his face.

'That's it, Carson. No tacos for you.'

He went into shock.

'No, Peña, come on, I was just kidding. It was a bad joke, okay?'

'Nope. You fucked up.'

The other agents abandoned Carson faster than street dealers when a black and white rolled up; loyalty took second place to breakfast tacos.

'Please. I love your mother's tacos. I'm sorry.'

Peña stared at Carson a moment. Her partner, Ace Smith, stood frozen next to her, as if waiting to see is she would punch, kick, or shoot Carson. The thought had crossed her mind.

'Ace,' she said to her partner, 'does that apology sound sincere?'

'No, it does not.'

'Pleeease.'

Peña sighed. 'It might sound more sincere if he was on his knees.'

'Might at that,' Ace said.

Carson hit his knees faster than a drunken sorority girl.

'Please. I'm really sorry. I'll never say that stuff again.'

'Well . . .'

Agent Beckeman walked in, grabbed his tacos, dropped his cash, and walked away with only a quick glance at Carson kneeling before Peña with his hands folded as if seeking forgiveness from the Lady of Guadalupe.

'I don't want to know.'

'The Feds submitted their detention brief,' Bobby said. 'Twenty-five pages with a five-hundred-page exhibit, including DVDs.'

'Bookman agreed to submit an *amicus* brief in the immigration case,' Karen said.

'I got donuts,' Carlos said. 'Krispy Kreme.'

'Bobby, you read the detention brief,' Scott said. 'Karen, call Bookman and tell him we need his brief ASAP. Oral arguments are today.'

'What do you want me to do?' Carlos asked.

'Give me a donut.'

Scott had arrived at the courthouse to find the gang gathered in his chambers and hundreds of emails in his inbox; apparently, every lawyer and human being he had ever met had sent an email of support, encouragement, and even congratulations, as if he had personally apprehended the alleged terrorists. He hadn't had that many messages since his college days from friends wanting tickets to the big game. Dozens of phone messages also awaited him, including one from a movie producer who wanted to do his life story and another from a TV producer who wanted him to star in a reality show.

'*Keeping up with the Fenneys*,' Karen said.

'*Hell's Courtroom*,' Bobby said.

'*Paralegal Wars*,' Carlos said.

'*The Bailiff Bachelor*,' Louis said.

Carlos looked sideways at Louis. 'You watch the *Bachelor*?'

'Uh, no. I, uh, I heard about it.'

Carlos wasn't buying what Louis was selling.

'Unh-huh. Looks like the big man wants a gal.'

Everyone laughed until Helen knocked on the open door.

'Judge, Frank Turner is here.'

'Show him in.'

Scott stood and went around the desk. Frank had come to Scott's aid; Scott could at least come around his desk. Frank walked in; Scott offered him an open hand and a big smile. But Frank did not seem in the jovial mood.

'Frank, you know Bobby, and this is Karen Douglas, my briefing attorney. She and Bobby are married, so don't ask her

145

out. This is Carlos and Louis, my paralegal and bailiff. They're not married. They're both available.'

Scott's attempt at humor fell flat with Frank.

'Sit down, Frank.'

Frank sat in front of Scott's desk; he sat behind it.

'Thanks for taking the case, Frank. I won't forget it.'

'Yeah.' Frank rubbed his face. He did not look well. 'Scott, I just filed a Motion for Pretrial Release. My duty as Mustafa's lawyer is to argue for his release pending trial, particularly since the Feds don't have a shred of evidence against him, but . . .'

'But what?'

'Don't do it. Don't release him.'

'Why not?'

Frank shook his head slowly. His mood was getting worse.

'So I figure I need to meet my clients, right? I mean, that's what criminal defense lawyers do, they go to the jail and meet their fucking clients.' He grimaced then glanced at Karen. 'Excuse my French, Ms. Herrin.' Back to Scott: 'So I meet the other defendants first. These people, they're scary. They remind me of the gangbangers I prosecuted. Cold eyes, look right through you, like you're not even a human being. Easier to cut your head off, I guess, if you're not really human. Anyway, I got nothing from them.'

Frank wiped his forehead free of sweat.

'Then I meet Mustafa. He looks like my goddamned grandpa or something. And I say, okay, Omar, I'm your lawyer and to defend you I need to know the truth, see, so why don't you be a good boy and tell me the truth. Well, his face changed. He wasn't my grandpa anymore, he was the devil himself. He said—'

Frank's eyes turned up to Scott.

'Scotty, I can't breach the attorney-client privilege, but don't let him out.'

'Frank, I've got to follow the law.'

'No, you don't. Not in this case.'

Frank wiped his face again. 'I feel like the guy who faced down the raptor in *Jurassic Park*.'

'The raptor ate him,' Bobby said.

'Exactly.'

Scott had never seen Frank Turner, famous plaintiffs' lawyer, afraid. But afraid he was.

'On the bright side, I'm getting lots of publicity. I've done interviews with every network and cable news program, and I'll be on O'Reilly next week.'

Frank's face was not bright with the bright side.

'Will you handle the detention hearing?'

Frank's expression said he was considering the request . . . and still considering. Finally, he nodded. Slowly.

'I'll do my job.'

'Thank you. I'll let you off the case after the hearing. I'll tell the imam that you have a conflict. Or you're sick. Or something.'

'Maybe I'll go into Witness Protection.'

He went away for a long moment. Then he snapped out of it and blinked hard.

'Scotty, I'll do that. I'll go away if I have to. But whatever you do, don't let that son of a bitch out.'

'The president – and only the president – decides who gets kicked out of America. He possesses the sole authority under the Constitution to enforce – or not enforce – the immigration laws. It's called prosecutorial discretion.'

'The president's discretion is absolute?'

'It is.'

'As in unchallengeable?'

147

'Yes, sir. Well, until the next election. The people can vote him out if they don't like how he exercised his discretion.'

'But there is to be no judicial oversight of his discretion between elections?'

'No, sir.'

'Then why are you here?'

The president's lawyer pointed at opposing counsel. 'Because the states don't agree.'

It was oral argument day in *The State of Texas, et al. v. The President of the United States of America, et al.* The executive order case. Immigration reform seemed more appropriate to the legislative branch; it was a political question, not a legal one. But, as often happens, when the politics prove difficult, one party makes it a legal case. The president had done so when he issued an executive order effectively granting amnesty to twelve million illegal immigrants without Congressional approval. Whether those people should be granted amnesty is a political question; whether the president exceeded his executive authority under the Constitution in granting them amnesty is a legal question. The first step to resolving such a legal question is the filing of a lawsuit in federal court. That the states had done. Whichever way Scott ruled, the case would not end in his courtroom. The loser would appeal to the Fifth Circuit Court of Appeals in New Orleans; the loser in the appeals court would then appeal to the Supreme Court in Washington. It would be a long legal journey. That legal journey began in Judge A. Scott Fenney's courtroom in Dallas.

'Mr. Daniels, what is the constitutional authority for that contention?'

'Separation of powers. The Constitution established three branches of government. The legislative branch enacts the laws, the executive branch enforces the laws, and the judicial branch interprets the laws. The president cannot tell Congress how to write the laws, they can't tell him how to enforce the laws, and neither can tell the Supreme Court how to interpret the laws. Enforcement of the law is vested exclusively in the executive branch. Enforcement is at the president's sole and absolute discretion – when, how, against whom, and to what extent.'

'To what extent?'

'Yes, sir.'

'The current immigration law requires persons residing illegally in the U.S. to be deported, is that correct?'

'Yes, sir, that's correct.'

'But the president exercised his prosecutorial discretion in deciding not to enforce that part of the law?'

'That's also correct.'

'Is that presidential authority limited to the immigration laws?'

'I'm sorry, Judge, I don't understand your question.'

'My question is, does the president also possess the sole authority to enforce – or not enforce – the tax laws?'

'Yes, sir, he does.'

'The tax code – written by Congress – specifies certain exemptions from the obligation to pay taxes, for example, universities and charitable hospitals. But you're saying that the president – on his own, without Congressional approval – may grant additional exemptions, that he may exempt certain people from paying taxes?'

'*Exempt?* No, sir, he can't exempt anyone from the tax law. But he can exercise his prosecutorial discretion and decline to enforce the tax law against certain people.'

'Just as he has declined to enforce the immigration law against certain people?'

'Yes, sir.'

'Isn't that just semantics? "Exempt" or "decline to enforce"? Isn't the bottom line the same: certain people don't have to obey the law, be it immigration or taxes? Is that the rule of law?'

'The president decides how to enforce the law. He may decide that enforcement of the tax laws against certain people, such as—'

'Persons residing here illegally?'

'—is not economically feasible. So he can decline to enforce the law against them. Many illegals work off the books. They get paid in cash, which is difficult to trace, so the president may decide that it's simply not worth allocating limited enforcement resources to chase those people.'

'And the same goes for the securities laws, the banking laws, the antitrust laws . . .?'

'Yes, sir. The president gets to decide when, where, how, and against whom to enforce the laws.'

'Really?'

'Really.'

'You're sure you want to bet your case on that contention?'

The government lawyer stared at Scott a long moment then sighed and turned his hands up.

'Judge, you do realize that we don't enforce the tax law against anyone. Or the securities law. Or the banking law. Or the antitrust law. Or the civil rights law. Or the environmental law. We don't enforce any laws anymore.'

'What do you mean?'

'I mean, since nine-eleven, we enforce one law: domestic terrorism. It's an honor code for all other laws. All federal law enforcement resources are spent on preventing another nine-eleven. Period. So while this is an interesting law school question – May the president decline to enforce the law? – it's a moot question. We haven't brought a dozen tax or securities or banking fraud cases in the last fourteen years. And the only antitrust case was that e-book pricing case, as if that were the end of the free world.'

'Why?'

'There's no money. Every dime goes to the terrorism task forces. So, even if you rule in favor of the states, the reality on the ground will remain the same – we don't have the money to deport all those Mexicans. Or any Mexican. The border is wide open and will remain wide open. The wall won't be built. Money, guns, drugs, and people will continue to flow across unimpeded. The president's executive order simply states the reality – we can't afford to deport Mexicans because we're spending all our money fighting Muslims.'

His shoulders slumped. A government lawyer who couldn't enforce the law was like a home run hitter forced to bunt; it wasn't his nature or training. He wanted to do his job. Swing for the fences. Or enforce the law.

'In summary, it is within the authority of the Executive Branch to set forth policy for the exercise of prosecutorial discretion in enforcement actions within the framework of existing law. This executive order is an exercise of that author-ity.'

He spoke with all the enthusiasm of a high school sopho-more reciting *Beowulf*.

'Thank you, Mr. Daniels.'

He closed his notebook and trudged to his seat. The court-room was empty except for a few journalists. This case was flying way under the radar. The lawyer for the State of Texas took his place at the podium.

'Your Honor, in 1986, President Reagan and the Congress granted amnesty to the three million Mexicans residing ille-gally in America. They deserved a path to citizenship, Reagan said. But, that was it. There would be no more amnesty. The

151

border would be locked down. Democrats hailed the move, assured that the new citizens would vote Democrat. Republicans warned that granting amnesty to illegal immigrants would only encourage more illegal immigration, that in twenty years there would be ten million Mexicans residing in the U.S. illegally. The Democrats were right; the Republicans were wrong. Today, *twelve* million Mexicans reside in America illegally. And get this – the Supreme Court said that under the Constitution illegal immigrants are entitled to state benefits such as education and health care even though they intentionally violated our laws in entering the U.S.' He shook his head. 'Is this a great country or what?'

'Mr. Thomas, this is a court of law, not the Sunday-morning political talk shows. Please refrain from editorializing.'

'My apologies, Your Honor.'

'So, your contention is that the president must deport every Mexican residing here illegally?'

'Yes, sir. The immigration law says "*shall* be removed," not "*may* be removed."'

'What if, as the government contends, there's simply not enough manpower or money to do so?'

'The federal government's budget is four *trillion* dollars. The Department of Homeland Security gets sixty *billion*. There's enough money. But that's what they always say. "We don't have the money." If they don't have the money to enforce the immigration laws, then why does the president's executive order grant legal status to twelve million illegal immigrants *and* all the government benefits that come with legal status? Those people will be entitled to social security numbers, work permits, health care, education, welfare, food stamps, unemployment benefits, and even earned income tax credits, which as everyone knows, is just a welfare payment since you can get a tax refund even if you never paid taxes. That credit alone will cost

152

one hundred fifty *billion* dollars for those immigrants. Every year. Two and a half times Homeland Security's budget. Deporting them would cost less and only once. This is all about politics, and the president wants the states to pay for his politics so he can win in November. Federal mandates to the states come without federal funds. They make the rules but don't provide the money.'

'We don't have the money,' Mr. Daniels said.

'Then don't make the rules,' Mr. Thomas said. 'And why the hell is the president letting in those Syrian refugees after Paris?'

Mr. Daniels shrugged.

'We're not taking them,' Mr. Thomas said.

'You have to.'

'The hell we do. States have rights, too.'

Mr. Daniels laughed. 'Since when?'

'Gentlemen, let's stay on topic,' Scott said.

'The president is playing politics,' Mr. Thomas said. ' "I'll get the Muslim vote, so let's admit sixty-five thousand Muslims even if some want to kill Americans. I'll get the Hispanic vote, so let's not deport twelve million illegal Mexicans." But he tells us we've got to pay for his politics. Texas has to pay billions each year for them. Five hundred thousand illegal immigrants cross the border each year and stay here because the president promises them free – free education, free health care, free homes, free food, free Internet, free everything. Who wouldn't come?'

'That's the law,' Mr. Daniels said.

'We're going to change the law.'

'How? The president must sign any law, and there'll never be another Republican in the White House. The demographics have turned on you.'

'And that's why you want twelve million illegal Mexicans to be given the right to vote – because they'll vote for you. That's why the president doesn't want to deport them.'

153

'And Republicans do? You control both houses of Congress. Why don't you guys pass an e-verify law that requires every employer in America to verify their workers' legal status? And fines the hell out of them if they don't? Take away the jobs, Mexicans will self-deport. They'll go home. But the ugly truth is, Republican businessmen want illegal Mexicans here for the cheap labor, they just don't want them to vote. You can't have it both ways.'

'All right, gentlemen, let's focus on the law. Mr. Thomas, doesn't the president have prosecutorial discretion?'

'He does. But the executive order goes beyond prosecutorial discretion. It changes the law, as the president himself said in his official press conference announcing the executive order. He said, and I quote: "I just took action to change the law."'

'He misspoke,' Mr. Daniels said.

'He misspoke the truth,' Mr. Thomas said. 'Congress clearly stated in the immigration law that persons residing in the U.S. *shall* be deported. The president's executive order clearly states that such persons shall *not* be deported. The law denies legal status to persons residing illegally in the U.S. The executive order grants legal status to them. The law states that such persons are not entitled to government benefits. The executive order states that they are. The president may exercise prosecutorial discretion. He may not change the law. But that is exactly what the executive order does. What the president publicly said he did. Change the law. The president issued the executive order like a child throwing a temper tantrum. He didn't get what he wanted from Congress so he tried to change the law himself.'

'How do we decide when he's crossed the line from exercising prosecutorial discretion to legislating the law?'

'We don't, Your Honor. You do. You decide. You're the judge.'

And so it was. When a society no longer shares common values, beliefs, traditions, languages, dreams – when society is simply a collection of strangers fighting for themselves, when 'we the people' becomes 'me, myself, and I' – there is friction. They rub each other the wrong way. They disagree. Your way or my way but never our way. But which way? They demand that judges decide. To referee their lives. To decide right or wrong, legal or illegal, winners and losers. Someone must win, someone must lose, and someone must decide. In America, that someone is a judge.

'Let us in.'

Jorge Romero released the intercom button. A voice came across.

'Who is it?'

'Jorge. With a special delivery from Hector.'

The overhead door to the warehouse lifted. Manny drove the pickup truck inside, and Jorge walked alongside. They had driven straight through the night. Jorge could not sleep; consequently, he was very tired when they arrived in Dallas eight hours later. They had texted the Arabs, but they refused to meet during the day. So Jorge and Manny had gotten food and a room. It was now seven-thirty that night.

The door shut behind them. It was a piece-of-shit warehouse located in a strip of piece-of-shit warehouses. But it was sizeable, large enough for an eighteen-wheeler. And in fact, parked in one corner was a ten-wheel truck without the eight-wheel trailer. It was a Peterbilt, a big rig, black with a massive chrome grill and low front panel that looked like it could plow snow. The cab sat high off the ground; a big two-step running board was fixed below the driver's door. Steel plates leaned against the side of the truck; next to the truck was welding equipment.

Which made Jorge wonder.

'Place stinks,' Manny said through the open window.

It smelled like a meth lab. In another corner stood a forklift and many barrels of the kind crude oil was transported in marked 'FERTILIZER' and 'AMMONIUM NITRATE.' Drums with the X over a skull and 'DANGER' and 'FLAM-MABLE' stamped on the side occupied the same corner. Flammable chemicals and fertilizer. He didn't figure Arabs for farmers. His *padre* had been a farmer in the Sierra Madre; some days – days like this one – Jorge Romero wished he had followed in his father's poor footsteps.

No, he figured the Arabs were building a bomb to kill the *gringos*. But being in the drug business, Jorge knew better than to ask the nature of a man's business. Still, he hated the fucking Arabs. So perhaps when he had crossed the Rio Grande back into Mexico, he would tip off the FBI about the contents of this warehouse.

Two young men appeared. One tall, wearing yellow sneak-ers, and one short, holding a large suitcase. The Arabs. Jorge was not so keen to deal with Arabs; he did not trust them. But he did not question *el jefe*. He only followed orders.

'We have your shipment.'

'Excellent,' the taller Arab said. 'Unload it.'

As if he were *el jefe* barking orders.

'Payment first,' Jorge said.

The taller Arab gave him a cold look. 'I would like to see what I have bought first.'

Jorge was tired from the long drive up from the border. He wanted to collect the money and find a whore for the night. He nodded.

'*Sí.*'

Jorge and Manny unloaded the containers and placed them on the concrete floor. The taller Arab counted the containers.

156

'There are supposed to be twelve.'

'My man, Pedro, he fell at the river. One container punctured on a rock.'

'Then I owe you only one-point-one million.'

'That shit killed Pedro and another man. Pay me in full, and we will call it even.'

Jorge and the Arab again exchanged cold looks. This time the Arab relented.

'Fine. I will pay you in full.' He turned to the other Arab. 'Little brother, bring the case.'

The other Arab stepped forward with the suitcase and placed it on the floor. He squatted and unlocked the case then opened the top. He rotated the case so Jorge could see inside. Manny stepped next to Jorge and whistled.

One-point-two million U.S. dollars.

Jorge Romero knew better than to look away from a customer. But he was tired and he was hungry and his thoughts were on a woman, a whore he would buy for the night with his cut of the cash. He knew he had made a grave error when his eyes came up from the cash to see the tall Arab holding a gun on them.

'What the hell is this?' he said.

'Payment in full.'

The Arab shot Jorge in the leg. The other Arab screamed with fright; Jorge fell to the floor. He had been shot before but it always hurt like hell. The Arab then shot Manny in the leg; he also went down.

'Abdul, what are you doing?' the short Arab said.

'If you kill us,' Jorge said, 'Hector will send many *sicarios* north to kill you.'

'Yes,' the Arab named Abdul said, 'but we will be in heaven with our father by the time they arrive.'

He turned to the shorter Arab. 'The masks.'

The shorter Arab walked away. Fucking Arabs. He wanted very much to kill them, but fate had turned against Jorge Romero that day. He had made a grave error, and now he would pay with his life. Hector had also made a grave error, to trust the Arabs. A people who would strap a bomb to their own children and send them out to die, those are not people one should trust. Killing was man's work, not the work for the children of God.

Jorge made the sign of the cross.

Beckeman sat in front of the television drinking a beer and watching *Saving Private Ryan*. He watched a lot of movies. Action. Adventure. Thrillers. Even dramas now and then. But never romantic comedies. There was nothing funny about romance.

He checked his watch: 8:00 P.M. Thirty-seven hours until the detention hearing, and they had found no evidence against Mustafa. It was like having to prove that Satan was bad.

Look the hell around!

He stopped the DVD and changed the channel to Fox News. On the screen he saw Attorney General J. Hamilton McReynolds III sitting on the front row with the other cabinet secretaries, the Supreme Court justices, and the Joint Chiefs of Staff, all gazing admiringly at the president and commander in chief.

'We won!'

The Constitution requires that the president 'from time to time give to the Congress information of the State of the Union.' So that night the president stood at the podium in the chamber of the House of Representatives in Washington, D.C., doing what every president since George Washington had done: inform the Congress of the State of the Union. George's speech in 1790 was the shortest on record, only 1,089 words.

158

That was George. Bill Clinton's speech in 1995 was the longest, 9,190 words. That was Bill. Thomas Jefferson sent written messages to the Congress. That was Tom. President Truman gave the first televised State of the Union address in 1947; and ever since, the annual speech to a joint session of Congress and the nation had become high political drama in America. The president offered his State of the Union, telling the people why he had done a standup job leading the country over the past year; the opposing party then gave a response telling the people why the president was full of shit. Politics in America.

'We defeated the terrorists who wanted to destroy our Super Bowl – our way of life! By God, that won't happen on my watch!'

Mac stood and applauded the president, as did every member of Congress on both sides of the aisle – Democrats sat on one side of the main aisle, Republicans on the other. The president was a Democrat, but Republicans knew the American people wanted the parties united in the war on terror. They wanted to be safe, at least in America. They didn't want the Democrats and the Republicans fighting each other; they wanted them fighting the terrorists. Both parties understood that sentiment. So the war on terror transcended politics. The president was twice as hard-ass as George W.; being Democrat gave him a free pass with the liberal press. He had increased drone strikes by 900 percent; he had killed more Muslims with drones than Bush had ever dreamed of killing. Guantanamo Bay was still hosting Islamic terrorists. Osama was dead, killed by American soldiers in Pakistan. As the president had so famously said, 'We have the right to kill anyone anywhere anytime.'

You've got to love him.

'Most presidents won't admit to their mistakes. I will. I made a mistake with Guantanamo. I campaigned on closing the camp. I thought it was wrong to detain human beings

159

without due process. It is. But after taking office and learning who the prisoners are, what they did and what they want to do – simply put, kill Americans until the day they die – I realized two things: one, they are not human beings. Human beings have consciences. They don't. They are evil beings. Human bodies possessed by evil. Pure evil. And two, we could not close Guantanamo. We can't send them to hell where they belong, so the next best thing is Guantanamo Bay. I authorized the release of several prisoners who are now commanders in the ISIL forces. We had them and let them go and now we must fight them again. That was my bad.'

Mac sighed. ISIS – the Islamic State of Iraq and Syria – or ISIL – the Islamic State of Iraq and the Levant? The media went with ISIS, the president with ISIL, for reasons that escaped Mac. Of course, the conspiracy theorists had their own take on the matter: the Levant comprises a larger area in the Middle East, including Israel; so, when the president says ISIL, he (a closet Muslim) is telling Muslims in the Middle East that he secretly does not recognize Israel as a sovereign nation but instead as a territory belonging to ISIL. Watch too much Fox News and that's what happens to your mind.

'In 2004, we had the current leader of ISIL, Abu Bakr al Baghdadi, in custody at Camp Bucca in Iraq. In 2009, we released him as not constituting a threat. Also my bad. Now he is the so-called Caliph Ibrahim. He's responsible for tens of thousands of innocent deaths, for hundreds of beheadings and crucifixions of civilians, for mass executions of Christians, for the use of sarin in Syria, and for thousands of women and girls being held as sex slaves. He personally and repeatedly raped the American girl they held as a hostage, Kayla Mueller, before her death. He said he owned her. *Owned her.* An American girl. Her abuse, her death, haunts me. And it will forever. I did not comprehend the evilness of the people we're fighting. I do now.'

The chamber was deathly silent. And then the president did something Mac had never seen him do: he abandoned the teleprompter. He strayed from the prepared text of his speech. He spoke from the heart, an organ Mac had thought did not inhabit his body.

'To al Baghdadi, I say this: You say you're a direct descendant of the Prophet Muhammad. You're not. You're a direct descendant of Satan. You are the devil incarnate. To do what you did to that sweet child in the name of God, that is the work of Satan. That is evil. You are evil. And I make a solemn oath – I will send you to hell where you belong. So look to the sky, Abu, because one day very soon, a drone missile with your name on it is going to give you a one-way ride to hell. As president of the United States of America, I guaran-damn-tee it!'

Mac exploded from his seat and clapped so hard his hands hurt. The entire chamber was deafening with applause and cheers and shouts of support. Tears rolled down his cheeks. He cried for little Kayla. He cried because after seventy-two years of life, he had finally witnessed an American president standing up to the evil in the world. Standing up for the innocent like Kayla. Throwing reelection concerns out the window and being the president of the United States of America. Being the leader of the free world. He had never felt so proud in his life.

On most issues of the day, Beckeman disagreed with the president. But he stood now, alone in his living room, and saluted his commander in chief.

Mac was the last person in the chamber to take his seat. The ovation had lasted ten minutes, maybe longer. There wasn't a dry eye in the place. And that said something, to get jaundiced senators and members of Congress to cry over anything except a reelection defeat. The president spoke again.

'Now we have Omar al Mustafa in custody. Not in Guantanamo. Not in Iraq. But in Dallas. I will not make the same mistake three times. I've learned my lesson in dealing with terrorists – when you have them in custody, keep them in custody. And that's exactly where he will remain.'

The members again applauded. The president raised a hand to quiet them.

'We won, this time. But we have to win every time. They don't. They just have to win once. Once a year. Once a decade. Once a lifetime. We had the tragic attack in California, an attack inspired by ISIL but not directed by ISIL. There has not been a major coordinated terrorist attack on the homeland since nine-eleven – and there won't be on my watch. That is my solemn pledge to the American people. But to fulfill that pledge, we need more funding for the FBI and Homeland Security. So we will never again be attacked here at home.'

That was a basic rule of politics: never let a good crisis go to waste. Seek more tax money. And when it came to protecting the homeland from terrorism, the people would pay. They would pay dearly to be safe in their homes and offices and sports stadiums.

'In other matters of state . . .'

The president moved on to the boring part of the speech – Mac had been given an advance copy to vet – so Mac's thoughts returned to Dallas. Beckeman had reported in: they had uncovered no evidence against Mustafa. It was now up to the judge. The detention hearing would be held Friday, and the judge would have to decide by Monday. Judicial independence was usually a good thing, but there were exceptions.

162

'. . . They are pursuing the American Dream, even if they are Mexicans. My executive order will keep families together, and that is what America is all about – families.'

Beckeman didn't have a family, Mexican or otherwise. So he sat alone in front of the television. He had resigned himself to a life alone; it was the job. He was good at it, and it needed to be done. It had to be done.

Looking at the president standing before Congress, he thought of the men who had created this country. They had put it all on the line to create America. The last sentence of the Declaration of Independence summed up what freedom was all about: 'And for the support of this Declaration, with a firm reliance on the protection of divine Providence, we mutually pledge to each other our Lives, our Fortunes and our sacred Honor.' Freedom wasn't free. It required sacrifice. It required a fight. Fifty-six men signed the Declaration, including Thomas Jefferson, Benjamin Franklin, John Hancock, and Samuel and John Adams. But not George Washington. He commanded the Revolutionary Army and was defending Manhattan Island against the British that day. He was a soldier, and he was doing what a soldier does: fighting for freedom. Putting his life on the line for America. Beckeman wasn't George Washington, but he was a soldier. He was fighting for freedom. He was putting his life on the line for America.

Some things are worth dying for.

The shorter Arab returned with two gas masks. The Arabs placed them over their heads. Then the Arab named Abdul shot the container nearest Jorge and Manny. Clear liquid oozed out of the hole. Jorge did not smell or taste anything. But he had seen Ricardo's and Pedro's dead bodies at the river. He knew something bad would soon happen. Thirty seconds later,

163

it did. Jorge's chest suddenly clamped down on his lungs, and he knew he would never wear another pair of cowboy boots handmade by Juan Castillo.

'Watch how they die,' Abdul said. 'It is a horrible death.'

He watched. In horror. As the Mexicans gasped for air. In their dark eyes, he saw the desire to kill the two Arabs standing before them; but their bodies could not fulfill that desire. Their bodies could only lie there and twitch. They clawed at their chests as if to open a hole through which to breathe . . . they clawed harder and harder until they clawed through their shirts and brought blood from their skin . . . drool escaped their mouths . . . followed by vomit, uncontrollable vomiting . . . their bodies convulsing and their pants turning wet with piss . . . and finally their eyes widening but their pupils constricting to pinpoints . . . and then it stopped.

They were dead.

The stench of puke was joined by the stench of shit. He felt his stomach turn and cramp; he ran to the far side of the warehouse, ripped off the mask, and threw up. This had gone too far. Abdul had often talked of killing, but never before had he killed. Until now. His big brother had just killed two men. Mexicans, sure, but still. He had thought this would go away, Abdul's obsession with killing and beheading and jihadism, that he would grow out of it, as he had grown out of his obsession with soccer. Of course, that had not happened until he became obsessed with jihad. He wanted to run away, to race out of this warehouse and drive away. Somewhere. Anywhere. He did not want to be a part of this madness. He wiped his mouth, replaced the mask, and returned to his brother.

'Abdul, why did you do that?'

'I wanted to see how it killed these two Mexicans. Now I know this death befits the Americans.'

★

164

'Mexicans die to come to America,' the president said. 'They risk their lives to cross the border. To give their families a better life.'

The other side of the aisle stirred. Immigration was red meat to Republicans, and the president had just tossed out a fresh carcass.

'I have asked this Congress for immigration reform since the day I took office. But Republicans have opposed every effort at compromise I've made. So I reformed the law myself. I changed the law myself!'

Mac grimaced. He really wished the president would stop saying that.

'I issued an executive order granting amnesty to the twelve million Mexicans living here in the shadows, hard-working, law-abiding, God-fearing people who want better lives. Twenty-six states have sued me in federal court to void my order. But I will win that fight as well. The twelve million Mexicans will win that fight. They will be put on a path to citizenship so one day they too can vote. Republicans should keep that in mind. One day, they will vote.'

And that was Diego Peña's dream: to vote in America once before he died. To be an American citizen when he died. To know that his wife, Sofia, was an American citizen. That she would never be deported.

Was that too much to ask of life?

He had often asked that question of God. For the last thirty-two years, the answer had been yes. That was too much to ask of life. So they lived in the shadows of America, neither here nor there, neither citizen nor voter, neither Mexican nor

American. And now the president promised that one day they would live in the sunlight, one day they would be American citizens, one day they would vote. He cried.

Cat Peña wiped a tear from her cheek. Her parents sat in front of the television almost in reverence, as if the president were the Pope saying Mass. He *was* offering salvation to them. Amnesty. Citizenship. Safety. Security. They had fled the cartels, north to safety; America accepted refugees from the terror wars in Somalia, Iraq, Iran, Egypt, and Syria, but not from Mexico. Perhaps that would require an unpleasant acknowledgement by America: Americans aided and abetted Mexico's terrorists. Americans funded the cartels; we sent $40 billion south each year, money paid for illegal drugs. Americans armed the cartels; we sold 10,000 high-powered weapons to the cartels each year. We were the cartels' customers and their co-conspirators; we fund them, we arm them, and then we deny any responsibility for them. If you know that your money will be used to corrupt police and politicians and purchase weapons that will be used to kill innocent Mexicans, are you not as guilty as the cartel *gauchos* who pull the trigger? If Americans were being killed in America, the answer would be yes. You would be charged with murder. But only Mexicans in Mexico were being killed, so Americans' drug use was just 'recreational.' Tell the families of the dead Mexicans that you were just having fun; that will make their pain disappear.

'Republicans love football, too, so we applaud the president in continuing the Bush policy in the war on terror. That policy saved the Super Bowl.'

The Senate Majority Leader gave the Republican response to the president's State of the Union address. Mac had to hear this.

'But we do not agree with the president on immigration. The Fourteenth Amendment that grants citizenship to any person born on American soil has been abused by too many people who come here just to have American babies. The FBI busted a citizenship tourism scheme that brought pregnant Asian women to California, put them up in luxury hotels, and took them on shopping sprees until their babies were born. Then they returned home, knowing that one day their children could return to America and enjoy the benefits of American citizenship even though their parents had never paid their dues – or taxes – in America. That is *not* the American way. We are a generous people, but we don't like being taken advantage of. And that's what these people are doing to us. We believe in the rule of law; they don't. So we must deport all twelve million illegal aliens. They should then apply for visas in accordance with the law, as millions of legal immigrants have done. We obey the law. We don't expect to intentionally break the law and then be rewarded for having done so. We expect to be punished. That is America, too.

'If we reward them with citizenship for breaking the law, how do I tell my children to obey the law? To respect the law? Why shouldn't they cheat at their taxes? Why shouldn't they run stop signs when no cop is around? Have you ever noticed how Americans stop at stop signs and red lights even when no cop is around? When no other cars are around? Why do we do that? Because it's the law. The law says stop, so we stop. We are not a nation of cheaters. We are law-abiding people. We respect the rule of law. Illegal aliens do not. They knowingly and intentionally broke our law, now they want to be rewarded rather than punished.'

Chapter 9

By Thursday, life had returned to normal – or at least as normal as life could be with twenty-three alleged Islamic terrorists residing ten floors below his courtroom and the FBI SWAT team standing guard outside. The protestors had decreased; only a few determined ones remained. The others had gone back to work. The girls' attention had died away, but Scott's speaking requests had not. He had been invited to speak at local, state, and national bar association meetings, civic clubs, and athletic banquets at local high schools and colleges. He declined them all.

'She wants another baby,' Bobby said. 'And to be a full-time mom. I created a monster.'

'She doesn't like working for the judge?'

'She doesn't want a nanny raising our child. Was Rebecca like that?'

'No.'

Scott and Bobby Herrin had been best friends since ninth grade, two renters in Highland Park. But Scott could play football, so he had moved up in the world and taken Bobby with him. They were Batman and Robin all through high school, college, and law school, right up until the day Scott hired on with Ford Stevens. They didn't see each other for eleven years, until Judge Buford appointed Scott to represent Pajamae's mother and he tried to punt her to Bobby. Shawanda refused. Scott lost everything, but regained his best friend. Bobby held no grudges; he was like that. Scott tossed him a toffee.

'What will I do if she quits?' Scott said.

'What will you do? What will I do? She makes eighty-five grand.'

'You need her paycheck?'

'Maybe not need. But it's nice to have. I mean, I make one eighty-five a year, that's a fortune by my standards. But the house is a money pit—'

They had bought an older home in the M Streets and were renovating room by room.

'—and if we have another kid . . .'

'Maybe she could work from home, come in for trials.'

'You think that would work?'

'She can think just as well at home.'

'Thanks, Scotty.' He relaxed, as if he had just been told he didn't have cancer. After a moment, he said, 'You ready for tomorrow?'

'As ready as I'll ever be. Mike Donahue, Frank Turner, and the most dangerous man in Dallas in my courtroom . . . it'll be interesting.'

'Think Mustafa will testify?'

'Frank's not that stupid. He won't give Mike Donahue a chance to bait his client.'

'Frank sure was scared. Wonder what Mustafa said to him?'

★

'Nothing?' the U.S. Attorney said.

'Nothing,' Beckeman said.

Mike Donahue had called him just before noon at FBI headquarters.

'So I'm walking into court tomorrow morning holding only my balls.'

'I'll be there with you . . . not holding your balls, but I'll be there.'

'You'd better be. You're the only witness I've got.'

He sighed as if his dog had been run over by a milk truck.

'Frank Turner is going to kick my ass.'

Bitzy's parents have lodged a complaint against Boo for punching her at the basketball game. Judge Fenney, I hate to bring this matter to you at this time. I know you're busy fighting those Muslim terrorists, but we have procedures for bullying that must be followed.

The principal's email pinged in just as Bobby walked out of Scott's chambers. The blonde girl bullied Pajamae, but now her parents claimed Boo bullied her. Seemed like the world was full of bullies these days.

' "I will cast terror into the hearts of the infidels." '

Omar al Mustafa held the Koran. He waved it. He jabbed the air with it. He wielded it like a weapon. Perhaps it was.

' "God is the enemy of the unbelievers" . . . "God does not love the unbelievers" . . . "The unbelievers are your inveterate foe" . . . "Do not grieve for the unbelievers" . . . "The only true faith in God's sight is Islam" . . . "God's curse be upon the infidels" . . . "Make war on them until idolatry shall cease and God's religion shall reign supreme." '

He paused for effect and held up the Koran to the camera.

'These are not my words. These are the words of God. Shall we ignore God's words? His will? His orders? The Americans

170

came to the Muslim homeland to spread democracy through violence. Why cannot Muslims go to the American homeland and spread Sharia through violence? If America can fire drone missiles into the Muslim homeland, why cannot Muslims detonate bombs in the American homeland? Why can Americans act violently against Muslims, but Muslims cannot act violently against Americans? The U.S. Army thinks it can outsource its war on Islam. They think they can hire Muslims to kill Muslims. They spent $25 billion to train and equip the Iraqi Army. But when ISIS forces marched into Mosul, the Iraqis threw down their weapons and stripped off their uniforms. Why? Because they knew the words on the ISIS flag speak the truth: *There is no god but God. Muhammad is the messenger of God.* Because the Koran forbids a Muslim to kill another Muslim. Because Muslims are united in their fight against the Christians and Jews. So they will die as the Koran informs. The messiah will come back to earth. He will defeat the Antichrist. He will purify the world of unbelievers. He will conquer the world for Islam. For Muslims. So it was written. So it will be done.'

The girls were sleeping, and Scott was watching the imam on a YouTube video cited in the government's detention brief. As an American, Scott did not appreciate Mustafa's point of view; as a U.S. district judge, he knew it was within the First Amendment's guarantee of free speech. The phone rang. It was the attorney general calling from Washington.

'You have my home phone, too?'

'And your cell.'

'What about my email?'

'Your girl sounds like a real pistol. Did she really deck Bitzy? Name like that, she's begging to be punched out.'

Mac chuckled.

'How'd you get that email?'

171

'It's called the NSA, Scott.'

Working for the federal government offered new disillusionment on a daily basis. He started to debate the right of privacy with the AG, but decided not to waste his breath.

'Did you watch the State of the Union?' Mac asked.

'I did.'

'The president sure was happy.'

'Seemed so.'

'Don't make him unhappy.'

'And how would I do that?'

'By releasing Mustafa.'

'This case has gone to the president?'

'It's been with the president since the tip came in. Scott, you're talking the Super Bowl. A credible threat goes straight to the top.'

'I'll hear the evidence tomorrow.'

'There is no evidence! I told you that! Were you not listening?' He exhaled heavily. 'Why are you so focused on the evidence?'

Now Scott laughed. 'Because I'm a judge. Because tomorrow we'll be in a court of law. Because the Constitution requires evidence to hold a person in custody.'

The AG said nothing, but Scott could hear him breathing.

'You're a young man, Scott. The Supreme Court justices are old men. There'll be a vacancy on the court soon. The president will nominate the next justice. Could be you. The judge who kept the Super Bowl safe. That would get you Senate confirmation on a voice vote.'

More disillusionment.

'Is everything political, Mac?'

'No. Who sits on the Supreme Court is, but who lives or dies on Super Bowl Sunday isn't. That's not political, that's not judicial. That's reality. Mustafa wants to kill Americans. The president isn't going to let that happen. He's asking for your help. I'm asking for your help. Scott, I serve at the pleasure of the president.'

'I don't.'

'I'd like to keep my job, but more important, I'd like to keep the American people safe.'

He sounded sincere, and Scott had no doubt he was. The AG had served in Vietnam; he had been a prisoner of war for two years. His country had abandoned him, but he had never abandoned his country. Karen had googled J. Hamilton McReynolds III and written a memo to Scott. She did not allow her judge to be uninformed.

'I'm watching Mustafa on YouTube,' Scott said.

'And do you think he's a good guy?'

'No. But he might be an innocent guy. At least of this crime.'

'Cumulative justice, Scott. One day he'll prove how guilty he is. And innocent people will die.'

Chapter 10

'*The United States of America versus Omar Mansour, also known as Omar al Mustafa, et al.* Detention hearing.'

Louis's booming voice reverberated through the crowded courtroom. Scott sat behind the bench; Bobby, Karen, and Carlos occupied their usual positions. U.S. Attorney Mike Donahue and Agent Beckeman sat at the prosecution table; Frank Turner and Omar al Mustafa at the defense table. Mustafa was shackled, as were the other defendants who sat in the jury box and in folding chairs in front of the jury box. But everyone knew that so goes the imam, so goes the other defendants. If the imam got out, they got out; if he didn't, they didn't. Scott spoke.

'The government has moved for pretrial detention of all defendants and has submitted a brief in support of its motion. Under the Bail Reform Act, a detention hearing must be held before the defendants may be detained pending trial. This hearing is not about the defendants' guilt or innocence of the charges on which they've been indicted. That matter will be determined at trial. The purpose of this hearing is to determine the defendants' eligibility for pretrial release, and if eligible, the conditions, if any, to their release. Two issues need be answered by the court to make that determination: One, are the defendants flight risks? And two, are the defendants dangers to the community? If both are answered in the negative, the defendants must be released on their own recognizance. If either or both are answered in the positive, I must set conditions to their release that will assure their appearance at trial and the safety of the community. Only if no such conditions exist may the defendants be detained. It is the government's burden to prove by clear and convincing evidence that the defendants are flight risks or dangers to the community and that no such conditions exist. However, under the Act, the charge of conspiracy to use weapons of mass destruction carries a presumption that no such conditions exist; therefore, the defendants must produce some relevant evidence that they are not flight risks or dangers to the community or that such conditions do exist.'

The imam's expression had not changed since the arraignment; the other defendants' expressions had. They no longer looked like fierce fighters; they looked defeated, resigned to their fate, students who already knew they had flunked the test. A week in jail will do that.

'The Act requires the court to consider several factors in determining the defendants' eligibility for and conditions of pretrial release. These factors are: one, the nature and circumstances of the offense, and particularly if it is a violent crime or an act of terrorism; two, the weight of evidence against the defendants; three, the defendants' history and character; and four, the nature and seriousness of the danger to any person or the community posed by the defendants' release.'

175

After hearing Frank's plea the day before, Scott found himself hoping the government had discovered damning evidence against the defendants.

'This is an evidentiary hearing. Each party may present evidence and witnesses. The other party may cross-examine opposing witnesses. However, if any defendant testifies on his own behalf, the government may not cross on the merits of the charges against him, only on the issues of flight risk and danger to the community. The rules of evidence do not apply. Hearsay is admissible. Evidence may be offered by proffer; no personal knowledge of the witness is required. This is an informal proceeding. Any questions as to the procedure?'

There were none.

'We will address the factors so as to dispense with the easiest first. The history and character of the defendants and the nature and seriousness of any danger their release would pose are essentially the same. The statutory characteristics include physical and mental condition, family life, employment, financial resources, length of time in the community and ties to the community, drug or alcohol abuse, and criminal history. The court assigned a Pretrial Services Officer to interview the defendants and make a recommendation as to release or detention of each defendant as well as to any conditions of release. Ms. O'Brien, please come forward.'

Sherry O'Brien walked forward and sat in the witness chair. She was middle-aged; she had done her job for fifteen years. She didn't put up with bullshit from either defendants or judges.

'Ms. O'Brien, did you interview the defendants and deliver release reports to the court and the parties with your recommendations?'

'Yes and no, Your Honor.'

That wasn't the expected answer. Scott turned to her.

'Please explain.'

'I attempted to interview each defendant. They all refused to talk to me.'

'Why?'

'They said you told them that they had the right to remain silent.'

Scott sighed. 'Well, I did say that, didn't I?'

'Yes, sir, you did. But I did write a report with the information I could find, the most important being that none of the defendants has a criminal history.'

'None at all?'

'No, sir. But without interviews, I could not make any recommendations to the court.'

'Anything else, Ms. O'Brien?'

'Yes. Three of the defendants are foreign nationals. They are citizens of Pakistan, and they have overstayed their visas and are residing in the U.S. illegally.'

One defendant jumped up from his chair. 'The president said we could stay!'

Louis made a move in his direction, but Scott stopped him with a raised hand. The defendant presented no danger in the shackles.

'Sir, whether you may stay in the country is a question for another day. The question today is whether you stay in jail.'

The defendant sat, and Scott turned back to Ms. O'Brien.

'Thank you. You're excused.'

She returned to her seat. Scott addressed the attorneys: 'Does either party want to present evidence on this factor?'

Mike Donahue stood. 'Your Honor, our evidence consists of testimony from the FBI agent in charge of the case. We'd like to address all factors at the same time during his testimony.'

'Any objection, Mr. Turner?'

'No, Your Honor.'

'The next factor is the nature and circumstances of the offense. The defendants have been charged with conspiracy to use weapons of mass destruction. As I said, this offense carries a rebuttable presumption of detention. Thus, the final factor, the weight of evidence against the defendants, becomes critical to the determination of release or detention. Mr. Donahue, please present the government's case.'

Donahue stood. 'The government calls FBI Special Agent Eric Beckeman.'

The tall agent strode to the witness stand like the Marine he had once been. Louis swore him in, and he sat erectly. Donahue questioned him from the podium.

'Agent Beckeman, you're in charge of the Joint Terrorism Task Force, is that correct?'

'I am.'

'It is your job to protect this nation against domestic terrorists?'

'It is.'

'And in that capacity you have captured or killed a number of Islamic terrorists?'

'I have.'

'And before that, you served as a captain in the Marine Corps in Afghanistan and—'

'Your Honor,' Frank said, 'we agree that Agent Beckeman knows what he's doing. Since there's no jury to be swayed, perhaps the government can dispense with his biography. In the interest of time.'

'That's up to Mr. Donahue . . . but less is more.'

'Fine, Your Honor,' Donahue said. 'Agent Beckeman, do you consider Omar al Mustafa a flight risk?'

'I do.'

'Do you consider him a danger to the community?'

'I do.'

'On what do you base your opinion?'

'On him. On his own words. What he's written and what he's said. He hates America and wants Americans to die.'

'Your Honor,' Donahue said, 'Defendant Mustafa's writings are exhibits to our brief. I can have Agent Beckeman recite portions, but if you've read our brief—'

'I have.'

'Then there's no need to repeat his words now.'

'Thank you.'

Donahue returned to his witness. 'Agent, is the Task Force particularly concerned about lone wolf attacks here in the U.S.?'

'We are.'

'Why?'

'Because ISIS has called for Muslims in America to, quote, "kill where you are."'

'How do you know that?'

'ISIS has posted numerous statements on Twitter—'

'Terrorists with Twitter accounts?'

'Yes. And hundreds of thousands of followers. Twitter suspends their accounts as fast as they can – which earned Twitter executives beheading threats from ISIS – but we estimate that at any time there are about forty thousand active pro-ISIS accounts.'

'And what did those statements say?'

The agent removed a paper from his coat pocket and read. 'This one in late twenty-fourteen was particularly direct. Quote, "Do not let this battle pass you by wherever you may be. You must strike the soldiers, patrons and troops of the *kuffars*. Strike their police, security, and intelligence members, as well as their treacherous agents. Destroy their beds. Embitter their lives. If you can kill a disbelieving American or European – especially the spiteful and filthy French – or an Australian, or a Canadian, or any other disbeliever, including the citizens of the countries that entered into a coalition against the Islamic State, then rely upon Allah, and kill him in any manner or way however it may be. Do not ask for anyone's advice and do not seek anyone's verdict. Kill the disbeliever whether he is civilian or military, for they have the same ruling. Both of them are disbelievers. If you are not able to find an IED or a bullet, then single out the disbelieving American, Frenchman, or any of their allies. Smash his head with a rock, or slaughter him with a knife, or run him over with your car, or throw him down from a high place, or choke him, or poison him. If you are unable to do so, then burn his home, car, or business. Or destroy his crops. If you are unable to do so, then spit in his face.'"

The courtroom had fallen silent.

'Chilling,' Donahue said.

'It is.'

'Agent, have you seen the consequences of this statement?'

'We have. Since this statement was released ISIS followers killed one hundred thirty civilians in Paris in the November attack and before that a dozen people at the Paris office of a magazine that printed cartoons they considered offensive to Muhammad. They killed four people at the Jewish Museum of Belgium, stabbed two police officers in Australia, and killed one Canadian soldier with a car and another by gunshot at the Parliament. The Swiss authorities stopped a plot to use poison gas, and the Australians stopped a plot by fifteen individuals to behead random people on the streets of Sydney, a plot run directly from Syria. Here at home ISIS followers killed fourteen in the San Bernardino attack and five servicemen in Chatta-nooga, and attacked two New York City police officers with a hatchet. We arrested a Florida man who wanted to detonate a backpack bomb on the beach. We have thwarted plots to deto-nate suicide bombs at Fort Riley, Kansas, and in New York City. We apprehended an Army National Guard soldier and his cousin who were plotting to kill fellow soldiers at an Illinois army base. The soldier had posted on Twitter: "I am already in the American infidel army and now I wish only to serve in the army of Allah alongside my true brothers. We would love to do something like the brother in Paris did. Hit here and then go to *dawlah insha'*Allah."'

'What does that mean? *Dawlah insha'*Allah?'

' "The caliphate, God willing." We have charged sixty-seven U.S. residents with domestic terrorism, including Muslim immigrants from Bosnia, Uzbekistan, Kazakhstan, Somalia, Iraq, Somalia, and Syria, we have hundreds of ongoing investigations of possible lone wolf attacks, and we're tracking thousands of potential jihadists in the U.S. Our intelligence community now regards ISIS as a greater threat to the U.S. homeland than al Qaeda, although al Qaeda recently called for lone wolf attacks against Bill Gates and Warren Buffett in an attempt to harm the U.S. economy.'

'Agent, I think we can all agree that ISIS is bad, but how is Mr. Mustafa connected to ISIS?'

'He recruits for them. And he's their cleric. He gives religious justification for their violent actions.'

'How does he do that?'

'Through his treatises and speeches that are printed in *Dabiq*, the online propaganda magazine of ISIS. He wrote one article stating that the Koran allows them to hold non-Muslim girls as sex-slaves. At this moment, ISIS holds five thousand women and girls as sex-slaves. *Five thousand*. These girls are raped every day of their lives. And we do nothing to stop it.'

There was a long moment of silence. Donahue finally blew out a breath for the entire courtroom.

'Agent Beckeman, how is Mr. Mustafa connected to the Cowboys Stadium plot?'

'We learned from a confidential source that Mustafa was the mastermind behind the plot.'

'Do you consider the other defendants flight risks and dangers to the community?'

'I do.'

'Why?'

'Because they're disciples of Mustafa. They follow his orders. And the same confidential source said they were participants in the plot.'

'Did the source identify the defendants by name?'

'Yes, sir. Their full names. All twenty-three, including Aabdar Haddad.'

'No further questions, Your Honor.'

'Mr. Turner.'

Frank Turner stepped to the podium. A great cross-examination of the government's witness is often the only way to overcome the presumption. Franklin Turner, famous plaintiffs' lawyer, never failed to deliver greatness; and he always made cross-examination high entertainment. But Scott did not expect either greatness or entertainment that day from Frank Turner. For the first time in his career, Frank wanted to lose.

'Agent Beckeman, do you know the name of the confidential source?'

'No. He kept that confidential.'

'Ah. So, what you really have then is an anonymous tip?'

'A source.'

'A source without a name, which is the definition of anonymous.'

'If you say so.'

'I think you did. So, Agent, this source called in to the terrorism hotline, is that correct?'

'Yes.'

'Did you answer the call?'

182

'Personally?'

'Yes.'

'No.'

'So the tipster told his tip to another person?'

'Yes.'

'Who?'

'That's confidential.'

'I won't tell anyone.'

'You're a lawyer. Of course you will.'

'Was that person a hotline operator?'

'Yes.'

'And did that person tell you?'

'No. He told our hotline chief.'

'And the chief told you?'

'No. He told another agent.'

'Who told you?'

'Yes.'

'So, an anonymous tipster told an operator who told the chief who told an agent who told you?'

'That's correct.'

'Kind of like a fishing story where the fish gets bigger each time the story is told.'

Frank's voice had risen. He seemed to be forgetting that he wanted to lose. Scott and Frank were different men and very different lawyers, but they had one thing in common: neither could stand to lose in a courtroom. The zealous advocate that resided within Frank Turner had awakened. He didn't want to win, but he couldn't help himself. He had to win. He was Michael Jordan in a pickup game.

'Agent, are you convinced of the veracity of the source?'

'I am.'

'Why?'

Beckeman shrugged. 'Why would he lie?'

'Let's see . . . perhaps he wants attention. Perhaps he's jealous. Perhaps he's the real terrorist who wants to lead you astray. Perhaps he's a rival imam.'

'A *rival imam*?'

'Agent Beckeman, did you conduct a search of Mr. Mustafa's house and mosque?'

'Yes.'

'Did you recover any bomb-making material?'

'No.'

'Any weapons of mass destruction?'

'No.'

'Any weapons of minor destruction?'

'No.'

'Any weapons of any kind?'

'No.'

'Perhaps a sharp kitchen knife?'

'No.'

'So you recovered no incriminating evidence of any kind whatsoever?'

'That's not correct. We did recover evidence.'

'What evidence?'

'His writings and his DVDs, and ISIS material, including *A Call to Global Islamic Resistance*, a treatise that urges lone wolf attacks in the West.'

'Incriminating means evidence directly connecting Mr. Mustafa to the bombing plot.'

'Under that definition, we did not.'

'Is there anything Mr. Mustafa has written or said that is not within the free speech protections of the First Amendment?'

'No. He is very careful not to advocate violence or to incite violence.'

'So his writings and speeches may be offensive, but they are not illegal?'

'They are not.'

'Did you tap his phones?'

'Yes.'

'Did you record any conversations in which he discussed the stadium plot?'

'No.'

'In which he discussed the use of weapons of mass destruction?'

'No.'

'In which he discussed committing any act of terrorism?'

'No.'

'Agent Beckeman, what evidence do you possess that Omar al Mustafa conspired to bomb Cowboys Stadium?'

'We have his writings.'

'His writings? He wrote about bombing Cowboys Stadium?'

'Not exactly.'

'Well, Agent, what exactly did he write about?'

'His desire for America to fail.'

'Fail? In what way?'

'He wants America to fail in Iraq and Afghanistan and Israel.'

'In the Middle East?'

'Yes.'

'And where is Cowboys Stadium?'

'In Arlington.'

'Which is to say, *not* in the Middle East.'

'Correct.'

'Did he mention Cowboys Stadium in any of his writings?'

'No.'

'Did he mention bombing any public structure in America in any of his writings?'

'No.'

'Did he mention the use of weapons of mass destruction in America in any of his writings?'

'No.'

'Again, Agent Beckeman, what evidence do you possess that Omar al Mustafa conspired to bomb Cowboys Stadium?'

'He is affiliated with ISIS.'

'And by "affiliated," you mean what?'

'He has aligned himself with ISIS.'

'And by "aligned," you mean what?'

'He believes in their cause.'

'Which is?'

'The Islamic State. What they call a caliphate.'

'Where?'

'In Iraq and Syria.'

'Which are where?'

'In the Middle East.'

'And where is Cowboys Stadium?'

'In Arlington.'

'Again, *not* in the Middle East?'

'Correct.'

'Do you have any direct evidence that he conspired with ISIS to commit any crime in the U.S.?'

'No.'

'Do you have any evidence that he financed or provided material support to ISIS?'

'No.'

'Do you have any evidence that ISIS conspired to bomb Cowboys Stadium?'

'No.'

'Agent Beckeman, what kind of bomb did the defendant intend to detonate in the stadium?'

'A big bomb.'

'Can you be a bit more specific?'

'No.'

'Why not?'

'We are pursuing leads as to the source of the materials.'

'But you testified that you recovered no bomb-making materials during your searches.'

'That's correct.'

'Then what leads are you pursuing?'

'Credible leads.'

'*Credible* leads? Agent Beckeman, do you have any evidence whatsoever tying Mr. Mustafa to the plot to bomb Cowboys Stadium?'

'I am not at liberty to divulge all our evidence at this time because it would threaten national security.'

'*National security?*'

'Yes, Mr. Turner. National security.'

He said it with a straight face. Frank stared at the agent a long moment then looked at Scott. He turned his palms up as if to say, *How do I respond to that?* He decided not to.

'Agent Beckeman, the only standard for his release or detention pending trial is whether he is a flight risk or danger to the community, correct?'

'That's what the judge said.'

'So you view his exercise of his right of free speech as a danger to the community?'

'The defendant wants to kill a hundred thousand people in two weeks. I think that makes him a danger to the community.'

'What has he done?'

'Plotted to blow up Cowboys Stadium.'

'How do we know that?'

'You'll know it when that stadium comes down Super Bowl Sunday.'

'And if it doesn't?'

'Then we got the right guy and prevented an act of terror.'

'So if the judge releases him and the stadium comes down, he's the right guy?'

'He is.'

187

'And if the judge doesn't release him, and the stadium doesn't come down, he's the right guy?'

'He is.'

'What if the judge releases him and the stadium doesn't come down?'

'Are you willing to take that risk? Or more accurately, are you willing for those one hundred thousands fans inside the stadium on Super Bowl Sunday to take that risk? Is the judge willing to take that risk?'

Was he? America had not suffered a major act of domestic terrorism since 9/11. If the Justice Department, the FBI, and the Department of Homeland Security had anything to say about it, America would never again suffer such a violation. They were good. They were aggressive. They defended America against all enemies, foreign and domestic.

But were they right? Did they have the right man? Was Omar al Mustafa just an American citizen who exercised his right to free speech guaranteed by the First Amendment to the U.S. Constitution? Or was he an Islamic jihadist who plotted to kill a hundred thousand Americans? Those were the questions. The answers would be revealed in that courtroom at trial. That was the assignment given U.S. District Judge A. Scott Fenney by the Constitution of the United States of America. But the trial would take place a month after the Super Bowl. A month after the event that could determine the defendant's guilt or innocence. A month after a hundred thousand people might die.

Was Judge A. Scott Fenney willing to take that risk?

'One last question, Agent Beckeman,' Frank said. 'What if the judge doesn't release Mr. Mustafa, but the stadium still comes down?'

Agent Beckeman glared at the lawyer questioning him; after a long moment, he exhaled and his expression softened. He spoke with an equally soft voice.

'Then I didn't do my job, Mr. Turner. And a lot of people died because I failed.'

'No further questions, Your Honor.'

Agent Beckeman stepped down from the stand and sat at the prosecution table.

'Any witnesses, Mr. Turner?'

'Yes, Your Honor. Defense calls Omar al Mustafa to the stand.'

Frank was like that. He possessed the ability and the balls to shock a courtroom. And everyone in the courtroom was shocked, including the presiding judge and the U.S. Attorney.

'Your Honor, may Mr. Mustafa's shackles be removed for his testimony?'

'Yes.'

The detention guard unlocked the shackles. The imam rubbed his wrists then walked to the witness stand. Louis swore him in.

'Do you swear to tell the truth, the whole truth, and nothing but the truth, so help you God?'

'As Allah is my witness.'

'That's a yes?'

'That is a yes.'

'Please sit.'

The imam sat. Frank stood at the podium.

'Mr. Mustafa, have you ever committed a crime?'

'No.'

'Nothing? Not even when you were a kid in Chicago? Maybe shoplifting Cheetos at a convenience store, buying beer when you were underage, pumping gas and driving off without paying?'

'No. Never. I was a good boy.'

'Are you a good man?'

'I try to follow Allah's path.'

'Have you ever traveled outside the U.S.?'

'Yes, when I was a young man, I studied in Jordan.'

'Which is an ally of America?'

'The last I heard.'

'Do you still have a valid passport?'

'I do not.'

'Hard to flee the jurisdiction without a passport?'

'I would think so.'

'Do you intend to show up for trial?'

'Of course. I must clear my name.'

'Would you agree to wear a GPS monitor?'

'Certainly. I will be at the mosque.'

'Do you own any weapons?'

'No.'

'No guns, no crossbows, no weapons of mass destruction?'

'No.'

'Would you agree not to go to the Cowboys games?'

'Yes. I do not like baseball.'

'Football.'

'Or that.'

Frank turned to Scott. 'No further questions, Your Honor.'

They held eye contact for a long moment then Frank walked to the defense table and sat down hard. Scott had expected a lengthy direct examination from Frank. Why had Frank not given one? Was he setting up the prosecution? Or was he cutting the direct short before his client confessed . . . or committed perjury?

'Mr. Donahue.'

Mike Donahue couldn't believe his good fortune. God was smiling on him that day. No way was Mustafa going to testify. But there he sat in the witness stand, legally obligated to answer any question Mike wanted to ask. Any question that might reveal a violent tendency. That might reveal that Omar al Mustafa was in fact the most dangerous man in Dallas. There was only one question: Would he take the bait?

'Mr. Mustafa, you conspired to blow up Cowboys Stadium on Super Bowl Sunday, didn't you?'

'Objection,' Frank said in a matter-of-fact tone – he was clearly expecting such a cross – 'the prosecutor cannot question the witness on the merits of the case.'

'Sustained,' Scott said. 'Mr. Donahue, please limit your questions to the issues at hand.'

'Why?'

'It's the law.'

'You allowed the defendant to testify that he was a good boy. Can't we show that he's not such a good boy?'

'You may at trial. Today, show me that he's a flight risk or a danger to the community. Show me something in his life, his character, or his past or present actions that indicates bad acts in the future. Show me how strongly the evidence weighs against him on the charges. Show me something. But don't question the witness on the merits of the case. The law doesn't allow that.'

The U.S. Attorney was not happy.

'Mr. Donahue, the defense subpoenaed the attorney general. I denied their request. We are sticking to the issue of detention.'

Donahue turned back to the witness. 'Mr. Mustafa, are you affiliated with ISIS?'

'No.'

Normally, Scott observed the demeanor of the defendant. But now he observed the demeanor of the defendant's counsel. Frank stared down at his hands.

'But your writings and speeches have been printed in the ISIS magazine?'

'Yes.'

'Did you give them permission?'

'No.'

'Did you sue to stop the publication?'

The imam smiled. '*Sue ISIS?* Are you serious?'

'Do you believe that America is waging war on Islam?'

'I do.'

'Why?'

'It is.'

'Do you believe ISIS is justified in killing civilians?'

'I understand the killing. ISIS would say, America kills Muslim civilians, why cannot Muslims kill American civilians? *Quid pro quo*, I believe you lawyers say. What you give, you get.'

'American civilians are noncombatants.'

'Are they? America is a democracy, is it not? Power resides in the people. ISIS would say, the American people put the president in the White House and thus in command of the army. The president gives the order to launch drones over the Muslim homeland and to kill Muslims with drone missiles. If the people put the president in office, are they not responsible for the president's actions? All responsible parties are combatants, counselor. I believe that is the law of war.'

'Do you support ISIS's acts of violence?'

'Do you support George Washington's acts of violence?'

'*What?*'

'How was America created? Through violent revolution. The king of England considered George Washington a terrorist, much as America today considers al Baghdadi a terrorist.'

'You're comparing George Washington to a guy who beheads innocent people?'

'Is a musket ball through the head a more humane way to kill than a knife through the throat?'

'George Washington wasn't a pedophile holding young girls as sex slaves!'

192

'How do you know? He was also a slave owner. At his death he owned one hundred twenty-three slaves. He treated his slaves harshly. He whipped them regularly. His slaves had children. Many were young girls. How do you know George did not partake of the girls? He is a white American legend so you paint him in soft tones. But you paint a Muslim legend in harsh tones.'

Mike Donahue was losing control of his cross; he had already lost control of his temper.

'Did ISIS have a right to kill one hundred thirty people in Paris?'

'Did France have a right to kill thousands of Muslims in Syria?'

'Does ISIS have a right to detonate bombs in America?'

'Does America have a right to detonate bombs in the Middle East?'

'Did you pledge allegiance to the caliphate?'

'Did you pledge allegiance to America?'

'Do you recruit for ISIS?'

'No. You do.'

'Who?'

'America. You created ISIS when you invaded Iraq. You took over the country and fired one hundred thousand Sunnis from government and the military. They had no jobs, no money, so they became jihadists. A man must take care of his family.'

'By killing people?'

'Are your soldiers not paid to kill? You recruit for ISIS every time your drones kill Muslims. You are providing material support to ISIS, not me.'

'I thought Islam is a peaceful religion?'

'And that is what America wants, is it not? Peaceful Muslims peacefully surrendering their homeland to the Christians and

Jews. But when Muslims stand up and refuse to peacefully surrender, when Muslims finally fight back, you are shocked. You ask, "Who radicalized them?" You did. The only weapons of mass destruction found in Iraq are the ones the U.S. dropped on Iraq. That is what radicalized Muslims in Iraq. No, Mr. Donahue, Islam is no longer a peaceful religion. Muslims will not go peacefully into extinction. Muslims will fight for their homeland and their religion because the Koran demands it.'

The U.S. Attorney's frustration was evident. But Mike Donahue hadn't boxed in college and put murderers on death row by not knowing how to land punches, particularly on a defendant who dared testify on his own behalf. He now walked to the prosecution table, picked up a small book, and returned to the podium. He unbuttoned his coat and held up the book. The bait.

'Let's talk about the Koran.'

'Certainly.'

'Mr. Mustafa, the Koran mentions a prophet. Who is that?'

'The prophet is Muhammad.'

'And God told these exact words in the Koran to Muhammad in visions?'

'That is correct.'

'But Muhammad, he didn't say, "Well, hell, God just told me all this neat shit, I'd better write it all down before I forget. I know if God told me all this, I'd sure as hell write it down. But in fact, Muhammad himself never wrote these words down, did he?"

'Careful, Mr. Donahue, freedom of speech does not extend to insulting the Prophet.'

'Under whose law?'

'Sharia.'

'Oh. So the Koran can state that Jesus was not the son of God, but no one can say that Muhammad was not the prophet of God.'

'That is correct.'

'And what is the punishment under Sharia for insulting Muhammad?'

'Death.'

'What about adultery by a woman?'

'Death.'

'Homosexuality by a man?'

'Death.'

'And those are the words of your god?'

'Those are the words of your god, Mr. Donahue. Allah is the god of the universe.'

'Your god isn't my god, Mr. Mustafa. Your god isn't God.'

'I will remember you said that.'

'You do that.' Donahue returned to the book. 'Let me read a few passages I found particularly interesting. "Prophet, make war on the unbelievers" . . . "Slay the idolaters" . . . "Fight for the cause of God" . . . "The true believers fight for the cause of God, but the infidels fight for the devil. Fight then against the friends of Satan" . . . "Believers, make war on the infidels who dwell around you" . . . "You will find that the most implacable of people in their enmity to the faithful are the Jews. And the nearest in affection to them are those who say, 'We are Christians'" . . . "Believers, take neither the Jews nor the Christians for your friends" . . . "Lay hold of them and kill them wherever you find them. Over such men We give you absolute authority."'

Scott knew what was coming. Did Mustafa?

'So, Mr. Mustafa, in the Koran, Muslims are the believers and the faithful?'

'Yes.'

'Christians and Jews are unbelievers, idolaters, infidels, and friends of Satan?'

'Indeed.'

195

'And your god commands all Muslims to slay all Christians and Jews until Islam rules the world?'

'Correct.'

'So jihadists are doing what your god commands?'

'They are. But I personally never advocate violence.'

'Oh, that's good to know. Here are a few other passages I found enlightening. "Blessed are the believers, who are humble in their prayers; who avoid profane talk, and give alms to the destitute; who restrain their carnal desires (except with their wives and *slave-girls*, for those are lawful to them)" . . . "Prophet, We have made lawful for you the wives to whom you have granted dowries and the *slave-girls whom God has given you as booty*."'

Donahue glared at the witness like a boxer staring down his opponent before a bout.

'So, Mr. Mustafa, your god told Muhammad, please don't say "fuck you" but it's okay for you to fuck young girls because I give them to you as slave-girls?'

The imam visibly recoiled, almost as if he had been slapped in the face. But he gathered himself.

'Only non-Muslim girls.'

'And ISIS is doing exactly that, aren't they, just as Agent Beckeman testified? Holding thousands of non-Muslim women and girls – some as young as seven years old – as slave-girls. And your god says it's okay for Muslims to be rapists and pedophiles, as long as they don't cuss!'

Donahue held up the Koran to the witness.

'Mr. Mustafa, is this a religion or a fucking cult?'

He flipped the Koran at the witness as if it were so much trash. The imam audibly sucked in air. His eyes showed his horror as they followed the book through the air; it fell short of the witness stand and landed on the floor with a thud. He stared at the book and started to reach out for it as one would an injured infant. His calm countenance changed, as if a storm cloud had crossed his mind. His dark eyes turned darker. His jaws clenched. His face reddened. He turned his eyes from the book to his inquisitor. He took the bait.

'You just signed your own death warrant, Mr. Donahue.'

'Are you threatening me with violence, Mr. Mustafa?'

'I most certainly am . . .'

His face trembled, as if his mind were fighting to restrain his mouth. His fists clenched in his lap. His body visibly shook.

'. . . *not.*'

He spit out the bait. He breathed out. After a moment, he was the Imam Omar al Mustafa again.

'I am simply cautioning you, Mr. Donahue. If you mock Muhammad, if you disrespect the Koran' – he gestured at the book on the floor – 'as you just did, there are those who might view that less than charitably. But I am not a violent person nor would I advocate anyone to act violently against you . . . or your pretty wife and two children.'

Prosecutor and defendant stared at each other a long moment.

'No further questions, Your Honor.'

The imam looked past the U.S. Attorney to the reporters in the spectator section.

'America was created through violent revolution against its oppressors but now America says no to anyone else's violent revolution against their oppressors—'

'You're excused, Mr. Mustafa,' Scott said.

'—which is understandable since America is their oppressor—'

'Stop, Mr. Mustafa.'

'—America wages war on Islam but Islam will prevail. The world will submit to Islam. The world will live under Islamic law. Sharia is coming to a neighborhood near you very soon and—'

Scott slammed his gavel down. 'I said stop!'

The imam stopped. Scott calmed and considered the witness. Federal judges seldom question witnesses, but they are empowered to do so. Scott decided to exercise that power.

'Mr. Mustafa, do you pray?'

'Daily.'

'What do you pray for?'

'The death of the infidels. The rise of the Muslim caliphate. A world under Sharia.'

'Really? I pray for God to watch over my daughters. So what about people who are not Muslims?'

'We invite unbelievers to believe.'

'To become Muslim?'

'Yes.'

'What if they don't want to?'

'They are free to live in peace under Sharia with us.'

'But they must live under Islamic law?'

'Of course.'

'Why?'

'It is our destiny. Your destiny. The world's destiny. It is written in the Koran. It is the—'

'Will of God.'

'Yes.'

'Your world is black and white, isn't it? There's no room for disagreement, is there? No room for other points of view? No room for tolerance? Christians and Jews in America are told to be tolerant of Muslims, but you don't seem very tolerant of Christians and Jews.'

'Why should we be tolerant of stupidity?' The imam pointed at the book on the floor. 'It is either written in the Koran or it is not. Either Allah said it shall be done or he said it shall not be done. Either it is right or it is wrong. God is not tolerant of Christians and Jews, why should we be?'

Scott studied the man sitting just a few feet away. He held a harsh view of the world, of his religion and others. He was a danger to religious tolerance, but was he a danger to the community?

'The witness is excused.'

The imam stood, stepped down from the stand, bent over, and picked up the Koran. He dusted it off as one might a historical antiquity then carried it to the defense table. His lawyer leaned away.

'Closing arguments. Mr. Turner.'

Frank walked to the podium.

'Your Honor, I will address the four factors set forth in the Bail Reform Act. First, the nature and circumstances of the offense. The defendants are charged with conspiracy to use weapons of mass destruction. We all agree it's an evil offense. The problem for the government is factor two, the weight of the evidence. The problem is, there is no evidence. The government's got nothing. I've had nothing before, so I know nothing when I hear nothing. And we heard nothing from Agent Beckeman in this courtroom today. The third factor, the defendants' history and character, clearly weighs in favor of release. The defendants have no prior criminal offenses on their records. They've never engaged in acts of violence. They've never possessed weapons of violence. They've never been charged with violent crimes, or any crimes. As Mr. Mustafa said, they were good boys. And they're good men. The defendants have nothing in their past or present to indicate that their release would pose any danger whatsoever to the community. These men should be released today on their personal recognizance. Failing that, we ask that you release them subject to conditions. Strap GPS monitors on them. Put them under house arrest. Do whatever is reasonable. But release them to their families. That is only fair when there is no evidence whatsoever of their guilt. Thank you.'

'Thank you, Mr. Turner. Mr. Donahue.'

The U.S. Attorney replaced Frank at the podium.

'On the website for the United States Attorney's Office for the Northern District of Texas, it states: "Our District's core priorities are, one, protecting Americans from terrorism and other threats to national security, both at home and abroad; two, protecting Americans from violent crime . . ." That is my job. That is what I do. That is what I'm trying to do today. Protect the American people from violent terrorism. Protect them from him' – he pointed at the imam – 'Omar al Mustafa. Mr. Mustafa has written and preached in favor of jihadist revolution for years. Yes, he has a right of free speech, but this is violent speech. And now he decided to practice what he preaches. Your Honor, a federal grand jury indicted Mr. Mustafa and twenty-three co-conspirators for conspiring to use weapons of mass destruction. They plotted to blow up Cowboys Stadium during the Super Bowl in just sixteen days. One co-conspirator, Aabdar Haddad, resisted arrest and was killed. Under the Bail Reform Act, indictment on such offense raises a statutory presumption that the defendants should be detained pending trial, that is, that there are no conditions that the court may impose on the defendants' release that will assure their appearance at trial and the safety of the community. Yes, under the Constitution, the defendants are presumed innocent until proven guilty. But, Your Honor, do you really want to put these men back on the street, twenty-three men under indictment, twenty-three men whom a grand jury said more likely than not planned to use weapons of mass destruction here in America? Yes, they have clean criminal histories. So did the nine-eleven hijackers – right up until they flew those planes into those towers.'

★

The drone pilots sat in Arizona and brought death to Arabs ten thousand miles away as if they were playing video games. After a day of killing Muslims, they went home to mama and the kids and watched sports on cable television, so happy with their lives in America, as if they had not destroyed entire families' lives in Pakistan and Afghanistan and Iraq and Syria. As if they were entitled to kill anyone anywhere anytime.

But they were not entitled to kill Abdul's father.

The errant missile had killed many fathers in the village, men who had been plotting the future of the village not terrorist attacks, just as drone missiles had killed thousands of innocent Muslims in the Middle East. But to the Americans, all Muslims look alike. All Muslims think alike. All Muslims want to kill Americans. All Muslims are terrorists in waiting. So America must kill all Muslims. They meant to kill terrorists; instead, they created terrorists.

'Judge Fenney has a big decision to make,' Professor Johnson said.

Abdul jabaar sat on the back row next to his little brother.

'I was just in the courtroom for the imam's detention hearing,' the professor said. 'I obtained a copy of the government's brief in support of detention and heard the FBI agent's testimony. The imam's anti-American and pro-ISIS statements were the only evidence introduced against him. The government produced no evidence whatsoever directly connecting him to the alleged plot to blow up the stadium. Apparently the government wants to detain him pending trial and then convict and imprison him for exercising his right of free speech.'

'When you tossed the Koran at him,' Agent Beckeman said, 'I thought Mustafa was going to come out of that chair and attack you.'

'That was the plan.' Mike Donahue turned to Scott. 'He's going to walk, isn't he?'

Scott had asked counsel to his chambers for a conference. Agent Beckeman had tagged along.

'I don't want to release him, but this *is* a court of law. I need evidence.'

'I want that son of a bitch bad,' Agent Beckeman said. 'And he is bad, Judge.'

'Why don't you just kill the motherfucker!' Frank Turner said. 'Don't you have a drone over Dallas? Scotty can let him out, and you guys can put a missile up his ass.'

The U.S. Attorney and the FBI agent gave Frank looks of confusion.

'Aren't you his lawyer?' Beckeman said.

'Only because Scotty appointed me!'

'I'm sorry, Frank.'

Frank waved him off. 'I'm a big boy.'

The four men breathed out a collective sigh and sat silent for a long moment. The FBI agent attacked the toffee bowl.

'I want that son of a bitch bad,' Beckeman said.

'Then get him!' Frank said.

'You made me look stupid on cross-examination!'

'It wasn't hard.'

'Fuck you, lawyer!'

'Easy, Agent Beckeman,' Scott said. 'Tell me what you know.'

'I can't!' Frank said. 'He'll behead me if I violate the attorney-client privilege!'

'How do you know?'

'He told me!'

Frank bent over and buried his face in his hands.

'I want that son of a bitch bad,' Beckeman said again. 'Hell, I'd arrest him for jaywalking just to keep him off the streets.'

Frank's head came up. He turned and stared at Beckeman with an odd expression.

'You ever watch *The Untouchables*?'

'With Costner?' Beckeman said. 'Only about a hundred times.'

'Watch it again.'

'Why?'

'Just watch it.'

Counsel and the FBI agent had just walked out of Scott's chambers when his phone rang. It was the attorney general. Again.

'Do you have me on your speed dial?' Scott asked.

'As a matter of fact, I do.'

'Ah.'

'Well?'

'Well, what?'

'What are you going to do?'

'Ponder.'

'*Ponder?* Who the hell ponders?'

'Judges.'

'I was a judge for twenty years. I never pondered.'

'I'm pondering this weekend and ruling Monday morning.'

'How'd the detention hearing go?' Peña asked when Beckeman walked into headquarters.

'We're fucked.' He sighed and looked around. 'Any tacos left?'

'What are you going to do?' Bobby asked.

The crew had gathered in Scott's chambers for the Friday-afternoon staff meeting.

'Hope the government finds some evidence against Mustafa by Monday at ten.'

Scott had adjourned the case until then. When he would have to make a hard decision. He ate a toffee and fired one to Louis.

'He's bad,' Carlos said.

'Yes, but I want the government to present evidence that ties his bad to this plot.'

'You read what he wrote, heard what he said,' Bobby said. 'Leave his ass in jail. No one's going to feel sorry for him.'

'I don't like him either, Bobby. But that's not the standard for detention pending trial. That's not the law.'

'That's not all Muslims,' Louis said. 'We're not all like Mustafa.'

'*We?*' Carlos said.

The room fell silent. Everyone stared at Louis for a long awkward moment then glanced at each other. Finally, Scott spoke.

'Louis – you're Muslim?'

'Yes, sir, I am.' He turned to his best buddy. 'Carlos, you're looking at me like I said I was gay.'

'That might've been better. Damn, big man, you never told me.'

'You never asked me.'

Carlos turned his palms up. 'You went to Hooters with me.'

Louis shrugged. 'I'm not a gay Muslim.'

'Were your parents Muslim?' Scott asked.

'No, sir. I converted when I was twenty-five. I was on a path of hatred and meanness, just wanting to hurt people to stop the hurt inside me. Then I read about Cassius Clay. He was the same way, until he converted to Islam and changed his name to Muhammad Ali. He found inner peace. I did, too.'

'The government screwed him,' Bobby said.

'Ali?' Carlos said.

'Oh, you've heard of him.'

'I'm alive. What'd they do to him?'

'Back in the sixties, he got drafted for the Vietnam War. Refused to serve, said his religion prohibited his fighting. Now, every white college boy got a CO – conscientious objector – status, but the government said no to Ali. He wouldn't enlist, so they stripped him of his boxing privileges. Couldn't fight for four years, right in the prime of his career. Because he was a celebrity, he was black, and he was Muslim.'

'I don't agree with Mustafa, what he says,' Louis said. 'I don't think that's Islam. He and those ISIS folks are taking a harsh view of the Koran.'

'Is there a point to all this?' Carlos said.

'There is,' Louis said. 'Muhammad Ali stood up for Islam the way it's supposed to be. Nonviolent. And he paid a heavy personal price because of politics. That was wrong. A federal judge could've righted that wrong, but nobody stepped up because they were scared to go against popular opinion. They were scared to do the right thing. They did what the people wanted.'

'And you think I should do the right thing with the imam?'

'I do, Judge.'

'So tell me, Louis, what is the right thing?'

'What did the judge say?'

Mac had called to update the president.

'He's pondering.'

'*Pondering?* Who the hell ponders?'

'That's what I said.'

Scott stepped inside the middle school gym for Pajamae's game; the action abruptly stopped. The gym fell quiet, and all heads on the court and in the stands turned to the door. To Judge A. Scott Fenney. From behind him, Bobby muttered,

'What the hell?' Every person in the place stood and started clapping, harder and louder, until the gym was filled with a thunderous applause. The last time Scott Fenney had received a standing ovation was back in college when he walked into each of his classes the Monday after his record-setting game against UT. It had been a heady experience. But not this heady.

'Judge,' Carlos said, 'is it your birthday?'

'See, A. Scott,' Boo said, 'you are a hero.'

'I'm just a judge.'

Scott found Pajamae on the court. She beamed with a broad smile and gave him a thumbs-up. After a time, the applause resided, and they climbed the stands to their regular spot. Men greeted Scott with handshakes and women with hugs. Everyone wanted to be in his company.

'Great job, Judge,' one man said. 'We need strong judges like you keeping those people off our streets.'

'ISIS in Dallas,' another man said. 'Unbelievable. I'll tell you one thing, Judge, I'll happily pay more taxes to buy more drones to kill more Muslims.'

Scott pushed onward.

'Scott, I should've never fired you.'

He stopped. Standing before him was Thomas J. Dibrell, rich real-estate developer and former rich client of A. Scott Fenney, Esquire. Tom was nearing sixty; he had given up on the comb-over and accepted his fate of baldness. He looked like an overweight Golomb. A model half his age stood next to him.

'Scott . . . Judge . . . you're the best lawyer I ever had. I was an asshole. Or maybe God wanted me to fire you so you'd be the judge on this case.'

Or maybe you were just an asshole.

'Thanks, Tom.'

Two more steps up the bleachers.

'Judge, thank you for keeping us safe,' a woman said. 'And for keeping my children safe.'

And then Kim Dawson was hugging him. 'Thank you, Scott. We're safe because of you.'

She released him and stepped aside to reveal Penny Birnbaum standing there. With that look on her face. She grabbed Scott and planted a hard kiss on his lips. She closed her eyes, but he did not. He saw Kim look away and other spectators smiling; everyone in Highland Park knew Penny. She finished the kiss and whispered in his ear: 'I'm so horny.'

He pulled away from her clutching hands and pushed onward and upward, climbing the stands. Millionaires and billionaires and the lawyers who served them greeted him like a hometown hero. Handshakes and hugs and slaps on the back. Expressions of thanks and appreciation, as if he had saved the world. Or at least their world. And it finally dawned on Scott: more than any other basic human need, we need to be safe. Safe in our homes, safe in our communities, safe in our country. We hire police, troopers, and agents for the FBI, DEA, TSA, NSA, CIA, and Border Patrol who will keep us safe. We appoint prosecutors and judges who will keep us safe. We elect presidents who will keep us safe. Our need to be safe transcends race, religion, creed, color, and socioeconomic standing; people in Highland Park want to be safe just as much as people in South Dallas. Which is to say, rich people are just as afraid. And that is the object of terrorism: to create fear in the population.

Fear had come to Big D.

Chapter 11

Saturday, 23 January
15 days before the Super Bowl

Scott ran the streets at seven the next morning. Men retrieving the morning paper called out to him—

'Judge Fenney!'

—people driving by waved to him—

'Judge Fenney!'

—everyone he encountered greeted him—

'Judge Fenney!'

And Penny stood naked in the second floor window at 4000 Beverly Drive.

'Blowing up Cowboys Stadium? Damn, Judge, that place cost one-point-two billion to build.'

Even the burly butcher at Whole Foods knew Judge A. Scott Fenney.

'*Dos pollos, por favor,*' Consuelo said.

Consuelo and Maria had come with them that Saturday. The butcher handed two chickens to Consuelo and his cap to Scott.

'Would you autograph my cap, Judge?'

As if Scott were Tony Romo. He handed Scott a sticky pen. Scott signed and handed the cap and pen back then wiped his hands on his jeans.

'Thanks, Judge. And thanks for keeping Mustafa in jail where he can't hurt anyone.'

'Judge, may I have your autograph?'

A woman held out an elegant pen and a brown-paper-wrapped package for him to sign. He took it and read the label: organic grain-fed rib eye steaks. He signed the brown paper. He handed the steaks and pen back to the woman, and he recognized her: George Delaney's trophy wife. Behind the counter, the butcher chopped meat with a cleaver.

'Hello, Judge.' George made an appearance. He glanced at Consuelo and Maria holding his hand. 'These all yours?'

'They are. This is Consuelo and Maria.'

George grunted a greeting. Consuelo pushed the basket to the dairy section.

'Your life sure as hell changed since last week.'

'It hasn't been boring.'

George's mood turned pensive. 'I don't get that guy, Mustafa. He's living in America, a country formed by men wanting religious freedom, but he wants to destroy America because we won't live under his religion. They're different from us, the Muslims. We're not a violent people. I mean, you don't see Baptists cutting people's heads off because they don't believe their way on abortion, do you? How can they cut through a person's neck with a knife? All that blood. But they're a blood-thirsty bunch, the Muslims.'

The butcher raised the cleaver then slammed it down on the thick red meat with a thud. They stared at the sight until Scott's cell phone rang. He didn't recognize the number – it was a 202 area code, Washington D.C., probably the attorney general again – but he answered anyway just to escape George.

'Excuse me, George, I've got to take this.'

He stepped away and answered. 'Hello.'

'Is this Judge Fenney?'

'It is.'

'Please hold for the president.'

'*The president?*'

Scott held. He heard George whisper to his trophy, 'The president called the judge!' And her response: 'You hate the president.' Scott stepped farther away so they couldn't eavesdrop. The voice Scott had heard deliver the State of the Union address came across.

'Judge Fenney.'

'Mr. President . . . sir.'

'I hear you're pondering?'

'Uh, yes, sir.'

'Well, ponder this: ISIL has recruited hundreds of Americans to join the cause, homegrown jihadists to attack us in the homeland. They're desperate for another nine-eleven. We're working twenty-four/seven to prevent that. It's not going to happen on my watch.'

He paused.

'Last summer, they called for attacks on the Fourth of July. So we rounded up every suspected jihadist in the country and held them until after the Fourth. It worked. We had no attacks on the Fourth. We're doing the same for the Super Bowl. Judge, I need you on the team.'

'What team?'

'The anti-terrorism team.'

'Sir, I'm just a judge.'

'Look, Judge, I've made mistakes with these terrorists, as I confessed to the nation Wednesday night. I didn't take ISIL seriously at first, called them al Qaeda's JV team. I thought that would sound pithy on the news. Now it sounds stupid. Really stupid, after they brought down that Russian jet and slaughtered a hundred thirty people in Paris. But I'm taking them seriously now, Judge. I can't make the same mistake again. I can't let Mustafa out of jail.'

'You wouldn't be, Mr. President. I would be.'

'You can't, Judge. You can't make that mistake. You won't be able to live with that mistake. I know. People have died because of my mistakes. Their deaths haunt me. If you release Mustafa – if you're wrong about him – you'll have a hundred thousand deaths to haunt you.'

'Sir—'

'Judge, ISIL is here, in America. They're not figments of our imagination. They're real. They're here. And they want to kill Americans. Imagine what will happen if they behead an American on the streets of New York or Chicago or L.A. Or Dallas.'

Saddam Siddiqui tossed the head of lettuce into the shopping basket. He loved shopping at Whole Foods. He loved Starbucks coffee. He loved Dick's Sporting Goods. He loved the Dallas Cowboys, America's Team. He had been born in Pakistan, but he loved America. He was now a naturalized American citizen. He wanted to live the American Dream. He had forgiven America for taking his father from him.

His brother had not.

Abdul was his father's first and favorite son, to be sure. He was the smart son and the athletic son and the handsome son. He was a star in school and on the soccer field. He had confidence and charisma. Their father adored Abdul. So his death crushed his first son.

Saddam, being the second and less favored son, had never felt his father's adoration; so he felt less of a loss than Abdul. He had recovered and moved on; Abdul had not. He could not. He missed their father; he cried for their father. Over time, his grief had turned to anger. His anger had increased with each passing year. He began reading harsh Islamic literature. His view of the world changed. Saddam did not like the changes he had witnessed in his brother, but his big brother was a force of nature that he could not resist. He turned and bumped into a man he immediately recognized.

'Pardon me,' Scott said.

The boy – a young man, actually – had the same appearance as the young Muslim defendants who had stood before Judge A. Scott Fenney the day before. He stared at Scott a long moment – or was it just his imagination?

'Have a nice day, Judge.'

Scott looked after the young man as he walked away. Why did the encounter give him pause? Bumping into an Arab in Whole Foods wasn't the most unusual event ever, but it wasn't usual. But was it just a coincidence? He was the presiding judge in a terrorism case against twenty-three Arab defendants, and he bumps into an Arab man in Whole Foods – was it a coincidence or a message? After a moment, he shook it off as a hazard of the job: paranoia.

Scott sat between two thirteen-year-old girls on the couch. Boo wanted to watch *Silence of the Lambs*. Scott vetoed her choice.

'But it won the big five Academy Awards,' she said. 'Best Picture, Best Actor, Best Actress, Best Director, and Best Screenplay.'

Scott had received emails and voicemails from high school, college, and law school classmates, teachers and professors, friends and lawyers he remembered and others he didn't remember, so many he felt as if he had won an Academy Award for Best Judge in a Leading Role.

'No.'

'It's a classic.'

America had been innocent before 9/11. Secure. Safe. So assured that the terrorists that afflicted the rest of the world would not – could not – cross the ocean that protected America. But cross it they had. And they took America's innocence.

They ate hamburgers, drank malts, and watched another classic, *Sense and Sensibility*. An old-fashioned, innocent, romantic movie. The way life is supposed to be, at least for thirteen-year-old girls. At least for a little while longer. The harsh reality of the world – of *Silence of the Lambs* and Islamic terrorists – would come to the girls soon enough. He was not going to hurry that day. A man keeps his family safe.

A judge keeps the people safe.

Black Hawk Down was Beckeman's second favorite movie of all time. His first was *Zero Dark Thirty* even though the hero was a woman; she fought for freedom. Watching the soldiers fight and die made him particularly sad. Good men died because a president could not make the hard decision. Some things are worth dying for. Mogadishu, Somalia, was not one of those things. Beckeman prayed the judge could make the hard decision Monday morning so innocent people didn't die.

Chapter 12

Scott sat in church. He practiced his freedom of religion as guaranteed by the First Amendment to the U.S. Constitution. Just as the imam practiced his freedom of speech guaranteed by the same amendment. They shared the same rights, but they did not share the same beliefs. Scott loved America; the imam hated America. Scott was Baptist; the imam was Muslim. Scott believed in separation of church and state; the imam wanted his church to rule the state. Scott believed in freedom of religion; the imam believed in his religion.

He did not believe in America.

He had a right to live in America but not believe in America. The Constitution guaranteed that right. Just as the Constitution prohibited detention pending trial unless the defendant was a flight risk or a danger to the community. There are no Guantanamo Bays in America. We cannot imprison an accused person because we think he might do

214

something bad in the future. The danger to the community cannot be at some unknown date in the distant future; it must be here and now: If he is released, he will harm someone.

Would the imam?

The Bill of Rights was written to protect people we don't like. People who don't agree with us, believe like us, or think like us. People with different religions, creeds, and colors.

People like Omar al Mustafa.

If Scott detained the imam pending trial despite the lack of evidence – that is, in spite of the Constitution – everyone would be pleased. The president, the attorney general, the U.S. Attorney, the FBI, the public, even Frank Turner – everyone except George Washington, Thomas Jefferson, James Madison, Alexander Hamilton, and Benjamin Franklin. The Founding Fathers would not be pleased with Judge A. Scott Fenney.

'Immigration and the Imam – it's all about Judge A. Scott Fenney today.'

Mac hated these Sunday-morning political talk shows, but he always watched. Part of the job description when you're a political appointee and wanted to remain so for another four years. The moderator of *Election 2016* introduced that morning's topics and then the talking heads around the table, all veteran political commentators whom Mac knew well. He knew them to be morons.

'Let's tackle immigration first since that's a high-stakes political case,' the moderator said. 'But let's start with a basic question. What exactly is an executive order? Stan, you're the constitutional law professor from Harvard, would you explain for us?'

Stan was middle-aged and wore a bowtie and tweed jacket. Mac never hired Harvard lawyers or lawyers who wore bowties.

'An executive order is a legally binding directive issued by the president to a federal agency pursuant to his authority under Article Two of the Constitution. An executive order cannot be challenged by Congress, but it is subject to judicial review. An executive order can be overturned if the president is making law, but not if he is enforcing the law.'

'What if he is refusing to enforce the law?'

'That's the question here.'

'And what's the answer?'

'Ask Judge Fenney.'

Ralph, another head, jumped in. 'The president's executive order is unprecedented!'

'Not at all,' Stan said. 'Prior presidents have issued hundreds of executive orders, but the opposing party always complains that he exceeded his constitutional authority. Lincoln's Emancipation Proclamation was an executive order. So was FDR's Works Progress Administration during the Depression and his internment of Japanese-Americans during World War Two, as well as Truman's desegregation of the military and nationalization of the steel industry, the latter having been subsequently overturned by the Supreme Court.'

'Then what makes this executive order so special?' the moderator said.

'It's an election year, and it involves immigration,' Stan said.

'It involves the president,' Ralph said, 'who is mad because the Congress won't change the immigration laws according to his desires, making law to suit himself rather than the American people.'

'So does Judge Fenney please the president or the Republicans?' the moderator asked.

'The president appointed him to the bench. He'll rule for the president.'

'Ralph?'

Ralph frowned. 'I'm afraid he's right. Judge Fenney will rule for the president. He's a lawyer, which means he's ambitious. No doubt he wants to move up in the judicial world. Rule for the president, and he will. Rule against the president – against twelve million Mexicans – and he'll never be Supreme Court Justice Fenney.'

Mac smiled. Their liberal guy was letting the judge know via television that his decision would affect his professional future. Play ball and move up. Don't play ball and sit on the trial bench in Dallas the rest of your life. Politics in America.

'He was appointed by the president, but more by the late Samuel Buford, the legendary federal judge in Dallas.'

'The legendary *liberal* federal judge in Dallas.'

'The president will have his victory.'

The heads nodded in consensus, and the show went to a commercial for an antidepressant. After the break, they took up the terrorism case.

'Will Judge Fenney detain Mustafa pending trial?'

'He'd better. This man is a danger to the community. We've all heard his ranting on YouTube – we've heard his ranting on this show. He's a radical Islamic cleric who wants America brought down.'

'But there doesn't seem to be any evidence against him.'

'Do you want him on the streets?'

'I want him in Guantanamo.'

On that all the talking heads agreed.

The priest talked, and the congregation listened. He spoke Spanish; they understood Spanish. The Cathedral Shrine of the Virgin of Guadalupe in downtown Dallas offered three English Masses and three Spanish Masses each Sunday, including this 10:30 service. Catalina Peña loved Mass; just to sit inside the magnificent cathedral was a religious experience. Perhaps it was the stark contrast of the cathedral and her job.

Mass offered hope; her job did not.

Or perhaps it was the setting itself: the stark white walls, pillars, and altar offset by tall stained-glass windows; the high arched ceilings; the carvings of the Stations of the Cross mounted on the walls; the brown wood tabernacle and pews. When she sat in a pew in the cathedral, she felt blessed. She wondered if the other members felt as blessed. Many if not most were illegal immigrants from Mexico, including Diego and Sofia Peña, whose only dream was the blessing of American citizenship that she possessed – because she had been born north of the river and not south. One hundred and sixty-eight years ago, the Treaty of Guadalupe Hidalgo ended the Mexican-American War and established the Rio Grande as the international border between the U.S. and Mexico. Ever since, Mexicans had tried diligently to give birth to their children north of the river; every Mexican knew that a child born north of the river would have a shot at the American dream, while a child born south would only dream. Cat glanced at her parents kneeling next to her in the pew; they had given her a shot, even if they had to live in the shadows. She worked for the FBI, enforcing the laws of America; one such law mandated that Diego and Sofia Peña be removed from America.

'Let us pray,' the priest said, 'that the president's executive order is upheld by the courts so that we can live in the sunlight and not in the shadows. The president is a good man. He cares about the lives of Mexicans.'

The poster nailed to the wall was of the president holding a cute Anglo baby at a political rally with the caption: *You're lucky you're an American baby because I kill Pakistani babies with drone strikes.*

Another poster showed a little Arab boy writing in blood on a wall below an image of an American Predator drone: *Why did you kill my family with a drone strike?*

Another showed a dead Arab child with the caption: *The American president has killed more children with drones than all other Nobel Peace Prize winners combined.*

Abdul jabbar felt the rage rise within him. He knew the statistics: 421 drone strikes in Pakistan; 2,478 Pakistanis killed; 423 civilians killed. Just numbers on a page – unless your father was among the 423. As his was. America had taken his father from him when he was just a boy. He had grown up without a father because America waged war against Islam. He hated America more every day.

'Touchdown!'

But his little brother loved all things American, and nothing more than the Dallas Cowboys. There he sat in front of the big screen television eating falafel like popcorn and watching the Cowboys play the Packers. He wore a white-and-blue Cowboys cap on backwards and a blue-and-white Tony Romo jersey. He was still a child at twenty-two.

'Come,' Abdul said. 'We have much work to do. Tomorrow is a big day.'

'Do we have to?'

His little brother was a bit of a whiner.

'Yes. We must. It is Allah's will. And remember, my brother, there is a reward: seventy-two virgins in heaven.'

'I would be happy with one on earth.'

'Well, you had better find her fast.'

His little brother muted the sound on the TV and turned to him. 'Abdul, you are my older brother, and I respect and honor you. I have always looked up to you for guidance, more so than our father. I have always followed you.'

'Then follow me now.'

'Abdul, I understand your anger, but I must advocate against this course of action.'

'You sound like a lawyer.'

'Abdul, please, I don't want to kill people. I want to love people. I want to love a girl. I want a girlfriend. I want to kiss her and hold her hand and sext her like other people do. I want to be a lawyer. I want a good life in America, not a glorious death. This is wrong.'

'*Wrong?* Was it wrong, my brother, for that drone missile to kill our father?'

'Yes, of course, but—'

'But what?'

'Is this what our father would have wanted for us? We are educated. We can have good lives in America.'

'How can our lives be good in America when America took our father's life in Pakistan?'

When the U.S. government had moved their mother and her two sons to America as recompense for killing her husband and their father, the younger son soon fell in love with America. The older son fell in with radical Muslims at the mosque. He watched other boys in the neighborhood playing soccer with their fathers, and his anger grew stronger each day. He could never forgive America. America had taken his father from him. One did not forgive such an act; one sought revenge for such an act. Neither ISIS nor the imam had radicalized Abdul jabbar; an American drone missile had.

'Come, brother. We must go to the law school. We can stop by Krispy Kreme on the way.'

A donut always lifted his little brother's spirits. But not that day. His brother sighed heavily and turned back to the television just in time to see the Cowboys score on a long pass. But he did not shriek like a little girl as he always did. His voice was soft.

'The Cowboys will go to the Super Bowl.'

'So will we, brother.'

Abdul wanted to kill Americans. Four days before, he learned that he had the intestinal fortitude to kill. His little brother, not so much.

'The Cowboys are going to the Super Bowl!' Pajamae shrieked. 'I wish we could go.'

She watched the game, Boo read her book, and Scott pondered his cases. His mind double-tracked between the immigration case and the terrorism case; the two most controversial cases in the country had found their way to his courtroom. He did not seek the cases; they had come to him. The parties came to him for a decision, and decide he must. He could not say, 'Go ask someone else.' In America, the people come to a judge for an answer. Judge A. Scott Fenney would have to give an answer at ten the next morning. His phone rang and jolted him from his thoughts. It was the attorney general.

'Wondering if you'd call.'

'Didn't want to disappoint you.'

'And?'

'Don't disappoint your country.'

'Mac—'

'Scott, we're fighting evil. These people want to end Western civilization, just like Mustafa testified. They want a world under Islamic law. We're looking to the future, they're living in the past. They want to rid the Middle East of Christians and Jews – "allies of the cross" they call us.'

'And then?'

'Then they're coming for us. Imagine a nine-eleven every year. Every month. Every week. Imagine suicide bombings every day in grocery stores, movie theaters, schools, subways, shopping malls, high school football games. Beheadings in the streets. That's the life we'll live. Is that the life you want for your girls?'

'How do we prevent that?'

'We kill or capture every jihadist in the world.'

'Is that possible?'

'No. But we have to try. We can't defeat ISIS in Syria because we can't kill civilians. The president wasn't a soldier. He doesn't understand that civilians die in war. The only question is which civilians – theirs or ours? We know the answer now: ours. So we have to kill the jihadists here at home. As fast as we can.'

'Mustafa says our drone strikes are creating more terrorists.'

'Then we'll kill them, too.'

'There's no peaceful resolution?'

'How do you negotiate for peace with people who will strap suicide vests to their children and send them to their deaths? We dream for our children. They kill their children. In the name of Allah.'

'Even if all that is true, Mac, the law requires some evidence to detain Mustafa pending trial.'

'I told you, there is no evidence. Not yet. But we'll find it before trial, I promise you. Just don't release him.'

'We could kill him.'

'You want to kill Mustafa if the judge releases him tomorrow morning?'

'I didn't say I want to kill him – well, actually, I do – I said we could kill him.'

Beckeman was on a conference call with the attorney general and the director.

'But what about the twenty-two other co-conspirators?' the director said. 'We can't kill them all.'

'Sure we can,' Beckeman said. 'Hell, I'll send Stryker, he can kill them all before lunch.'

'I know we *can* kill them. What I mean is, we can't *politically* kill them.'

'Might be a bit of a PR problem.'

'You think?'

The three men sighed in unison.

'Did the president's call do any good?' the director asked.

'He's pondering,' Mac said.

'The president?'

'The judge.'

Beckeman snorted. 'We're fighting terrorists and he's pondering. That's what's so damn frustrating about this job. We got the bad guys. We won. Now a judge might tell us we lost and they won. Can you imagine the boost Mustafa will get among Muslims if he walks out of the federal courthouse? He beat the U.S. government. Hell, it'll be on *Al Jazeera* all across the Muslim world. He'll be a fucking folk hero.'

'Fenney is a good man trying to do the right thing,' Mac said. 'He just doesn't understand that right and wrong changed on nine-eleven.'

'It's like Vietnam, liberals thinking we could win the people's hearts and minds. We couldn't then, and we can't now. These people's hearts and minds are with Muhammad.'

Beckeman was a good guy/bad guy type of guy. You were either good or bad, right or wrong, black or white. There was no grey in his life. But judges were colorblind: all they saw were shades of grey.

'What the hell is it going to take for him to realize what we're dealing with? For him to understand that this is a goddamn war. That we're fighting for his freedom. His children's freedom.'

Chapter 13

Monday, 25 January
13 days before the Super Bowl

Scott woke the next morning with his decision firmly in mind. He would follow the Constitution and the Founding Fathers and not public opinion – or the president, the attorney general, the FBI, or even Frank Turner. God help him if he were wrong.

'Morning, Judge! How 'bout the Boys?'

Scott waved at the man picking up his newspaper. The morning news was all Cowboys that day. ISIS had been defeated in Dallas; now Dallas had to defeat the Patriots in the Super Bowl. It was seven the next morning, and his feet pounded the pavement of Highland Park but his mind remained focused on Omar al Mustafa. The FBI had presented evidence that he was guilty of hating America but no evidence that he was guilty of conspiring to blow up the stadium where America's Team played or that he was a danger to the community. Under the Constitution and the Bail Reform Act – under the law of the land — the imam was entitled to release on personal recognizance, or at least with conditions attached. United States District Judge A. Scott Fenney had sworn an oath to uphold the Constitution, and not just in the easy cases. The Constitution was written not for the easy cases but for the hard cases.

Omar al Mustafa was a hard case.

Scott prayed the attorney general wasn't right about cumulative justice. That the imam wasn't the bad guy in this case because of his past conduct. That he would not use his freedom to execute a plot to blow up the stadium. That—

Tires screeched.

A white box van swerved hard in front of him.

Scott had run into the intersection without looking both ways. The van didn't hit Scott, but he hit the van. He instinctively turned his body; he took the blow with his shoulder, but his head snapped forward and banged against the van. The impact staggered him. He almost fell to the pavement but managed to stay on his feet. He grabbed his knees for support and stared at the concrete and shook his head to clear his vision but without success. Brakes squealed, a door creaked open, and footsteps came close. Neon yellow Nike sneakers appeared in his line of sight.

'You okay, Judge?'

His mind, his body, the world moved in slow motion. He blinked hard and turned his eyes up from the yellow sneakers to red nylon sweat pants to a number nine Tony Romo jersey to . . . *Ronald Reagan?* Scott had suffered several concussions in college, and he felt concussed now. Numb . . . fuzzy . . . he again tried to shake his head clear. He heard metal scraping against metal . . . the side door sliding open . . .

'Let me help you, Judge.'

But Ronald Reagan didn't help him . . . instead he grabbed Scott around the neck and slammed him hard against the

225

van . . . another arm wrapped around his neck from behind and a wet cloth covered his mouth . . . he felt dizzy . . . his body being pulled into the van . . . his head went back against the floor of the van . . . he saw a face above him . . . a familiar face . . . *George W. Bush* . . . his felt sleepy . . . his eyes closed . . .

Boo sat at the kitchen table with the stethoscope around her neck, the blood pressure cuff in her hand, a glassful of kale smoothie on the table, and tears running down her cheeks. She wiped her eyes and checked the clock again: 7:45.

'Do not worry, Boo,' Consuelo said from the stove. '*Señor* Judge, he will be back.'

But Boo was worried. She knew she was worried because her finger tapped the table at a furious pace without her even thinking. A. Scott could have suffered a heart attack, a stroke, a broken ankle, an asthma attack (although she didn't think he had asthma), a deep vein thrombosis, early onset Alzheimer's, a migraine . . . or, oh God, a car could have hit him. At eight sharp, she called Louis.

Louis Wright lived east of the expressway but only ten minutes away from the judge's house. He figured if he was supposed to watch out for the judge, he'd better live close. His house was small, two bedrooms and one bath, but it was his. He had never figured on owning a home. People in South Dallas rented their entire lives or lived in the projects. Home owner-ship was not a common topic of conversation while strolling down Martin Luther King Boulevard; more like home inva-sions. But the judge had taken Louis Wright out of South Dallas and offered him a different life. A better life. He had gotten his GED and was working on his college degree, one night course at a time at the community college. He wanted to be a lawyer. Like the judge. His life had changed when A.

226

Scott Fenney had pulled up to the projects in that red Ferrari. He smiled at the thought, but his cell phone ringing interrupted his thoughts. It was Boo.

'Louis, it happened again.'

Boo looked up when Louis entered through the back door. She wiped her tears.

'Please find him, Louis.'

'Which way did he go?'

She held out a piece of paper. 'I made him draw his route and promise to run the same way every day. In case he had a heart attack.'

Louis took the map. 'I'll find him.'

He didn't find him. An hour later, he had traced the judge's entire route through Highland Park, but he was nowhere to be found. He had found him that day a year and a half before on the beach in Galveston, bloodied and bruised, but he could not find him on the streets of Highland Park that day.

'If he frees Mustafa, I'm gonna fucking throw up,' Beckeman whispered to the U.S. Attorney.

He felt as if he were in church. The congregation whispered even though court had not yet been called into session. Even though the judge was late. They sat at the prosecution table; Mustafa and Frank Turner sat at the defendant's table. The other defendants sat in the jury box and on chairs next to Mustafa. They waited for the judge.

Abdul jabbar slapped the judge's face repeatedly until he stirred. They had blindfolded him and tied his hands behind his back. He gagged then rolled over and threw up.

'Stop the vehicle, brother!'

His little brother stopped the van they had stolen that morning. Abdul helped the judge into a sitting position so he did not choke on his vomit. That would not further the plan.

Louis stood at the corner of Lovers Lane and Hillcrest Avenue just north of SMU, a big black man in a small white town. He feared the worst. Not from the white people and not for himself. But from those Muslims and for the judge. He had no doubt they had taken the judge. Followers of Mustafa. There were good Muslims and there were bad Muslims, just like there was good and bad people of all faiths and color; but these Muslims were beyond bad.

They were evil.

Louis Wright had seen stone-cold bad before, up close and personal, but he had never imagined bad like these folks. Cutting folks' heads off. Burning folks alive. Killing women and raping children. That's pure evil, the devil's doing. His mama had always said that the devil was real, an evil force in the world; he had always figured she was just exaggerating, as she often did to make a point to her son about staying out of trouble in the 'hood. But he knew now that she had been right. His mama had been right about most things, except one. She had always said he was to never trust a white man. She had been right about the devil but wrong about the man. Of course, she never met the judge before she died.

'You lost?'

Louis snapped to the moment. A Highland Park police cruiser had stopped next to him at the curb. A big black man standing on a busy corner in Highland Park attracted attention. The white cop said again, 'You lost?'

'No, I ain't . . . I'm not lost.'

'What are you, a security guard?'

Louis wore his uniform.

'Bailiff. Federal court.'

'Really?'

Really. He had to remind himself as well each morning when he put the uniform on. He was a federal court bailiff making $50,000 a year. Working in a courthouse. Until a year ago, he made it a practice to avoid courthouses; nothing good happened to a black man in a courthouse, especially in Dallas. He had had issues with the Feds back then; but the judge – before he became the judge – had resolved his issues. Now Louis Wright no longer had to look over his shoulder. He had only to look out for the judge.

'I'm looking for the judge I work for.'

'What judge?'

'Judge Fenney.'

'The federal judge? On the terrorism case?'

Louis nodded. 'He went running, didn't come back. I traced his route, didn't find him. I think he was grabbed.'

'*Grabbed?* You think Judge Fenney was abducted?'

The cop called in to the station.

'Bobby, I'm worried,' Karen said. 'He's never late.'

It was ten-thirty. She and Bobby stood huddled next to the bench. Carlos joined them.

'Where's Louis?'

Bobby's cell phone vibrated. He checked the caller ID: 'Louis.'

'Something ain't right,' Beckeman said to the U.S. Attorney.

They stood and walked to the judge's assistants standing to the side of the bench. The magistrate judge's back was to them; he was whispering into a phone. After a moment, his hand holding the phone dropped. The woman grabbed him.

'Bobby . . . what is it?'

'What's going on?' Beckeman said.

'Where's the judge?' Mike Donahue said.

The magistrate turned to them. His face was pale.

'Someone grabbed him off the street this morning while he was running.'

Beckeman ran out of the courtroom with a gruesome image in his mind: the judge's beheaded body dumped on a Dallas street.

'They abducted the judge?'

'Yes, sir.'

'Arabs?'

'Who else?'

'Why didn't we have security on him?'

'He refused.'

'Jesus.'

'Yes, sir.'

The president of the United States of America sat behind his desk in the Oval Office in the White House. The director of the Federal Bureau of Investigation stood across from him. The president shook his head.

'We don't kidnap judges in America.'

'They do.'

'What if they behead him? In America?'

'Well, if I were Muslim, I'd get the hell out of town.'

Abdul slid the sharp knife along the judge's neck, right over the carotid artery.

'I would like nothing better than to cut your fucking head off.'

'Brother, no. He is a federal judge.'

'So?'

'Where am I?' The judge spit bile. 'Who the hell are you?'

Abdul sighed. There would be another time.

Scott felt hot breath on his face and a foul smell in his nostrils and a whisper in his ear.

'Judge, do you see how easily we can take you? We can do it again, any time we want. We can take you away from your daughters, your friends, your life. We can take your life. We can cut your head off and put the video on YouTube. We can mail your head back to your daughters to put on the mantle like a trophy. We can do that, Judge – and we will unless you release the imam.'

'You're in this with him?'

'He is our leader. He is a prisoner of war.'

'What war?'

'The American war against Islam. You have forty-eight hours to release him. Or else.'

'Or else what?'

'You do not want to know "or else," Judge. I promise you.'

Metal scraped against metal again, and Scott felt a cold breeze. Hands grabbed him and pushed him. He hit the ground hard and rolled over. He heard the van speed away. He lay there a moment and assessed himself: his head was clear; he had not suffered a concussion. Satisfied with his mental condition, he struggled to a sitting position, but he couldn't free his hands or his eyes. He heard a boy's small voice.

'Why you tied up, mister?'

'Please take this blindfold off.'

Fingers grasped at the blindfold, and it was soon off. Scott blinked against the light until his eyes had adjusted. He looked around. Three young black boys surrounded him, their hands on their knees, regarding him as one would a stranded shark on the beach. Interested, but wary.

'You endorse Under Armour?' one boy said. 'I'm gonna get me a Nike contract when I'm in the NBA.'

'I'm a judge. Two men kidnapped me. Please untie my hands.'

The boys did as he asked then helped him to his feet. Scott had been dumped in the projects of South Dallas. He had been there once before but in a red Ferrari that had attracted a sizable crowd. A blindfolded and bound white man dumped from a van had attracted only three boys.

'You boys know where I can borrow a cell phone?'

One boy reached to his back pocket and held out a cell phone to Scott.

'You can use my iPhone. It's a six.'

'A. Scott!'

Boo barreled out of the house and down the sidewalk and into Scott's arms just he stepped out of Louis's car. Pajamae followed on her heels. Both girls cried into his shirt. As he cried. He was not afraid for his own personal safety; perhaps it was all the football, too many hits to the head, to worry about his own future. But he was afraid for the girls' future without him. They depended on him. They needed him. To raise them. To take care of them. To watch over them. A man protects his children.

Beckeman slammed on the brakes and skidded the sedan to a stop in front of the judge's house. He stood outside embracing his daughters. The big black bailiff stood next to them. Beckeman got out and ran over.

'Judge, you okay?'

'I think so.'

But his face was red and scratched, his hands were scraped, and his clothes torn and dirty. As if he had been thrown out of a moving vehicle.

'We need to take you to the ER, get you checked out. And debrief you.'

'No. You can debrief me on the way to the courthouse.' The judge stood tall and faced Beckeman. 'I have a decision to render.'

'Thank God the judge is okay,' the president said. 'Now find those Arabs.'

'Yes, sir.'

'Is your man up to it?'

'Yes, sir. Beckeman is the best we've got. And he's not afraid of bad PR if he kills Muslims.'

'Good. Because I want those two Arabs dead before kickoff.'

'Sir, we now know there are more conspirators out there. Perhaps we should consider canceling the Super Bowl.'

'No. If we shut down the Super Bowl, they win. That's not going to happen, not on my watch. The Super Bowl will be played on February seventh.'

The president pointed a finger at the director.

'Find the Arabs. Or find a new job.'

'Mr. President, if we don't find them, we'll both be looking for new jobs.'

By noon, Scott had exchanged Under Armour for Brooks Brothers; he addressed the packed courtroom from the bench.

'In our legal system, judges have an important role: to uphold the Constitution. That role often requires a judge to make hard decisions, rulings that are unpopular with the public, rulings that protect an individual's rights seemingly at the expense of society's morals and traditions. Terrorism is the latest arena in which the individual's constitutional rights seem to be pitted against society's best interests. Terrorist attacks scare us. We want to be safe, at least here at home. We want our government to keep us safe from terrorists. The easiest way to do that would be for the government to arrest every suspected terrorist and throw him in prison. But that would not be the constitutional way to keep us safe. That would not be the American way.'

The U.S. Attorney and Agent Beckeman squirmed at the prosecution table.

'Omar al Mustafa and twenty-two co-defendants were indicted and arrested on terrorism charges. The government requested they be detained pending trial. As required by law, this court held a detention hearing on Friday. At that hearing, the government failed to produce any credible evidence that Mr. Mustafa and his co-defendants are flight risks or dangers to the community, the only two bases for pretrial detention in federal court. At seven this morning, I had decided to grant pretrial release to all defendants.'

Beckeman hid his face in his hands. The imam restrained a smile.

'But at seven-thirty this morning, credible evidence came to my attention, evidence that more likely than not connects Mr. Mustafa to the stadium plot and that irrefutably establishes that he presents a clear and present danger to the community. I was abducted off the streets of Highland Park by two men who claimed they work for Mr. Mustafa.'

The crowd gasped. Word of Scott's abduction had apparently not reached his courtroom until now.

'These men threatened to behead me unless I release Mr. Mustafa. That is not going to happen. The court finds the following facts pursuant to the Bail Reform Act:

'One. That on this date the presiding judge was abducted by two men who claimed allegiance to defendant Omar al Mustafa;

'Two. That the two men demanded Defendant Mustafa's

234

release from federal custody under threat of additional unlawful acts against said judge;

'Three. That such abduction of the presiding judge in Defendant Mustafa's federal criminal case evidences a willingness of persons aligned with Defendant Mustafa to commit violence acts, with the apparent blessing of Defendant Mustafa; and

'Four. That such unlawful conduct can properly be attributed to Defendant Mustafa.

'Therefore, based upon the facts found by the court, the court states the following conclusions and reasons for the pretrial detention of all defendants:

'One. Omar al Mustafa is a danger to the community;

'Two. The other defendants are also dangers to the community because they are obedient to Defendant Mustafa;

'Three. The evidence establishes by clear and convincing proof that the defendants are dangers to the community and likely to intimidate or threaten jurors or witnesses; and

'Four. The defendants failed to rebut the presumption of detention set forth in section thirty-one forty-two-e-three of the Act.

'Therefore, the defendants are ordered detained by the U.S. Marshal's Service pending their trial in federal court. However, due to the publicity attendant to this case and the public animosity toward the defendants, which will no doubt be heightened due to this morning's events, the court orders that the defendants be held in the federal detention center in the Earle Cabell Federal Building in Dallas, Texas, for their own safety.'

'Scott, are you okay?' Karen asked.

Scott had collapsed into his chair in chambers. He was mainlining toffee. Karen and Bobby stood on the other side of the desk.

'Shit,' Bobby said. 'Kidnapped in broad daylight in Highland Park. These guys got balls.'

'I'm okay. It was scary, but mostly I was scared for the girls.'

'That someone would take them, too?'

'No. That they'd be okay without me.'

'Don't say that, Scott,' Karen said.

She started to cry; Bobby embraced his wife. Scott's phone rang. It was the attorney general.

'Cumulative justice, Scott.'

'You were right, Mac.'

'The Constitution wasn't written for people like them. They're barbarians, living in the Dark Ages. The Founding Fathers created this country for civilized people who believed in freedom and justice. These people believe in oppression, abduction, beheadings, terror. In the name of Allah. Now you see what we're dealing with every day, trying to keep this country safe.' Mac sighed heavily. 'You okay, Scott?'

'I am. Thanks for checking in.'

'Thank you for detaining those people. You're doing the right thing. You're protecting the American people.'

'And the judge.'

Mac laughed. 'Helps to keep a sense of humor.'

'Hopefully, this case will calm down now.'

Mac fell silent for a moment. Then he spoke in a soft voice.

'Scott, you watch out for yourself. These people won't quit until we kill or capture them.'

Abdul and his little brother watched the evening news account of their morning activities.

'Breaking and frightening news on the Omar al Mustafa case. Presiding Judge A. Scott Fenney was abducted this morning while out for a jog in Highland Park by two unidentified men in a white van, men who told the judge that they are followers of Mustafa.'

'See?' Abdul said. 'It worked.'

His little brother had not wanted to kidnap the judge, but Abdul had insisted, and his brother had followed. As he always had. As he always would.

The reporter on the television: 'The judge was released two hours later in South Dallas. He was blindfolded and bound but unhurt. Three boys came to his aid.'

The screen cut to a street scene with three black boys.

'This white van, it stop right here, the door swing open, and they throw this white man out. Then it speed off. So me and Rodney and Isaiah, we run over here and ask the man if he need help. He be wearing some cool Under Armour, say he a judge, asked to borrow my phone. I got me an iPhone Six – *un*locked. He called Louis, we all know him, and he was here in no time. Judge, he say thanks and got in the car and they leave.'

Back to the reporter: 'I showed the boys a photo of Judge Fenney, and they said that was the man they helped. This case is getting more frightening by the moment.'

Anchor: 'We go now to FBI headquarters in Dallas where a press conference is just beginning.'

'I'm FBI Special Agent Eric Beckeman. I'm in charge of the Joint Terrorism Task Force. I can confirm that U.S. District Judge A. Scott Fenney was in fact abducted this morning by two Arabs we believe are connected with the stadium plot.'

Beckeman stood in front of a clump of microphones and a firing squad of cameras.

'Agent, how did the FBI allow a federal judge to be abducted? That doesn't happen in America.'

'Judge Fenney declined our offer of a security detail.'

'But he's presiding over the trial of the most dangerous man in Dallas. Who's in control? You or him?'

237

'That's still an open question.'

'What if they had beheaded him?'

'They didn't.'

'What if they had?'

'They didn't.'

'Will the judge have a security detail going forward?'

'He will.'

Another reporter shouted: 'So there are more plotters at large?'

'Apparently.'

'Do you have any leads as to their whereabouts?'

'No.'

'So the stadium bomb plot is still active?'

'Possibly.'

'What do you plan to do about that?'

'Find the two Arabs and kill or capture them.'

'In twelve days?'

Beckeman checked his watch. 'And ten hours.'

'Was the judge hurt?'

'No. They did not harm the judge. In fact, he is back in his courtroom at this time.'

'Tough judge.'

'So it would seem.'

'What about Mustafa?'

'He's not going anywhere. The Arabs demanded that Judge Fenney release Mustafa, or else, in their words. That backfired on them as the judge ordered his detention pending trial. These Arabs underestimated the judge.'

His little brother gave Abdul a questioning look.

'We will see about that,' Abdul said. He checked his watch. 'I must go to the law school.'

★

'Our targets are two Arab males, both in their twenties, one tall, one short. The tall one wears yellow Nike sneakers. They were last seen wearing Ronald Reagan and George Bush masks.'

'Senior or junior?' an agent asked.

'What?'

'George senior or George junior?'

'W.'

Beckeman had exited the interview room, marched down the corridor, and entered the war room. He stood before the whiteboard. On the board were twenty-four photos: Mustafa at the top and lines drawn to his twenty-two co-defendants and one Aabdar Haddad. A red X had been drawn across Haddad's face. Beckeman drew two circles on the board and wrote '25' and '26' inside the circles.

'People, this is *Zero Dark Thirty*. You've all seen the movie. Now you're living it. We know the date, the time, and the place. We just don't know the enemy. We've got to identify them, find them, and kill or capture them. And we've got twelve days to do it.'

'How?'

'As the judge's abduction proves, this plot begins and ends with Mustafa. They work for him. Go back to the top and work down. Tear the mosque apart, find every male who's ever prayed there.'

'Boss, we checked every male at the mosque.'

'Check them again. We're missing two men. The judge said they referred to themselves as brothers.'

'They're all brothers and sisters.'

'They might be.'

'This is exactly what they want,' Agent Peña said.

'Exactly what who wants?' Beckeman said.

'It's a diversion.'

'What is?'

'Grabbing the judge.'

'They grabbed the judge to get Mustafa out.'

'Then why'd they release him? Why didn't they hold him hostage until we released Mustafa? It's a diversion.'

'From what?'

'The plot.'

'The plot begins and ends with Mustafa.'

'The plot begins in Syria and ends at the Super Bowl.'

Agent Baxter ran up. 'Chief, we located the white van. They torched it, but the Evidence Response Team is on it, see if they can find anything.'

'We won't find them in this world,' Peña said. 'They're in the dark Net talking to ISIS in Syria.'

'Because Mustafa's in jail,' Beckeman said.

'Because they're the bad guys. They're running this op, not Mustafa.'

'Bullshit. This plot is too complicated for two lone wolves.'

'Why don't we just waterboard Mustafa?' Baxter said. 'He knows them. He knows everything.'

'We enforce the law, so we obey the law,' Beckeman said.

But he wanted to waterboard the son of a bitch himself. He sighed. How does a civilized society fight uncivilized barbarians? Politics say we fight by the rules; but reality says there are no rules, not in this war. This was a war of ideology. Beliefs. Religion. There's only dead or not dead. Survival or extinction. Victory or fear. What rules apply when you're fighting for your way of life? When they are fighting for their god?

FBI Agent Eric Beckeman had fucked up.

He had assumed he had all the bad guys in jail. That he had won. If not the war, at least this battle. But he had assumed wrong. The battle was not yet won. That wrong assumption could have cost a hundred thousand people their lives. Because he had forgotten the most basic rules when fighting Islamic jihadists:

1. There will always be more of them.
2. They will never lose.
3. They will never win the war, but they will never quit the fight.
4. We can beat them, but we cannot defeat them.
5. Because they are fighting for God.

FBI Agent Catalina Peña stared at the photo of Aabdar Haddad with the red X across his face. She had searched his life from birth to death. Twenty-two years on this earth, now he was part of the earth. He had been born to Bedar and Fatema Haddad of Houston, Texas. They were Muslims, but mainstream. The father owned an ethnic restaurant; the mother had raised their six children. Aabdar was the oldest and the first to attend college. His Facebook page contained nothing related to ISIS or jihadists. He had uploaded no videos to YouTube. Nothing had been tweeted from his Twitter account in over a year. He had a steady girlfriend. He was an A student studying architecture at the University of Texas at Arlington. He had good friends – college kids, grad students, law students at SMU. Muslim kids who were going somewhere, not Muslim kids who wanted to kill someone. He had prayed at the imam's mosque, as had apparently every Muslim in the Dallas-Fort Worth metroplex. As Agent Beckeman himself had said, 'Mustafa, he's the Joel Osteen of Muslims.' The search of his apartment had uncovered no ISIS propaganda, no jihadist recruiting videos, no evidence that he was involved in the stadium plot or any terrorist plot. He was just a college kid. Beckeman had killed the wrong guy.

'Bullshit!'

241

Which was Beckeman's only response when Cat had submitted her report, that and he threw the report back at her and told her to rewrite it. She stared at her boss. He had fucked up. He had killed the wrong guy. He had arrested the wrong bad guys. He had not stopped the plot.

'We have twelve days, people, to find them and kill or capture them. This is twenty-four/seven. Task force meetings twice a day, nine and six. Vacations, leave, and sleep are revoked. We don't sleep, we don't rest, we don't stop. Until we've stopped them. Find the Arabs.'

'Captain, what about the judge?' Agent Stryker said.

'Twenty-four/seven security detail.'

'How many agents? Two?'

'One. He ain't the president.' Beckeman hesitated then said, 'No, two. I'm not going to have a dead federal judge on my record.'

That night, a black sedan with two FBI agents sat parked on the street outside the Fenney house in Highland Park. Scott peeked out through the blinds then checked on the girls.

Chapter 14

Tuesday, 26 January
12 days before the Super Bowl

When a horse bucks you off, you have to climb back into the saddle. Fast, or fear will get the best of you. Scott had always heard that cowboy saying, but he wasn't a cowboy so he didn't know if it were true. But it sounded true. So at dawn the next morning, Judge A. Scott Fenney got back on the horse. He dressed in his running gear and headed to the back door.

'A. Scott . . . don't go.'

He turned back to Boo standing in the hall and rubbing her eyes.

'Don't worry, honey, the FBI agents will be with me.'

'I'm scared.'

He went to her and squatted before her. 'Boo, if I let these men bully me into not running, it'd be like the bullies at school running Pajamae out of Highland Park. She's staying, and I'm running. We're not going to let the bullies win.'

She wrapped her arms around his neck.

'We can't lose you, A. Scott.'

'You won't.'

When Scott came around to the front of the house, the door to the FBI car opened and two white males in black suits got out.

'Uh, Judge – where are you going?' one agent said.

'I'm going for my run.'

'You really think that's a good idea?'

'I can't live in fear, Agent . . .'

'Jones. This is Agent Smith.'

'Smith and Jones.'

'We're assigned to protect you.'

'Then run with me.'

'A, we're not dressed for that, and B' – he patted his well-fed belly – 'I'm not in shape for that. And Smith is too old for that.'

'Well, Agent Jones, if I live in fear and hide out in my house, the terrorists win. I'm running.'

Scott ran west. Two blocks down, he glanced back. The FBI car followed slowly behind him.

'This is bullshit,' Agent Jones said to Agent Smith. 'We're here to protect his judicial ass, not to follow him around like his private bodyguards. This ain't happening tomorrow morning.'

The judge turned the corner so Agent Smith turned the corner.

'What are you going to do?'

'Talk to the boss. Because I don't run. Hell, I don't even run after bad guys, I just shoot their ass. Now I've got to jog with a judge? I don't think so.'

★

'Are you okay, Scott?' Karen asked again.

She sat across his desk from him.

'I'm fine.'

He went back to the bowl for another toffee.

'You were abducted . . . and you finished off the whole bowl this morning.'

She gave him a concerned look.

'So, what did you think about oral arguments?' Scott asked.

She realized he wasn't going to talk about the kidnapping and gave up.

'The government made a good point about enforcement resources,' she said, 'but that's not the point.'

'What's the point?'

'The point is, your job isn't to rule on whether Congress will fund immigration enforcement. That's a political question. Your job is to rule on the constitutionality of the executive order. That's the legal question. Nothing else matters in this room.'

She pointed at the window.

'Not those protestors, not public opinion, not politics, and not the president who appointed you.'

The attorney general called at ten.

'I missed you,' Scott said.

'I'm sure you did.'

'What now? I detained Mustafa.'

'The president is on my ass about the immigration case.'

'Are you going to call me every day about that case, too?'

'Are you going to dismiss the states' lawsuit?'

'You're kind of pushy, aren't you, Mac?'

'The president put you on that bench, Scott.'

'He still wants to jog?' Beckeman said.

He had been reading the latest arrest log for the Muslim

roundup. Agent Jones had knocked on his door immediately after the morning manhunt meeting. He wanted off the judge's security detail.

'Apparently. But I don't jog.'

'Obviously.'

Beckeman studied his round agent. Jones had actually once been a fit man, but the divorce had put him on a liquid diet. Alcohol is fattening. But even with the extra weight, Jones was a good agent. And right now he needed good agents giving him good news. They had none that morning. It was as if the two Arabs had vanished into thin air. The president had called the director; the director had called Beckeman. As if he needed more pressure than the pressure presented by one hundred thousand lives at stake Super Bowl Sunday. But he was a Marine; he could handle the pressure.

'Replace me, boss.'

Beckeman sighed and gazed out through the glass walls of his office at his agents in their cubicles. His gaze paused on a pretty face.

'I've got just the agent for the job.'

Chapter 15

Wednesday, 27 January
11 days before the Super Bowl

'This is bullshit.'

'What are you pissed about?' her partner said. 'It's easy money, babysitting a judge. Let the other guys chase the Arabs. Me, I want to finish out my twenty, then bass fish the rest of my life.'

Ace Smith was close to retirement. She was not. So she was pissed. Special Agent Catalina Peña had signed on with the Joint Terrorism Task Force to hunt down terrorists, not to babysit a half-senile, decrepit old judge on his morning walk. But she had opened her mouth to Beckeman once too often, and he had exiled her to the judge's security detail.

Unbefuckinglievable.

She hadn't met or seen Judge Fenney, but no doubt he looked like every other federal judge she had met and seen: white hair, black reading glasses, brown liver spots, and grey suit. Old white men. Senior citizens who had earned enough political favors to warrant a lifetime appointment to the federal bench living out their lives at taxpayers' expense. And now she had to jog with the judge, which would be about as enjoyable as jogging with Donald Trump.

The air was crisp and cool, a perfect morning for a run. Scott walked out the back door and around to the front of the house. He did not find Agents Smith and Jones but instead Agent Smith standing next to the black sedan and a young female perched on the hood. She wore running clothes; he wore a suit. She was drinking a Starbucks coffee; he was eating a breakfast taco. She did not abandon her perch when he arrived. She did look him up and down with a bemused expression.

'You like Under Armour?'

Scott checked his attire; he was wearing all Under Armour except his shoes.

'Uh, Cat . . .' Agent Smith said.

'I must,' Scott said.

'You running with the judge, too?'

'Pardon me?'

'Uh, Cat . . .' Agent Smith said again.

'You work for the judge?'

Scott glanced from her to Agent Smith and back to her.

'I am the judge.'

She had taken a big drink of the coffee but froze. Her eyes got wide; she swallowed hard then slid off the hood of the sedan.

'*You're* Judge Fenney?'

'You're an FBI agent?'

'You're not what I expected, sir.'

'Neither are you.'

They regarded each other a moment, then she abruptly backhanded Agent Smith hard across the chest.

248

'Why didn't you tell me, Ace?'

'I tried.' Agent Smith grinned and said through a mouthful of taco, 'But you were doing such a good job making a fool of yourself.'

'Thanks. I'll remember that next time a bad guy tries to shoot you in the back.' She turned back to Scott and stuck a hand out. 'Agent Catalina Peña, sir. You've met Agent Smith.'

He looked every inch the FBI agent; she did not. Her inches were lean and muscular and covered by a long-sleeve yellow running shirt, white running tights, red running shoes, and a black waist pack. Her brown hair was pulled back in a ponytail.

'I hear you need a runner?'

'Apparently.'

'Track team at UT. Two and four hundred meters.'

As if applying for employment.

'You're over-qualified for the job.'

'Did you run in college?'

'On a football field.'

'You don't look big enough.'

'I survived on stupidity and speed, at least before the knee operations.'

'How many?'

'Two.'

'Ouch.'

'You ready to run?'

'Judge, I was born to run.'

Agent Smith waved them off with the taco. 'I'll watch the home front. But don't worry, Judge, Cat can shoot.'

Competitive athletes moved differently than normal people. Even past their prime – she figured the judge was twenty years past his prime and she was ten – their bodies still retained the grace and gait of their competitive days. The judge ran with

249

grace, his long legs keeping pace with her track team stride. They ran past other runners, lawyers and businessmen who were born lawyers and businessmen plodding hard on the concrete as if their feet were pounding nails, men who ran each morning because it was good for them, not because they had been born to run. Cat Peña had been born to run. She loved to run. Her feet felt light, as if they barely touched the ground. She always felt that she glided more than ran, and she always ran alone. A competitive athlete could not run with an amateur; consequently, she hadn't run with anyone in a very long time. She kept an eye out for bad guys, but she enjoyed running with a man. This man. An athlete. A judge.

It wasn't bullshit after all.

'That is a lot of shit,' his little brother said.

'Actually,' Abdul said, 'it is not shit. It is better than shit. Spread it on fields, and the crops will grow. Add some diesel fuel and a detonator, and it will explode.'

Abdul had studied the Oklahoma City bombing in detail. That seven-thousand-pound bomb had worked perfectly. But he needed a bigger bomb. So they had amassed fifty thousand pounds of ammonium nitrate.

'We will soon be ready, my brother, to bring death and destruction to America.'

His brother sighed. 'You know, Abdul, I liked you better when you wanted to be a professional soccer player.'

'Get to the photo shop.'

Two hours after his run with Agent Peña, Scott sat at his desk. Karen sat across from him.

'We got Bookman's brief,' she said.

'And?'

'Not what I had expected.'

'Seems to be the day for the unexpected.'

She studied Scott a moment. 'Okay.'

'I'll read it tonight.'

'You'll enjoy it.' She hesitated then said, 'Are you okay, Scott?'

'This ain't fun and games, people. This is a fucking manhunt.'

The task force had assembled for the morning meeting. So far the status had not changed. His agents had found exactly nothing. Again. And time was running out. The door to the war room opened, and Agents Smith and Peña entered. You'd have thought the Playmate of the Year had walked in buck-naked. The agents bolted from their chairs and fought to get to her first. Because she had more to offer than big tits and a tight ass; she had breakfast tacos.

'Finally,' Agent Carson said. 'What took you so long?'

'I had to run with the judge,' Peña said. 'And watch your tone of voice, Carson, or these'll be the last breakfast tacos you ever eat.'

'Sorry.'

Beckeman sighed. Hungry agents were worthless; and this would be the best meal they had that day. Hell, the tacos did smell good. So he pushed through to the front before the bastards took all the eggs, cheese, and bean tacos.

'How was the run with the judge?' Beckeman said.

He bit into a taco.

'He wasn't what I expected,' Peña said. 'He's young. Handsome. Fit. He was a star football player in college.'

The other agents reverted to their college frat days and gave her an *ooooh*. She gave them her middle finger just as Agent Stryker barged in.

'Captain, we got an interesting statement from a male at the mosque. Said there were two men he didn't know hanging

251

around now and then. One tall, one short. Thought he heard them say they were brothers. And get this – the tall one played on the mosque soccer team a few times. He was really good.'

'And that means what to me?' Beckeman said through a mouthful of eggs, cheese, and beans.

'He wore yellow sneakers.'

'Dude, you really love your beer.'

He stood at the counter in the photo shop as Abdul had instructed.

'It must measure exactly one hundred inches wide and one hundred ten inches tall,' he said.

'The hell you gonna do with it?'

'Uh . . . I will place it on my living room wall.'

'Your woman okay with that?'

'What woman?'

'Amen, brother.'

The law mandates that persons residing illegally in the U.S. be deported. The president does not agree with the law. He could not convince the Congress to change the law. So he changed the law via executive order. That he may not do. As the Supreme Court said in *Youngstown Sheet and Tube*, when President Truman seized the steel mills by executive order, 'In the framework of our Constitution, the President's power to see that the laws are faithfully executed refutes the idea that he is to be a lawmaker. The Constitution limits his functions in the lawmaking process to the recommending of laws he thinks wise and the veto-ing of laws he thinks bad. And the Constitution is neither silent nor equivocal about who shall make laws which the President is to execute. The first section of the first article says that "All legislative Powers herein granted shall be

252

vested in a Congress of the United States . . ." After granting many powers to the Congress, Article I goes on to provide that Congress may "make all Laws which shall be necessary and proper for carrying into Execution the foregoing Powers, and all other Powers vested by this Constitution in the Government of the United States, or in any Department or Officer thereof." . . . The Founders of this Nation entrusted the lawmaking power to the Congress alone in both good and bad times.' The president's executive order violates the Constitution.

Professor John Bookman taught constitutional law at the University of Texas School of Law. He claimed to be the last known practicing Jeffersonian in America. Maybe, maybe not. But he knew the Constitution. He cited the Constitution, Supreme Court cases, and the Federalist Papers, articles written by James Madison, John Jay, and Alexander Hamilton and published in American newspapers advocating ratification of the Constitution by the thirteen states; the articles explained the intent of the Constitution by the men who wrote it. The phrase 'human nature' was mentioned over and over again in the papers. The Founding Fathers understood human nature, man's natural desire for more – more money, more power, more everything. As Madison so famously wrote, 'If men were angels, no government would be necessary.' But they knew men were not angels, and they understood human nature. So they limited the power of man and government in the Constitution. Since 1788 when the Constitution was ratified, federal judges have been called upon to decide whether the president or the Congress exceeded their express powers under the Constitution. Now it was Judge A. Scott Fenney's turn to decide. Did the president exceed his power under Article Two when he issued an executive order that suspended all deportations of persons residing illegally in the U.S.? Perhaps his intentions were good; but good intentions don't count. Either the Constitution granted him that power or it did not. The president claimed that he possessed that power. That his discretion was absolute.

Human nature, it seemed, would not be denied.

Chapter 16

Friday, 29 January
9 days before the Super Bowl

Agents Peña and Smith had been waiting out front Thursday morning and were again that morning. He again ate a breakfast taco; she again wore running gear – black tights, white shirt, and the same red shoes and black waist pack. Scott again wore Under Armour apparel. She again looked him up and down with the same bemused expression.

'Judge, do you endorse Under Armour?'

'Heartily.'

'Lots of money?'

'Yes. I pay lots of money to wear their clothes.'

She laughed. It was a good laugh. They ran west on Lovers Lane. Agent Smith again waved them off with the taco.

'Any progress in finding those men?'

'The Arabs? No, sir.'

'Can they execute the plot without Mustafa?'

'Beckeman says no.'

'And what do you say?'

'I . . . follow orders.'

'I doubt that.'

Scott had always enjoyed his runs, quiet time alone to ponder life and the law; it was no longer quiet time. Agent Peña talked nonstop. But he had to admit: it was nice to have someone to run with. He had always run alone. Rebecca had not been a runner. She had been a climber. A social climber. Lunches, dinners, and society balls. That was her course in life.

'Did your wife really run off with the golf pro at your country club?'

Coming from her, the question did not offend Scott. Of course, everyone in America now knew his life story.

'She did.'

'And then she was charged with murdering him?'

'She was.'

'And you defended her?'

'I did.'

'What kind of man defends his ex-wife who left him for the golf pro?'

He had no answer. So she asked another question.

'Where is she now?'

'Somewhere with a man.'

Cat Peña pulled the FBI sedan into the carpool lane behind the judge's big Expedition then felt silly for having done so. They could probably have ensured the judge's safety by pulling up to the curb just outside the carpool lane. Ace rode shotgun and carried one. He glanced around at the kids chatting and laughing.

'I feel dumb,' Ace said.

'You look dumb, too.'

'I mean, sitting in the carpool lane when we don't have kids to drop off.'

'I'll drop you off. You're probably the same mental age as these kids.'

The judge's two girls jumped out of the Expedition but not before kissing him goodbye. They were cute kids carrying backpacks that looked like they were ready for an Arctic expedition.

'You believe he adopted a black kid?' Ace said. 'A hooker's daughter, no less.' He chuckled. 'Must have caused quite a commotion among these Highland Parkers.'

All the Mercedes-Benzes, BMWs, and Lexuses in the carpool lane were occupied by white people. Other than the judge's daughter, Cat saw no children of color. Or adults of color, except for the Latino men tending to the school landscape.

'The judge doesn't seem to care what people think,' Cat said.

'A good trait in a judge.'

'And in a man.'

An Anglo teacher whom some men might find attractive – if a man went for a twenty-something with shiny black hair, five-five, one-twenty, full round breasts, and a tight ass – held the back door for the judge's daughters. After they had exited the vehicle, she ducked her head and gave the judge a coy little smile. She said something to him. Cat leaned forward and squinted; she tried to read the woman's lips.

'Did she say, "Call me?" What the hell's that all about? He can't even drop his kids off at school without some horny teacher coming on to him like a drunken prom queen?'

Ace seemed amused. 'Do I detect a twinge of jealousy in your voice, Agent Peña?'

'I mean, how old is she? Twenty-five? The judge is forty. He doesn't want to date a girl that young.'

Cat was thirty-one.

'I don't know, she looks mighty fine from where I'm sitting.'

'Fuck you. And the fucking horse you rode in on.'

Ace whistled. 'You've got a mouth on you, girl.'

'I haven't had my coffee yet.'

'Cat, you can't get a crush on our protectee. That's against the rules.'

She caught a glimpse of the judge's blue eyes in the side mirror as he checked for oncoming traffic before exiting the carpool lane. After running with the judge the last three mornings, Cat did have a crush on him. He was handsome, smart, and single; he had defended his ex-wife against a murder charge; and he had adopted a black girl. What's not to like?

'Thought you were pissed 'cause Beckeman put you on the judge's security detail?'

'I was. I am.'

'You don't look pissed off . . . except at that cute teacher.'

They followed the judge out of the carpool lane – Cat fought the urge to shoot the finger (or her Glock) at the cute teacher – and the two miles to downtown and the courthouse garage entrance where the SWAT team took over his security. The night-shift detail would escort him home. But she would see him the next morning. And every morning until the Arabs were captured or killed.

They were Arabs; thus, they were presumed guilty. The law school had become their Guantanamo Bay – no grand jury indictments, no trial by jury, no incriminating evidence, no presumption of innocence. They were treated as enemy combatants by conservative students and liberal professors alike. Fear transcended political affiliation. They felt the hot glare of suspicion, the noose tightening around their neck. Perhaps Abdul was right. Perhaps they would never really be Americans. Perhaps they would always and only be Muslims.

'Do not be afraid, little brother,' Abdul said. 'Allah is with us.'

He wished he were as sure as Abdul that Allah was with Saddam Siddiqui. He had never been as devout or as determined as his older brother. He had always been more carefree, the type to go with the flow, to let the wind take him where it may. Making his mark on the world had never been a priority with him. That attitude had always infuriated his father. And then his father had been killed. Since their father's death, Abdul had been the strong wind in his sails.

'Come on, people, find the Arabs!'

'Captain, we're tracking down every Muslim male in Dallas,' Stryker said. 'But it takes time.'

'We don't have time. The clock's ticking.'

The president had called the director at 8:00 A.M. Eastern time; the director had called Beckeman at 7:15 A.M. Central time.

'Are you going to call me every morning?' Beckeman had asked.

'Yes. Because the president calls me every morning.'

'That's why you make the big bucks.'

'Is the task force working this weekend?'

'You really have to ask that?'

'Sorry. Please find the Arabs.'

'Searching for Arabs is all I do.'

He had hung up with the director and walked into the war room. His agents were drinking coffee and eating donuts; caffeine and sugar, the basics of a manhunt.

'Where's Peña with the tacos?' he asked.

No answer was forthcoming, so Beckeman bit into a chocolate-glazed donut.

'Chief,' Agent Jenkins said, 'I've been thinking.'

'Your first mistake.'

259

'My six-year-old son plays soccer. I go to his games, it's like the fucking Academy Awards, all the cameras. Mommies and daddies capturing every moment of Baby Jesus's life.'

Agent Jenkins stuffed a donut into his mouth but did not stop talking.

'The taller Arab in the yellow sneakers, he played on the mosque soccer team. Maybe other Muslims taped the games. Maybe someone captured his image on their cell phone or camcorder.'

'And you think they'll just hand over their phones and cameras?'

'I asked a few to check their phones, but they're not exactly cooperating with us.' He shrugged. 'We did arrest their imam. But we could get search warrants.'

'How many?'

'Could be hundreds.'

'It'd take several days to get all the names and the warrants, right?'

'Probably.'

'So by that time, what do you think would happen to any images on their phones?'

'Deleted?'

'Exactly.'

Agent Jenkins glanced over Beckeman's shoulder and shot off as if to jump between a bullet and the president. Which meant only one thing.

'Tacos!'

Agent Peña had arrived. She carried a box of tacos; Agent Smith followed behind like a bodyguard. Beckeman muscled his way to the front; these sons of bitches weren't eating all the eggs, cheese, and bean tacos that day. He grabbed two and dropped his cash in the box.

'Peña, Smith,' Beckeman said, 'any security problems with the judge?'

260

'Chief,' Peña said, 'it's a diversion, the judge's abduction. We're looking in the wrong direction. We—'

'No, sir,' Ace said. 'No problems.'

'Good. 'Cause you two got the night shift. Meet the judge at the garage exit at four-forty-five, one of his girls has a basketball game at five.'

'I'm betting the black girl,' Agent Smith said.

Peña gave him a look.

'*What?*'

'You're a regular Sherlock Holmes.'

Scott sat in the gymnasium stands. Alone; no one wanted to be in his company, except for his crew. The fans that had greeted him so warmly the week before now acted as if he had Ebola; they had crowded into the adjacent section of the bleachers, as if expecting Islamic terrorists to burst through the doors and open fire at him. His abduction had taken him from hero to potential target. No one wanted to be collateral damage. To his left sat Louis, Carlos, Bobby, and Karen bouncing Little Scotty on her knees; to his right sat Boo and Agents Peña and Smith. He had not expected them to work his evening security detail, but he had not been disappointed when they were waiting at the garage exit. Scott stood.

'Come on, Boo, concession stand run.' He pointed out the orders. 'Root beers for Carlos, Louis, and Bobby, coffee with cream for Karen, and prunes for Little Scotty.' He patted the boy's head. 'Sorry, bud. Agents Peña and Smith, what can I get for you?'

'I'll take a root beer, too,' Agent Smith said. 'And ice cream, if they got some. I love root beer floats.'

Agent Peña rolled her eyes at her partner then stood. 'Agent Smith seems to have forgotten that we're here to protect you, sir, not eat ice cream. I'll go with you.'

Agent Smith offered a bemused expression. 'I don't think a

middle school basketball game in Highland Park is going to attract a crowd of Islamic jihadists.'

'The game won't, but the judge might.'

Scott looked from Agent Peña to Agent Smith and back to Agent Peña.

'Do you two need a moment?'

Agent Peña sighed. 'I need caffeine, and he needs sugar.'

Louis stood. 'I'll go with you, Judge Fenney.'

'It's okay, Louis. Agent Peña's got a gun.'

'I've got your back.'

Louis led the way down the stands. Scott, Boo, and Agent Peña followed. They stepped onto the floor and turned toward the concession stand – and came face to face with Penny Birn-baum.

'Hello, Scott.'

'Oh, uh, hi, Penny.'

Her eyes went from Scott to Agent Peña. She frowned. 'Is she with you?'

Agent Peña recoiled. '*She—*'

'—is an FBI agent,' Boo said. 'She's guarding A. Scott's body.'

'Oh, really?'

The two women gave each other once-overs as women do.

What the hell are you looking at?

First the cute teacher and now this little tart. What, is the judge starring in *Highland Park Bachelor*? Cat returned the favor and gave her a possible perpetrator eyeballing.

Wonder how you'd feel if I strip-searched you, see if you're wearing Spanx under that tight-knit dress to make your ass look so round and firm?

Cat needed no help in that regard.

The two women eyed each other like prizefighters at the offi-cial weigh-in. Boo's eyes darted back and forth between the women as if she were watching a tennis match. She was clearly enjoying this. Scott decided to break it up.

'Enjoy the game, Penny.'

Penny started to walk past him but abruptly put her mouth to his ear away from Agent Peña and whispered, 'I'm not wearing panties.' She blew in his ear and squeezed his hand. He felt his face turn hot. Agent Peña noticed.

'Five root beers, two coffees with cream, a jar of prunes, and ice cream.'

The judge ordered, the big black bailiff hovered like a Mexican mother, and Cat eyed the civilians loitering around the concession stand . . . no one looked Muslim or armed or dangerous except that tart named Penny . . . but her attention was abruptly drawn to Boo and another girl, blonde, five-two, a little snot by the looks of her. There was apparently bad blood between them because they immediately got in each other's face.

'How's your nose, Bitzy?'

'My dad said he's going to sue you.'

Boo threw a thumb at her dad. 'Call my lawyer.'

'Uh, Judge, sir . . . your daughter . . .'

'She's fine.' To the attendant: 'Better make that six root beers.'

'Oh, that's right, your dad,' the blonde said with a wicked sneer. 'The *liberal* federal judge.'

'Uh, Judge . . .'

'She's fine.'

'She decked the blonde.'

'She does that.'

'I ain't never dated an FBI agent,' the judge's assistant named Carlos said.

'I've never dated a man with five priors,' Cat said.

'*Ay-yi-yi*. You ran a criminal background check on me?'

'On everyone near the judge . . . except these two girls.'

Cat sat across the table from Carlos and between the judge's daughters.

'You've got a crush on him, don't you?' the daughter named Boo whispered to her.

'Who? Carlos?'

'No. A. Scott.'

'Why do you say that?'

'I observe.'

'Your father seems to have quite a few girls.'

'Oh, no, he's the hunk of Highland Park, but he doesn't have anyone.'

'The hunk of Highland Park?'

'We think he is.' Her eyebrows bounced. 'Do you think he is?'

'I'm on the job.'

'But you look at him.'

She was observant.

'Don't worry about that Penny girl,' Boo said. 'She's an oral sex kind of girl, and A. Scott doesn't want that.'

Agent Smith spit out his pizza so as not to choke.

'Why not?' he said.

'*Ace*,' Cat said.

'Oh. Sorry.'

He ducked his head to his pizza. Cat shook her head at him.

'She's not his type,' Boo said.

'What's his type?'

'You.'

The judge's other daughter nodded. She had scored thirty-two points; her team won handily. They all went for pizza after the game, a Friday-night tradition for the Fenney family. Cat ate one piece and a salad. Ace was finishing off a large meat-and-cheese deluxe pizza all by himself.

'Best meal I've had all week,' he said.

He was fifty-five and divorced with no prospects. Certain jobs made personal relationships difficult, if not impossible. The FBI was one such job. The magistrate judge walked over and whispered in Cat's ear.

'Please watch out for Scotty.'

Each of the judge's people had made the same request to her that night.

'I will. I'm armed and Latina.'

'Good.'

The magistrate walked to his place on the other side of the table next to the bailiff who sat next to the judge. He was apparently willing to take a bullet for the judge.

'Have you ever shot anyone?' Boo asked.

Cat pointed a finger at her partner. 'I want to shoot him all the time.'

They talked and laughed and even joked about the judge's abduction only five days before. The Arabs remained at large.

You shot the Mexicans?

Abdul jabbar sat in front of a computer at the law school and typed in Arabic.

In the legs.

A response came quickly: *Why?*

He typed again: *To test the product.*

A response came: *And was it effective?*

He typed: *Very. But they brought only eleven containers. Now only ten.*

That will be sufficient.

It is effective.

265

Did you acquire the Tovex?

Yes.

Excellent. From who?

A disgruntled former employee of a mining company.

Was the price high?

Indeed it was.

Did you pay him in full?

Indeed I did.

Very good, Abdul. You are proving yourself a capable lone wolf.

Indeed I am.

A lone wolf. He liked that image of himself. One dangerous man bringing death and destruction to America. If he brought that stadium down on one hundred thousand people, his name would live on in history. Like Osama bin Laden.

This is a one-time shot, Abdul. Like 9/11. Succeed or fail, you are dead. It is a suicide mission either way. Is your little brother up to the task?

Abdul thought a moment then typed: *Yes.*

He waited for a response. It came soon.

Of that you are certain?

He typed: *Yes. He is just . . .*

Just what?

A nice boy.

Yes. He is. But nice is not a good trait in a jihadist. He must be able to cut his best friend's head off if necessary. Can he do that?

Abdul pondered the words on the screen. He would have to drag his little brother kicking and screaming to meet Allah. And he would. He typed.

No. But I can do it for him.

The response was a long moment in coming. Finally, words appeared on the screen.

Do not fail me, Abdul.

★

266

Cat walked in the back door of her house in East Dallas to find her parents sitting at the kitchen table. She sighed at the sight.

'You don't have to wait up for me. I'm past my *quinceañera*.'

Her parents offered innocent expressions, like suburban drug buyers caught in the act.

'We are not waiting up for you, are we, Diego?'

'That was a glorious day,' he said. 'Your *quinceañera*.'

He looked as if he might cry.

'Your father wanted a snack.'

He held up an Oreo cookie. He kept the company in business.

'Sit,' her father said.

She sat and took the Oreo. Her mother poured a glass of milk. She dipped the cookie in the milk and ate it whole. Her parents regarded her as one does a newborn.

'So who did you meet?' her mother asked.

'I didn't meet anyone.'

Her mother gave her a look. She was a human polygraph machine.

'Okay, I met someone.'

Her mother nodded knowingly at her father.

'And who is he?'

'He's a judge.'

'A judge? Like on *American Idol*?'

'No, not like on *American Idol*. Like a real judge. A federal judge.'

'Have we heard of him?'

'No, but you will.'

'Why? What did he do?'

'He didn't do anything. He's presiding over the stadium terrorist case.'

'I thought the Muslims kidnapped that judge,' her father said through a mouthful of Oreos.

'They did. That's how I met him. I'm on his security detail.'

'You are protecting him?'

'Yes.'

'But you are also in love with him?'

'Yes . . . No . . . I don't know.'

Her father grunted and gave her another Oreo. Her mother patted her hand.

'Bring him over Sunday for lunch. I will cook for him. So you don't have to.'

Cat did not cook.

'We're not there yet, meeting my parents.'

'How old is he?'

'Forty.'

'He's forty and never been married?'

'He's divorced.'

'Does he have children?'

'Two girls. Thirteen.'

'Twins?'

'Not exactly.'

'Do they live with their mother?'

'No. They live with him.'

'Where is their mother?'

'She ran off with a golf pro.'

'Oh, my.'

'Did he win any majors?' her father asked.

Chapter 17

Saturday, 30 January
8 days before the Super Bowl

The alarm went off at seven. Scott jumped out of bed and ran down the hall to the living room. He peeked out the front blinds. Agent Peña sat perched on the hood of the black FBI sedan; Agent Smith was nowhere in sight.

Scott ran back down the hall to his bedroom. He dressed quickly in his running gear then checked on the girls. They formed one big lump under their comforter. He shut their door then went to the back door but realized he hadn't brushed his teeth. He ran back down the hall to his bathroom and brushed. Then back down the hall and out the door. He tried to appear nonchalant when he rounded the corner of the house and saw Agent Peña. And she saw him.

Her heart jumped. She couldn't believe it, but it actually did. As it had the last three mornings. She tried to hide her excitement.

269

'Morning, Judge Fenney.'

'Morning, Agent Peña. Where's Agent Smith?'

'Too much pizza. Or the flu. Everyone else is hunting for the Arabs, so it's just me today. Your body is in my hands . . . so to speak.'

'You know, Agent, I was thinking. Perhaps we should dispense with the formalities and the "sir" and go with Scott and Cat. At least while we're running. Since we're going to be running every morning until the trial.'

'Are we now?'

'I hope so.'

She stared openly into his eyes from a distance of five feet.

'I hope so, too, Judge . . . sir . . . Scott.'

Their gaze remained steady for a long moment then she suddenly felt awkward. She broke eye contact.

'Shall we?'

'We shall.'

They ran west on Lovers Lane. After they had both gained their rhythm, Cat spoke.

'You were quite a football player in college, sir . . . Scott. I googled you. And watched that game against Texas on YouTube.'

'You can do that?'

'I can. So can you.'

'I've never watched a replay of that game.'

'Why not? You were incredible.'

'I don't live in the past.'

'Except with your ex?'

Scott's first instinct was to tell Cat that she was wrong, dead wrong, that he was past his past when it came to Rebecca. Way past. Never thought about her, never wondered about her, never imagined her with other men. But she wasn't wrong.

She was right. Dead right. He had taken a vow: *Till death do us part.*

The scene reminded Beckeman of *The Godfather*, when the Corleone family went to the mats to fight a mob war. The FBI had gone to the mats to fight a holy war. They knew the date this war would be won or lost: Super Bowl Sunday. They knew the time and the place and the plan. They just didn't know the enemy. They couldn't find the enemy. But they would not stop searching until they did. Until they found the enemy and killed or captured the enemy. And won the war. Or at least this battle. The entire task force was fighting for America that Saturday morning. Except Agent Peña.

An hour later, Scott and Cat returned to the house. Cat retrieved a bottle of water and a thermos from the FBI sedan.

'Coffee,' she said.

'How about breakfast?' Scott said. 'The girls would love it if you joined us.'

'And you?'

'I would, too.'

She smiled. 'Beckeman told me not to let you out of my sight, so I'd just be following orders.'

She locked the car and followed Scott around the house. They entered through the back door to find Consuelo cooking and Boo waiting with the blood pressure cuff and a glass full of something green.

'Consuelo, this is Agent Catalina Peña. Cat, this is Consuelo de la Rosa-Garcia and her daughter, Maria.'

'*Buenos días,*' Consuelo said.

'*Buenos días.*'

'Hi again, Agent Peña,' Boo said.

She tried to rub the sleep out of her eyes but without much effect. Cat raised her fists as if boxing and said, 'The boxer.'

271

'I don't box,' Boo said. 'I fight.'

'Oh, yeah,' Scott said. 'You hit that girl last night. I thought all the attention had ended the bullying.'

'Just for a few days. Then it got worse. The mean girls, they're jealous of the attention we got.' She looked at Cat. 'Because A. Scott is a hero.'

'I'm not a hero, Boo. Cat and the other FBI agents, they're the heroes. They saved the Super Bowl, not me.'

He sat at the table and extended his left arm to Boo. She strapped on the cuff. Cat frowned.

'Are you okay, Scott?'

'One-ten over seventy,' Boo said.

'What? Oh, yeah, I'm fine.' He nodded at Boo. 'She's not.'

'Funny,' Boo said. To Cat: 'Someone's got to take care of him.' She pushed the green concoction in front of Scott. 'Drink your smoothie.'

'What's in it?'

'Don't ask.'

'Did you put broccoli in there? I hate broccoli.'

'You really think I would put something you hate in your smoothie just because it's good for you?'

Father and daughter eyed each other.

'Yes, I do.'

Boo rolled her eyes at him, but winked at Cat. Scott picked up the green smoothie and considered it. Cat did as well.

'That looks awful,' she said.

'You're not helping,' Boo said.

'What's in it?' Scott asked.

'Stuff.'

'What stuff?'

'Good stuff. Come on, try it, you'll like it.'

He tried it. He didn't like it.

'It tastes terrible.'

'It can't be good for you and taste good.'

She stood and kissed Scott on his forehead. 'Drink. It's good for you.'

Scott downed the smoothie; Cat grimaced at the sight.

'Thank you,' Boo said.

She padded down the hall.

'Cute kid,' Cat said.

'I like her. Not so much her smoothies.' He stood. 'I need some coffee to get that taste out of my mouth. You want some?'

'Please.'

'Cream?'

'A little.'

He poured two cups and took them to the table.

'Cat, would you like to clean up? I can find something for you to wear.'

'Your ex's clothes?'

He shrugged. 'It's all designer stuff. I might be able to find one of her Cattle Barons' Ball outfits, maybe fringed suede short-shorts and a matching halter top . . . and cowboy boots.'

'Rich Highland Park wives wear stuff like that?'

'Mine did.'

'I don't. I've got an overnight bag in the car with a spare set of clothes. I always pack one. Never know with this job.'

Cat walked out front to the vehicle and stood still a moment. She inhaled the cold air to clear her head. She needed to gather herself. She was an FBI agent; he was federal judge under her protection. She had a huge crush on him; he seemed to have a crush on her. She found herself sexually attracted to him; if she knew men, and she did, he was sexually attracted to her. What the hell was she doing?

273

Risking her job, that's what she was doing.

But she would.

For him.

She would die for him; that was her job.

She would lie with him; that was her desire.

She would protect the judge; she wanted the man.

Shit.

Scott showered in his bathroom and Cat in the girls'. He returned to the kitchen first and set the table. Cat returned clad in snug jeans, the red running shoes, a burnt orange Texas Longhorns sweatshirt, and the waist pack; her dark brown hair hung loose to her shoulders. Her skin was smooth and tan; her eyes were chocolate brown. Her lips were red. She looked too young for how old he felt.

'I'm starving,' she said.

Pajamae stumbled into the kitchen followed closely by Boo. Consuelo's *huevos rancheros* worked better than an alarm clock.

'Pajamae,' Cat said, 'you played a great game last night.'

'Thank you, ma'am.'

'Do you want to play college ball?'

'Yes, ma'am, I do.' She gestured at Cat's sweatshirt. 'I'd love to play at Texas.'

'I ran track at UT.'

That impressed Pajamae. 'You *did*? Were you fast?'

'Pretty fast. I ran the relays, two hundred and four hundred.'

'Did you run in the Olympics?'

'I wasn't that fast. But one of my teammates did.'

'Black girl?'

'Yes.'

Pajamae nodded. 'We dominate track and field . . . and

274

basketball . . . football . . . tennis with Serena . . . golf with Tiger but not so much lately . . . soccer and baseball belong to the Latin American players.'

'I take it you love sports?'

'I do. I want to be a professional basketball player.'

'Well, work hard, maximize your talent, and see where you end up. But always have a plan B.'

'What was your plan B?'

'The FBI.'

'Do you have a badge?'

'Yes, I do.'

'May we see it?'

'You may.'

Cat pulled her badge out of the waist pack and handed it to Pajamae. She and Boo studied it then handed it back.

'Do you have a gun?'

'Yes, I do.'

'May we see it?'

'No. We only take our guns out when absolutely necessary to subdue a bad guy.'

'Have you ever shot a bad guy?'

'Uh, Pajamae,' Scott said. 'That might be—'

'Yes, I have.'

'Did you kill him?'

'No. I shot him in the leg.'

'Because you missed where you were aiming?'

'Because I hit where I was aiming.'

'Did you arrest him?'

'Yes.'

'What did he do bad?'

'He robbed banks.'

'No, shit?' Boo said.

'Boo,' Scott said.

'I mean, no kidding?'

'No kidding. He had robbed fifteen banks. We caught him coming out the sixteenth. He shot at us, we shot back. He was a good bank robber, but a bad shooter.'

'What happened to him?' Pajamae asked.

'He's in prison.'

'My daddy went to prison. Not Judge Fenney, but my biological dad. His name was Eddie.'

'What did he do?'

'Drugs. Dealing. Got my mama hooked on heroin. He was a white boy.'

'Where is he now?'

'Dead.'

'The president wants the Arabs dead before kickoff!'

The president had yelled at the director, so the director now yelled at Beckeman. As if that would further the search for the Arabs.

'I've got to find them before I can kill them. These guys are ghosts.'

'What do you need?'

'I need wiretaps, sneak and peeks, NSA email and phone surveillance – I need it all.'

'You've got anything you need.'

'I need to waterboard Mustafa.'

'Except torture.'

'He knows the Arabs. Who they are and where they are.'

'How do you know?'

'Do you know me? Do you know where to find me?'

'Yes.'

'Why?'

'You work for me.'

'Exactly. They work for him. Give me thirty minutes alone

with him, he'll talk. He's not a soldier, he's a fucking PhD. A professor. He'll talk.'

'The president has a strict policy against torture.'

'And I have eight days to find the Arabs.'

'Do you have any tattoos?' Boo asked the FBI agent named Cat.

'No.'

'Are you thinking about getting one?'

'No.'

'I love tattoos but I'm scared of needles.'

'Good.'

They had walked into Whole Foods. Pajamae tore Consuelo's list in half. The girls went one way with a basket, Cat and Scott the other way with another basket. Cat glanced back at the girls.

'You think they're safe? Maybe we should shop together.'

'It's Whole Foods. They're safe as long as they stay away from the cupcakes.'

The White House sat only six blocks up Pennsylvania Avenue from the J. Edgar Hoover Building. The FBI headquarters was named in honor of a closet gay paranoid whack job who scared the hell out of every president for forty years. Well, maybe not LBJ. He was an even bigger whack job. But not gay. Director Paulson stood in the Oval Office fifteen minutes after hanging up with Beckeman.

'Sir, we haven't had a major attack on the homeland since nine-eleven. We can't have one on your watch. Not if you want this job for another four years.'

The president stared out the window at the Rose Garden. These were the make-or-break decisions presidents had to make. If Mustafa talked and the Arabs were captured or killed before the Super Bowl, the president would be a hero. If Mustafa didn't talk and word got out that he was tortured – and word would get out – the president would go back home after the election. The president turned back to the director.

'No.'

'Mr. President, you're trying to be a good man fighting evil.'

'You want me to fight evil with evil?'

'I want you to keep those people at the Super Bowl alive.'

'Will this prevent a heart attack?'

Boo stood in the Whole Life department. She knew it well. This department was where she kept A. Scott healthy. She held the container up to the clerk.

'Heart attack? Guar gum with psyllium? No, I don't think so. But it'll prevent constipation.'

'That's what Elvis died from.'

'Heart attack?'

'Constipation.'

Scott pushed the basket past the Whole Life department; he spotted Boo talking to a clerk.

'Let's see what Boo found,' Cat said.

'No. You'll only encourage her.'

'I take lots of supplements.'

She ignored his advice and walked over to Boo. Scott followed. Reluctantly. It was like feeding a stray cat.

'What'd you find, Boo?' Cat asked.

'Guar gum with psyllium.'

'I take that.'

'You do?'

'Yep. Fiber. Prevents constipation. Elvis died of that.'

'I know!'

278

She tossed the bottle into the basket. Scott retrieved the bottle, put his glasses on, and checked the price.

'It's twenty-five dollars, Boo.'

'Do you want to die from constipation?'

Boo and Cat stared at him waiting for an answer.

'I'm going to the meat market,' he said.

He dropped the bottle into the basket and headed to the meat market. *Constipation?* He heard Boo and Cat giggling like girls behind him then felt her next to him.

'I like your glasses. Makes you look smart. And I like Boo.'

'Me, too.'

'Is she like your ex?'

'Only her looks.'

'She's beautiful. Was your ex?'

'She was.'

She was thirty-seven, but she looked twenty-seven. Hector Calderon was sixty years old and felt it – except when he was inside her. In such moments he felt young again, in the spring of life, full of the sap. He looked over her and upon the Gulf of Mexico through the open doors of his Cancun beach villa. He was vastly wealthy and could buy anything he desired, but he could not buy youth.

Oh, youth is surely wasted on the young, they say, and so true it is.

Hector prided himself on being educated and erudite, suave and sophisticated, handsome if not hard-bodied. He had had many beautiful young women in his life – they came with the money – but never had he been with a woman who was so like him. Who knew how to dress, how to speak, how to present herself in public. She did not embarrass him in public or disappoint him in private. He felt proud to have her on his arm. She was accustomed to the finer things in life, that was obvious. She had lived a high life in her prior life. She was a bit of a mystery, but he liked that. And he did not worry about her wearing a wire in their private moments because, as now, she was always naked in their private moments.

His eyes returned to her. He had not cared about a woman in so long. They had just been bodies to have sex with. Nothing more. But after a year together, he cared about this woman. His phone rang. Ah, perhaps it was Jorge with his money.

'*Buenos días, patrón.*'

It was not Jorge. It was Pablo.

'What is it, Pablo? I am busy.'

'Jorge, he is still not back from America.'

'Was he arrested?'

'No. I do not think so.'

Jorge Romero would not run off with Hector's $1.2 million. He was too loyal. And he was not that stupid.

'Perhaps he has found an American woman,' Pablo said.

He laughed; Hector did not.

'I will make inquiries,' Hector said.

He hung up the phone and stroked his woman. He soon forgot about Jorge Romero . . . but not about his $1.2 million.

Cat whispered to Scott, 'We're being followed.'

'What?'

She nodded behind him. Scott turned and spotted a six-foot-six, 330-pound black man trying to appear inconspicuous in Whole Foods. Scott walked over.

'Louis, what are you doing here?'

'I'm shopping, Judge Fenney.'

'Where's your basket?'

'Uh, I'd better go get one.'

'Louis, I appreciate your concern for my well-being, but I'm safe with Agent Peña. She's got a gun.'

'I got your back.'

'I know you do. But if you spend too much time in Whole Foods, you'll have tattoos. Go enjoy your weekend.'

Louis' big chest rose and fell with his breath. 'You sure, Judge Fenney?'

'I'm sure. They won't kidnap me again.'

The Whole Foods meat market was a long glass counter filled with sirloin, rib eyes, T-bones, buffalo, chicken, pork, sausage, bacon, shrimp, salmon, and crab.

'You ever eat ostrich?' Cat asked.

'I didn't know you could,' Scott said.

'You can. It tastes great, and it's very lean.'

'I'll try it.'

'We don't have ostrich,' the butcher said over the counter.

'Or not. *Dos pollos* then.'

'You speak Spanish?' Cat asked.

'No.'

Scott hadn't shopped for groceries with a female above the age of thirteen whose name wasn't Consuelo in . . . well, he couldn't remember the last time. Rebecca never shopped for groceries; social climbing did not occur at the grocery store. So she had delegated that duty to Consuelo. And since grocery shopping was not billable time – except for trial lawyers – Scott had had no time for that chore.

He had time now.

And he had a woman above the age of thirteen with him. Of course, she was an FBI agent assigned to protect him, but it almost felt as if they were a couple.

'And four buffalo patties,' he said to the butcher.

'Four?' Cat asked.

'You're staying for dinner.'

'I am?'

'Aren't you?'
'Yes.'

Saddam Siddiqui collected the falafel and walked toward the checkout counters. He cut through the produce department; as he walked past two young girls investigating the bananas, a bag of broccoli fell from their overloaded basket. He stopped and picked up the broccoli.

Scott always checked on the girls, and he did now. He spotted them in produce examining the bananas. Boo was very particular about the bananas she bought. A young man walked up to them, bent over, and handed something to them. He smiled and spoke to them. He looked too old for them.

Scott walked that way.

When he was halfway to the girls, the young man walked away. He looked like the young man Scott had run into there the Saturday before. He had the same dark skin and the same Arab features. When Scott arrived, he said, 'Who was that boy?'

'Oh, I dropped the broccoli,' Boo said. 'He picked it up for us.'

'What did he say?'

'"You dropped your broccoli."'

'That's all?'

'Unh-huh.'

'Oh. Okay.'

Scott turned away but stopped and turned back.

'Is that broccoli for my smoothies?'

'No.'

The director had called Beckeman to relay the president's answer. There would be no enhanced interrogation of Mustafa.

'It's his call.'

'Nothing?'

'Less than nothing.'

'Shit.'

'Only one man knows where the Arabs are holed up.'

'You think he's a bad guy?' Cat said.

'That boy?'

'What boy?'

'Same Arab-looking boy I bumped into here last week. And now today, he was talking to the girls.'

'You think he's stalking you?'

'Seems an odd coincidence.'

'Too odd. Scott, he might be one of the Arabs.' She unzipped her waist pack. 'Show me.'

They left the basket and hurried up and down the aisles and ended their search outside. He was gone. They stood outside the exit doors and stared at the parking lot. Cat zipped up her waist pack.

'I don't like this,' she said. 'I don't like this at all. Why would they abduct the presiding judge? Why would they stalk you?'

'I don't know. Why?'

'To divert our attention. I think the two Arabs who grabbed you are running the plot. I think ISIS is directing them from Syria. I think that's always been the plot. Not Mustafa.'

'What do you think about crepe myrtles along the back fence?'

'What color?'

'Yellow.'

'Yellow's my favorite color.'

'Then yellow it is.'

They were sitting outside on the patio. Scott was drinking a beer, Cat an iced tea. She was still on the job. Buffalo burgers cooked on the charcoal grill. They had talked more about Cat's concerns that his abduction had been to create a diversion, but they had dismissed concerns about the Arab boy at Whole Foods as paranoia, a job hazard for FBI agents and federal judges alike.

'Scott, do you have anyone in your life?'

'My girls.'

'Above the age of thirteen?'

'No.'

'What about the cute teacher at carpool?'

'Kim? No.'

'Or that woman at the game?'

'Penny? Hell, no.'

'Why not?'

'She scares me.'

Cat laughed. 'I mean, why don't you have someone?'

'Oh. The job.'

She nodded. 'It's always the job.'

'What about you? Do you have anyone?'

'My parents.'

'A man?'

'No.'

'Why not?'

'The job.'

Scott drank his beer, she her iced tea. They sat close enough to hold hands, but they did not look at each other.

'Scott . . . do you want someone in your life?'

'Desperately.'

That had come out too honestly. As if he were testifying in court. He cringed with embarrassment . . . until he felt her hand on his. The touch of another human being – not sexual, just a touch that said, *You matter to me,* felt good.

★

'Have you seen *Silence of the Lambs*?' Boo asked Cat.

They ate burgers and baked sweet potato fries on trays on the couch. Scott and Cat bookended Boo and Pajamae.

'Yes.'

'Is it as good as the book?'

'You've read the book?' A. Scott said.

'I didn't say that.'

'Sounded like you said that.'

'A. Scott, I know you wouldn't want me to read a book about a guy named Hannibal the Cannibal and a serial killer named Buffalo Bill even if the heroine is a role model for young women like Clarice Starling.'

Boo smiled at her father.

'I became an FBI agent because of Clarice,' Cat said.

'You're not helping,' A. Scott said.

'Oh. Sorry.'

But she grinned.

'Let's watch *Silence of the Lambs*,' Boo said.

'I don't want to watch a movie about cannibals,' Pajamae said.

Boo sighed. 'Fine.'

They watched *Casablanca*. Boo loved Ingrid Bergman.

'Show Cat how you dance,' Pajamae said. 'She's not going to believe it.'

'I don't think she wants to—'

'I love to dance.'

Boo played country-western music on their phone. The Dixie Chicks. Scott stood and pulled Cat up. He took her in his arms; it felt as if she'd been there all his life. They danced country swing. When the song ended, she threw her arms around his neck.

'Now that's dancing,' she said.

She did not release him. She gazed into his eyes without blinking. For a long, quiet moment. Which was interrupted by Boo's voice.

'Um . . . we're going to bed now.'

Cat released him and appeared embarrassed.

'But it's only nine-thirty,' Pajamae said. 'We can stay up late on weekends.'

Boo gave her sister a stern look.

'Oh, yes, we're very tired. Time for bed.'

They jumped up from the couch.

'We'll probably be asleep in like, two minutes,' Boo said.

'You won't see us until the morning,' Pajamae said.

'Guaranteed,' Boo said.

'Go to bed,' Scott said.

They kissed him and Cat goodnight then ran down the hall.

'They want you to have someone,' Cat said.

'They do.'

'That's sweet.'

'They are.'

The moment turned awkward, then she turned to him.

'You can have me, Scott. You can have me right now.'

She kissed him then pulled back a moment. Her expression changed. She grabbed his face with both hands and kissed him hard. He kissed her back. All the desire he thought had died long ago came alive. She grabbed at his shirt; he pulled her sweatshirt over her head and tossed it aside. Then her bra. They kissed and touched and felt and wanted. She unzipped her jeans and pushed them down. Then her panties. She unzipped his jeans and pushed them down. Then his under-shorts. She led him to the couch and sat him down; then she climbed on top of him and guided him into her. He breathed her in; he had forgotten a woman's scent. He had forgotten how wonderful a woman smelled and felt, how exhilarating it

286

felt to be one with a woman. To feel alive that way. They wrapped their bodies tightly together and clutched each other so close that they seemed to meld into one body, one mind, one soul, one life. For a brief moment on a Saturday night, they were one.

'That was nice,' Scott said.

She frowned. '*Nice?*'

'Uh . . . really nice?'

The frown remained.

'Great?'

A fracture in the frown.

'Incredible?'

A smile.

'That's better.' She kissed him. 'It was. Incredible.'

They sat naked and silent.

'So, what do we do know?' she said.

'We could have sex again. Slowly this time.'

'Could we? You *are* forty.'

She reached down to him. Her eyebrows shot up.

'Oh, we could.'

They did.

'That was nice,' Cat said.

'*Nice?*'

She laughed. 'That was fucking incredible.'

She held this man tight for a few more minutes. She hadn't been with a man in two years . . . or was it three? The job. A 24/7/365 job chasing Islamic terrorists left little time for love or romance or even sex. She ran and worked out to burn up her desire. But when he walked outside that first morning – his eyes as blue as the sky, the uncombed blond hair falling onto his face, the lean, muscular body . . . *shit* – the desire returned with a vengeance. Each day the desire built until she thought she would explode sitting next to him on the couch watching the movie. Then they exploded together. Could it last beyond that night?

'I'd better get home. My folks will be worried.'

'You live with your folks?'

'They live with me.'

She stood and got dressed. He did as well.

'I'll walk you to your car.'

'Better not.'

She checked outside. 'Night shift just arrived. We don't need to start rumors. See you in the morning.'

She went to the back door but stopped.

'Scott, would you and the girls like to come to my house tomorrow for lunch? Meet my folks? My mother wants to cook for you.'

'We'd like that very much.'

She kissed him goodnight.

'That might have been the best day of my life,' she said. 'Well, except when I won the two hundred meters at the NCAA.'

'Of course.'

Beckeman read the latest terrorism briefings while *Body of Lies* played on the big screen. DiCaprio got it right. The CIA had gotten it wrong. All wrong in Iraq. Al Qaeda had been replaced by ISIS. Just when you thought things couldn't get worse, they had. Much worse. The president had called them the JV team, but they were the varsity now. The Russian jet. The Paris attacks. San Bernardino. It was no longer a question of if, only of when. When they killed more Americans in America. A lot more.

Chapter 18

Sunday, 31 January
7 days before the Super Bowl

Scott's phone pinged at 6:45 A.M. It had never pinged before. He reached over to the nightstand and grabbed the phone and his glasses. A red circle with a white '1' inside hovered over the 'Messages' icon. He tapped it. A 'Messages' page came up. There was only one message, from a number he didn't recognize. He tapped it, and the message came up.

Scott, last night was amazing. Both times.

Cat had texted him. He had never before received a text from a woman. Or a man. Or anyone. He was a federal judge. He didn't text.

But she had texted him.

Last night was amazing.

The president wasn't happy when he called the director at 8:00 A.M. at home.

'And?'

289

'Nothing, sir.'

'Nothing at all?'

'No, sir. Mr. President, if you allowed enhanced interrogation—'

'No.'

He hung up on the director.

'Soooo . . . how'd it go last night?'

Boo looked innocently at Scott from across the table. Pajamae stared at her breakfast; she stifled a giggle.

'Fine.'

'*Fine?*' Boo said. 'That's all we get? We went to bed an hour early for *fine?*'

Women needed strong adjectives, Scott decided.

'Cat and I had a wonderful evening.'

That brought a big grin to both girls' faces just as his phone pinged.

'What's that?' Boo asked. 'Is that your phone? Is she texting you?'

Scott checked his phone. She was. He read the text: *I have a surprise for you today.* He could not restrain a smile.

'She is!'

The girls high-fived.

'Now, A. Scott, whatever you do, don't sent photos with both your face and your private parts?'

'*What?*'

'We had an assembly about sexting – you know what that is?'

Scott nodded.

'Well, it seems very yukky to us' – Pajamae nodded emphatically – 'but kids send each other pics of their private parts all the time. So the speaker, she said don't put your face in any photo with your private parts.'

'Keep your face and your privates separate,' Pajamae said.

'Good rule if I've ever heard one,' Scott said.

'That way,' Boo said, 'if the photo gets out on the Internet, no one can put your face with your privates, which would be embarrassing.'

'Very.'

They stared at him.

'Well?' Boo said.

'Well, what?'

'Aren't you going to text her back?'

'Uh . . . no.'

'You've got to.'

'Why?'

'That's how it's done.'

'Eat your breakfast.'

'Why didn't you text me back?'

'Uh . . .'

Cat frowned but shook him off. This was new territory for Scott: a relationship. What he had had with Rebecca had been more of a financial arrangement: he got a trophy; she got a mansion, a Mercedes, designer clothes, and social standing.

'So this is the family room,' Cat said. 'And yes, that is a near-life-sized nativity scene in the corner.'

Cat had come over and gone to church with Scott and the girls – in her professional capacity – and then had taken them to her house in East Dallas for lunch – in her personal capacity. She lived with her parents in a Tudor-style house in the M streets not far from Bobby and Karen, a gentrified area of town north of downtown and east of the expressway. It was about the size of Scott's house – federal employees don't live in McMansions – and had been renovated to perfection by her father. His name was Diego. He lived and died the Dallas

291

Cowboys. A big-screen television hung on the wall opposite the nativity scene and below a massive crucifix. He sat in a leather recliner watching the Super Bowl pregame show, which began a week before the game.

'Look, the Patriots, they arrived in town this morning,' Diego said.

On the television, the players entered their hotel in downtown Dallas to a crowd of their fans who had made the two thousand mile trip from Boston. Scott and Cat walked over to the nativity scene.

'I found the statues in Nuevo Laredo,' Diego said. 'The burros, they are lifelike, are they not?'

'They are,' Scott said. He regarded the scene a moment. 'Well, you don't see that every day.'

'Oh, you haven't seen anything yet,' Cat said.

She led him down the hall to the master suite, which her parents occupied. It was a large room with a modern bathroom at one end and an alcove at the other. She hit the lights and took him into the alcove.

'A shrine to Our Lady of Guadalupe complete with a working fountain made to look like a grotto.'

A life-sized statue of the Virgin Mary stood above the fountain. A rack of prayer candles stood beside the fountain.

'My mother lights every candle every day.'

'Do you have fire insurance?'

'Of course.'

'It's quite a house.'

'It's not a house. It's a shrine. You want to see my car?'

'Is Jesus driving?'

'Funny.'

He followed her back down the hall and through the kitchen – Cat's mother was teaching the girls how to make churros, long deep-fried fritters sprinkled with sugar and cinnamon;

292

they had powdered sugar all over their hands and faces – and out the back door. The patio and backyard had been made into a hacienda-style walled courtyard featuring more religious statues. A door in the wall led into a detached garage. Cat turned the lights on; in the middle of the garage sat a bright yellow two-door coupe.

'It's yellow,' Scott said.

'Dodge Challenger. Six-point-four liter HEMI V-eight with a six-speed stick.'

'It's yellow.'

'Four hundred eighty-five horses under the hood.'

'It's yellow.'

'I know it's yellow. I told you, yellow is my favorite color.'

'That's a lot of yellow.'

She opened the driver's door.

'And red leather upholstery,' Scott said.

'I'm Mexican. Get in.'

Scott glanced from the red seats to her brown eyes. 'In the car?'

'The back seat.'

'Why?'

'It's your surprise. I always wanted to have sex in the back seat of a car, but I never did. Today's the day. Get in.'

'I'm a federal judge.'

'You're a man. I'm a woman. Get in the fucking car.'

He hesitated.

'Do I have to pull my weapon?'

He got in. She pulled her jeans off and followed him in. She unzipped him and straddled him; the car smelled of leather and Cat Peña. And for a little while on red leather seats in a yellow muscle car parked in a garage in an East Dallas Catholic shrine, they were teenagers at the drive-in movie.

★

'My son, he was only thirteen. The cartel in Nuevo Laredo, they abducted him because he would not run the drugs for them. They use boys because they cannot be tried as adults. They shot Raul in the head.'

Sofia stood. 'I must light a candle.'

She walked out. They were sitting in the nativity room. The girls were sitting *in* the nativity, astride the burros.

'Sofia, she still suffers. As do I. The *policia*, they did nothing because they were all on the cartel payroll. I realized that I could no longer protect my family in Mexico. A man must protect his family. Sofia, she was pregnant with Catalina. I wanted to protect my family. So we came to America. We knew it would take years to do so legally, but the cartels would not allow us that much time. They took over Mexico with money and guns from America, so they drive Mexicans north to America. Thirty-two years ago, we crossed the river outside Nuevo Laredo.'

An awkward silence filled the room.

'Scott, my parents, they're here illegally.'

'I'm a judge, not ICE.'

Immigration and Customs Enforcement.

'Thank you.'

'Odd, is it not?' her father said. 'Americans don't want us here, but Americans fund and arm the cartels that drive us here. What they call, unintended consequences.'

'We're so concerned about ISIS ten thousand miles away,' Cat said, 'but we're completely unconcerned about Mexican cartels only a hundred and fifty feet away across the Rio Grande.'

'The cartels haven't tried to blow up a football stadium filled with a hundred thousand Americans,' Scott said.

'True. But they've killed a hundred thousand Mexicans in the last ten years, just on the other side of the river. And they

294

send *sicarios* north to kill in America. We had a case in an affluent Dallas suburb three years ago, man and his wife sitting in their car outside a Victoria's Secret. White SUV pulls up, masked man gets out, walks to the car, and shoots the man nine times in the head – victim had been a lawyer for the Gulf Cartel, tried to hide out in suburban America. Shooter gets back in the SUV and disappears. We nabbed them just last month, trying to come back into the U.S. in Matamoros. Father and son, Mexican cops, coming up for another hit. We have an entire task force chasing *sicarios*.'

'I didn't know.'

'No one does. Point is, the cartels have killed more, beheaded more, and terrorized more people than ISIS. We give Syrians fleeing ISIS terror refuge in America – why not my parents? They fled terror, too. But we say they're "illegal aliens" instead of "political refugees." Look at them. They're not alien at all.'

'They don't look like aliens to me,' Pajamae said from the burro.

'That was a scary movie,' Boo said.

'You saw *Alien*?' Scott asked.

Pajamae nodded; she could not lie.

'We claim the Fifth,' Boo said.

'Are my parents guilty?' Cat asked.

'Of what?'

'Entering the country illegally.'

'We are innocent,' Diego said. 'We were running for our lives.'

'They've waited thirty-two years for justice,' Cat said.

'Catalina had to be born in America to be an American,' Diego said, 'so we made our way to San Antonio. There she was born. I was trained in carpentry, so I began working with homebuilders. Eventually, I started my own business renovating homes. We moved here three years ago when Catalina was

295

assigned to the task force. I am now seventy-two, so I have retired except for my daughter's house. And I build shrines in other houses.'

'Is there a demand for that?'

'Oh, yes. I could work full time building shrines.'

'You've got a niche market.'

'Yes, and I get paid in cash so I don't have to pay taxes.'

'Uh, Dad . . .' Cat gave her father a look. 'He's a federal judge.'

'Oh, so he is.' Diego turned to Scott with a half smile: 'I was just kidding.'

'I'm not the IRS either.'

'I am glad your kidnappers did not kill you.'

'Me, too.'

'So my daughter, she now protects you?'

'Yes.'

'She is a very good shot with her guns.'

'*Guns?*' Scott turned to Cat. 'How many guns do you have?'

She shrugged. 'A few.'

'Is that more or less than ten?'

'Do bazookas count?'

'Is this a date?' Boo asked.

Cat sat with the girls on the back patio.

'What?'

'Us coming over? Are you and A. Scott on a date?'

'Well . . .' She thought of their tryst in the car. 'Maybe . . . no, it's not a date.'

'Then ask him on a date.'

'Isn't the man supposed to ask the woman?'

'If you wait for him to ask you out, we'll be out of college before we have a mother.'

'You want a mother?'

'We do. Or at least a big sister. We think you'd be a good one. Either one.'

Pajamae nodded.

'You do?'

Boo reached to the back pocket of her jeans and pulled out a cell phone.

'We could text.'

'Okay.'

She held the phone out to Cat. 'You put your number in our phone, and we'll put our number in your phone.'

Cat took the phone and typed.

'But no sexting,' Boo said. 'Save that for A. Scott.'

'Is that Baby Jesus?' Pajamae asked.

She was pointing at a statue of the Virgin Mary holding Baby Jesus.

'It is.'

'I've never seen that in someone's backyard.'

'You've never been to Mexico.'

Lunch consisted of chilies rellenos, enchiladas, tacos, chalupas, guacamole, refried beans, flautas, tortillas, flan, and churros. Food crowded the table, and they crowded around the table. Cat stuck a long churro in her mouth and gave Scott a brown-eyed look across the table.

'So, Judge Fenney—'

Diego waved a churro at him.

'Scott.'

'So, Judge Scott, have you heard about the president's executive order granting amnesty to illegal Mexicans?'

Scott glanced from Diego to Sofia to Cat to Diego.

'I have.'

'And now Texas has sued him to stop the amnesty.'

'Yes, they have.'

'We are praying the president wins. If he wins, we win.'

'I light six candles each day,' Sofia said.

'Do you know the judge who will decide?' Diego said.

'Dad, he can't talk about that.' Cat turned to him. 'Sorry, Scott, their lives hang in the balance with that case, so they're living and dying it.'

'Oh. I am sorry, Judge Scott,' Diego said.

'Diego, Sofia . . . Cat . . . do you watch the Sunday-morning political talk shows?'

'No. We go to church.'

'A smart choice. Do you read the newspapers?'

'We stopped taking the paper. I read the sports online.'

'Why do you ask, Scott?' Cat asked.

He again studied their faces. Everyone in Dallas knew that he was the presiding judge in the terrorist case; perhaps everyone didn't know that he was also the presiding judge in the immigration case.

'Because I know the judge on the case.'

'Is he a fair judge?' Diego asked.

'I hope so.'

'Who is he?' Cat asked.

'Me.'

'Scott, I'm sorry,' Cat said. 'I didn't know. If I did, I wouldn't have let my dad go on and on.'

They had said goodbye to her parents. Cat had walked them out to the car.

'You didn't know.'

'Is Consuelo here illegally, too?'

'She was. She got a green card.'

'How?'

'I don't know. I think Judge Buford had something to do with it.'

'He was the judge before you, the one that died?'

Scott nodded. 'I think he went to bat for her.'

'Lucky her.' She sighed. 'My folks don't have a federal judge batting for them.'

The moment suddenly felt awkward.

'Cat, is the case going to be an issue between us?'

'No, of course not, Scott. That's your job. I would never hold your job against you.'

'Good.'

'I mean, if I had to shoot your dad because he was a bad guy, you wouldn't hold that against me, would you?'

'Maybe I'll be another Clarice Starling when I grow up,' Boo said. 'Or another Cat Peña.'

'I'll hire you as my private bodyguard,' Pajamae said, 'like Cat guards Judge Fenney.'

'That'll be cool.'

Scott was tucking the girls into bed.

'A. Scott, we love Cat.'

'You do?'

'Do you?'

'Little early for that, Boo.'

'You do. Good. Because she's the one. You've got to marry her.'

'Boo . . .'

'We need a mother.'

'She's too young to be your mother.'

'A big sister then. We're coming into our YA years.'

'YA?'

'Young adult.'

'Am I not doing a good job?'

'You're a great father. But you're not a mother. Or a big sister.'

'I try.'

'Try with Cat. Please.'

'She likes to run,' Pajamae said.

'She does.'

'And she's beautiful.'

'She is.'

'So what's not to love?'

'Is she paying you two?'

'*Pro bono*,' Boo said.

'Whereas, Judge Fenney.'

Boo gave him a devious look. 'She can sleep over.'

'Stop saying that.'

'The judge, he will decide the case? The president's executive order?'

'Yes, Father, he will.'

Her father smiled. 'Then surely he will save us.'

'Why do you say that?'

'Because he loves our daughter.'

That night, lying in bed, Scott thought about Catalina Peña. Out of his abduction came Cat. For the first time since Rebecca, he had a woman in his life, and it felt good. She seemed to have bonded with the girls, and they with her. Did she want to be their mother or at least their big sister? And more important, could he rule against the president – against her parents – and still have her?

He wanted her.

His phone pinged. He put on his glasses and opened the message. A photo was attached. He opened the photo and inhaled sharply. The photo was of Cat lying on her bed with a long churro in her mouth. He made a mental note to tell Cat the girls' sexting rule: no face and private parts in the same photo.

★

A black sedan occupied by two FBI agents sat outside the Fenney home. They drank coffee to stay warm and awake.

'You really think Peña's screwing the judge?'

'Word is, she was in the house late last night, and the judge and his girls went to her house for lunch today.'

'Her mom makes the best breakfast tacos.'

'That's not the point.'

'What's the point?'

'We're not supposed to fuck on the job.'

'Just fuck up on the job.'

The two agents laughed.

'Like Waco.'

'That was a big fuckup.'

'And Hanssen.'

'Also a big fuckup.'

'And that hair analysis fiasco, two hundred convictions bounced because agents enhanced their testimony, said they were positive matches when they were maybes at best.'

'Stop, you're depressing me.'

'I'm so bored.'

'You sound like my five-year-old boy.'

'Two crack agents like ourselves, we should be searching for those Arabs that snatched the judge, not sitting out here in the cold all night so he doesn't get snatched again.'

'Those guys are ghosts. Gone back to Syria. They're not within a thousand miles of the judge. Guaranteed.'

Two cars behind the FBI car, Abdul jabbar and his little brother sat in a Kia.

'The judge is not going to release the imam,' Abdul said.

'As you predicted,' his little brother said.

'Yes. It is time for "or else."'

'No, Abdul, I really do not want to do that. It is very wrong.'

301

'There is no right or wrong in our fight for freedom.'

'*Freedom?* We are free. We live in America. I love America!'

Abdul slapped his brother's face.

His face stung from his brother's hand but more from his disapproval. He had not pleased his father; he wanted to please his brother. He had yearned for his father's love, but it had never been forthcoming; he desperately needed his brother's love. So he had followed him to Dallas. How far would he follow him?

'America killed our father. To love America is to dishonor our father. We must avenge our father's death.'

'Brother, I don't want to live in the Islamic caliphate in Syria. I want to live here in Dallas. I want to be a lawyer.'

'You will not be a lawyer, and you will not live in Syria or in Dallas.'

'What will I do?'

'You will die in Dallas.'

Chapter 19

Monday, 1 February
6 days before the Super Bowl

'Are you fucking the judge?'

'*What?*'

'You heard me.'

Cat Peña glared at Beckeman. She wanted to punch him. She had just walked into the FBI headquarters after running with Scott and escorting him to the courthouse; Beckeman hadn't allowed her a cup of coffee before attacking her.

'Yes. As often as I can.'

The two special agents of the Federal Bureau of Investigation locked eyes like kids seeing who would blink first. Neither did.

'Sex on the job?' he said. 'This ain't the Secret Service.'

'A, I'm not having sex on the job. And B, what I do off the job is none of your fucking business.'

'Your fucking is my business when you're fucking a federal judge under FBI protection.'

'Then put me on the fucking manhunt.'

Cat could tell his military mind was working through the implications of having her on the hunt for the Arabs – and her mouth in the twice-daily meetings.

'I don't think so.'

'So I can keep fucking the judge?'

Her boss glared at her a moment then turned and marched away. She gave his back the finger.

'I'm sexting him, too!'

Karen entered the judge's chambers but did not find Scott. She heard noises from his private restroom – *how could men make such noises?* – so she walked around to his side of the big desk and placed the various case orders on the desk pad for his signature. Routine court matters. Discovery. Trial settings. Denials of motions for summary judgment. His cell phone sat on the desk; it pinged. She often answered his personal phone, in case the girls or the school were calling. She was as close to a wife as Scott had now. She picked up the phone; it was open to the message page. There was a message . . . and a photo . . . of a woman's bare bottom. The restroom door opened; Scott emerged and came over to the desk. Karen held the phone out to him.

'It's for you.'

He took the phone and looked at the photo. His blond face turned red.

'Uh . . .'

'I don't want to know.'

Karen walked around to her side of the desk and sat.

'I'm seeing Agent Peña.'

Karen was his court clerk, briefing attorney, friend, moral compass, and surrogate mother to the girls. He punted most sex questions to her; she never complained. He would not be a good father without her. Or a good judge.

'By seeing, you mean having sex?'

'Yes.'

'That's her butt?'

Scott nodded.

'I bet she can't even spell cellulite,' Karen said.

'Is this how relationships work these days? Sexting?'

Karen blushed.

'Wait . . . no . . . not you and Bobby?'

She shrugged. 'Sometimes, you know, to spice things up after a long week.'

'I feel like the world left me behind,' Scott said.

The phone pinged again. Another photo from Cat. Of Cat. He blew out a breath. He looked up to Karen grinning.

'You're catching up fast. But no face and body parts in the same photo.'

Scott nodded. 'The girls told me. I need to tell Cat.' He held the phone out to Karen. 'See?'

Karen threw her hands up as if he had thrown the phone at her.

'No! Please, I don't want to see that.'

Scott put the phone face down on the desk.

'You like her?' Karen asked.

'I do. But there are issues.'

'She's got a great butt and carries a gun. What could be an issue?'

'Her parents are residing here illegally.'

'You've already met her parents?'

'We went to her house yesterday, for lunch.'

'The girls, too?'

Scott nodded. 'They love her.'

'Is she going to take my job?'

'She's not a lawyer.'

305

'As their mother?'

'Too early to tell. But the thought has crossed my mind. Maybe God's giving me a second chance at love.'

'I hope so, Scott. I really do. But now you're conflicted?'

He nodded. 'Her parents are good people.'

'I'm sure they are. But they're irrelevant to the case.'

'The case will affect them. My decision will affect real people.'

'It's called being a federal judge.'

Scott pondered her words a moment. 'Do you get tired of always being right?'

'No. Bobby gets tired of my always being right, but I don't.'

Karen stood and walked to the door. She turned back.

'The parties are pestering me for your ruling. You want me to write a first draft?'

'Yeah.'

'Which way?'

'Both ways.'

Carlos entered at a fast clip. Scott had asked Karen to send him in.

'You need me, boss?'

Scott opened his desk drawer and removed an envelope. He tossed it to Carlos.

'For you and Louis.'

Carlos opened the envelope. He removed the contents and stared as if he were looking at Willy Wonka's Golden Ticket (the girls loved that movie as well). For a moment, Scott thought Carlos might cry on his leather jacket.

'Super Bowl tickets,' Carlos said. 'On the fifty-yard line.'

'The NFL gave me two tickets.'

'Thanks, boss. I gotta find the big man.'

He ran out. Scott had run with Cat, dropped the girls off at school, and driven to the courthouse. He had no morning hearings, so he had reread the briefs in the immigration case. He thought of Diego and Sofia Peña. If he ruled in favor of the president, he would give them amnesty. Once the president's order was implemented, there would be no putting the genie back in the bottle. A decision in favor of the president would give the Peñas what they had waited thirty-two years for. How many others like them were out there? Good people seeking safety or a future. His decision would affect real people's lives all across America. A state judge's decisions affected only the parties to the lawsuit and sometimes the citizens of that state. A federal judge's decisions affected every person in America. A federal judge didn't rule only on the law of Texas or California; he ruled on the law of the land. Such was the power of a federal judge. And the responsibility. A. Scott Fenney was feeling the weight of that responsibility when his secretary's voice came over the intercom. It was almost noon.

'Judge, the attorney general is on line one.'

Scott picked up the receiver. 'Hello, Mac.'

'Scott, how are you? No one tried to snatch you off the streets lately, have they?'

'Not so far.'

'Don't worry. I hear Peña's a shooter. And pretty.'

There was a pause in the conversation, as if Mac expected a manly reply from Scott; he resisted.

'So what can I do for you, Mac?'

'Dismiss the lawsuit.'

'Which one?'

'The immigration case.'

'We've had one round of oral arguments, another next week. I've read the briefs, including an *amicus* by Bookman at UT.'

'He rides a Harley.'

'He knows con law.'

'And he said the president exceeded his authority?'

307

'He did.'

Mac laughed. 'It's not the first time in history a president has done that.'

'How does the president have that authority under the Constitution?'

'He doesn't.'

'Then why did he exercise that authority?'

'Off the record?'

'Sure.'

'Because he can. Unless a federal judge stops him. Not many judges do. Him or any prior president. Only two executive orders in history have been overturned by the courts – Truman's seizure of the steel mills and Clinton's one about strike-breakers working for federal contractors. That's out of thousands of executive orders.'

'Why only two?'

'Because federal judges are lawyers first, and lawyers are ambitious by nature. District court judges want to be appeals court judges. Appeals court judges want to be Supreme Court justices. So not many will stand in the president's way, not when the president must nominate them to a higher bench. You're young, Scott. You've got a long judicial career in front of you. Do you really want to fuck it up so soon?'

'My duty is to the Constitution, not the president.'

'Please don't make me mad, Scott.'

'You said I'm a federal judge, so someone will always be mad at me.'

'I didn't mean me.'

'Mac, I can live with your being mad at me.'

'I'm sure you can. But can Agent Peña's folks? They're good people, Scott. I'd hate to see them deported.'

It took Scott a moment to gather himself.

'Is there anything about me you don't know?'

'If there is, I don't know it.' Mac chuckled. 'Scott, dismiss the lawsuit. I've got enough problems dealing with Muslims, I've got no time for Mexicans.'

Boo waved at the brown-skinned workers tending the gardens in Highland Park – even in February – and skipped along the sidewalk being very careful not to step on a crack and break her back. Pajamae jogged alongside; the girl never walked or skipped or hopped. She ran.

'It's so nice living here,' Pajamae said. 'Down in the projects, you can't walk home from school. Men say nasty things to you and try to seduct you.'

'Do you mean seduce or abduct?'

'Both.'

It was nice to live in Highland Park, Boo had to admit. She had never felt scared or nervous without Scott. She always worried about him when he wasn't with them, but never about herself. She was safe in Highland Park. She . . . knew something wasn't right the moment she walked in the back door.

First, the door was open.

Second, Maria had dirtied herself; the stink hit Boo like a fist to her stomach.

And third, Consuelo was gagged and bound to a chair.

'Consuelo!' Boo screamed.

'Oh, sweet Jesus!' Pajamae said. 'A home invasion! Did they rob us?'

'We don't have home invasions in Highland Park.'

Consuelo tried to scream through the gag, but all that came out was a muffle. Her eyes were wide like she was scared, and she shook her head violently. Boo and Pajamae ran to her. But she looked past them.

They turned and knew what she was trying to say.

★

The voice of Scott's secretary again came over the intercom. It was almost one.

'Judge, the school is on line one.'

He punched line one and put the receiver to his ear.

'This is Judge Fenney.'

'Hello, Judge. This is Ruth Williams, the principal.'

'Oh, I'm sorry, Ms. Williams, you're calling about the speaking invitation. I apologize, I was—'

'Abducted.'

'Yes. A bit tied up.' She chuckled. 'So what's the date?'

'Judge, I wasn't calling about that.'

'No? Then what about?'

'Your girls.'

Scott sighed. He knew what was coming. Another kid had taunted Pajamae, so Boo had jumped in to defend her sister, which usually involved her fists. She had a good right cross for a kid. Her standard response upon being sent to Ms. Williams' office was, 'Call my lawyer.' Ms. Williams had.

'Was anyone hurt?' he asked.

'*Hurt?* Who?'

'The kid that Boo punched.'

'Boo punched someone? Again?'

'Isn't that why you're calling?'

'Oh. Well, usually, but not this time. I was just inquiring about your girls.'

'What about my girls?'

'Their family emergency. Why they had to go home in the middle of the day.'

The back door to the house was ajar.

After throwing down the phone and calling for Louis, Scott had sat still for a few moments to gather himself. He wasn't

310

given to panic, and he couldn't give in to panic; but panic threatened to overwhelm his thoughts. He took several deep breaths until his breathing calmed. He knew the girls would either be at home or gone, taken by the same men who had taken him. If they were at home, he would kiss them and hold them and never forget the fear of losing them that he now felt. If they were not at home, if they were gone, if they had been taken by the men who had taken him, he would search for them, he would find them, and he would kill the men who took them. He knew it was within him to do such a thing and that knowledge scared him. On the elevator down to the garage, he had said a simple prayer.

Please God, let them be at home.

He also decided that he didn't want to bring the FBI into the matter or his house. He wasn't sure why. But if God answered his prayer, the FBI would not be needed. If God did not answer his prayer, he would need to assess the situation himself first. And he did not need their protection; he had Louis. So Louis had driven them in his black Dodge Charger; Scott had ducked his head when they exited the garage past the SWAT team.

Scott and Louis stood just outside the house. No sounds came from inside. Scott gave the door a slight push. The door swung open slowly to reveal the kitchen sink and counter, the stove and oven, the refrigerator, the table, Maria sleeping in her high chair, and Consuelo bound and gagged in a chair. Her eyes got wide when she saw Scott.

'Is there anyone in the house?' Scott asked her.

She shook her head. They stepped inside.

'Louis, check the house.'

Scott removed the gag from Consuelo first.

'*Señor* Judge, *dos hombres*, they took the girls!'

Scott dropped to his knees. *No.* Fear clamped down on his mind like a vice. Fear for his girls. Fear of what he would do when he found them. And find them he would. God had not answered his prayer. Instead, He had set Scott on a path that would lead him to kill. And kill he would.

'Did they hurt them?'

'No, *Señor* Judge. They put the rag over their mouths, and the girls, they went limp. They carried them out like sacks of potatoes.'

Louis returned to the kitchen. 'The house is clear, Judge.'

'Consuelo, what did the men look like?'

'*El presidente.*'

'What?'

'They wore the masks like Bush and the dead president, and they wore the gloves.'

'Same two men. They're smart. No ID and no fingerprints.'

'They left the note.'

On the table sat the girls' cell phone on top of a single piece of paper laid flat. Scott patted his pockets for his glasses; he had left them in his chambers. He handed the note to Louis. He read it aloud.

'Judge, we have your girls. If you go to the FBI, we will cut their heads off and send them back in boxes. Tell the FBI nothing, except that your girls are sick with the flu. Do nothing different. Run each morning with your FBI girlfriend. Go to court. Hear your cases. Do your job. But release the imam. This is the "or else," Judge. Release him or you will never see your girls alive again.'

'I'm scared, I'm scared, I'm scared, oh, dear Lord Jesus, help me I'm so scared.'

'*Shh*,' Boo said to her sister. 'Calm down.'

'I can't.'

Boo whispered. 'Pajamae, we'll be okay. A. Scott will save us.'

'I know.'

'Then why are you freaking out?'

'Because being tied up freaks me out.'

'Why?'

'When I was little, my mama tied me up when she got sick so I didn't wander off. When the sickness passed, she untied me.'

Their hands were tied and blindfolds covered their eyes, but they were not gagged. The men had said they would not gag them because they might throw up from the chloroform, whatever that is; her tummy did feel yukky. But only if they were quiet. Thankfully, the men had the TV on loud; it was in a foreign language, but not Spanish.

'Hey,' Boo called out. 'We need a little help over here.'

She heard footsteps on the wood floor.

'What?'

It was the good brother. The other boy – she could tell from their voices and the words they used that they weren't grown-ups – was mean. He was the bad brother.

'Can you untie my sister? She's freaking out.'

Boo recounted Pajamae's childhood story for him.

'That is so sad. Her mother was a heroin addict?'

'She died of an overdose.'

'I will my ask my brother.' He did not walk away. Instead he shouted. 'Abdul, can I untie the little black girl? She is scared to be tied up. When she was a small child—'

'No names!'

'My bad.'

'And tell her to shut up before I cut her fucking head off and send it to the judge in a box!'

The good brother whispered to Boo. 'I think that is a hard no.'

'Why are y'all doing this?'

'So your father will release the imam.'

'But he wants to bomb the Super Bowl.'

'Exactly.'

Pajamae cried, 'I'm so scared.'

'She's having a panic attack.'

'Maybe cat will help.'

'Cat's here?' Pajamae said.

'What?' Boo said. 'No, Cat's not here. I think he has a cat.'

Boo heard the purr of a cat.

'Here,' he said, 'I'm putting the cat in your lap, little black girl. Maybe the cat will calm you down.'

The phone pinged, but Scott did not open the message. Bobby read the abductors' note; he shook his head then handed the note to Karen. She sobbed. She passed the note to Carlos, who read it and gave it to Louis. He had driven Scott back to the courthouse.

'Since I became a Muslim,' Louis said, 'I haven't wanted to kill another man. But I want to kill those two men.' He turned wet eyes up to Scott. 'I want to kill them bad.'

'Badly,' Karen said softly through tears.

'No, Ms. Herrin. Bad. I want to hurt them bad, taking our girls.'

Everything Scott had in the world had been ripped from him. He was a federal judge. He wielded great power in his courtroom. But he felt powerless. How would he get them back?

'What if they hurt the girls,' Karen said. 'I read about what those ISIS men do to . . .'

So had Scott.

'They didn't hurt me,' he said. 'They won't hurt the girls.'

Or so he wanted to believe. But what if they did? What if they hurt his daughters? A. Scott Fenney was not a violent

314

man, but he could be. He would be. If they hurt his daughters, he would be very violent.

'Let's search for them,' Carlos said.

'Where?' Bobby said. 'They could be anywhere.'

'We can GPS their cell phone.'

Scott pulled the girls' cell phone from his pocket.

'They don't have their phone.'

'Shit.'

'Scotty, we've got to go to the FBI,' Bobby said. 'We're amateurs. We need professionals.'

'FBI's been looking for these two guys for two weeks,' Carlos said, 'since they kidnapped the judge. They can't find their butts with both hands.'

'Scotty, what are we going to do?'

'Beg.'

'I'm begging you.'

Federal judges do not speak privately with criminal defendants. That's a rule. But what rules apply when terrorists take your children? Scott stood outside the detention cell; the imam sat inside. Iron bars separated the two men, but their religious beliefs divided them. Scott had handed the abductors' note to Mustafa. He read it then handed it back to Scott.

'Shame.'

'Please release my girls.'

'I cannot do that.'

'They're just little girls. They didn't hurt anyone.'

'Judge, I cannot release your girls because I did not take your girls.'

'Your men did.'

'They are not my men.'

'They kidnapped me to get you released. Why would they do that if they're not your men?'

315

'I do not know. You should go to the FBI.'

'They said they'd behead my girls.'

'And they will.'

'So you know them?'

'No. Beheading is part of the plan.'

'What plan?'

'The plan to put terror into the hearts of the unbelievers.'

'But we want to live in peace with Muslims.'

'We don't want to live in peace with you. We want to live under Sharia.'

Scott sighed and pulled a chair next to the bars. The imam held the key to his daughters' freedom. He knew the men holding them; he could order them freed. Scott had to find a way into his heart, a father-to-father connection with this man. For his girls.

'I've watched your YouTube videos and interviews. Here in America, you have the freedom to say all that.'

'Then why am I in this jail for saying all that?'

'You're in this jail because the government thinks you conspired to use a weapon of mass destruction.'

'And what do you think?'

'I think your men kidnapped my children to get you released.'

'Are you going to release me?'

'No.'

'Then why would I take your children?'

Scott's shoulders slumped. 'Why?'

'Why what?'

'Why all of this? Why terrorism?'

'Why are you asking me? Ask the Christian and Jewish terrorists.'

'What Christian and Jewish terrorists?'

'The American and Israeli armies. The biggest terrorists in the world are the Americans, followed closely by the Jews.'

'Omar, my children are innocent.'

'Oh, we are on a first-name basis now? Well, Scott, innocent Muslim children die every day in the Middle East, killed by weapons made in the USA. Why should American children be exempted from death?'

And Scott realized that there was no way into this man's heart. Hate had turned his heart to stone. Scott stood and walked to the door but stopped at the imam's voice.

'So, Judge, are you going to release me to save your daughters?'

'No. They want you out because they can't execute the plot without you. If I release you, you'll bomb the stadium. You'll kill a hundred thousand people.'

'You would sacrifice your children for strangers in a football stadium?'

'No. I'm going to find my girls and kill your men. Then I might release you so I can kill you, too.'

The imam smiled slightly and looked at Scott over his reading glasses.

'When I get out of this cell – and I will, you know that, you are a judge – my standing among Muslims around the world will rival the caliph. Omar al Mustafa defied America and won. And you will help me win.'

'Why would I do that?'

'Because you are a man of principle. A true believer. In the Constitution. That it was meant to protect people like me.'

'Abdul, those people are disgusting. Why do you watch those videos?'

Abdul watched ISIS beheading videos like his brother watched football. After his father's death, his path in life had blurred. But when he had first watched the ISIS video, *The Clanging of the Swords, Parts 1–4*, it was as if his path had come

317

into focus. He knew his destiny in life, which was death. Abdul removed the video from the player and tossed the remote to his little brother.

'Watch football.'

His little brother changed the channel to ESPN but he was not his same giddy self. It was media day at the Super Bowl. Reporters interviewed the players. Rich athletes. 'The life of this world is but a sport and a diversion,' the Koran said. They should be praying to Allah. Soon they will. For mercy. His little brother looked so sad, Abdul felt obliged to cheer him up.

'So, brother, who do you think will win, the Cowboys or the Patriots?'

'The Muslims.'

'How can you not find two Arabs in Dallas, for Christ's sake?' the director yelled at Beckeman. 'I mean, how many Arabs can there be?'

'About a hundred fifty thousand.'

'In *Dallas*?'

'Yep. We've cleared hundreds of males at the mosque. We have hundreds more to clear.'

'We have six days.'

'I know. Ask the president again—'

'I did. He said no again.'

Scott tried to focus on the lawyers, but he could think only of his daughters. He had eaten breakfast with them and taken them to school. They had kissed him before jumping out of the car. He had watched them run up the sidewalk and disappear inside the school. What if they had disappeared from his life?

'What do you want us to do?'

Scott snapped to the moment. He realized every person in the courtroom was waiting for him to speak.

'I'm sorry, what?'

His cell phone vibrated. He checked the number: 'Unknown.'

It was the girls. They had escaped and borrowed a phone. They were calling their father to come get them. He jumped up.

'Thirty minute recess.'

Scott bounded down from the bench and through the rear door leading to his offices and chambers. The crew followed on his heels. Carlos shut the door behind them. Scott placed the phone on his desk and activated the speaker. Everyone gathered around.

'Boo?'

'Hello again, Judge.'

A man's voice he recognized. The girls had not escaped.

'We have your daughters.'

'If you hurt my girls—'

'You are threatening me? When I can slit your daughters' throats any time I want? Judge, threats at this time are not wise.'

'Please don't hurt them.'

'That is much better.'

'What do you want?'

'You know what we want – release the imam.'

'Let me speak to them.'

'Okay. I will do that for you.'

The bad brother whispered to Boo, 'You say anything to give us away, I will cut your throat from ear to ear.'

'I won't.'

'I am putting the call on the speaker. Talk. Your father can hear you.'

319

'A. Scott?'

'Are you okay, honey?'

'Yeah.'

'Don't be scared.'

'I'm not. Pajamae is, but I'm not.'

Scott could hear Pajamae's voice in the background: 'Judge Fenney, help us! I'm scared!'

They were alive. Scott breathed out with relief. Karen buried her face in her hands and cried.

'Calm down, Pajamae. It'll be okay.'

Boo came back on the phone: 'Panic attack. She can't stand to be tied up.'

'You're tied up?'

'And blindfolded. But they took the gags off. We can talk.'

'Are you hungry?'

'They gave us food. Falafel. Whatever the heck that is.'

'Boo, be brave. I'll find you. I'll come for you.'

'Will you please kill this asshole?'

'I will.'

'I'd really appreciate that.'

Scott heard a man's laughter and then his voice.

'She is a real pistol, the redheaded one. Judge, do hurry and release the imam. Before I send her pretty little red head back to you in a box.'

In August 2014, ISIS beheaded American journalist James Foley and posted the video on the Internet. The executioner warned the president that more American blood would flow if the U.S. continued airstrikes against ISIS.

The U.S. did.

ISIS beheaded American journalist Steven Sotloff and British aid worker David Haines in September; British aid worker

Alan Henning in October; American aid worker Abdul-Rahman Kassig in November; and two Japanese in February. They burned a Jordanian pilot alive because of King Abdullah's alliance with the U.S. Three ISIS jihadists (two of whom were British citizens) plotted to kill the Queen of England on VJ Day, but the Brits killed them with a drone strike before they could carry out their attack.

Now ISIS had abducted his daughters. It didn't seem possible. ISIS had been on the television, not in Dallas. Not in their lives. But now they were. Because of Omar al Mustafa.

Abdul jabbar sat before a computer screen in the law school library and typed a message.

We have his girls.

Chapter 20

Tuesday, 2 February
5 days before the Super Bowl

Boo woke to odd sounds. Chanting. In the distance, but not outside. Maybe from a television in another room. She couldn't understand the words; they were in that same foreign language.

'Allahu Akbar . . . Allahu Akbar . . . Allahu Akbar . . .'

The chanting made her feel cold. She said a silent prayer.

Please, A. Scott, come for us.

Scott opened his eyes to a new world. Life had changed. Irrevocably. Irreparably. His bedroom was not the same as the day before. Or the bathroom. Or the house. Everything was different. The girls were gone.

He was afraid for them – that the men would hurt them.

He was afraid for himself – that he would never see them again.

And he was mad. The shock had worn off and been replaced by anger: *They took my girls! They came into my house and took my daughters!*

His entire being burned with anger.

But he had to keep up appearances. He had to keep the girls' abduction secret – from the neighbors, the school, their friends, the FBI . . . and from Cat. He had no choice. So he dressed for his run and walked down the hall, but he stopped at the girls' bedroom door. Their bed was empty.

Where did they sleep last night?

He entered their empty room and sat on their empty bed. He picked up a framed photo from the nightstand; it was of the girls, Shawanda, Louis, Bobby, Karen, and Scott on the court-house steps after the verdict three and a half years before. Two months later, Shawanda was gone from his life. Now Pajamae and Boo were gone from his life. He had been wrong; there was still something fame could take from him. His daughters.

And take them it had.

He went out the back door and walked around front; he nodded at Agent Smith eating a breakfast taco and forced a smile in response to Cat's. She stepped to him as if to kiss him, but he couldn't kiss her. If he kissed her, if he touched her, if he embraced her, he would tell her. And his daughters would die.

So he ran. Normally, they got into a nice rhythm for the five miles. But not that day. That day Scott *ran*. The anger propelled him forward. He didn't talk. He didn't think. He ran. Hard. Violently. Angrily. The anger drove him.

'Are you mad at me?' Cat asked when they arrived back at the house.

'No.'

'Why didn't you text me back last night? Or answer my phone calls?'

'I was . . . occupied.'

'With the girls?'

323

'Yes.'

He wanted to tell her the truth, but instead he turned and went inside. Cat waited outside with Agent Smith. When Scott walked in the back door, he found Consuelo sitting in a chair and saying the rosary through silent tears; and he saw Boo's blood pressure cuff and stethoscope on the kitchen counter with her little notebook and pencil. He wrapped the cuff around his left arm then pumped it up. She had explained the process to him before; he recorded his blood pressure in the notebook for that date: 120/80.

'Aren't the girls going to school today?'

Scott had seemed distracted on their run that morning; he hadn't been his normal self. He had said nothing during the run. Cat had that kind of morning now and again, so she had left him to his thoughts. She just enjoyed the moment, running with a man she cared about.

A man she . . . loved?

She had waited outside while he dressed for court; she didn't feel that having sex with him gave her carte blanche in his life. He had walked out of the house dressed for court but alone. He shook his head.

'They're still not feeling well.'

He turned toward the Expedition in the driveway.

'Did you get them the flu shot?' Cat asked.

Scott wheeled on her. His face was suddenly stern. His voice more so.

'Of course, I got them the vaccine. Do you think I'm not a good father? That I don't take care of my girls? That I can't protect them? Is that what you think, Agent Peña?'

Cat almost dropped her coffee. *Agent Peña?*

'No . . . no, that's not what I think. You're a great father, Scott. I'm sorry, I . . . I didn't mean anything.'

Scott's stern face slowly dissolved. He started to say something but abruptly turned and climbed into his Expedition. Cat realized she was trembling.

'Shit, he sure got up on the wrong side of the bed today,' Ace said.

You only die once. Why not make it martyrdom?

The ISIS motto inspired Abdul jabbar. It was now his personal motto. His path in life. He was not the uneducated, unemployed, disaffected, alienated, angry Muslim male portrayed in the American media as the typical Islamic jihadist.

He was just angry.

He wanted revenge. When the Super Bowl had first been played in Cowboys Stadium in 2011, he had learned of the arches that supported the roof and the massive HDTV screen hanging from the roof. He began plotting his revenge. He decided on a fertilizer bomb like Oklahoma City, only bigger. Much bigger. Big enough to buckle one arch. Big enough to bring the stadium down. The plot was five years in the making. Not five months or five weeks or five days. But five years. Revenge will drive a man a long distance indeed.

'Five days, people,' Beckeman said.

An hour later, Cat and Ace had deposited the judge at the courthouse and sat in the war room at FBI headquarters in Dallas. Agent Beckeman stood before the whiteboard. Cat still had not recovered from Scott's harsh words that morning. It was so unlike him. She had never met a more even-tempered, gentle man. Perhaps he was worried about his daughters. But still, the flu was not life threatening.

'Mustafa knows the men,' Agent Stryker said. 'A little enhanced interrogation and—'

'The director talked to the president again this morning,' Beckeman said. 'The answer is still no.'

Scott's anger threatened to get the best of him. He had arrived at the courthouse and gone straight to the detention center.

'Where are they?'

The imam looked up from the Koran. 'I do not know.'

'Help me!'

'I cannot.'

'You release my daughters, or I swear to God you'll rot in that cell. You'll never see the light of day again. Or your children. You take my children from me, I'll take your children from you.'

'I would really like to cut off their heads and send them to the president,' Abdul jabbar said.

'Why? They're just kids.'

'And the president kills kids in Pakistan and Iraq and Syria every day with drone missiles. Look.'

Abdul pointed at the television. CNN reported another drone strike in the Middle East, this one in Syria. The missile supposedly killed an ISIS commander – and a dozen children. The missiles could not choose between the good and the bad, so often the good died with the bad and often instead of the bad. As their father had died.

'I really want to do that,' Abdul said. 'Behead someone. Feel what it is like to take a human life.'

'You killed those two Mexicans.'

'That is not the same as cutting through a person's flesh and veins and the blood spurting out. That is real killing. And one day, I will do that.'

His little brother stared at him.

'Abdul, you scare me.'

★

Louis stood in the courtroom next to the judge. He was like his father, the girls like his sisters. They were the only family he had ever had. Life without the girls, that wouldn't be a life. He fought back tears and tried to focus on the lawyers.

'Your Honor, the states do not have standing to contest the president's executive order.'

Scott was going through the motions of life – dressing in a suit, driving to the courthouse, presiding in the courtroom over the second oral arguments in the immigration case . . . but none of it seemed real. It was as if he were watching another person living his life.

'We have standing,' the states' attorney said, 'because A, we are the ones forced to pay for the president's executive order, and B, the principle of abdication gives us standing.'

Scott's eyes were focused on the lawyer standing before him, but his mind was focused on his daughters: *Were they hungry?*

'Your Honor, we've addressed the cost issue extensively in the briefs. Would you like me to address the abdication issue?'

Had they slept last night?

'Uh, Your Honor?'

Were they being treated well?

He heard Karen's voice, but it seemed distant. 'Please do, counsel.'

'Yes, sir . . . ma'am. The federal government has claimed – with the backing of the Supreme Court – sole authority over immigration and border security. That is, federal law preempts all state laws respecting immigration and border security. The states can take no action in that regard. But then the federal government refuses to act. We can't act, and they won't. But they force the states to pay for the consequences of their refusal. We have to pay the cost of their inaction.'

'That's the law,' another lawyer said.

'That's not fair.'

'Cry me a river.'

Scott was supposed to be a judge. But he couldn't. At that moment, he was only a father.

'Mr. Daniels,' Karen said, 'the government does not dispute that in order to combat terrorism it is abandoning enforcement of the immigration laws?'

'No, sir . . . ma'am.'

How did they use the restroom bound and blindfolded?

'I've got to pee,' Boo said.

'Again?' the good brother said.

'It's only my second time today.'

'Oh. Seems like more with both of you going.'

She heard footsteps come close to her and felt his hands on her shoulders.

'If it would be easier for you, we can go together.'

'I do not care' – he whispered now – 'but Abdul . . . my brother would go apeshit.'

Boo shrugged. 'Have it your way.'

'Let the little bitches piss their pants,' the bad brother named Abdul said from a distance.

'No,' the good brother said, 'I will help them.'

They had worked out a pee routine with the nice brother. He helped Boo to her feet then led her a short distance; when her socked feet came off the hard wood and slid on the slick tile, she knew she was in the bathroom. He untied her hands but did not remove her blindfold. She could never see their faces; if she did, the bad brother Abdul would cut their heads off. So she waited until she heard the door close, then she knew it was safe to remove the blindfold. Then she peed. He always waited right outside the door, which made her nervous. He could hear her peeing. Yuk.

'I'll be a little longer this time.'

328

'Why?'

'Because I have to, you know, go number two. That falafel runs right through me.'

'Oh. Okay, I will come back in a few minutes. But please do not come out until I return.'

'I won't. I promise.'

She didn't really have to go number two. But she wanted a few minutes to look around the bathroom without him listening at the door. So she peed quickly then pulled up her undies and pants. She wore jeans and a sweater.

The bathroom was small but very nice. It had a fancy toilet and pedestal sink and a walk-in shower. There was a window in the shower, but she couldn't see outside and no one could see in; it was made of those glass blocks like in the gym bathrooms at school. She could not climb out the window or wave for help to anyone outside.

She searched for something sharp to use as a weapon or to cut the bindings, but there was nothing. Just liquid soap in a squirt bottle and a nice little hand towel. There was no cabinet under the sink like in her bathroom. Where did they put their toothbrushes and toothpaste and stuff? Then she remembered A. Scott's bathroom; there was a medicine cabinet behind the mirror above the sink. She tugged on the mirror, and it opened. Tucked into the wall was a shallow cabinet. On the little shelves were toothbrushes, toothpaste, dental floss, tweezers, and a nail clipper. She took the clipper and put it in the back pocket of her jeans where she could reach it with her hands tied. She shut the mirror and stared at her reflection. She looked older.

Pajamae saw his face. Abdul, the bad brother. He didn't see her seeing him. Her blindfold had slipped down just enough for her to see everything. Until her view was suddenly blocked.

'What are you doing?' the good brother whispered.

329

He quickly stood between her and Abdul then squatted, and she saw his face, too. He had green eyes. He replaced her blindfold and tightened it.

'Please do not tell your sister. If Abdul finds out that you have seen our faces, he will cut your head off, and hers too. And your father's. Maybe even your maid's and her baby's. Promise me you will not tell.'

Pajamae was so scared she thought she would wet her pants. But the wet came from her eyes.

'I promise. I promise I won't tell anyone. Please don't let him cut our heads off.'

Abdul abruptly stood. 'Where is the little white girl?'

'She is in the bathroom.'

Abdul handed the remote to his little brother. 'You watch the football on TV, I will check on her.'

'Why?' He stood; his voice sounded loud to his own ears. 'Why, Abdul?'

'Because she is old enough.'

'For what?'

'To be my *sabaya*.'

For the first time in his life, he stood up to his big brother.

'No, Abdul.'

'Yes.'

'No.'

'She is an unbeliever. It is allowed. It is *halal*.'

'By whom?'

'The Koran. Al Baghdadi. The caliph himself took the American hostage as his *sabaya*.'

Their father had always been Abdul's man of *haqq* – the truth. Now the caliph was that man.

'You are not al Baghdadi. This it not Syria. We are not ISIS. And she is not your sex-slave!'

330

'I am Muslim. I am ISIS. I have pledged *bayah* to al Bagh-dadi.'

'I will not allow it.'

Abdul snatched a paper off the table and read with great anger. ' "Enslaving the families of the *kuffar* and taking the women as concubines is a firmly established aspect of the Sharia – that if one were to deny or mock, he would be deny-ing or mocking the verses of the Koran and the narrations of the Prophet." That was in *Dabiq,* the words of great Islamic scholars. Are you a great Islamic scholar, little brother? Do you deny or mock the Koran?'

'If the Koran truly allows that, then I do deny it. And I do not want to be a Muslim anymore.'

Abdul slapped him. His face burned, but he did not flinch.

'Why is that little girl supposed to be raped by you? Why am I supposed to die at twenty-two? Because someone wrote words in a book fourteen hundred years ago that says God hates Christians and Jews and so I must hate Christians and Jews as well? I do not. I do not hate Christians or Jews or anyone. I do not care if they believe in Islam. I am no longer sure I believe in Islam. Not if this is what it means to be a Muslim in the age of ISIS – I must be a jihadist, I must take innocent little girls as sex-slaves, I must kill innocent people in a football stadium. So sit down, Abdul jabbar! I will check on the girl!'

He walked off, but he heard Abdul's voice.

'No one is innocent, brother.'

'You finished?'

He was back.

'Just a sec.'

She flushed the toilet then replaced the blindfold.

'I'm ready.'

331

She heard the door open. He retied her hands and checked her blindfold to be sure it wouldn't slip down. He led her back to her sister.

'You okay, Pajamae?'

'Whereas.'

She did not sound whereas. But the good brother giggled.

'Whereas. You sound like a law student.'

Boo froze: *They're law students!* Which made her think. A. Scott was always giving them teaching moments when he tried to explain the choices in life and help them make good choices instead of bad choices. Maybe she had a teaching moment with the good brother.

'You know, you don't have to help your brother kill people.'

Abdul was a man. A bad man. He was just a boy. A good boy.

'Abdul, he hates Americans. Me, I like them.'

'You're not American?'

'No. We were born in Pakistan. We have been here thirteen years. We're naturalized citizens.'

'Then you're Americans. Just like us. You belong here.'

'We do not belong to any country. We belong only to our religion. That is what Abdul says.'

'Oh. See, that's the problem. We're Baptists on Sundays, the rest of the week we're Americans.'

'We are always Muslims.'

Cat texted Scott for the sixth time at three.

Scott, please talk to me. I gave myself to you because I care for you. I might even love you. Please don't shut me out.

He shut her out.

The call came at four.

'Release the imam.'

He hung up.

'Scotty, we need to call in the FBI,' Bobby said.

'Beckeman said they communicate over the dark Internet.'

'What's the dark Internet?' Louis said.

'A place you can't google,' Scott said.

'We need a hacker,' Carlos said.

'I know one.'

Louis drove; Scott evaded the FBI security detail at the garage exit by hiding in the back seat of the Dodge Charger. They arrived at the federal minimum-security prison in Seagoville south of Dallas at five. What the press had dubbed a 'Club Fed' prison, as if the inmates were lounging poolside reading the *Wall Street Journal* after a round of golf. There was no golf course; there were tennis courts and white inmates. This penitentiary was home to cheats, crooks, conmen, and other white-collar criminals – white men who had committed financial crimes. Black criminals were in state prison. Scott had called ahead. The warden was waiting for him. Louis stayed in the car; prisons scared him.

'Uh, Judge, this is a bit unusual – okay, it's never happened before – a federal judge coming to see an inmate he sentenced. What's up?'

'I need his help.'

'What kind of help?'

'It's a personal matter. And a confidential one. But nothing illegal. Nothing that would get you in trouble.'

'You sure?'

'I'm sure. I'm just visiting an inmate.'

Denny Macklin didn't seem as cocky as he had the day Scott had sentenced him. Prison will do that to a man. It's hard to be cocky when another man tells you when you can shower.

'Denny, I need your help.'

Denny lay on his bed. It was a metal bed with a shallow mattress; it did not have a pillow top and a soft down comforter. The ten-foot-by-ten-foot cell offered a metal toilet and sink. The walls were bare; the floor was concrete. Scott sat in a chair on the free side of the bars. The warden had given them privacy.

'Why would I help you? You put me in here.'

'No, Denny, you put yourself in here. When you understand that fact, you'll be ready to live outside again.'

Denny sighed, almost a cry. He spoke in a soft voice.

'You get carried away, with your own genius. How smart you are. How clever. Untouchable. Smarter than the Feds. Smarter than anyone. Once you know that, your next step is over a cliff.'

'You're on the right track, Denny.'

'Thanks, Judge.'

'For what?'

'Putting me in here.'

'I helped you?'

'You did.'

'Will you help me?'

'How?'

'My two daughters were abducted by terrorists.'

Denny snapped up. '*What?*'

'The people who plotted to blow up Cowboys Stadium—'

' "ISIS in Dallas" – I saw that on CNN in the lounge.'

'—they abducted me and demanded I release Mustafa.'

'He's the most dangerous man in Dallas.'

'So I've learned. I refused to release him, so they took my daughters.'

'That wasn't on CNN.'

'No one knows. They left a note, said they'd behead my girls if I went to the FBI.'

'So you came to me?'

'Yes.'

'Why?'

'Because you're smarter than the FBI.'

'True.'

'I need your help to save my daughters . . . and a hundred thousand people in that stadium.'

'I thought the plot was thwarted?'

'Two bad guys are still out there.'

Denny stood and came to the bars. 'They're going to blow up the stadium? Can they do it without Mustafa?'

'Apparently they're going to try.'

'What about the FBI?'

'They can't find them.'

'No surprise there.'

'That's where you come in.'

'What do you want me to do?'

'Find them. In something called the dark Net.'

'That's the part of the Net where bad people play.'

'You know it?'

'Very well. That's where I played bringing down the company.'

'The FBI says that's how they communicate with ISIS in Syria. Cat . . . I mean, the FBI figures ISIS is directly running this plot, talking to these two guys. But they use software to route their messages though a dozen different countries to evade tracking. If you can find their location in Dallas, we can stop them from killing all those people – and my daughters.'

Denny paced the cell.

'This kind of operation would require lots of man-hours.'

'It's just you, Denny.'

'I'm not going anywhere, not for two years. You got a pen?'

Scott pulled a pen from his shirt pocket and handed it to Denny through the bars. He pulled off the top.

'Felt tip. Perfect.'

He stepped to the white wall and drew an outline of the North American continent and a dark spot at the Dallas location; then he drew an outline of the African continent and a dark spot in Syria. He added Europe and the UK. The Atlantic Ocean lay between the continents.

'So we got bad guys in Dallas and bad guys in Syria talking to each other but running their messages all over the world before hitting the final destinations. No doubt they use end-to-end encryption. Hacking the encryption would be easy enough, but finding the message in the first place, that's the tricky part. Only way would be to trace a live feed . . . be in the dark Net same time as the bad guys . . . find the message . . . then jump aboard and hitch a ride. And to find the bad guys in Dallas, we have to ride a message from Syria.'

He drew a line from Syria to Europe to the UK to Canada and down to Dallas.

'We figure the bad guys in Dallas are taking orders from the bad guys in Syria,' he said, 'so they're working on Syrian time, not Dallas time.'

'What do you mean?'

'I mean, Syria is eight hours ahead of us. It's five P.M. here but one A.M. in Syria. So one of the parties must work in the middle of the night. I don't figure the ISIS boss is missing any sleep. So that puts the Dallas party in play from say, midnight to noon our time. That's our window of opportunity.'

'Smart thinking, Denny.'

'Those ISIS, they're smart people, too.'

'And bad people.'

Denny stopped and faced Scott. 'Taking kids, that's bad. I read that they use young girls for . . .'

336

'Can you do it, Denny?'

He stared at his work on the wall a moment then nodded.

'I did it myself. Routed messages all over the world to evade the authorities. I know the software inside and out. I can do it, Judge. I can find them. But that's not the question.'

'What's the question?'

'Question is, can I find them in time?'

'You can save a lot of innocent people, Denny. You can save the world. Like you did in those video games.'

'Except this is real.'

'This is real, Denny. Will you try?'

'I will. How will we communicate?'

Scott pulled out the girls' cell phone and handed it to Denny.

'It's their phone. My girls.'

'Oh, nice – a Hannah Montana screensaver.'

'They're thirteen. When can you start?'

'Let me check my daily planner.' He gave Scott a look. 'Right now.'

'What do you need?'

'Laptop, twenty-four/seven high-speed Internet connection, and a subscription to Starbucks. I won't be sleeping for a while.'

Abdul jabbar sent the message then glanced around the law library. The computer cubicles were mostly empty in the evening. He always took the computer cubicle in the corner, not to catch a bit of porn in private but to communicate with Zaheed. A message came back.

Has he gone to the FBI?

Abdul typed: *Not yet. But no doubt he has told his FBI girlfriend.*

A return message came quickly: *He must.*

Abdul typed: *He will.*

A return message: *Proceed with the plan. Talk again tomorrow.*

Abdul logged off. In five days, a hundred thousand Americans would die.

Cat walked in the back door. Her parents sat at the kitchen table. She hung her FBI jacket on the rack, unbuckled her waist pack and dropped it on the table, and then reached under her shirt, unsnapped her bra, and pulled it through the armhole of her shirt. Her father shook his head.

'I am still amazed at how women can do that.'

He held out an Oreo to her. She shook him off. He frowned.

'What's wrong, my dear?' her mother said.

Cat sat down hard. Her mother patted her hand. She took an Oreo.

'The judge . . . Scott . . . he was short with me this morning.'

'What about?'

She recounted their morning together.

'Perhaps he had a bad day.'

'His day hadn't started yet.'

'Perhaps he was worried about his daughters.'

'It's the flu. I texted him six times today, he never responded.' She stuffed a whole Oreo in her mouth and said, 'It's me. It's always me. I scare men off.'

Her father gestured at the waist pack. 'Perhaps it's the gun.'

'Perhaps it's my personality.'

'Why don't you sext him?' her mother said.

'*What?*'

'Send him a text with a sexy photo. Like the kids do.'

'*Mother . . .*'

She gave Cat the human polygraph look.

'I tried. It didn't work.'

'Shame.'

338

'You could try naked,' her dad said.

Cat regarded her parents with an open mouthful of Oreos.

'What are y'all watching on TV?'

'I will make churros for the girls,' her mother said.

'So, Catalina,' her father said, 'when will the judge rule on our case?'

Boo woke to that same chanting in that same language.

'Allahu Akbar, Allahu Akbar, Allahu Akbar . . .'

But it wasn't in the distance or on the other side of the house. It was very close.

And then it stopped.

She heard footsteps on the wood floor . . . coming closer now . . . all around her . . . next to her. She swung her legs around in a circle until they hit something.

Someone.

'Who is that?'

'You are my *sabaya*.'

Abdul. The bad brother.

'I have prayed to Allah, and Allah approves. He gave me you as booty.'

'*Booty?*'

'You are my sex-slave.'

'*What?* Don't you even think about it, Abdul.'

She felt hands on her feet, pulling her socks off then rubbing her feet. She yanked her feet away.

'Get away from me!'

His hands touched her legs below her knees. They slid up and down her calves. Then they surrounded her knees. His breathing became deeper and faster. He panted like a dog.

'Get your hands off me! Help! Help!'

Hands grabbed at her waist, at her jeans, at the button and zipper. Boo kicked and screamed.

339

'Help! Pajamae! Wake up!'

'What is it, Boo?'

'Abdul, he's trying to pull my pants off!'

'Why?'

'He's trying to sex me! Kick him!'

She kicked, and Boo could feel the air move as Pajamae's legs swung wildly around. The hands still grabbed at her pants. Then she heard a grunt and the hands left her.

'Shit, you kicked me in the mouth, you little bitch! I think I'm bleeding.'

'Abdul!' It was the good brother. 'What are you doing?'

'He tried to sex me!' Boo screamed. 'He tried to pull my pants off! He said I was his booty!'

'Abdul,' the good brother said in a strong voice, 'I told you no!'

'The Koran says yes. She is my booty. I own her.'

She heard footsteps and their voices grow dim. She calmed. She cried.

'A. Scott, please hurry.'

Chapter 21

Wednesday, 3 February
4 days before the Super Bowl

Denny Macklin woke to the pinging of the cell phone. He checked the messages.

My mother made churros last night. Want some? Make you feel better.

Denny typed a response.

Yes!! Love churros!! Thanks!!

He had worked all night. He closed his eyes and thought, *The judge is such a nice guy. Much nicer than when he sentenced me to two years in this stinking prison.*

'Mr. President,' the director said, 'if you would just consider—'
  'No.'

Scott stepped into the girls' empty bedroom. He sat on their empty bed. He looked at the same framed photograph and

341

then at their stuff. Their clothes – Pajamae's neatly hung and folded; Boo's strewn about – and their DVDs and their boom box and their books and their new Dallas Cowboys jerseys. The stuff of their lives.

It was the third day they were gone.

He kept up appearances. He went outside and ran with Cat. They ran the five miles in silence; not a word was spoken. He tried to gauge her, but her brown eyes were hidden behind Oakley M Frames. When they returned to the house, she got a small paper bag out of her car and held it out to Scott like a peace offering.

'Churros. For the girls. They said they wanted some.'

'They did?'

'We text.'

She followed him around back. At the door, he turned to her; she could not come inside; inside she would learn the truth. She embraced him and kissed him, but he did not kiss her back. She pulled away.

'Hey, you're not playing fair. If you're pissed at me, say so.'

'I'm not mad at you.'

'But you don't want to kiss me or touch me or . . .'

'Cat . . . I can't.'

'Is it a physical thing? They have drugs for that.'

She smiled; he did not. He could no longer force a smile.

'No.'

'Mental? Are you feeling guilty about your ex?'

'No.'

'Then what is it?'

'Cat . . . I just can't.'

'Tell me, Scott. Please.'

He took her face with both hands. He felt the wet in his eyes.

'I can't! They'll—'

'*They?* Who? The girls?'

342

He wanted to tell her. But he released her, walked inside, and shut the door.

Beckeman's intercom buzzed. He hit the button.

'What?'

'Chief, the warden at the Seagoville prison is on line one.'

Beckeman picked up the receiver and pushed line one.

'Beckeman,' he said.

'Agent Beckeman, this is Warden Pitt down in Seagoville. Thought you should know, the judge paid a visit to one of my inmates yesterday.'

'*Judge?* Judge Fenney?'

'Yes, sir.'

'Were two of my agents with him?'

'No, sir. He was alone.'

'What inmate?'

'Denny Macklin.'

'Never heard of him.'

'Geek. Almost brought down that public company 'cause they fired his daddy.'

'Oh, yeah. I remember. What did the judge want with him?'

'I don't know. All he said was to give the geek whatever he wanted. Well, he didn't call him a geek. What do you want me to do?'

'Give the geek whatever he wants but keep me in the loop.'

'Yes, sir.'

Warden Pitt had more to say.

'What is it, Warden?'

'A favor. Keep me in the loop for a job. I hate this fucking prison.'

The attorney general called at ten.

'Scott—'

'Not now, Mac.'

There was silence for a long moment.

'You okay, Scott?'

'No.'

He hung up.

'Kareem Abdul-Jabbar was a legend in the NBA,' the little black girl said.

'How do you spell that?' his brother asked.

'What?'

'Jabbar.'

'Uh . . . j–a–b–b–a–r. I think.'

'Ah. Same as Abdul's name.'

Abdul had just walked into the house. He sighed. His little brother was feeding falafel to the two blindfolded girls and the cat. He looked up at Abdul.

'Is he pleased?'

'Very. He says we will be heroes.'

'Dead heroes.'

'What is the girl telling you?'

'About someone with your name.'

'Who?'

'Kareem Abdul-Jabbar,' the little black girl said.

'And who is he?'

'He was an NBA legend.'

'A basketball player?'

'Yes. He was named Lew Alcindor, but he changed his name when he became a Muslim.'

'She is right,' his little brother said. 'I googled him. He wrote an op-ed in *Time*.'

'You googled? Here?'

'Oh. Sorry.'

'We must stay off the grid.'

'I didn't google ISIS. The NSA won't flag a basketball player. Listen.' His brother read off his laptop. ' "For me, religion – no matter which one – is ultimately about people wanting to live humble, moral lives that create a harmonious community and promote tolerance and friendship with those outside the religious community. Any religious rules should be in service of this goal. The Islam I learned and practice does just that . . . Terrorism is actually an act against the very religion they claim to believe in. It's an acknowledgement that the religion and its teachings aren't enough to convince people to follow it. Any religion that requires coercion is not about the community, but about the leaders wanting power." Abdul, I like this Kareem. I like his Islam.'

Abdul laughed. 'Brother, we do not follow the teachings of a basketball player. We follow al Baghdadi. He is a direct descendant of the Prophet.'

'Does he play basketball?' the little black girl said.

'*What?* No, you stupid little girl. He is the caliph.'

'What's a caliph?'

'Leader of the caliphate.'

'Makes sense. What about Cassius Clay?'

'Is he also a basketball player?'

'No, you dope. He's Muhammad Ali.'

'Who?'

'The boxer. He became a Muslim and changed his name, too.'

'Athletes. American gods.' He snorted with disdain. 'We will bring the stadium down on Super Bowl Sunday. The holiest day of the year for Christians and Jews in America.'

Pajamae felt someone come close and then smelled a foul body odor and hot breath on her face – and a strong hand grabbing her throat. He squeezed.

'Be careful who you call dope, little black girl. I would like nothing better than to send your head to your father in a box.'

Pajamae struggled to breathe. She was sure she would die at that moment. But the good brother spoke.

'Uh, Abdul, let us call the judge.'

Scott's cell phone rang. The room snapped to attention. Scott checked the caller ID. He nodded and put a finger to his lips. He answered and put the call on the speaker.

'Hello.'

'Did you release the imam?'

The same voice.

'No.'

'Why not?'

'I need time. If I suddenly change my mind and release him, the FBI will get suspicious. May I talk to my daughters?'

'You may hear that they are alive . . . so far.'

There was silence then Boo's voice. 'Whereas, A. Scott?'

The room breathed out with relief. They were still alive.

'Boo, are you okay?'

'A. Scott, he tried to—'

The man's voice came back on: 'Release the imam.'

The call was disconnected.

'When A. Scott finds out you tried to sex me, he's going to kill you, asshole.'

Her face suddenly stung, and she fell to the floor. He had slapped her.

'If the judge comes for you, I will cut his head off.'

The bad brother named Abdul laughed in that mean way he laughed. She heard his footsteps and a chair groan when he plopped down in it. She could hear the good brother breathing next to her.

346

'Are you okay?' He helped her to a sitting position. 'Abdul, he has anger issues.'

'No, shit.'

Her face hurt, but she refused to cry. She would not be afraid. The three of them whispered in the corner like the snotty girls in the lunchroom at school.

'What's he mad about?' Boo said.

'America killed our father with a drone missile.'

'In Dallas?'

'No. In Pakistan.'

'My mother was like that.'

'America killed your mother with a drone missile?'

'No. She was mad.'

'Oh.'

'Then she left.'

'Where did she go?'

'I don't know.'

'How can you not know where your mother is?'

'She ran off with a golf pro.'

'Really? Is he any good?'

'He's dead. She killed him – or they said she killed him. A. Scott, he proved she didn't.'

'And where is she now?'

Boo shrugged. 'Somewhere with a man.'

The good brother sighed. 'I wish I could leave my brother.'

'Why don't you? And take us with you?'

'Because he is my brother.'

'But he wants to do something very bad.'

'Yes.'

'And you don't.'

'No. He has lost his soul to hate.' He breathed out. 'But he is my older brother.'

'We're sisters, but I wouldn't hurt people just because Pajamae wants me to.'

'I don't want you to hurt anyone,' Pajamae said.

'If you did.'

'I don't.'

'It's just an example.'

'Oh.'

'You know, my dad, he'll come for us.'

'He will never find you.'

'Will you let Abdul sex us? Or kill us?'

'No. I will not let that happen.'

'He'll try again.'

'I know.'

He felt as if his heart and mind were ripping him in two. His heart would always love his big brother; he bordered on hero worship. Abdul had always been his hero. Bigger, stronger, smarter, tougher. A man when he was still a boy. But Abdul had been happy; he always laughed and joked and dreamed of the future. He wanted to be a professional soccer player. He wished they were still boys in the village in Pakistan. Before the drone came.

That happy boy was still inside Abdul.

Perhaps he could find that boy. He took a deep breath, hoping to find the necessary courage. He walked across the room and sat across the table from his brother.

'I have been thinking,' Abdul said. 'There are one-point-six billion Muslims on the planet. If each Muslim killed just four or five infidels, Islam would rule the world. And we could afford to live on the beach in southern California – for nothing.'

'Uh, yes, that is an interesting idea. But brother, are you sure that Allah truly wants us to kill a hundred thousand people?'

'No. He wants us to kill six billion *kuffars*.'

'Every non-Muslim is an infidel who deserves to die?'

'Yes.'

'Could we not just behead a few Jews? Would that not make you happy?'

'It would make me very happy, and I might do that as well. But have you forgotten what the Christians did to our father?'

'No. But those people in the stadium, they did not make that missile, they did not fly that drone, they did not give the order to fire that missile. The president did. Let us kill him instead.'

'Ah, if only we could. Then we would be heroes for sure. But we cannot. So we will kill a hundred thousand Americans instead.'

'But they are innocent.'

'No, they are guilty. All Americans are accomplices to murder, to genocide, because they do not demand their government stop waging war against Islam. They sit here in America and watch football games while their president sends drones to kill Muslims, so they can take our homes and our land and our oil, so they can subjugate us to their rule. They have made a choice. And every choice has consequences. We will strike a blow for all Muslims.'

'But there will be children in that stadium. They know nothing of that.'

'They must pay for their fathers' sins. My brother, if we take down that stadium, we will be heroes, as Zaheed said.'

'We will be dead.'

'We will die an honorable death.'

He stared at his older brother. The happy boy was gone.

'Let's go to Starbucks.'

'You go,' Abdul said. 'Get me a grande coffee Frappuccino, no whip.'

'Let's go together.'

Abdul smiled. 'Ah, you are worried I will take the girl. You are right, I would.' He stood. 'Come, we will go together, brother. As we will die together.' He glanced at the girls. 'Tie them down.'

'Hey, guard!'

Denny Macklin tapped the keys on the laptop at a furious pace – *Where are you hiding, asshole?* – until he heard the heavy footsteps of the overweight guard named Buddy.

'What do you want?'

Denny's eyes did not leave the screen or his fingers the keyboard.

'Did someone deliver churros for me?'

'Churros?'

'Yeah.'

'No.'

Dang. Denny loved churros with hot coffee. Guess he'd just have the coffee.

'Get me another skinny vanilla latte. Pronto.'

'Fuck you.'

'You want me to report you to the warden?'

The judge had spoken to the warden, and the warden to him. Whatever he wanted or needed was his for the asking. And he was asking for a Starbucks. He gave the guard a moment to reconsider; he finally surrendered, as Denny knew he would.

'Venti or grande?'

Karen typed through tears. Working kept her sane. The thought of never seeing the girls again threatened to break her heart. She could not imagine never seeing Little Scotty again. To lose him would kill her. To lose them would kill Scott. He would be a broken man. Forever.

★

'Ah, Judge, I was hoping you would stop by. I have enjoyed our talks.'

Scott stood outside the imam's cell. 'My girls are being held hostage, but you're enjoying our conversations? Don't you care?'

'Do you care that Muslim children are being killed by American drone missiles as we speak?'

Scott sat on the stool and slumped down.

'Judge, do you pray to God to save your daughters?'

'I do.'

'You believe in God?'

'I do.'

'Why?'

'Because I don't believe in coincidences.'

Mustafa scooted his stool closer to the bars. 'Please explain.'

'Not now.'

'Yes, now. I must understand the man who sits in judgment of me.'

Scott again held out hope that he could find some human connection with this man. This Muslim. So he answered.

'Is it just a coincidence that an ocean of oil lies beneath the Middle East, the exact spot where the three major religions of the world were founded? And that today the world depends on that oil, which dependence has brought those three religions into mortal conflict on that same spot?'

'Ah, very good, Judge. And no, it is not a coincidence. It is the end of days. Go on.'

Scott summoned the strength to go on. 'It's not a coincidence that humans share the same physical attributes – it's evolution. But evolution cannot account for our psychic similarities. So is it just a coincidence?'

'I do not understand.'

351

'As a lawyer, I traveled quite a bit overseas. I met people. I talked to common people – cabbies, waiters, clerks. And everywhere I've traveled people share the same psychic desire – to work hard to improve their lot in life, but more important, to improve their children's lot in life.'

'Interesting.'

'But I've never traveled to the Middle East.'

'Meaning?'

'Meaning parents there strap bombs to their children. We dream for our children. Your people kill their children. I don't understand that.'

'Because you are not Muslim. You have not lived a life oppressed. You have lived free in America.'

'Which is the third reason I believe in God: America.'

'This I must hear.'

'Is it a coincidence that five of history's greatest men – George Washington, Thomas Jefferson, James Madison, Alexander Hamilton, and Benjamin Franklin – came together at the same time and place – literally in the same room – to create America? What would the world be today without America?'

'There would be fewer terrorists.'

'There would be chaos. Less freedom. More oppression. Disease. Poverty. And the Nazis would control most of Europe. We don't always get it right, but we try to. Without America, the world would be worse. Much worse.'

'So you think God created America?'

'I do.'

'My, you are a true believer, Judge. Which is good for me, I suppose.'

'Why is that?'

'Because you will set me free.'

★

Boo got her fingers on the nail clippers in her back pocket and pulled them out. She worked the clippers around until she felt the clipper on the rope that bound her wrists. She squeezed. The clipper squeaked.

'What's that?' Pajamae asked.

'Nail clippers.'

'How can you cut your nails blindfolded?'

'I'm not cutting my nails. I'm cutting the rope.'

'Is it working?'

'No.'

Abdul wanted to sex her. She had to escape and take Pajamae with her.

'Hector, I have made inquiries. Every day for two weeks. I have received no responses. Jorge, Manuel, the shipment, the money . . . they all just disappeared.'

Tomas Guzman was Hector's man in the Middle East. He sighed over the phone.

'It is not like the old days. Dealing with the Taliban for the heroin from Afghanistan, they were very professional. It was all about the money for them, so you could depend on them. There was respect. These ISIS Muslims, they are different. They want the money, but they want to rule the world – who has time for that? They have no respect for anyone.'

'They will have respect for me when I am through with them.'

'They are religious fanatics. It is never a good thing to mix religion and money. Like money and women.'

Hector gazed out the sliding glass doors at his woman lounging by the pool. She looked like a glamorous Hollywood movie star from the sixties with a white one-piece bathing suit, a white wide-brimmed sun hat, and the big sunglasses. She drank iced tea through a straw.

'Yes, that is true.'

'Hector, if I have made a mistake in judgment, I will pay you what you have lost in this matter.'

'How can you pay me for four dead men?'

'I cannot.'

'No, Tomas, you cannot. There is only one method of repayment for death. And that is more death. These people, they think they are terrorists. But I will show them true terror. We have cut off more heads than they can dream of cutting off. We have seized control of our country while they dream of an Islamic State. We have spread terror in America with our drugs while they still dream of an attack on this continent. We, *mí amigo*, have experience in this sort of thing. Their men in America must die. And die they will. So help me God.'

Denny sat before an Apple laptop connected to a twenty-four-inch flat-screen LED monitor. The Hannah Montana phone rang. Denny answered.

'Hello.'

'Is Boo there?'

A kid's voice.

'No.'

'Will you take a message?'

'No.'

Denny disconnected. The phone rang again. The same voice.

'That was very rude. My name is Audrey. I want to ask Boo if I can borrow her study notes from history class—'

Denny disconnected again. The phone rang again.

'Look, I don't have time to take—'

'Denny, it's Judge Fenney.'

'Oh. Sorry. Kids have been calling your daughter.'

'Anything?'

'Audrey wants to borrow Boo's study notes—'

'On finding the Arabs.'

'Oh. No. Takes time, Judge.'

'We don't have time.'

He must go to the FBI!

Abdul typed a response to Zaheed.

I have tried everything! You said if I told him not to go he would go. That reverse psychology bullshit.

He sent the message and waited for a response. He looked around the computer lab in the law school library. Students studying for their future. Little did they know their future was about to end. Zaheed's response soon came.

Behead his daughters.

Chapter 22

Cat Peña arrived at Scott's house early that morning with a plastic container of her mother's tortilla soup. It would be good for the girls. She parked the government sedan at the curb and got out with the soup. Agent Smith had been taken off the security detail. Beckeman had decided that the threat against the judge had diminished enough to warrant only one agent. He needed Ace on the manhunt for the two Arabs; he did not need her mouth. She walked around to the back door and knocked; the door swung open. Even in Highland Park, that wasn't good. And at the house of a federal judge who had been abducted just ten days before, that was not good at all.

She drew her weapon.

She stepped inside. There was no beeping alarm system. There was no noise at all in the house. No Consuelo cooking, no girls giggling. It was quiet. Too quiet. She placed the soup

356

container on the kitchen table. She put her back to the wall and stepped silently down the hall. She stopped at the girls' bathroom. The door was ajar. She gently pushed on the door; it swung open.

Their bathroom was empty.

She stepped to their bedroom just down the hall. She stood next to the open door. She heard a sound from inside. She raised her weapon, jumped in front of the door, and pointed her weapon at—

Scott.

He sat on their bed, bent over, his elbows on his knees. He looked up at her. Tears rolled down his face. She lowered her weapon. She stepped inside.

'Where are the girls?'

'My knees hurt,' the little black girl said.

'Shut up.'

Abdul jabbar bit off half the Krispy Kreme glazed donut. He stood in front of a green screen set up in the kitchen. He would insert the background before sending the video to Zaheed; perhaps he would make it a scene from Disneyland. Zaheed would get a kick out of that.

'Can I stand up?'

'Shut up.'

He wore all black, including a black headscarf and bandana he would pull across his face so only his eyes would be visible, but he wore the yellow sneakers. He had checked himself out in the bathroom mirror; he thought black suited him well. The black ISIS flag hung on a stand to his side. The hostages knelt in front of him, blindfolded with black cloths and bound hands and feet. They were not gagged. He wanted the camera to capture their screams. Abdul held a sword.

'Brother – what is this?'

His little brother had just showered and dressed and entered the room.

'Exactly what it appears.'

'Why?'

'Orders from Zaheed.'

'No, brother. This is not happening.'

'Yes, little brother, it is. I must behead the unbelievers.'

'They are not unbelievers. They are children.'

'They are the children of the unbelievers. If we kill their children, the unbelievers will submit to Islam as the Koran requires.'

'Fuck the Koran! Fuck Zaheed! Fuck you, Abdul! If you want to kill them, you will have to kill me first.'

'*Kill?*' the little white girl said. '*Them who?*'

'Oh, Lord Jesus!' the little black girl said.

His brother came and stood between Abdul and the hostages.

'Have you no conscience? That is what separates humans from animals. Animals have no conscience, so they can kill without feeling. Humans cannot. Because we are not animals. You killed those two Mexicans, but you feel no guilt, do you?'

'Why should I?'

'Because you are human – humans suffer guilt when they do something wrong.'

'A, guilt is for the weak of mind. And B, I did nothing wrong.'

'This is wrong.'

'This is Allah's will. This is my destiny.'

'God wants you to kill these two little girls?'

'*Kill?*' the little white girl said again.

'No, Abdul, this is not what God wants. If your god wants that, he is not my God. If I must kill to be Muslim, I will not be Muslim.'

'You will be an apostate. We kill apostates.'

'Then kill me, brother. Behead me.'

Abdul could not raise his sword to his brother. The Koran forbade that. His little brother was weak. Weak in body and mind. He wanted to be a lawyer. Live the American Dream. Watch football and barbecue organic meat from Whole Foods. Drink Budweiser. Another year in America and he'd be a regular at NASCAR races. His brother had forgotten from where he had come and what had happened there. He had, as they say, moved on. Abdul had not. He stuffed the last of the donut into his mouth, pulled the bandana across his face, and said, 'Stand aside, brother.'

'Do you still think it's a diversion?'

Scott had given the abductors' note to Cat. She had read it and dropped down hard into a chair at the kitchen table. It took her a few minutes to gather herself.

'When did this happen?'

'Monday.'

'Why didn't you tell me?'

She wasn't mad; she was hurt.

'You read the note.'

She nodded. Her face changed from hurt woman to hard FBI agent.

'Scott, I've got to tell Beckeman.'

'They'll kill the girls.'

'If we don't find them and stop them, they'll kill a hundred thousand people in three days.'

'Beckeman knows these two men are out there, they abducted me. He just doesn't know they abducted Boo and Pajamae. How would that knowledge change his manhunt?'

'It wouldn't.'

'Exactly. That's why I haven't told the FBI. It doesn't matter. Except to me.'

359

'Child abductions matter to us.'

'But those hundred thousand people matter more. And they should. Those two girls matter to me. So I'm going to find them.'

'How?'

He told her about Denny Macklin.

'I can help.'

'This stays between us. For now.'

She nodded. 'For now. But if it gets to the point of affecting the manhunt for the Arabs, I'll have to tell Beckeman.'

'Agreed.'

'We need help.'

'We've got help.'

Denny Macklin was a pain in the ass. A genius, but still a royal pain in Buddy's butt. Buddy, the cellblock C guard, had already delivered a fancy chair and a second laptop and big screen to Macklin's cell that day. Now he delivered a large pepperoni pizza with black olives.

'Have a piece,' Macklin said.

'Really?'

'Sure. I can't eat a whole pizza for breakfast.'

But Buddy could and often did.

'The president won't let us do our job,' Beckeman said to the Task Force assembled in the war room, 'so we're not going to find the Arabs by game time. Our focus now is to secure the Super Bowl. If we can't find them, we've got to keep them out of that stadium. Set up a perimeter at the street all the way around the parking lot with checkpoints at every entrance. Every vehicle gets searched, every occupant frisked, and every purse examined. Every delivery truck is searched by an FBI agent. We're gonna get dirty. We've been author-ized a drone—'

'With hellfire missiles?' Agent Stryker said.

'You wish.'

'—that will be over the stadium the entire day. We're on site at daybreak.'

Denny ate pizza and drank coffee and rubbed his eyes. His brain was fried, his butt numb, and his eyelids felt like sandpaper against his eyeballs every time he blinked. He had stayed up all night, again, but had come up empty, again. He was trolling the dark Net, but there was nothing but—

'Well, well, well . . . what do we have here?'

A message from Syria.

'I see you, asshole. Now I'm going to ride you all the way to Dallas and—'

What the hell? The asshole disappeared.

'Oh, okay. You think you're good, huh? Smarter than Denny Macklin. We'll see about that.'

Scott sat behind his desk in chambers. Cat and the crew occupied the chairs and couch. It was three. They had waited for a call all day. But none had come. Until now.

His phone rang.

Scott snapped forward in his chair. Everyone gathered around the desk. Scott put the call on the speakerphone. A familiar voice came across.

'So, Judge, have you released the imam?'

'No.'

'Are you going to release him?'

'Yes.'

'When?'

'Soon.'

Sound could be heard in the background. Was it music? In the distance? Everyone leaned in close to hear.

'Let me talk to my girls.'

'No.'

'Why not?'

'They are not . . . available. You will see them soon enough.'

He hung up.

'Oh, God,' Karen said. 'Did he hurt them?'

'No,' Scott said.

But did he?

'What was that sound in the background?' Cat said. 'Music?'

'Must have had a radio on,' Bobby said.

'Didn't sound like radio music,' Cat said. 'And it didn't sound as if it were coming from nearby. It was a distant sound.'

'Maybe a neighbor was playing their music loud.'

'But what kind of music was that?'

'Wasn't country western.'

'Or rock.'

'Wasn't soul,' Louis said.

'Or Latino,' Carlos said.

'Or jazz,' Bobby said. 'Not with that *boom boom boom* sound. What was that?'

'Tuba.'

They all turned to Frank Turner standing in doorway.

'It's marching band music,' he said.

'How do you know?' Cat said.

'I played tuba in the band for four years. What the hell's going on, Scotty?'

'Shut the door, Frank.'

Frank shut the door and stepped to the desk.

'Same people who grabbed me, they kidnapped my girls.'

'*Your daughters?* When?'

'Monday.'

'Are they alive?'

'They were yesterday.'

Frank faced Cat. 'What's the FBI doing to find them?'

'I didn't go to the FBI,' Scott said.

'Why not?'

'They left a note, said they'd behead the girls if I did. I begged Mustafa to tell me where they're at. He refused.' Scott turned his palms up. 'We don't have a clue where they're at.'

'They're in Highland Park.'

Frank pointed at the cell phone on the desk but looked at Scott.

'That was the SMU marching band, practicing in the stadium on campus.'

'There are no Muslims in Highland Park,' Bobby said.

'There are two,' Scott said.

The Town of Highland Park comprised two square miles. It was the hole in the donut that was Dallas. SMU sat in the middle of Highland Park, and the football stadium sat on the campus. The girls were being held in Highland Park. Everyone stood around Scott's kitchen table.

'Check the Highland Park phone book,' Louis said.

'There isn't one,' Bobby said. 'Highland Park is included in the Dallas phone book.'

'I checked our databases for the males at the mosque,' Cat said. 'None had a Highland Park address.'

'They're here,' Frank said.

Scott spread a town map on the kitchen table. He drew a circle around the stadium then marked off search grids starting at the stadium.

'What are we looking for?' Carlos asked. 'Them Muslims, they know the FBI is looking for them, so they ain't gonna just walk around.'

'The FBI's not looking for them in Highland Park,' Cat said.

'We're not looking,' Louis said. 'We're listening.'

'For what?'

'Prayers. Evening prayers. They'll face toward Mecca, that's east. So listen for chants on the east side of the houses.'

'What'll the chants sound like?'

'Allahu Akbar.'

'Shit, what are the odds of finding them?'

'There are no odds,' Scott said. 'But we have to try. We'll search in pairs. Cat carries a gun so—'

'I've got a gun, too,' Carlos said.

'How'd you get a gun with your prior convictions?'

'Arrests. No convictions.'

'I carry a gun,' Frank said.

'Why?'

Frank shrugged. 'Plaintiffs' lawyer.'

Scott turned to Bobby. 'Do you have a gun?'

'No . . . but Karen does.'

'Louis?'

'No, sir. I'm big enough not to need a gun.'

The Gerald Ford Stadium – named not after the former president but after a billionaire banker; it *is* Dallas – stands at the south end of the SMU campus. To the east of the stadium are campus buildings, a retail strip center, and the George W. Bush Presidential Library abutting North Central Expressway. The Arabs weren't holding the girls hostage in a dorm room, the Starbucks, or the library.

The campus stretched north of the stadium eight city blocks, close to a mile; only there did a residential area begin. That the band could be heard a mile away was doubtful. But residential areas began only two blocks west of the stadium and just south

364

of the stadium on Mockingbird Lane. Everyone had agreed that the search should focus south of the stadium.

They had marked off the map and divided up into teams: Scott and Cat; Bobby and Carlos; Louis and Frank. Each team carried a map, a flashlight, a cell phone, and a gun. It was 1:00 A.M. and cold. Scott and Cat were bundled up in Under Armour, coats, gloves, and knit hats.

'I'm trying to be an FBI agent,' Cat said, 'but the girls . . . you do know I love them?'

'I know you do.'

'If these men hurt them . . .'

'I know you will.'

They were walking east on Mockingbird across from the stadium when a Highland Park police cruiser pulled alongside. They stopped. The officer spoke to them through an open window.

'You folks okay? Don't see many people taking a walk this time of night.'

'I'm Judge Fenney.'

The officer shone a flashlight in Scott's face then quickly averted the light.

'Sorry, Judge. Little cold for a walk. What brings you out so late?'

'With all the attention of the case, this is the only time I can walk in peace. And I'm not sleeping very well.'

'You're not worried about getting abducted again?'

'This is Agent Peña. FBI.'

Cat flashed her badge to the officer.

'Dedicated. Okay, enjoy your walk, Judge. And try melatonin. It'll help you sleep.'

'They're dead, but they're still walking?' Carlos said.

'Yes,' Bobby said. 'That's the definition of zombies.'

They turned east on Cornell Avenue.

'A series about zombies been on TV for six seasons?'

'No. A series about what happens to the world when zombies take over has been on TV for six seasons.'

'Everyone dies.'

'A lot do, but some humans learn how to kill zombies and survive.'

'I'd kick their undead asses.'

'Carlos, do you even know how to kill a zombie?'

It made no sense for them to be talking about *The Walking Dead* while searching the streets of Highland Park for two girls held hostage by Islamic terrorists. And not just any two girls, but Boo and Pajamae. Bobby and Carlos loved those two girls like their own; they would both gladly trade places with the girls. They would both die for the girls.

If the girls were still alive.

The human brain could not focus on something so evil and so awful – the image of Boo and Pajamae lying dead with their heads cut off – for very long and remain sane. So, in self-defense, the human brain switches gears to a lighter image – killing zombies – to ease the pressure of the moment. It was like people making jokes at funerals. You can't think about death for very long.

'A wooden stake in the heart.'

'No, no, no, that's how you kill a vampire. With a zombie, you've got to kill its brain. You stick a stake in a zombie's heart, he'll still eat your ass for lunch.'

'Shit, I would've fucked that up.'

'I feel like I'm in a Shakespearean tragedy,' Franklin Turner, famous plaintiffs' lawyer said to the bailiff.

'You read Shakespeare?' Louis said.

'Every word he wrote. You?'

'Just starting. Ms. Herrin, she's teaching me grammar and literature. Didn't get a lot of Shakespeare down in South Dallas.'

'Just the tragedy.'

Frank pulled out the flashlight and checked the map for their grid. They had walked west on Beverly and south on Hillcrest; now they would go east on Princeton. So far they had seen nothing suspicious. Of course, it was Highland Park. This wasn't a white-trash trailer park where every other resident cooked meth and pit bulls roamed the neighborhood.

'Is that a pit bull?' Louis asked.

'Where?'

Louis pointed east; Frank shone the flashlight that way. The light found the dog. It was a pit bull.

'A fucking pit bull in Highland Park,' Frank said.

The dog obviously didn't know that it didn't belong in Highland Park. It broke into a run . . . toward them!

'Shit.'

Frank fumbled about his three layers of garments for his gun. He was scared, but Louis was apparently terrified. He stood frozen in place. He faced the dog with no attempt to evade it. Frank got the first layer unzipped and was working on the second layer when the dog growled and bared its teeth from only ten feet away, and Louis—

—growled back. He spread his massive arms and growled at the dog.

'*Graaaaaaa!*'

The pit bull pulled up short. He eyed Louis, as if thinking, *What the hell?*

'*Graaaaaa!*'

The dog turned tail and hauled ass down Princeton Avenue.

'See,' Louis said, 'I don't need a gun.'

★

367

Cat entered through the back door of her house just as the sky was brightening with the dawn. They had searched through the night and come up empty. But her kitchen was not empty; her parents sat at the table in their bathrobes. Her mother drank coffee; her father ate Oreos. She felt like a suspect caught in the act.

'So, did you and the judge make up?' her mother asked with raised eyebrows.

'Yes.'

'Oh, that's nice.'

'Did he rule on our case?' her father asked.

'No.'

Cat sat at the table. Her father offered an Oreo, but she shook him off. He frowned.

'What is it, my child?'

She exhaled. 'The Arabs that kidnapped Scott . . . they took the girls.'

'*No! When?*'

'Monday.'

'Little Boo and Pajamae?' Her mother started crying then stood and ran down the hall. 'I must light candles and pray for them.'

Her father slowly set the Oreo on the table. He took her hand.

'Do you think you will . . .?'

'Yes. We will find them. Alive.'

Chapter 23

Friday, 5 February
2 days before the Super Bowl

'Damnit, Mr. President!' the director said. 'The Super Bowl is Sunday. We've got to find those Arabs! These are desperate times. Desperate times require desperate measures.'

Beckeman's phone rang at 7:15 A.M. It was the director.

'The president designated Omar al Mustafa as a Law of War detainee. He is now the property of the United States government. The president also authorized thirty minutes of enhanced interrogation techniques against the detainee in order to prevent an attack on the homeland. Just you, Beckeman. No one else is in the loop on this – or in the room. Understood?'

'I've done this before.'

'So you have. Ground rules: No waterboarding. No pliers. No car batteries. No nail guns. No cigar cutters. No—'

'How about a Taser?'

'I didn't hear that.'

Denny sat in the leather captain's chair in his command center. The travel pillow wrapped around his neck gave him spinal support. Rap music played on the boom box. *Star Wars* posters adorned the walls. A nice throw rug made the concrete cell-block feel warm. The little fridge was filled with Mountain Dew and ice-cream sandwiches. Two flat-screen monitors stared back at him. On one monitor he was playing *League of Legends*. On the other he was tracking the Arabs. He couldn't help thinking what he had thought since he was thirteen and realized he would always be the smartest person in the room: *I'm the master of the whole fucking universe.* He heard the guard named Buddy walking by his cell.

'Hey, Buddy, can I shower now?'

'No.'

Buddy walked on. Okay, Denny was still the smartest person in the room, even if there was only one person in the room these days. Denny focused on the second screen. He was waiting for the asshole. He was a morning guy. And an every-other-day guy. This was the day.

Come out and play.

'Play time, Omar,' Beckeman said.

The guard unlocked the cell door then locked it behind Beckeman.

'Get lost,' Beckeman said to the guard.

He got lost. Mustafa lay on his cot with his eyes closed. Dreaming of killing innocent Americans, no doubt. His eyes opened.

'Did the judge send you?'

'The *judge*? No. The president did. He sends his regards. I need answers, Omar. Who are the Arabs?'

'I do not know them.'

'They work for you.'

'They do not.'

Beckeman removed the Taser from his coat pocket and test-fired it. The electrical volt across the arc contacts crackled.

'You'll tell me.'

Abdul read the message from Zaheed: *The caliph sends his personal regards and prayers. He said he is honored by your martyr-dom. You make him proud.*

Abdul typed a response: *Please give my regards to the caliph.*

Zaheed replied: *I will. Did you send the beheading video?*

Abdul typed: *Yes.*

Denny sat up straight. The words were in Arabic, but he used translation software. In English, they read: 'Beheading video.'

No. It couldn't be. They killed the judge's daughters. Beheaded them. And now they would upload the video to the Internet so the world could see their deaths. And the judge. He would see his daughters' heads being hacked off.

Denny wasn't going to let that happen.

He couldn't save the judge's daughters, but he could find the video and delete it from the Internet. Knock it down as fast as they put it up. It wasn't as if he had anything else to do with his time.

And he owed the judge that much.

Scott sat at his desk in chambers. Louis filled the couch. The others were searching for the girls, but Scott had to come to court to tend to urgent matters then he would return to the search. He would find his girls. He would kill the men who took them. Of that he was certain.

'Judge?'

371

He looked up to a detention center guard standing in the doorway.

'Yes?'

'Judge, this ain't right.'

Beckeman put the imam to the concrete floor and his right knee in the imam's chest. He lowered the Taser to his arm. First the arm, then the chest.

'Get the hell out!'

Beckeman turned to see the judge, the guard, and the big black bailiff standing outside the cell.

'Open this cell,' the judge said.

The guard unlocked the door. The judge stepped in. The black man followed him in. The cell seemed small now.

'You get out, Judge. I'm authorized by the president. National security.'

'I'm authorized by the Constitution. This man is in federal custody by my order, not the president's. Get out now – unless you want your own cell. Unless the president wants the press involved.'

Beckeman stared down the judge.

'It's a war, Judge.'

'Out there, maybe. But not in here. This is a courthouse.'

Beckeman released Mustafa and stood; he stared at the judge then slapped the Taser into his hand. He walked out.

Scott helped the imam to his feet.

'Are you okay?'

The imam sat on his cot. 'Yes. I think he was bluffing.'

'I don't think so.'

'I thought you sent him.'

'To torture you?'

'What would you do to save your girls?'

372

Scott studied the Taser. 'If I thought it would work, I might. But I'd do it myself. I wouldn't send someone to do it for me.'

He again studied the Taser. Would it work? The imam read his mind.

'Go ahead, Judge. Do it. We would do it to you without a second thought. We would cut your head off and send it to your family.'

'Why?'

'You are an unbeliever.' He held up the Koran. 'God said, "Do not grieve for the unbelievers."'

Scott stared at the imam then at the Taser. He hit the button and the volt popped. Why shouldn't he? The imam knew where his girls were being held. He took a step toward the imam but felt a big hand on his arm. He turned; Louis shook his head. Scott lowered the Taser.

'I'm not you. And this isn't Syria or Iraq. This is America. We're better than that. We're better than you.'

The imam smiled. 'We will see about that. We will see if you are better than us when ISIS strikes in America, time after time, when Americans are beheaded on the streets of America. We will see then, Judge, if Americans are truly better than us.'

Denny found the video. It had just been uploaded to the Internet. He clicked on it. The scene was all too familiar: the black ISIS flag, a man dressed in black and holding a sword, a hostage kneeling before him. But there were two hostages. Two young girls. The judge's daughters. The video played. Denny watched in horror. He covered his eyes. He couldn't watch the ending. He deleted the video.

'Well?'

It was the director.

'The judge stopped me.'

'You didn't wait until he went home for the day?'

'No, I didn't. He threatened to go to the press if I didn't stop.'

'You think he will?'

'No.'

'Did you get anything from the imam?'

'No.'

'God help us.'

Beckeman hung up. Agent Stryker barged into his office carrying a laptop.

'Captain, you gotta see this.'

'Okay,' Scott said, 'I've marked off the search grids for tonight.'

Everyone stood around the kitchen table.

'We have twelve hours till sunlight. We can cover a lot of ground tonight.'

Someone banged hard on the front door. Scott walked to the door and looked out; Agent Beckeman and a dozen other men in suits stood on his porch. He opened the door. Beckeman did not seem happy.

'Agent Beckeman.'

'Judge, may we come in?'

He didn't wait for an answer. He stepped inside; the other agents followed. They crowded the small living room. Beckeman glanced toward the kitchen.

'Come on out, Peña.'

Cat emerged from the kitchen; the others followed.

'You knew about this? His girls getting abducted?'

'How do you know?' Scott asked.

Beckeman looked from Cat to Scott. 'You're a federal judge. You can do whatever you want.' He pointed a finger at Cat. 'You're an FBI agent. You do what you're told.'

'How do you know?' Scott said.

374

'You're suspended, Peña. Gun and badge.'

Scott grabbed Beckeman's lapels and yelled in his face, 'How do you know?'

Beckeman stared at Scott a moment then dropped his eyes. Scott released him. Beckeman nodded at another agent. The agent placed a laptop on the coffee table and sat in front of it. He typed then turned the screen toward Scott. On the screen stood a man dressed in all black with a black scarf concealing his face except for his eyes; he wore yellow sneakers. He held a long sword. Kneeling before him were Boo and Pajamae; they were bound and blindfolded. Scott's knees buckled; he dropped to the floor and closed his eyes.

'No . . .'

'Play it,' Beckeman said.

'Hold on,' Frank said. 'That's not right. Scott's—'

'Play it!'

The agent activated the video. Scott opened his eyes at the sound. He wanted to hear his daughters' last words. He wanted to see them alive once more. He wanted to kill the man with the sword.

'We are here in America,' the man said. 'And we are here to stay until America leaves the Middle East. It is our land, our lives, our oil. Get out of the Middle East, and we will get out of America. You leave us alone, we will leave you alone. Until then, we will bring death and destruction to Americans just as America has brought death and destruction to Arabs. This war will be like Vietnam for America; before this war is over, you will beg for a truce.'

He raised his sword.

'We will show you no mercy. We fight for Allah. For our homeland. For Muslims around the world. You have killed our children. Now we kill yours.'

'Oh, please . . . don't kill us!' Pajamae cried.

'A. Scott's gonna kill you, asshole!' Boo shouted.

The man grasped the sword with both hands and swung it down hard at Pajamae's neck—

'No!' Louis screamed.

—but he stopped the sword an inch away from her skin. He looked up at the camera.

'Judge Fenney, release the imam immediately or the next time I will not stop the blade.'

The screen went black. Scott's hands were trembling, and his heart racing. Boo was right; he would kill him.

'Run it back,' Beckeman said.

The agent manning the laptop ran the video back to where Pajamae said, 'Oh, please . . . don't kill us.'

'She said something,' Scott said.

Beckeman nodded. 'They edited it out. She said "Abdul."'

'Thanks for not letting Abdul kill us,' Boo said.

The good brother had brought them more falafel.

'My brother, he has lost his soul.'

'You know, if you let us go, A. Scott, he'd help you. He's that kind of man.'

'But we kidnapped you.'

'My mother ran off with a golf pro, and he defended her.'

'True.'

'Then let us go.'

'I cannot. I could not let Abdul behead you with his sword—'

'*Behead?*' Pajamae said. '*Sword?* Oh, sweet Jesus.'

'—but to save your life, I had to make a pledge to him, on our father's soul.'

'What kind of pledge?'

'To help him bring the stadium down on Sunday.'

'You saved us by promising to kill a lot of other people?'

'Yes.'

'But they'll die.'

'But you will not.'

'If Abdul killed us, would you still help him kill all those people?'

'No.'

'Then let him kill us.'

'You would die for them?'

'Yes.'

'Me, too,' Pajamae said.

'It would not matter. Those people will still die.'

'Even if you don't help him?'

'Yes.'

'We can't let them behead those girls and put it out on the Internet!' the president said. 'It'll be open season on Muslims in America.'

'YouTube must've pulled it,' the FBI director said. 'It went down as soon as it went up.'

'Find those girls!'

Denny sat with his head in his hands. He had deleted the video fifty-two times so far. As fast as it went up, he knocked it down. Like playing whack-a-mole. It was the least he could do for the judge. He still couldn't watch the ending.

Beckeman had watched *Taken* a hundred times. It was 3:00 A.M., and he needed a good movie. He often watched a movie to decompress after a stressful day, which is to say, he watched a movie every night. Till he fell asleep. Usually in the recliner.

If he had a daughter and someone grabbed her, he'd go after her with everything he had. He'd find the bad guys and kill them. He'd rescue his daughter. They'd live happily ever after. Just like in the movie.

He often wished life had happy endings like Hollywood.

He slid the *Taken* DVD back into its slot on the shelf and thumbed through the rest of the T's. He had organized his extensive collection alphabetically. He started into the U's. *Unfaithful . . . Unforgiven . . . Untouchables.* He pulled that DVD out and plugged it in. He needed an Eliot Ness moment.

Why had Frank Turner told him to watch it again?

Beckeman dropped into his recliner and started the movie. Mustafa was going to get off scot-free. The son of a bitch was a bad guy, but he would walk out the courthouse a free Muslim. Because Special Agent Eric Beckeman couldn't find any evidence that he committed any crimes.

Damn, Costner was so young when he made the movie. Sean Connery was fantastic as the Chicago cop and Andy Garcia was cool and a dead shot, but who was the hero? The nerd accountant. Al Capone killed people and made millions bootlegging, but Ness could never nail him. But the nerd did.

Beckeman jumped out of his chair.

Scott rolled over in bed. It was dawn, but he could not sleep. They had searched through the night but had found nothing. They might have walked right past the house where the girls were being held. An arm fell over him. She held him tight from behind.

'I'm not leaving you until we find them,' Cat said. 'We'll sleep a few hours then search all day and night. We will find them.'

Chapter 24

Saturday, 6 February
The day before the Super Bowl

'You find the guys. We'll find the girls.'

It was nine the next morning. The FBI team had met at Scott's house for breakfast and strategy; Consuelo had fed everyone through tears and three rosaries. The FBI could not conduct a manhunt in broad daylight in Highland Park. It would be too obvious. Someone would call the media. Once the TV trucks arrived, the manhunt was over. And chances were good that the Arabs would spot them; if they did, they would kill the girls and run. If they had not already killed them.

'How are you going to find your girls?' Beckeman said.

'I've got help.'

'Macklin?'

The judge nodded.

'What's he doing?'

'What the FBI can't.'

★

Denny Macklin sat up straight in the leather captain's chair with lumbar support.

He couldn't save the judge's daughters, but he could still save a hundred thousand people at the Super Bowl tomorrow. He grabbed the Bausch & Lomb and squirted the saline solution in each eye; he wasn't even going to blink while he had the asshole on the screen. He hadn't seen the asshole in two days, and then suddenly he's there. Another message from Syria that . . . disappeared before Denny could climb aboard.

'What the hell is he doing?'

Beckeman stood outside the judge's house with Agent Stryker. Peña and the judge had left to search for his girls.

'The president and the director, they both ordered us to find those girls,' Stryker said.

'It's a diversionary tactic.'

'What?'

'They grabbed the girls to keep us occupied looking for them while they bomb the stadium.'

'That's what Peña said when they snatched the judge.'

'I know.'

'So what do we do?'

'Secure the stadium.'

'What about the Arabs?'

'Tomorrow is Super Bowl Sunday. They're coming to us.'

'You go to them. And you kill those fucking Arabs.'

It was all he thought about these days. Hector stared across his desk at José and Gilberto, his top two *sicarios*, who stood before him in his hacienda.

'These are my orders: Cross the river into America tonight. Drive to Dallas without delay. Find Jorge and Manuel. Collect my money. And kill the fucking Arabs.'

Hector held out his prized machete. José took it. He and Gilberto had flown to Cancun from Nuevo Laredo that morning on one of Hector's Gulfstream jets. They would fly back, enter America, and then drive to Dallas. They would arrive early the next morning and kill the fucking Arabs. Of that, Hector had no doubt. They had completed numerous assignments in America without apprehension or identification; their faces existed on no law enforcement database. In America, they were ghosts.

'Bring me their heads, *por favor.*'

'Oh, Hector—'

The woman walked into the office with her pretty head in a glossy magazine. She looked up and squarely at José and Gilberto. She saw their faces. Did she hear Hector's order?

'I'm sorry. I didn't realize you had company. We'll talk later.'

She twirled and bounced out. José and Gilberto stared at her butt. They quickly realized their error and became red-faced. They now stared at the floor with embarrassment. But Hector stared with sadness at the open doorway through which she had walked. They had been together for a year; she had lived with him for the last ten months. It had been the best ten months of his life. But just like that, it had come to an end. He sighed.

'So*, mí muchachos,* do you have any questions regarding your assignment?'

Gilberto raised his hand like a schoolboy.

'*Sí?*'

'I have two questions.'

'Okay.'

'*Jefe,* I have killed many men for you, but never before have I cut a man's head off.'

'Ah. Are you reluctant due to your religious beliefs?'

Gilberto had been an altar boy before he became a *sicario.*

381

'Oh, no, *jefe,* it is not that. I'm just wondering if we should kill them before we cut their heads off or after?'

José rolled his eyes.

'Well, Gilberto,' Hector said, 'once you cut off their heads, they will be dead, you see, so there is no after.'

Gilberto nodded. 'Ohh. That makes sense.'

'There is less chance of getting blood on your boots if you kill them first and let the blood settle then cut off their heads,' José said.

Hector gestured at José. 'See, a practical *hombre.* That is why José is *mí sicario numero uno.* He never lets emotion affect his judgment. He is all business.'

José shrugged. 'I never liked Jorge that much anyway.'

Hector grunted in response. 'So, Gilberto, what is your second question?'

'*Jefe,*' Gilberto said, 'tomorrow is the Super Bowl. The Cowboys are playing. I love the Cowboys. Can we not kill the fucking Arabs on Monday? I want to watch the game.'

José again rolled his eyes and started to reprimand his young protégé, but Hector stopped him with a raised hand. Gilberto was only nineteen, so Hector had to be patient. He was just a boy. A stone-cold killer, but still just a boy.

'If you kill the fucking Arabs tomorrow morning, you can go to the game tomorrow afternoon. I have season tickets, so I got two tickets on the fifty-yard line for the Super Bowl.'

'You have season tickets to the Cowboys games? How many games did you go to this year?'

'Unfortunately, none. The outstanding federal warrants for my arrest in the U.S. prevented my attendance.'

Hector tossed the Super Bowl tickets on the desk.

'The tickets are yours upon completion of your assignment.'

Gilberto snatched the tickets off the desk and regarded them as some men do gold.

'*Jefe, sí*, we will kill the fucking Arabs tomorrow. And then go to the game. I always wanted to see the Super Bowl live. *Gracias, jefe. Gracias.*'

He was just a boy. Hector pulled out his wallet and counted out one thousand U.S. dollars for each *hombre*.

'For the game.' He then added another five hundred. 'For my children. Please buy them Cowboys jerseys, I think maybe Tony Romo.'

Agent Stryker stood at the fifty-yard line on the second level. The stadium was not just a football stadium; it was a multi-use venue. It hosted rodeos, pro wrestling, soccer, college Final Four basketball, concerts by the Rolling Stones and George Strait, the American Country Music Awards, motocross rallies, monster truck competitions, and Boy Scout sleepovers. The floor could be transformed from a football field to a monster truck dirt course in hours. And the dirt, props, turf, goal posts, stages, lighting, and equipment for each event were stored in dozens of huge storerooms below where Stryker stood. Store-rooms large enough to store a massive bomb. The FBI had searched every storeroom in the stadium. There was no bomb in the stadium.

It was 7:00 P.M. They had searched all day. Walking the streets and alleys around the SMU campus. Looking for any sign of the girls or the Muslims. Of course, trying to find a Muslim in Highland Park was like trying to find a Democrat in Highland Park. It was a 'needle in a haystack' type of thing. Knowing that his daughters were near, maybe in this house or that house, threatened Scott's sanity that day. He had to find his girls. He had to save them. A father protects his children.

★

So you did not behead the hostages as I instructed?

No.

Why not?

It was not feasible.

Did your brother interfere?

Yes.

You allowed your little brother to prevent you from following my orders?

He said if I killed the hostages, he would not help me with the stadium. I need him. So I secured his pledge on our father's soul that he would carry out the stadium mission if I spared the girls' lives.

Ah. He has grown attached to the hostages. That can happen, particularly when they are young and female. It is always a better practice to abduct older white males, preferably Jews, as there is little chance of becoming attached to them.

But the emotional impact of two little girls as hostages is critical.

That is true. Just make sure your brother does not lose his nerve tomorrow.

He wants to be a lawyer.

I wanted to be the next Rinaldo. Allah had other plans for me.

Beckeman gazed upon the green artificial turf on the playing field. He had played football in high school, as most boys do, and he had dreamed of playing pro ball, as some boys do.

But God had other plans for him.

Playing football for a living. How simple that life must be. Play one game a week every week for six months. Each game is contested within the white stripes delineating the field. Referees call fouls and impose penalties. The game is played according to rules set out in a rulebook. Everyone played by the rules, more or less. The biggest rules violation the commissioner had to worry about was that a quarterback might deflate the football for a better grip.

He did not have to worry that an Islamic terrorist might blow up the stadium.

In less than twenty-four hours, one hundred thousand spectators would fill the stands. They would wear their team colors, jerseys, and face paint. They would drink beer and margaritas, eat nachos and corn dogs, cheer and boo. They would watch the action on the field and replays on the video screen hanging above the field. They would be happy and free and alive. They would not know that their lives were in danger. That their lives were always in danger. How comforting it must be to live in utter ignorance of the danger all around. In blissful innocence. Beckeman felt like Agent Kay in *Men in Black*, the first one where he says to Agent Jay, 'There's always an alien battle cruiser or a Korilian death ray or an intergalactic plague about to wipe out life on this planet, and the only thing that lets these people get on with their hopeful little lives is that they do not know about it.'

'Captain, we found brothers at the mosque. Named Siddiqui.'

Stryker had walked up.

'And?'

'They're law students at SMU.'

'And?'

'One is tall, one short.'

'And?'

'Tall one plays soccer.'

'And?'

'His name is Abdul.'

A hundred thousand people might die the next day because Denny Macklin had failed to find the bad guys. He sat in the captain's chair in his command center; his two laptops were up and running, and the software scanned every word coming out of Syria on every message board and every chat room.

Nothing.

It was 9:00 P.M. in Dallas and 5:00 A.M. in Syria. The prior messages he had seen had all been sent from Syria in the 4:00–7:00 P.M. range. They were way out of range now.

Shit.

He was the smartest hacker in the world. But he was in this cell because he was too smart for his own good. He had finally figured that out. He had failed his father. Himself. The world. And now he had failed the judge's daughters. Denny Macklin was a failure.

Allahu Akbar, Zaheed.

At first the words on the screen didn't register with Denny's brain. Too many sleepless nights, too many hours staring at digital text on the screens, too many Starbucks.

Allahu Akbar, Abdul.

Now the words registered. Denny jumped up in his chair and on board the message. This time he stayed on. They bounced from Syria to Cairo to Casablanca to Lisbon to London to Quebec to Chicago to Dallas to—

Shit.

Scott and Cat were walking east on University Boulevard on the west side of the SMU campus. Walking. Searching. Hoping. Praying. It was night, but Highland Park had street lights. His cell phone rang. He answered.

'Judge, it's Denny. I found them. They're law students at SMU. One is named Abdul. And he's on a computer in the library right now talking to someone named Zaheed in Syria. Get over there and grab that asshole. And Judge – I'm sorry about your girls.'

'They're alive, Denny. He didn't kill them on that video.'

'Oh, thank God.'

Scott disconnected the call and said to Cat, 'One of the

386

Arabs is in the law school library, on a computer. His name is Abdul.'

They broke into a run. They were only a block from the law school. They dodged oncoming traffic on Hillcrest and crossed onto the campus. They turned north and cut between the buildings and ran up the stairs to the main entrance of the Underwood Law Library.

Abdul glanced out the third-story window and saw the judge and his FBI girlfriend running through the illuminated quadrangle and up the steps to the library entrance on the second floor. *Shit.* They had found him. Somehow.

It was time.

He logged off the computer and stepped outside the computer lab and to the adjacent atrium. He could see down to the entrance. The judge and the FBI agent stood one floor below him; would they take the stairs or the elevators? He waited and watched; they stopped a student. The student pointed up. Abdul ducked back then peeked out. The judge and the agent walked toward the elevators beneath him. He pulled his knit cap down low on his face and ran to the stairs on the other side of the atrium. He joined a group of students heading downstairs.

Cat stepped into the elevator. Scott followed then stopped.

'You take the elevator,' he said. 'I'll take the stairs.'

Scott backed out. The elevator doors closed; he jogged to the stairwell. He took the stairs two at a time. A group of students hurried down past him; nothing about them caught his attention. He arrived at the third-floor and—

—he froze.

One of the students wore yellow sneakers.

387

He looked down the stairwell to the second-floor landing; he saw yellow sneakers. That was the man who took his daughters. The man who swung the sword at his daughter's neck. The man he was going to kill. The man stood only fifteen feet below Scott.

'Abdul!'

The man hesitated but did not look up. He ran.

'Shit!'

Scott ran back down the stairs and into the lobby. He stopped and looked around. He didn't see the man. He ran out the main entrance and spotted the yellow sneakers; the man ran fast across the law school quadrangle and into the dark trees. Scott ran after him.

The elevator doors opened, and Cat stepped out. She drew her weapon from her waist pack. She held it against her leg to avoid attention. The computer lab was adjacent to the elevators. She stepped to the door. LAW STUDENTS ONLY the sign read. She stepped inside and scanned the room. Only a few heads were visible above the cubicles. She walked down the center of the room and checked each cubicle. No student appeared Arab. She glanced out the window and saw Scott running under the lights outside the building and into the trees.

'I lost him.'

Scott had chased Abdul but had lost him in the dark on the treed campus. He returned to the law school to find Cat chasing after him.

'What do we do now?' she asked.

'Call the dean.'

'Why?'

'Abdul's a law student.'

★

They met the dean at his office in the main law school building. He arrived just minutes later; he lived only a few blocks away. When a federal judge says it's an emergency and needs his help, the law school dean helps. Scott knew the dean personally; he introduced him to Agent Peña.

'Scott,' the dean said, 'it's after ten. What's the emergency?'

'Richard, the same men who kidnapped me took my daughters from my house Monday. They're holding them right here in Highland Park. They're part of the conspiracy to blow up the stadium tomorrow, and we just learned that they're law students.'

'*How?*'

'Long story. But we need your help.'

'Of course. What can I do?'

'Do you have any Muslim law students?'

'A few.'

'Any brothers?'

'Two. Abdul and Saddam—'

'Siddiqui,' Beckeman said as he entered the dean's office.

'And you are?' the dean said.

'Special Agent Beckeman, Joint Terrorism Task Force.'

The dean gestured at Cat. 'I thought she was FBI.'

'She's suspended. We need to find the Siddiqui brothers. Fast.'

'They're the terrorists?'

'They are.'

The dean sat behind his desk and consulted his computer screen.

'They haven't been in school the last week.'

'Any idea why?'

'No.'

'Do you have photos of them?'

389

He again looked at his screen. 'No. Nothing in their files. But they're just normal-looking law students.'

'They don't dress in traditional Muslim attire?'

'No. They dress in traditional Highland Park attire.'

'Phone numbers?'

'This is what we have on file.'

He wrote numbers down on a notepad and handed the page to Beckeman.

'Address?'

On the drive to the Siddiqui brothers' home, the FBI agents talked excitedly, but Scott sat in the back seat with a single thought in mind: *I'm going to kill Abdul Siddiqui.*

The phone numbers were no longer working, so they drove to the address. Stryker drove the sedan; Beckeman sat up front, Peña and the judge in the back. They pulled up to a house on Lorraine Avenue; it was on the other side of Highland Park, a long way from the SMU stadium. Too far to hear the band playing. The judge had told him about the music on the phone call. They knocked on the door, and an older woman answered in her night robe. Beckeman flashed his badge.

'Ma'am, I'm Agent Beckeman with the FBI. Do you know Abdul and Saddam Siddiqui?'

'Yes, I do. They're nice boys. Are they okay?'

'We're trying to locate them. Do they live here?'

'Not anymore. They rented the guesthouse out back, but they moved out before Christmas.'

'Did they leave a forwarding address?'

'No. They didn't do anything wrong, did they?'

They returned to the sedan.

'How'd we miss them?' Peña asked.

'They moved.'

'And they're law students,' Stryker said. 'Who'd figure law students for jihadists?' He was checking his iPad. 'Here they are. We interviewed them back in November. They were clean. No criminal histories, no ties to any jihadist groups . . .'

'They were tied to the imam,' Beckeman said.

'A lot of Muslim men prayed at the mosque.' He tapped the iPad. 'And we did a sneak and peek on the follow-up, just to make sure.'

'When?' Beckeman asked.

'Ten days ago, after the judge was grabbed.'

'But they haven't lived here since before Christmas.'

Stryker frowned and checked the iPad again. 'Oh, we didn't do it here. We did it at another house. On Drexel Drive.'

Carlos and Bobby walked down the sidewalk on Drexel Drive.

'So if I meet a zombie,' Carlos said, 'I'll stab it in the head with my switchblade.'

'You carry a switchblade?' Bobby said.

'You don't?'

Bobby regarded Carlos a moment then sniffed the air. 'That you?'

'I didn't fart.'

'Is that your aftershave?'

There was a sweet smell in the air. Carlos sniffed.

'No, man, that ain't me.'

Carlos gave a suspicious look around and then above them. He pointed up.

'That's him.'

Bobby looked up. A kid sat high on a limb in a big oak tree that hung over the sidewalk. Highland Park was known for its canopy of oak trees. But not for kids smoking dope in oak trees.

'What are you doing out here?' Bobby asked. 'It's after midnight. And it's cold.'

'I'm not cold,' the kid said.

'Get down from that fucking tree,' Carlos said.

'Fuck you,' the kid said.

'I'm a cop. Undercover. Now get down.'

'You don't look like a cop.'

'That's why they call it undercover, you little dope.'

'Let me see your badge.'

Carlos flashed a badge to the boy but whispered to Bobby, 'Got it at flea market. Figured it might come in handy one day.'

The kid climbed down the tree. He looked about fifteen. He continued to suck on the joint.

'What do you want?' he said.

'We're looking for a couple of Arab dudes,' Carlos said, 'selling drugs to minors.'

'Cool. Like on TV.'

'Yeah. Like on TV. You seen anyone look like that around here?'

'Yeah.'

'Where?'

'Behind my house.'

'*What?*'

'We've got a guesthouse out back. We rent it out to rich college kids. Since my dad left us to shack up with his secretary, we need the money. They pay my mom in cash, that way she doesn't have to pay taxes. It's the law.'

'Is that so?' Bobby said.

'Yep. Mom said if Mexicans mowing the grass don't have to pay taxes on their cash, why should she?' He looked at Carlos. 'No offense.'

Carlos shrugged. 'When I was roofing houses, we got paid in cash. I never paid a dime in taxes.'

'What are their names?' Bobby asked.

'The Mexicans who mow our grass?'

That's why they call it dope.

'No. The Arabs living in your guesthouse.'

'Ohh. Abdul and Saddam. They're law students.'

'Just them two?'

'Yeah.'

'You see anyone else with them? Maybe two girls?'

'We never see them. The guesthouse is behind the garage, can't see it from the street or the house. They come and go through the alley. I think all they do is study.'

'They give you this dope?'

'Yep.'

'Why?'

'So I don't rat 'em out to my mom. They got a cat in the house.'

'A cat?'

'Yeah. My mom has a strict no-pets policy. She'd kick them out if she knew. So they give me weed to keep my mouth shut.'

'Extortion. A criminal in the making.'

'Don't tell my mom, okay? She's already in therapy because of the divorce. This is my therapy.'

The boy took a drag on the joint.

'Give me that.' Carlos snatched the joint from the boy's mouth. 'Smoking dope in front of a cop. This shit can fuck up your brain. Tell you what, I won't tell your mom if you get me a key to that guesthouse.'

'A key?'

'Yeah, a key to the front door.'

'Well . . . okay.'

The boy turned and ran into the house. Carlos shrugged and sucked on the joint. He inhaled, held it, and exhaled slowly.

'Good shit.'

The boy returned with a key and gave it to Carlos.

'Give me my joint.'

'Sorry, kid. Evidence. Now get your ass inside. And stay there.'

The boy muttered, 'Fucking cops,' but went inside. Carlos finished off the joint, and Bobby called Scotty. The call was still ringing through when a black sedan drove up fast and stopped next to them. Scotty jumped out. Three FBI agents followed him out. Carlos dropped the joint and stomped it out.

'We walked right past this place,' Scott said. 'The first night we searched.'

'You can't see the guesthouse from the street,' Cat said.

Beckeman had snuck off to conduct a quick surveillance of the house. Scott stood on the sidewalk talking to Judge Herrin and the Latino guy named Carlos. Cat addressed Agent Stryker.

'We've been searching Highland Park for these girls since Thursday when we learned they were being held near SMU.'

'You should've told us.'

'Why didn't you tell me you had done a sneak and peek at a Highland Park house?'

'It was stated in a manhunt meeting.'

'I didn't get that information.'

Stryker nodded toward Scott then lowered his voice. 'Maybe you were fucking the judge that morning.'

Cat fought the urge to punch the bastard and was losing the fight when Beckeman returned. He shook his head in answer to their unasked question.

'It's dark. Shades are drawn. Can't see inside. Can't hear anything. They're probably asleep.'

'The girls are in there,' Scott said. 'Let's go in. We've got a key.'

'Maybe they're in there, maybe not. But maybe they booby-trapped the house. We hit a tripwire, we could blow the place up, kill everyone inside, including your daughters. We need to call in the pros.'

He turned to Stryker.

'Call in HRT.'

Chapter 25

Sunday, 7 February
Super Bowl Sunday
7:00 A.M.
9 hours before kickoff

The Hostage Rescue Team stood massed outside the small guest-house in Highland Park. They were waiting for first light. The HRT operators wore helmets and body armor and wielded assault weapons. They would go in hard, they would go in fast, and they would rescue the two hostages and capture or kill the two bad guys.

That is, if they were lucky.

If they were not so lucky, if the bad guys knew they were coming and opened fire when they kicked in the door or had rigged the house with explosives, some of them would die; the bad guys would hopefully die; the hostages would surely die. Hostage Rescue Team leader Roger Dedman lived for these moments. And one day he would die in these moments.

Was today that day?

★

'Today is the day, my brother. Today, we meet Allah.'

His big brother actually seemed excited. They had both bleached their hair blond and shaved clean, the better to look American and not Arab. Abdul stood in front of the full-length mirror in the bedroom. His little brother lay on the bed watching the morning news; he was already dressed in his uniform. He stared at his big brother's bare torso. Across his chest two words had been tattooed: *Allahu Akbar*. Across his back in fancy script were more words: *We will put terror into the hearts of the unbelievers – The Koran 3:151*. His brother was definitely a committed jihadist, he had to give him that. He was not. But he had no choice. He had pledged on his father's soul to help his brother if his brother did not kill the girls. Abdul did not kill the girls; so he would honor his pledge. He ate his Honey Nut Cheerios, but he thought he might throw up.

Ten minutes later, the sky had brightened enough to see the small guesthouse. A Kia Sorrento registered to Abdul Jabaar Siddiqui sat out front. The Hostage Rescue Team stood ready to make entry into the house. The entire block had been evacuated in case the suspects had set explosives in the house – in case they chose to meet Allah rather than face American justice. Everyone knew this could be a suicide mission – for the suspects, the rescuers, and the hostages. Beckeman turned to HRT operator Roger Dedman, the man in charge of this rescue mission, the man who would be first through the door, and said, 'Go get the hostages.'

'We'll bust the door,' Dedman said.

'Wait.' Beckeman dug deep in his pocket and pulled out a key. 'Here.'

'You've got a key to the house? How?'

'Long story.'

Dedman turned to the judge and said, 'I'll bring your girls out myself.'

Dedman walked off, and Beckeman regarded the judge. The man was pale with fear. But not for himself. For his girls. The judge had wanted to go in himself when they found the house; Beckeman – and Peña – had convinced him that it was safest for his girls to wait for HRT.

'Judge, we've got EMTs and an ambulance on standby to take your girls to the hospital.' He turned and stuck an open hand out to Agent Peña. 'Gun and badge, Peña.'

She hadn't surrendered either yet. She started to say something, but the sound of a news helicopter hovering overhead drowned her out. Beckeman pointed at the nearest agent.

'Get that helicopter out of here!'

The media had gotten word and descended on the scene. Which didn't make Beckeman happy. But at least the American people would see the FBI in action, risking their lives to save lives.

Inside the house, Boo held the nail clippers and clipped the rope holding her hands. She had been working most of the night. She could hear Pajamae stirring next to her.

'Mama?'

Pajamae often called for her mother while sleeping.

'It's me, Pajamae. Boo.'

'Oh, no, I thought it was a nightmare. But it's real. We're still tied up.'

Pajamae started crying. Wailing. Loudly.

'*Shh*, you're going to wake up the brothers.'

Boo worked the clippers even faster.

The HRT entry team stood on the front porch. Two operators held bomb blankets; upon entry into the house, their job was to locate the hostages and cover them with the blankets and their bodies before the bomb exploded. If there were bombs. Roger Dedman put his ear to the door.

'They're crying,' he said in a low voice. 'We need to get inside. *Now.*'

Abdul jabbar admired himself in the bedroom mirror.

'Father would be proud of us today. Allahu Akbar, my brother.'

'Allahu Akbar,' his brother said, as if he were about to swallow a deadly pill.

'Pajamae, don't cry.'

Boo worked the clippers on the rope fast. She needed to get her hands free before the brothers woke up. She needed to free herself and then her sister so they could escape! Before Abdul cut their heads off!

Beckeman watched the entry team fifty feet away at the door but listened to their communications over the handheld radio. The judge and his people had gathered around.

'They're crying?' the big black bailiff said.

Dedman inserted the key into the front door lock. He turned the key. The key wouldn't turn.

Dedman's voice came over the radio: 'Key is a no go. We're going in hard. Bring up the battering ram.'

Beckeman heard the bailiff's voice again: 'They're crying?'

'Today, my brother, we strike a blow for our father. For all Muslims. For . . .' Abdul cocked his ear. 'Brother, did you hear something?'

'I don't think so.'

'Check the front door.

'I'm eating my Cheerios.'

Abdul sighed and walked to the front door.

'They're crying?'

Louis Wright could take it no longer. His girls were crying, and he was doing nothing about it. He decided to do something about it.

'I don't need a battering ram.'

Louis broke for the front door.

'Big man!'

Carlos saw Louis's massive body making for the door like cops were chasing him. He followed his friend.

'I'm coming, big man!'

Louis weighed three hundred thirty pounds; Carlos only two hundred. Consequently, Carlos caught up with him halfway to the front door. They ran harder. Ten feet from the door, the HRT guys saw them and dove out of the way.

'Let's kick some ass!' Carlos shouted.

Scott looked at Louis and Carlos running toward the house then at Cat; they both broke ranks and ran after them.

Boo's hands came free of the ropes. She yanked the blindfold off. She blinked against the light. She looked around. She pulled the blindfold off Pajamae.

Abdul arrived at the front door. He put his hand on the doorknob. He turned the knob.

★

Louis and Carlos threw their bodies at the door, five hundred and thirty pounds of pissed-off black and brown Americans. The wood splintered on impact.

CRACK! The front door crashed in; it sounded as if the home were crashing down on them. Boo and Pajamae screamed.

Abdul stood at the open front door. He grunted. Must have been the paperboy. He leaned down and picked up the morning newspaper on the doorstep. He shut the door and returned to the bedroom.

Louis and Carlos fell through the shattered door, rolled, and jumped up like commandos. Carlos pulled his switchblade.

'Come and get me, you crazy-ass Muslims! You ain't never tried to behead no Mexican!'

Louis saw the girls. 'Pajamae! Boo!'

'Louis? Carlos?' Boo said. 'What the heck are y'all doing here?'

He dove on top of them and waited for the bomb to explode.

Dedman jumped over what was left of the front door and ran inside. They were in a small main living area with a kitchen at the far end. He saw only the big black man and two girls huddled on the floor. Well, there was no bomb.

'No suspects in the first room,' he said into his mike.

The black man sat up. The white hostage threw her hands into the air like a bank robber caught in the act. Dedman realized he was pointing his weapon at her; he lowered the gun. The black hostage lay bound on the floor; she was curled up in a ball and sobbing.

★

Scott and Cat followed HRT into the house. Scott ran to the girls and dropped to his knees; Boo jumped into his arms. Cat untied Pajamae and hugged her. Then Pajamae came to him. They all cried. Scott embraced his girls. His life.

Beckeman entered the house. Agents were running through the house; he heard no gunshots or explosions. The agents returned to the main room with their weapons down.

'The house is clear.'

Beckeman stood next to the judge's Mexican man and said, 'Put the blade up before you hurt yourself.'

Karen watched the news at home. Her phone rang. It was Bobby.

'The girls are safe.'

She dropped the phone and sobbed on the floor.

Consuelo had said four rosaries that morning. She had lit so many prayer candles that the night had turned to day an hour early in her house. When the TV person said the girls were alive and well, she fell to her knees and thanked God.

Denny Macklin and Buddy cried in front of the TV in his cell. Buddy slapped Denny on the shoulder.

'Denny, you made your dad proud.'

Beckeman stood in the center of the room with the hostages, the judge, the black bailiff, the Mexican matador, and Agent Peña. His agents searched the house but came up empty. Beckeman turned his hands up.

'Where the hell are they?'

★

'Look,' Abdul jabbar Khalid said.

He pointed at the television. The scene was from the Siddiqui brothers' house. The FBI had stormed the house and found the girls. But not them.

'See, it worked,' Abdul said. 'The FBI is stupid and arrogant and prejudiced. They accepted our anonymous tips on Haddad and the imam and our setting up the Siddiquis without question. They are Muslims, therefore they must be terrorists.'

'The imam *is* a terrorist.'

'All the better for our plan.'

By tipping off the FBI to the bomb plot, to Aabdar Haddad, and to the imam, the FBI thought they had apprehended the terrorists, so they had unconsciously relaxed, like soccer players when they know they've won the game. Then they kidnapped the judge and demanded the imam's release; kidnapped the girls and demanded the imam's release; posted the YouTube video and demanded the imam's release. That reinforced their conclusion that the imam was the mastermind. The FBI had focused all of their attention on the imam, which allowed Abdul and Saadi Khalid to fly under the radar. They framed the Siddiqui brothers for this moment: the FBI was there, and the Khalid brothers were here. And truth be known, he enjoyed taunting the FBI, a lone wolf evading their high-tech surveillance. *Catch me if you can!* They could not catch Abdul jabbar Khalid.

'Come, brother, let us take a hundred thousand Christians and Jews to meet Allah.'

Abdul and Saadi walked out of the house they rented in East Dallas and got into their Honda Civic. Destiny awaited the Khalid brothers.

'I hope the girls are okay,' Saadi said.

'We're bleeding,' Boo said.

'*Bleeding?*' Scott called out to the agents. 'They're bleeding! We need some help over here!'

403

Two EMTs rushed over with a medical case. They dropped to the floor and opened the case then pulled on latex gloves.

'Lay down, honey,' one said to Boo.

He took her shoulders and gently laid her down. The other EMT did the same with Pajamae. They checked the girls for obvious blood but found none.

'Tell me where you're bleeding,' the first EMT said to Boo.

'No,' she said.

'Boo, where are you bleeding?' Scott said. 'He needs to know.'

'No.'

'Boo—'

'I'm not telling him. I'll tell Cat.'

Cat pushed in and dropped to her knees. Boo gestured her closer. She put her head close to Boo's then her ear next to Boo's mouth. Boo whispered something; Cat came up with a relieved expression. She addressed the EMTs.

'Do you have any feminine hygiene products in that case?'

They both exhaled.

'Uh, no, ma'am.'

'Let's go to the bathroom, girls.'

They helped the girls up. The three females walked off. The three males looked helpless, as men do in these situations.

'Single father,' Scott said.

'A man can't raise women,' the older EMT said.

Agent Beckeman came over but gestured in the girls' direction. 'They okay?'

Scott nodded. 'Female matter.'

'Ah.'

Beckeman turned to a dozen agents in body armor and plain clothes standing in a circle in the middle of the room.

'Where the hell are the brothers?'

404

His question was answered with silent shrugs and confused expressions. The silence lingered until broken by a new voice behind them.

'Oh, no, we've been robbed!'

All eyes turned to the opening where the front door once hung. Two young Arab men stood there with suitcases in hand. Scott pointed at them.

'That's them! I saw that one in Whole Foods!'

The agents pointed their guns at the men. They dropped their suitcases and raised their hands.

An agent entered the room carrying yellow sneakers, a black ISIS flag, and a sword. Which brought the anger back inside Scott. He stepped to the men.

'Which one of you is Abdul?'

'I am,' the tall one said.

Scott punched him in the face, knocked him to the floor, and jumped on top of him. He punched him again and again until he was pulled off by FBI agents. He sat on the floor breathing hard. Agent Beckeman stood over him with a bemused expression.

'Judge, you can't beat up suspects. It's unconstitutional.'

Beckeman turned to Agent Stryker. 'You did a sneak and peek and didn't find the sword?'

'Maybe it wasn't here.'

'Maybe you fucked up.' He turned to the Siddiqui brothers. 'Confess now, and you might not get the death penalty.'

'That's not our sword,' the shorter brother said.

'Oh, right. Someone framed you.'

'You were stalking me in Whole Foods!' the judge said.

'I was shopping!'

★

Boo walked into the living room with Cat and Pajamae. Two older boys sat on the floor handcuffed. One seemed familiar. Where had she seen him?

'Who are they?' Pajamae asked.

'The men who kidnapped you,' Scott said.

'Which one is Abdul?' Boo asked.

Beckeman pointed at the bigger boy. 'Him.'

Boo walked over to Abdul and punched him in the face; he fell over backwards. She pointed a finger at him.

'That's for trying to sex me!'

'He tried to sex you?' A. Scott said.

Before she could answer, he dove on top of Abdul. All she could see was his fist swinging down.

'Hit him! Hit him!' Boo yelled. 'You want a golf club?'

Two FBI agents grabbed A. Scott and pulled him off Abdul. Her father was red-faced and breathing hard, just like that day at the Village, when he beat up the big bald man's car with a nine-iron. That was the day Mother left them.

'I didn't try to sex her.' The agents lifted Abdul up. His face was red, his nose was bleeding, and he sobbed like a baby. His mean voice was gone. 'As Allah is my witness, it was not me.'

Boo hugged A. Scott. Boy, she loved that man.

'Judge,' Beckeman said, 'you gotta stop beating him up. There'll be nothing left to prosecute.' He turned to his agents. 'Clean him up, before we perp walk them. The press will think we did that.' He turned to the brother named Saddam. 'You expect me to believe you were in New York City the last week?'

'Yes. We can prove it.'

'Why?'

'So you don't arrest us for a crime we didn't commit.'

'No. Why were you in New York?'

'Our brother, he got married.'

'Why did you come back today?'

'We're going to the Super Bowl.'

'To blow up the stadium?'

'To watch the game. We have tickets.'

A cat came over and jumped into Saddam's lap.

'Oh, kitty,' he said. 'Did you get fed?'

As if he were talking to a newborn.

'What the hell is going on?'

A middle-aged woman stormed into the house. She glanced around at the bashed-in door and the mess in the house. She was not pleased.

'Who did this damage?' she said.

'Who are you?' Beckeman said.

'I own this property. Who did this?'

'We did.'

She pointed a finger in his face. 'You're going to pay for this.'

'Ma'am, we're the FBI and this is a crime scene.'

'A crime scene? What crime?'

Beckeman pointed at the men. 'Your tenants plotted to blow up Cowboys Stadium.'

She turned to them. Her mouth fell open. 'Oh – my – God!'

'Yes, ma'am,' Beckeman said. 'They—'

'Have a cat! In the house!'

Saddam grimaced and said, 'Aw, shit.'

The woman stepped to him and pointed that finger in his face. 'I have a strict no-pets policy. You just forfeited your deposit!'

'Get her out of here!' Beckeman said.

Two agents dragged the woman out; she was still screaming about the cat. What a fucking zoo. Beckeman gestured at another agent and then the brothers.

'Take them to headquarters. We'll question them there.'

The agent led the brothers outside. Agent Stryker held a cell phone out to Beckeman.

'It's the president.'

Beckeman put the phone to his ear. 'Mr. President.'

'Agent, are the girls safe?'

'Yes, sir. The hostages are safe and unharmed, and we apprehended the bad guys. The Super Bowl is safe.'

'You're safe,' Louis said.

Boo wiped tears from his face. He gave her and Pajamae a big bear hug. Carlos pushed in.

'I want some of that,' he said.

He was a tough guy, but not too tough to cry.

'Damn, y'all kicked the shit out of that door,' Boo said.

Agent Beckeman ended the call with the president then stepped over to them.

'Judge, I need to ask your girls a few questions. We can do an in-depth briefing in a few days, but I need some answers now.'

'Girls,' Scott said, 'are you up to answering a few questions for Agent Beckeman?'

'As long as you and Cat are with us,' Boo said.

Scott nodded to Beckeman, who turned to the girls.

'Did you hear them talking about blowing up the stadium?'

'Yes, sir,' Boo said. 'Abdul, he's the bad brother, he wants to kill everyone in the stadium because we killed his father.'

'We who?'

'You. The government. In someplace called Pakistan. With a drone. Whatever that is.'

'Ah. This is about revenge.'

Boo nodded. 'That's what Abdul said. They would avenge their father's death. The good brother, he doesn't blame us. He said it was an accident.'

'Did you hear them talking about the bombs, where they would place them, how they would get them into the stadium?'

'No, sir.'

'Anything else you heard them say that you think might be important?'

'I think you should play good cop/bad cop with the brothers. Abdul is mean, he won't break. But the one with the cat, he's a nice boy. He'll spill his guts.'

'Good cop/bad cop?'

'I heard that on TV.'

Beckeman grunted then turned to her sister. 'Pajamae, do you have anything to say?'

Her eyes dropped to the floor; she shook her head.

'No, sir. I don't know anything.'

'There is one thing,' Boo said.

'What's that?'

'Their voices just now, they sounded different than before.'

'They were probably talking in a different tone before, so you wouldn't recognize their real voices.'

'Ohhh. That's smart.'

'They're smart. All right, thanks, girls. In a few days, I'd like to talk to you more about all this, when you feel up to it.'

'Okay,' Boo said.

Pajamae nodded without enthusiasm. Beckeman stuck a hand out to Scott.

'Judge, thanks for your help. I don't know if we would have found them without your hacker.'

'How did you find us?' Boo asked.

'A hacker traced messages from Syria to the law school,' Scott said. 'They're law students.'

409

'*Duh*. Why do you think I said "whereas" on the phone that day?'

'That's what you were trying to tell me?'

'Took you long enough to figure that out. We could have died on that falafel they were feeding us.'

The adults laughed. Beckeman turned to Cat and stuck an open hand out to her.

'Gun and badge, Peña.'

She glared at him then slapped her badge into his hand then held out her gun to him. He took it.

Carlos wiped his eyes on his sleeves then slapped Louis on the back.

'We kicked some ass, big man. Or at least a door.'

They looked back at what was left of the door.

'We smashed the shit out of that door,' Louis said.

'What do you say, big man? Our work here is done. Let's go to the Super Bowl.'

Chapter 26

9:00 A.M.
7 hours before kickoff

FBI Special Agent Gene Manning admired Cowboys Stadium. There was much to admire. He had never seen anything like it in his thirty-four years of life. He normally worked the Los Angeles division, but he had been assigned to the Super Bowl that year. He had seen the stadium on television, but it was like seeing the Grand Canyon on TV; a camera couldn't capture the reality of it. Standing there and looking up at the stadium reminded him of the first time he had stood on the steps leading up to the Capitol in DC; it was a monument to man. What man could dream. What man could build. What man could achieve if he put his mind and $1.2 billion to the task.

'Agent Manning!'

Another eighteen-wheel tractor-trailer had arrived at the delivery entrance on the north side of the parking lot. The FBI had set up a perimeter around the entire parking lot; no truck, van, car, motorcycle, man, woman, or child would enter the

411

parking lot that day without being searched. One hundred thousand fans and ten thousand law enforcement personnel would be in attendance that day. Police, police with dogs, SWAT teams, police and FBI helicopters overhead, a Defense Department drone way overhead – they had the place locked down.

Manning's assignment that day was to search every delivery truck entering the stadium premises. The bomb plot may have been thwarted with the arrest of Mustafa and his followers – and he had heard some reports that Beckeman and the Task Force had captured two other Muslims that very morning – but the FBI would not let their guard down. They could never let their guard down. Other agents led bomb-sniffing dogs around the perimeter of the truck and stuck mirrors under the truck. Manning checked out the driver.

'Sir, please step down from the truck.'

The driver opened the door and climbed down. He was young, medium build, ethnic, perhaps Eastern European.

'Name?'

'Hu. H-U.'

Or Asian. Manning checked his iPad for 'Hu.' The Bureau had run background checks on every executive, employee, staffer, security guard, cheerleader, coach, player, referee, ball boy, and hot dog vendor. No one except the fans got inside that stadium that day without a criminal background check. On the iPad he saw the driver's name and photo: *Hu, Al A.* Employee of the beer distributor servicing the stadium. On the job for almost two years. His employee photo on file with the company matched his face and description. Blond hair, green eyes, somber expression.

'This your rig?' Manning asked.

It was a big black Peterbilt hooked up to a trailer with a beer logo painted on the sides.

412

'Yep. All the drivers, they made us independent contractors so they don't have to give us benefits. And we had to buy our own trucks. Cheap bastards.'

'Hey, cheer up, buddy. You look like you're going to a funeral. It's the Super Bowl.'

He waved a hand at their surroundings: smoke rising into the sky from the RV'ers tailgating at the far end of the parking lot; happy fans arriving early to buy out the pro shop; the big exterior screens on the stadium previewing the game, a marquee matchup between the two most loved and hated football teams in America; the world's media present and accounted for – hell, it was Mardi Gras with endorsement contracts. But Manning got no response from the driver. Some people were just that way.

'Mr. Hu, please open the trailer doors.'

Manning followed the driver to the rear of the trailer where Agent Bryan waited. The driver unlocked the double doors and swung them open. Inside the trailer, crates of beer were stacked almost to the ceiling and all the way to the front. Bryan wore sneakers, nylon sweats, and gloves; the container was refrigerated. He was junior to Manning; hence, he had the dirty duty that day. Bryan climbed into the forty-foot-long container and crawled over the tops of the beer crates with a flashlight. He disappeared into the darkness.

'That's a lot of beer,' Manning said.

'They sell them for eight bucks a bottle,' Hu said. 'If I got a dime for each bottle, I could retire.'

Agent Bryan reappeared and jumped down. He rubbed his hands together.

'Damn cold in there.'

'Anything?' Manning said.

'Beer.'

The agents with the dogs and mirrors gave Manning a thumbs-up. He turned to the driver.

413

'You're good to go, Mr. Hu.'

The driver shut and locked the doors then climbed back into the cab and drove toward the tunnel entrance where deliveries and players arrived.

'Are we there yet?' Gilberto asked.

'No,' José said. 'Check the map.'

It was past ten. The drive up Interstate 35 had been slow; apparently all of Texas was going to the Super Bowl today. You would think the state would tip toward Dallas. Now they were driving around Dallas like two blind men. They needed GPS. Gilberto spread the map of Dallas across his lap. The map was very large.

'Where the hell is this place?'

'Uh, somewhere in Dallas.'

'We should have gotten a GPS.'

'Gosh, I am so excited.'

'About killing the fucking Arabs?'

'No. About going to the Super Bowl. I want to get to the game early. I want to buy a Cowboys jersey. And perhaps we can get Tony Romo's autograph.'

José sighed. Gilberto was just a boy.

Louis pulled up in front of Carlos's house in the black Dodge Charger. It was 10:30. He honked. Carlos wanted to go to the game early so he could meet some of the cheerleaders, maybe get a date; the boy lived in a fantasy world, but he seemed happy there. Carlos's mother opened the front door and waved him in. Louis cut the engine, got out, and walked to the door.

'Louis, come have breakfast. I am cooking for Carlos now.'

'Thank you, Mrs. Hernandez.'

Louis Wright wanted a Mexican mother.

★

414

'Turn right,' the boy said.

The man did as the boy instructed. That was a mistake. José checked the street sign.

'Martin Luther King Boulevard?'

Gilberto frowned. 'I do not think this is the place. There are only the black people here.'

The vehicle hit a pothole and bottomed out; when it came out of the hole, the right front tire clunked.

'I think we have a flat tire,' José said.

He steered to the side of the road. They got out and examined the tire. It was flat.

'You fix the tire,' José said. 'I will figure out where we are.'

'Okay.'

Gilberto never complained. He had come up from the farm to the border; he had grown up dirt poor, so he was thrilled to work for the cartel. Hector paid good wages to his men, particularly his *sicarios* willing to risk a lifetime in an American prison. Gilberto retrieved the spare tire from under the vehicle and jacked the front end up. José studied the Dallas map.

'What you greasers doin' in the 'hood?'

José looked up from the map. Two Mexicans fixing a flat tire had attracted a crowd. There must not be much to do in the south of Dallas, José assumed. Ten black males faced them. José decided to play dumb.

'*No habla ingles.*'

The leader of the black posse laughed. 'Don't speak no English, he say. Dumb fuckin' Mescins.'

He was big and muscular and without a shirt, which seemed odd since it was quite cold at that time of the morning. Perhaps he had warmed himself with the alcohol or the drugs or both. He took a step toward José. Which was a mistake, although he did not know that yet. José reached inside the vehicle and pulled out two Uzis. He pointed both at the man.

415

'You want trouble, *hombre,* you have come to the right Mescins, as you say. If you wish to die, here and now, take one more step forward. If you wish to live, then walk away. It is your choice. Once Gilberto changes the tire, we will leave your neighborhood.'

The man stared at the twin barrels staring back. He made the correct choice.

'Yeah, well, you better leave.'

'Come on, Louis,' Carlos said. 'Let's go. The cheerleaders are waiting for me.'

Louis finished his breakfast while Carlos's mother checked him out: black leather boots, black leather pants, black leather jacket over a black tee shirt, black hair slicked back. Carlos could be going to church or court or Cowboys Stadium for the Super Bowl. She smoothed his hair and kissed his cheek and sent him on his way, like a mama sending her little boy to his first day of school. Mrs. Hernandez's little boy wouldn't last a day in South Dallas.

She took his plate and went into the kitchen. Louis had eaten three servings of her tacos, enchiladas, tortillas, and refried beans. It was a little early in the morning for dinner, but he had been starving; he hadn't eaten since . . . he couldn't remember since. All he had done the last week was search for the girls.

'You got any weapons on you?' he asked Carlos.

'You expecting trouble at the game?'

'No, man. They're going to search us.'

'Oh.'

'Well?'

Carlos shrugged. 'I have my gun.'

He pulled a nine-millimeter Glock from his back waistband. Louis sighed. 'You got to leave it here.'

'Damn. I feel naked without my gun.'

He placed the gun on the table.

'Anything else?'

Another shrug. 'My blade.'

'Can't take it in.'

'They won't let me take a switchblade into the stadium? This is America!'

'Leave it.'

Carlos pulled the blade from his boot and put it on the table next to the gun.

'That it?'

'Yep.'

Louis gave Carlos a suspicious look. Carlos gave Louis his innocent look.

'What?'

Louis didn't blink. Carlos surrendered.

'Okay.'

He pulled a pair of brass knuckles from his coat pocket and dropped them on the table. He shook his head and sighed.

'You've clearly never been to a bullfight in Juarez.'

'Good thing you didn't have to shoot all those black people,' Gilberto said. 'We'd really be late for the game.'

José grunted. It was one. They were finally heading north to the warehouse where they would kill the fucking Arabs.

'We meet again, Mr. Hu,' Agent Manning had said.

It was three hours before kickoff. The same driver had returned with another load of beer. These beer truck drivers were making run after run.

'Football and beer, like apple pie and ice cream,' Manning said.

Mr. Hu offered only a lame smile and said, 'Yep.'

The dogs and the mirrors circled the truck.

'Let's take a look at your load.'

The driver opened the trailer doors; Agent Bryan climbed up but didn't scramble over the top of the crates all the way to the front this time. He had climbed into so many refrigerated containers that day that he might soon suffer frostbite. So he only crawled over a few crates then shone the flashlight to the front of the container. He returned and jumped down.

'All beer,' he said.

'You're good to go, Mr. Hu.'

The driver locked the doors, returned to the cab, and drove toward the tunnel.

'We had a good day, big man.'

'Indeed we did.'

'And it's gonna get better.'

'Indeed it is.'

'Indeed. I like the words you use these days.'

'You should ask Ms. Herrin to teach you, too.'

'Shakespeare? I don't think so.'

'That's not Shakespeare. That's just English.'

'Close enough.'

They were almost to the stadium. Traffic on the interstate was bumper to bumper. The drive had taken almost two hours. Carlos rode slouched in his seat.

'You know, I used to want to be famous like the judge,' Carlos said. 'I don't no more.'

'Anymore.'

'Don't start with me.'

Carlos suddenly sat up straight and pointed out the front window.

'There it is.'

The stadium rose before them.

★

418

'We are close now,' José said.

'Good,' Gilberto said. 'Because I have to pee.'

'Thanks for sharing.'

'And the kickoff is in just one and a half hours. We must kill the fucking Arabs fast. No talking.'

'Do I ever talk?'

'I'm just saying.'

'Well, don't.'

Saadi Khalid loaded the bomb – actually, five bombs – into the back of the beer truck with the forklift. He had pulled the truck and trailer into the warehouse and closed the overhead doors; he had then unloaded the shipment of beer he was taking to the stadium. He climbed into the container and pushed the crates holding the bombs forward; the rollers made the job easy. He locked the rollers and secured the crates in place. Abdul had vacuum-wrapped the bombs in plastic to evade the bomb-sniffing dogs. His brother was very smart.

He jumped out of the trailer and went over to the tall package wrapped in brown paper leaned against the wall. He removed the wrapping and stepped back to admire the photo panel. It was perfect. He carried the panel to the trailer and set it inside; he climbed up and maneuvered the panel in place. It fit precisely; one hundred inches wide and one hundred ten inches tall. He secured the panel in place in front of the bomb. Standing only five feet away, he would swear he was staring at crates of beer. He had to give Abdul credit; he was a very smart jihadist.

He jumped down from the container and fired up the fork-lift. He loaded the crates of beer all the way to the door. When he finished, he stood where the FBI agent would stand; he shone a flashlight into the container. All he could see were crates of beer, back to front. The bomb was completely concealed behind the photo panel. Abdul Khalid's Plan A might actually work.

Which would be a much better death than Plan B.

'There it is. That is the warehouse.'

José parked the vehicle. They checked their weapons. They got out and walked to the entrance door. It was open. They stepped inside. A partition blocked their path. On top of the partition was a shelf; on the shelf was a bell. They held their weapons down their legs; Gilberto slapped the bell. Once. Twice. Again.

'I hear you!' They heard a voice from the back. 'Yeah, yeah, I'm coming. Hold your horses.'

An old Anglo man appeared from around the corner.

'Yep?'

'Uh,' José said, 'we are looking for Abdul and Saadi.'

'Who?'

'The Khalid brothers.'

'No such folks here.'

'But is this not one-nine-zero-zero?'

'It is. What street?'

'Sixth.'

'That's your problem. This is Fifth. Sixth is that way.'

The Anglo pointed to the entrance.

'Oh, we are very sorry.'

'No problem, partner.'

'Can I use your restroom?' Gilberto said.

Saadi sat in the driver's seat. He had been to a Cowboys game. He knew what the people in the stadium would be doing when the bomb detonated. Most would be watching the half-time show. Some would be shopping in the pro shop, paying $100 for jerseys and $50 for shirts and $25 for caps. Others would be drinking beer at $8 a bottle or margaritas at $12 a glass. They would be eating nachos and hot dogs and hamburgers. They would be alive.

For a few more minutes.

Then the bomb would detonate. They would hear the massive explosion; the glass walls at that end of the stadium would shatter and shards would fly through the air and impale tens of thousands. The stadium itself would shudder, and then the arch would buckle. The weight of the video screen would pull the roof down. They would see the roof come down upon them. Bury them as the entire structure collapsed upon itself, much as the floors of the Twin Towers had collapsed upon the one below. It would all drop into the massive hole in the ground. When the dust cleared, the stadium would be a mass grave. The thought of that made Saadi nauseous. He did not want this. He wanted to be a lawyer. He had hoped to finish college and get into law school, perhaps at SMU with the help of the Siddiqui brothers. He had plans; but his brother had other plans. He wanted desperately to walk away from his brother, walk away from all this madness, but he had made a pledge in order to save the girls. At least they would be far away when the bomb detonated. He had that at least.

And even if he walked away, would it matter?

The madness was already in motion. Those people were going to die, if not from this bomb, then from a more horrible death. There was no stopping the madness.

José and Gilberto arrived at the warehouse.

'One nine zero zero. Sixth Street.'

'Let us kill these fucking Arabs and get to the game,' Gilberto said.

José parked the vehicle next to the warehouse. The two *sicarios* exited the vehicle. The boy was all business now. He had that look in his eye that told José the stone-cold killer had returned. They checked their weapons and walked to the front door. José figured on a small amount of C-4 to blow the door, but Gilberto grabbed the doorknob and turned. The door swung open.

'Could be a trap,' José said.

They drew their weapons and entered the warehouse. Again they were surprised. The place was lit up like a whorehouse on Saturday night. And it was vacant except for a forklift, several dozen crates of beer and two steel barrels sitting in the center of the floor.

'Where the hell are the fucking Arabs?' Gilberto asked.

'They are gone.'

'How are we supposed to kill them if they are not here?'

They walked to the barrels.

'And where are Jorge and Manuel?'

Gilberto looked around the warehouse while José tried to open the top of one barrel. It was on tight. He reached down to his ankle and pulled his jeans up. He grabbed the Rambo knife strapped to his leg. He put the blade under the lid and gave it a rap with his pistol. The lid popped open. He removed the lid.

'I have found Jorge,' José said.

Jorge Romero stared at José from inside the barrel. His eyes were wide. And his pupils, they were just tiny black pinpoints. His hair was matted and clothes were wet as if liquid had been poured over him.

'What the hell happened to him?'

José felt a sudden tightness in his chest. He tried to take a deep breath, but he couldn't. He couldn't breathe. He grabbed at his chest. He sucked for air but none would come into his lungs. His body began twitching uncontrollably.

★

'What the fuck are you doing?' Gilberto said.

He laughed but quickly realized that José was not playing. He went to José and grabbed him by the shoulders; but José looked right through him. He clawed at his chest. Gilberto released him, and he fell to the floor.

'What the—'

And now Gilberto felt his chest tighten like a vice. He too clawed at his chest and gasped for air. He too fell to the floor. And he realized he would never see the Super Bowl live.

Chapter 27

3:00 p.m.
1 hour before kickoff

'Hamburgers and root beer floats for the Super Bowl,' Scott said.

'Perfect,' Boo said.

Pajamae said nothing. The girls did not want to spend a night in the hospital for observation, so Scott had taken them home. Consuelo's cooking would be better for them than a night in the hospital. She had come over to welcome them home with a big breakfast. They had then showered and slept for several hours. Now the entire crew – Scott, the girls, Bobby, Karen, and Little Scotty – and Cat, she was suspended, sat in front of the television watching the Super Bowl pregame show. The stadium was almost full. One hundred thousand people, including Louis and Carlos.

The pregame show was interrupted for a news brief. The reporter updated the audience on the stadium plot case. Cameras caught the Siddiqui brothers in a perp walk from the house to the FBI sedans. They carried shocked expressions.

The younger boy looked into a camera and said, 'We're innocent. We're not the jihadists. They are still out there.'

Pajamae started crying. Scott put his arm around her shoulders and pulled her close. She hid her head in his chest.

'They said they would cut my head off,' she said.

Scott glanced at Cat and shook his head.

'Honey, they're not going to hurt anyone ever again.'

'And Boo's head. And yours. And Consuelo's and Maria's.'

He held her tight. He didn't know how to comfort her, convince her that she was safe.

'Pajamae, the bad guys are in custody. You saw them in handcuffs. We got them.'

'No, Judge Fenney. We didn't get them.' She turned her face up to Scott. In her eyes was fear. 'But they're going to get us.'

'What are you talking about?'

She pointed at the Siddiqui brothers on the television.

'That's not them.'

'What do you mean? Those are the men who kidnapped you and Boo. I saw that one at Whole Foods, and I saw Abdul wearing the same yellow sneakers at the law school.'

'Did you see his face?'

'No.'

'I did.'

'You did what?'

'I saw his face. Abdul's. And his brother's.'

'We were blindfolded,' Boo said.

'My blindfold slipped down one day, when you were in the bathroom. The good brother pushed it back up, made me promise not to tell you, or Abdul would cut all our heads off. I saw them, Judge Fenney. I saw the bad guys.'

She again pointed at the television.

'That's not them.'

★

425

Two FBI agents hurried Scott, Cat, and the girls down a corridor to a door marked 'Interrogation Room.' They could see inside through a two-way mirror. The Siddiqui brothers sat side-by-side at a table facing the mirror; their hands were on the table and cuffed. On a side table sat the sword, the black ISIS flag, and the yellow sneakers. Agent Beckeman sat opposite the brothers with his back to the mirror. One of the agents knocked on the mirror. Beckeman stood and came outside.

'What's this all about?'

'Tell him, Pajamae,' the judge said.

'Those boys in there, they're not the bad guys.'

'How do you know?'

'I saw the real bad guys.'

'But—'

'My blindfold slipped down. I saw them. That's not them.'

Beckeman studied her a moment. 'Come on.'

He opened the door to the interrogation room and gestured them inside. He led them to the Siddiqui brothers.

'Take a close look at these men,' he said to the judge's daughter. 'Have you ever seen them before?'

She pointed at Saddam Siddiqui. 'I saw him.'

'Aha!'

'In the produce department at Whole Foods. He picked up our broccoli.'

'Broccoli?'

'I did,' Saddam said.

'Look, are these the men who kidnapped you?'

'No, sir.'

'Why didn't you say so at the house?'

'She was scared,' the judge said. 'They told her they'd behead her.'

'And cut my head off.'

'I told you we were in New York the last week,' Saddam said.

'Then how do we have Saddam Siddiqui logged in to a computer at the law school almost every night during that time period? How'd you do that when you were in New York?'

'I gave Abdul my passcode. He cannot afford a laptop. He talks to friends back home in Pakistan.'

Beckeman turned to Abdul Siddiqui. 'So you were in Dallas the whole time?'

'Not me. Abdul jabbar.'

'That's you. Abdul jabbar Siddiqui.'

'No. I am Abdul jabaar. J-a-b-a-a-r. He is Abdul jabbar. J-a-b-b-a-r.'

'Where the hell do you people get these goofy names?' Agent LeCharles D'Wandrick Jefferson said.

Beckeman turned to the agent. 'Seriously?'

Agent Jefferson shrugged. Beckeman turned back to the Siddiqui boys.

'Abdul and Saadi Khalid, they are brothers,' Abdul Siddiqui said. 'We met them at the mosque. They were from our village, but we did not know them there. They moved here from Pakistan with their mother about the same time we did. Their father was also killed by the same drone missile that killed our father. The U.S. government moved us to New York City and them to Minneapolis. I have struggled with my father's death. I became angry. Very angry. But not angry enough to hurt anyone.'

'You didn't try to sex me?' the judge's other daughter said.

'No. It was not me.'

'Sorry I hit you.'

'You hit hard for a girl.'

'Go on,' Beckeman said.

'Abdul and Saadi, they moved down here a few years back. We became friends playing soccer. Abdul is a skilled player. Saadi, not so much. He wants to go to law school.'

427

'I think he can cross that off his bucket list now,' Beckeman said.

'What about those yellow sneakers?' the judge said. 'I saw you at the law school wearing those sneakers.'

'What size are they?' Abdul asked.

Beckeman grabbed a sneaker and checked. 'Twelve.'

Abdul held his foot up. 'I wear a nine. Look at my shoe.'

Agent Jefferson pulled Abdul's shoe off. 'It's a nine,' he said.

'Wait,' Peña said. 'I checked out every male in the mosque records. There was no Abdul jabbar Khalid or Saadi Khalid.'

'Aliases,' Beckeman said. 'No doubt they're off the grid. No credit cards, no utilities in their names . . . not even Internet. Fake IDs, fake social security numbers, fake driver's licenses, prepaid cell phones . . . They're ghosts.' Back to the brothers. 'What were they doing in your house?'

'They said their house was being painted, asked if they could stay there for a few days while we were in New York. We said okay. They drove us to the airport.'

'When?'

'Sunday.'

'The day before the girls were abducted,' the judge said.

Agent Carson entered with a document. 'Boss, we got these boys on a time-stamped ATM machine at LaGuardia last Sunday. And their tickets on American.'

'Shit. We've got two sets of brothers and two Abduls.' To the Siddiqui brothers: 'Where do they live? Abdul and Saadi.'

'We don't know. We don't know where they're at.'

'I do.'

'Where?'

'They're at the stadium.'

Chapter 28

3:45 p.m.
15 minutes before kickoff

Cowboys Stadium offers thirty-five hundred television screens strategically placed throughout so no fan will miss a second of the game. You can watch the game in line at the concession stand or in the restroom, in the corridors looking at the art collection, in the pro shop buying Cowboys jerseys, and even outside on massive screens mounted on the stadium's exterior. All thirty-five hundred monitors plus the massive HDTV screen hanging above the field are controlled by one laptop. The technician manning that laptop wore an employee badge that identified him as Sam Taylor. To his brother, he was Abdul jabbar Khalid.

'The chopper's waiting on the roof,' Beckeman said. 'Let's go.'

  'Where?' Scott said.

  'To the stadium.'

They stood outside the interrogation room.

'She's not going to the stadium.'

'I need her there.'

'I need her safe.'

'She's the only person who can ID the Khalid brothers.'

'Who might have brought a bomb into the stadium.'

'If they did, only she can find them so we can stop them.'

'How can she see everyone coming in?'

'Facial recognition software. We've got everyone's face on film.'

'Evacuate the stadium.'

'If we evacuate, they'll detonate. We have to find them before they detonate.'

'Chief,' Cat said, 'you need to call the president. He needs to make that decision.'

Beckeman sighed. 'I know.'

'She's not going,' Scott said.

The judge stared down the FBI special agent a long moment until the moment was broken by a soft voice from below.

'Judge Fenney, I have to go.' Scott closed his eyes. He knew she was right. 'If I don't go, all those people will die.'

Scott squatted before his daughter. 'But you might die.'

She shrugged. 'I'll be in heaven with Mama.'

'If she's going, I'm going,' Boo said.

'But I want Cat with me,' Pajamae said.

Cat smiled at Beckeman.

'Fine,' Beckeman said.

'I want my gun and badge,' Cat said.

'Fine.'

'Mighty fine,' Louis said.

'Damn fine,' Carlos said.

They had settled into their seats on the fifty-yard line.

430

'Super Bowl, autographs, dates with the cheerleaders . . . I'm probably gonna have to get a calendar to schedule them all in.'

'You live in a nice little fantasy world, don't you?'

'Yes, I do. And I'm very happy there.'

Carlos eyed every girl in sight. Louis eyed the stadium. It was amazing.

'She is,' Carlos said. 'Amazing.'

'A feat of engineering genius,' Louis said.

'You don't think hers are real?'

Abdul jabbar Khalid was a structural engineer by training and an Islamic jihadist by choice. He had obtained the stadium's architectural plans from Aabdar Haddad and studied them diligently. Every structure had a weak spot. He had determined that the arches were the point of attack.

Abdul had calculated that a fifty-thousand-pound fertilizer bomb detonated directly beneath one arch just before it entered the concrete supports might buckle if not break the steel of the arch. Render the arch unstable. Unable to transfer the force of gravity into the ground. Perhaps the arch would succumb to gravity, just as the Twin Towers had. The arches were 65-grade steel, supposedly indestructible. Perhaps. The Twin Towers were also supposed to be indestructible. But no one had anticipated commercial jets flying into the towers; they had not anticipated the heat a jet fuel fire could generate. Perhaps no one had anticipated a fifty-thousand-pound bomb detonating just feet from an arch. The 9/11 hijackers were very lucky that day. Perhaps Abdul Khalid would also be lucky this day. One unstable arch could bring the roof down on the spectators; if he were very lucky, it could collapse the entire stadium and render it a mass grave of infidels. And render Abdul jabbar Khalid a hero for all time.

That was Plan A.

★

The FBI director had briefed the president. There was a chance – albeit a small chance – that a bomb had been placed in or about the stadium.

'I agree with Beckeman,' the director said. 'If we evacuate, they'll detonate.'

'First sign of trouble, cut the TV feed,' the president said. 'I don't want the world to see a hundred thousand people killed on live television.'

'Anything else?'

'Can we cut the spot?'

'No, sir. It's too late.'

Abdul Khalid sat in his perch between the HDTV screens that hung ninety feet above the playing field. It was a steel grid box with screens on four sides and in the space between there were catwalks, a control booth, and a retractable elevator for the technicians to gain access. Once he rode the elevator up, he was there for the duration of the game. The only way down during the game was to jump. His laptop was in his hands and his destiny at hand. From his vantage point, he could see the entire stadium below him; but no one could see him, no one could shoot him, no one could stop him.

Down below a hundred unbelievers unfurled a massive American flag and held it above the playing field. A military honor guard marched onto the field, and Abdul thought, *Oh, good, we will kill some enemy soldiers as well today. This day just keeps getting better.* Three girls called the Dixie Chicks stood at a microphone and started singing.

'Oh, say, can you see, by the dawn's early light, what so proudly we hailed, at the twilight's last gleaming, whose broad stripes and bright stars, through the perilous fight, o'er the ramparts we watched, were so gallantly streaming, and the rockets' red glare, the bombs bursting in air, gave proof through

432

the night that our flag was still there. Oh say, does that star-spangled banner yet wave. O'er the land of the free and the home of the brave?'

Abdul jabbar Khalid thought, *I will show you the land of the free.*

Louis Wright wiped a tear from his face. He loved the Dixie Chicks, he loved the national anthem, but more important—

'I love this country,' Carlos said.

'Me, too.'

'Would you die for this country?'

'I hope so.'

Saadi Khalid steered the truck to the side of the road and stopped. He checked his watch. Timing was critical. It was almost time for kickoff. The first half would run just over an hour. Then the halftime show would start. Detonation had to occur during the halftime show when everyone would be in their seats in the stadium and in front of their televisions at home. When the whole world would be watching.

As one hundred thousand Americans died.

His hands trembled. The gravity of what he was doing hit him again. He knew that once he arrived at the stadium, there would be no turning back. Al Qaeda had killed three thousand people on 9/11. The Khalid brothers would kill thirty times that many that day. Their names would be said in the same sentence with Hitler and Stalin and bin Laden. He wiped a tear from his face. His cell phone rang. It was Abdul.

'Saadi, are you in position?'

'Yes, my brother.'

'Stay there until I call. I will tell you when it is time. Do not let me down, Saadi.'

'I will honor my pledge, brother.'

'Allahu Akbar.'

He could not stop the madness.

The president's face appeared on the video screen hanging above the field. The crowd hushed.

'My fellow Americans. I come to you from the Oval Office in Washington, D.C. As you may have heard, ISIL tried to destroy our football game, just as they have tried to destroy our way of life. They failed on both counts. We defeated them today, and we will defeat them every day. We have them on the run!'

The crowd cheered. Abdul Khalid laughed. 'Oh, yes, Mr. President, we are running away.'

On the screen: 'So enjoy the game knowing that you are safe. That America is safe. God bless America!'

In the old days, they would have played the game outside, in an open-air stadium, in the freezing temperature that enveloped Dallas that day. Like the Ice Bowl, the 1967 NFL championship game between the Cowboys and the Packers played in Green Bay in minus-fifteen-degree temperature and minus-forty-eight-degree wind chill. The field was an ice rink. It was too cold for the referees to put whistles in their mouths, so the game was played without whistles. Football was meant to be played outside in the elements. It wasn't tennis. You played in ice, snow, rain, and heat. It was messy and it was ugly, but that was football. But it made for bad TV. No one wanted to watch games where the players slipped and fell instead of ran and caught. And television rules the NFL. So now the Super Bowl is played in climate-controlled sealed stadiums. Seventy-two degrees of air-conditioned comfort.

Beckeman gazed down at the stadium as the chopper approached the landing pad. The translucent roof panels were shut tight. The glass gleamed in the sun. The parking lot was packed. Tailgaters barbecued beef and drank beer and watched the game on the giant screens on the outside of the stadium. Super Bowl Sunday was a bright, shining day, cold but sunny. Perfect for America's game. Or a terrorist attack. The chopper came in for a fast landing.

Carlos and Louis stood and cheered. The Cowboys took the kickoff and were marching down the field when Louis's cell phone vibrated in his pocket. He pulled it out and read the message.

'What the—'

'What?' Carlos said.

'The judge is here. Says to meet them in the control room on the concourse level.'

'The judge is here?'

'And the girls.'

'That don't sound good.'

'Doesn't.'

'Don't start with me.'

Two dozen video screens hung on the wall of the control room in front of computer stations. It looked like the NASA control center in *Apollo 13*. Beckeman had called ahead to summon his agents for an emergency briefing.

'Our suspects are Abdul jabbar Khalid and Saadi Khalid. They are in the stadium. They didn't carry a fifty-thousand-pound bomb in a backpack.'

'Maybe it's in a bus,' Stryker said.

Beckeman thought for a moment. 'No. They planted the bomb weeks ago.'

'How?'

'They work here. Search every storeroom, every space big enough to hold a bomb.'

435

'We searched every inch of this place.'

'Search it again. They're watching us. They know our search patterns. They're watching then moving the bomb.'

Agent Stryker checked his iPad. 'Captain, there are no employees, vendors, or anyone else named Abdul or Saadi Khalid working in this stadium today.'

'They're working under false IDs.'

'Several thousand people work here. How will we find them?'

Beckeman pointed at the judge's black daughter. 'She will. She's going to find them on these monitors.' To the technicians: 'Put up the employees' photos on one monitor, the interior and exterior cameras on the others.'

The technician pointed to one screen. 'The employee photos will run on that monitor, they're in alphabetical order.'

'When she spots the brothers, we have to move in fast and hard. So spread out and be ready. Check every male who looks Arab, but await my call.'

The agents exited the control room. Beckeman came over to Scott and Cat.

'Peña, you stay here with the girl.' To the judge: 'I need your girl in here checking the employees' faces and the stadium monitors. They're here. They're in the stadium. These cameras can see a face three hundred feet away. And the software will pull up anyone with Arabic features.'

'Your software racially profiles?' Scott said.

'Yes, and there's no Santa Claus.'

'*What?*' Pajamae said.

Carlos and Louis ran up to the entrance to the control room. Two FBI agents blocked their path.

'We work for the judge.'

The door opened, and other agents walked out. The agent named Beckeman saw them.

'Let them in,' he said.

They entered the room and went over to the judge.

'What's going on, Judge?'

Pajamae focused on the monitor that showed the employees' faces. The others focused on the other monitors. Whenever they saw someone suspicious, they called to her and she checked the face out.

'What about him?' Louis said.

'No,' Pajamae said.

'Him?' Louis said.

'No.'

'Him?' Carlos said.

'That's a her.'

By halftime, she had looked at hundreds of faces. She was up to the employees whose names started with S.

Saadi's cell phone rang. He answered.

'It is time, brother. We will be together till the end.'

Saadi plugged the cord into his phone and pushed the ear bud into his ear. Abdul was in his ear. In his head. In his heart.

Saadi shifted the truck into gear.

Beckeman stood at the railing outside the control room. Detonation would happen during the halftime show. He was sure of it.

Inside the control room, Louis said, 'Him?'

'No,' Pajamae said.

'Him?'

'No.'

437

'Him?'

'No.'

'Welcome back, Mr. Hu,' Agent Manning said.

The familiar black Peterbilt truck had pulled up to the delivery entrance with another load of beer. The driver spoke down to Manning through the open cab window.

'Yep, my last run. They stop selling beer at the end of the third quarter. If you're not drunk by then, you gotta get drunk somewhere else.'

Manning laughed. 'And all those drunks will hit the road after the game. Okay, let's take a look at the back.'

Mr. Hu unplugged his phone from his ear and climbed down from the cab. The agents led the dogs around the vehicle and examined the underside with mirrors.

Pajamae had looked at hundreds of employees' face, but none resembled the brothers, the good brother or the bad brother. She rubbed her eyes then glanced at all the other screens. Most showed places inside the stadium, but some showed outside. One screen caught her attention. She stood and pointed.

'Zoom in!'

'Which one?' Cat said.

'That one. The big truck.'

The technician moved his mouse, and the shot on the screen zoomed in close, first on a man in a suit.

'Not him. The other man, the one in the uniform.'

The camera caught the man's face close-up. Pajamae sucked in air.

'That's him! That's the good brother!'

'Are you sure?' Cat said.

'Yes. They're green.'

'What's green?'

'His eyes.'

Agent Manning followed the driver to the rear of the truck. The driver again unlocked the back doors. Agent Bryan began to climb up, but Manning waved him off. They had checked this driver twice before. He was clean. So he gave the inside a cursory search with the flashlight. Beer all the way to the front. Manning walked with the driver to the cab. The agents with the dogs and mirrors gave him an all-clear.

'You're good to go, Mr. Hu.'

The driver climbed into the cab and started the big diesel engine. Manning got a call on his radio.

'Manning, come in!'

'This is Manning.'

'This is Agent Peña. Hold that driver!'

'Hu?'

'Me?'

'No. That's the driver's name.'

'Hold him there!'

Manning banged on the truck door. The driver opened up.

'Mr. Hu, hold tight just a minute. They've got a backup in the tunnel.'

'Sure thing.'

Shit! Saadi plugged Abdul into his ear.

'What do I do?'

'Stay calm, brother. Allah is with you.'

Saadi fought to control his emotions. He took deep breaths.

Beckeman entered the control room on the run.

'What do we have?'

439

Peña pointed at the screen that showed a beer truck at the delivery entrance.

'She says the driver is one of the brothers.'

Beckeman turned to Pajamae. 'Are you sure?'

'Yes, sir. That's him.'

Beckeman turned back to Peña. 'Get me that agent on the radio.'

Peña spoke into her radio. 'Manning, come in.'

'Manning here.'

'Here's the chief.'

Peña handed the radio to Beckeman.

'Manning, who is that driver?'

'Mr. Hu.'

'His full name.'

On the monitor, Beckeman saw Manning checking his iPad.

'Al A. Hu.'

'Al A. Hu?'

Beckeman grabbed a pen and wrote the name on a notepad.

'Al A. Hu. Alahu. Allahu. As in Allahu Akbar. They're taunting us. That's him.'

'Why is he delivering beer?' Pajamae asked.

'He's not. He's delivering a bomb.' He spoke into the radio. 'Manning, get that man out of the truck and cuff him. But watch out, he's assumed armed and dangerous. He's one of the Khalid brothers. There's a bomb in the truck. I'm sending the bomb squad and SWAT team over.'

Beckeman grabbed his radio.

'All agents, this is Beckeman. The bomb is not in the stadium. It's in a beer truck outside. Agent Manning is apprehending the suspect. All agents on the north side of the stadium proceed to the delivery entrance. Evacuate the area. Seal it off.'

Agent Manning banged on the door again. This time he jumped onto the running board and pointed his weapon through the open window. The driver saw the barrel and recoiled.

'Get out of the truck!' Manning shouted.

'Whoa, hold on. Don't shoot. I'm getting out.'

'Do not get out!' Abdul said in Saadi's ear. 'Knock him off the truck with the door!'

Saadi Khalid took a deep breath. When the agent pulled the gun back, he swung the door open hard and knocked the agent off the running board. He fell to the ground. Saadi shifted the truck into first and floored the accelerator.

'Drive!' Abdul screamed in his ear. 'Drive to the arch! Allahu Akbar!'

'Shit!' Beckeman shouted in the control room.

He watched Manning hit the ground then fire his weapon at the truck driving away. He screamed into his radio.

'Stop that truck! Shoot the driver!'

On the screen, the truck veered away from dozens of cops and FBI agents shooting at it. The truck drove fast along the north side of the stadium, toward the—

'He's heading for the arches on the west side!'

Beckeman ran out the door and down the main concourse of the stadium. He picked up other agents along the way.

'Faster!' Abdul screamed. 'Faster! They cannot stop you!'

Saadi steered through tears. Toward the arches. Toward the madness. It was too late now. They would all die. He would die. He must die. He saw the police shooting at him, but their bullets could not kill him, could not penetrate the steel plates Abdul had installed in the doors. Bullets shattered the side window but whizzed past above his head. Still, he ducked his head.

★

Cat watched the monitor as the big rig raced across the parking lot at high speed, knocking cars out of the way, people diving out of the way, police shooting at it. But with no effect. It was an armored vehicle. The police on the ground had to shoot up at the tall truck; their bullets impacted the driver's door but did not penetrate. The bullets shattered the side window but the shooting angle up at the tall truck prevented a hit on the driver. There was only one way to kill the driver. She turned to Scott.

'Stay here with the girls.'

She ran out the door. The control room was on the east side of the stadium. The truck was headed for the west side. She had to run over a hundred yards faster than the truck was moving. She had to beat the truck to the arches. She ran.

'Allahu Akbar!' Abdul screamed in his ear. 'Get to the arch and detonate! They cannot hurt you! Allah protects the faithful! The believers!'

Bullets popped against the door. Saadi was scared shitless.

'Don't be scared, brother! I am with you! We will soon meet Allah together!'

Cat caught up with Beckeman and the other agents at the fifty-yard line. She passed them at the forty-five yard line. They were older and slower; she was young and still fast. She was born to run. All her running was for that moment in life. This was her moment. To do her part. For America.

'Turn!' Abdul screamed.

Saadi turned the wheel hard and aimed the truck directly at the arches.

★

442

Cat ran through the west exit just as the truck rounded the corner and headed directly at the arches. She pulled her weapon and ran to a point directly in the truck's path. To a police car parked in front of the arches. She jumped onto the hood and then onto the roof. At that height, she had the necessary shooting angle. The truck barreled directly at her. She saw the driver, and he saw her. She aimed the weapon.

Saadi saw the FBI agent named Peña directly in front of him, standing on a police car between him and the arches, aiming her gun at him. The windshield around him suddenly popped with holes . . . one, two, three . . . *shit, she can shoot!* . . . the fourth bullet hit him in the left shoulder and knocked him back against the seat. The pain was excruciating; it felt as if his arm had been ripped off. He fell sideways onto the seat. He let go of the wheel. His foot came off the accelerator.

Cat jumped off the police car just before the truck slammed into it. She rolled then vaulted to her feet. The impact caused the truck to veer right just enough to miss the arches. The truck plowed into cars parked in the lot until it came to a stop. Cat ran to the truck, jumped onto the running board, and opened the driver's door. She pointed her gun at the driver. He held one hand up. The other hand was bloody.

'Thank you,' he said.

'I shot you.'

'Now my brother cannot blame me for failing him.'

Beckeman and the other agents arrived.

'He's alive!'

Beckeman climbed into the cab and confronted the Arab.

'Did you start the detonation sequence?'

The Arab shook his head. 'No.'

'Where's the detonator?'

'Under the seat.'

Beckeman found the detonator box under the seat and pulled it out. Wires led from the box to the back of the truck. The lights on the box were unlit. He blew out a breath.

'Well, fuck.'

Abdul listened through the phone and watched the scene on his laptop. An outside security camera captured the moment. His brother had failed him. He had not detonated the bomb. He was such a disappointment.

Saadi Khalid knew his big brother was watching and listening. He knew what Abdul was thinking. He grabbed the cell phone off the floor with his right hand and yelled into it: 'I honored my pledge, Abdul!'

'Abdul's on the phone?' the male agent said.

'Yes.'

'Saadi?'

He heard his brother's voice over the phone. He put the phone on speaker.

'Yes, Abdul?'

'I knew I would have to drag you with me to meet Allah, but meet him you will, little brother.'

'Abdul Khalid,' the male agent said, 'your plot failed. Give it up.'

'Is that you, Agent Beckeman? When will you learn? We will never give up. And the plot has not failed. It has just begun.'

Abdul had planned for just such a possibility, that his little brother might wimp out at the moment of truth. Abdul pulled out his other cell phone and dialed a number.

★

444

The lights on the box lit up.

'Aw, shit,' Beckeman said.

The countdown had begun. Ten minutes.

'Abdul,' the Arab yelled into the phone, 'did you activate it remotely?'

'Yes, brother.'

'Stop it! I will die!'

'I will see you in heaven, little brother.'

'Can we cut the wires?'

'If you cut the wires, it will detonate immediately. I set it for ten minutes so I can finish my work here. I won, Beckeman. You lost.'

Beckeman thought for a moment, then muted the cell phone and spoke into his radio: 'Cut the feed to all exterior cameras.' He then yelled down to a local cop, 'Where's the nearest deep lake? With a bridge?'

'Mountain Creek Lake.'

'How far?'

'A few miles.'

'We've got a bomb in the back of this truck. Clear a path to the lake and get me there in nine minutes. I need a driver.'

The Arab pushed himself up. 'I will drive.'

'Why?'

'To stop this madness.'

Abdul's laptop went blank. He tried to access the other exterior cameras, but could not. The FBI had blinded him. Nice try, but it would not alter destiny.

'What are you going to do?' Cat asked Beckeman.

'We're going to drive the bomb into the lake.'

'But . . . you'll die.'

'I took an oath, Peña. So did you.' He turned to the Arab. 'Where's Abdul?'

445

'In the booth. In the big screen. He has a Plan B.'

'What is it?'

'Sarin.'

Beckeman turned back to her. 'Peña, evacuate the stadium.'

'A hundred thousand people? There's not enough time.'

'Then kill Abdul before he releases the sarin.'

Beckeman tossed the cell phone to her. She unmuted it.

'You still there, Abdul?'

'Yes.'

'I'm coming.'

'I'm waiting, Catalina.'

She disconnected Abdul, jumped down, and ran into the stadium.

Beckeman swung the door shut.

'Drive.'

The Arab backed the truck away from the wrecked cars then followed a police escort out of the stadium parking lot. Eight minutes until detonation.

Cat ran back through the stadium to the control booth.

'Scott, get the girls out of the stadium. Fast.'

'Why? Is there another bomb in the stadium?'

'No.' She lowered her voice. 'Abdul's got sarin in the stadium.'

Scott went to his daughters. He kissed them both. Louis and Carlos stood close.

'Boo, climb onto Carlos's back.'

She did.

'Pajamae, on Louis's back.'

She climbed on, but said, 'Judge Fenney?'

'Yes, honey.'

She pointed at a monitor.

'That's Abdul.'

On the monitor was a man with bleached blond hair and dark skin.

'Louis, Carlos, get them out of the stadium.'

'And then what?' Louis said.

'Run.'

'Guess we're starring in *Thelma and Louise*,' Beckeman said to the Arab.

'Who are Thelma and Louise?'

'Just drive. Faster.'

They followed the police cars south on Highway 360. The speedometer hit ninety. Five minutes till detonation.

Cat and Scott ran to the stairs that led down to the field. The players had left the field. It was halftime at the Super Bowl. Workers were prepping the field for the big halftime show. Beyoncé was scheduled to appear.

'Lower the elevator!' Cat yelled into her radio.

'Abdul's mine,' Scott said.

Abdul sat in the video booth above them. On his monitor, he saw the FBI agent named Catalina standing below waiting for the elevator to descend. The judge stood next to her. Why was he there? But it was of no concern. They were coming to him. He had to hurry; he had to get the halftime show started.

They exited the highway and turned east on Pioneer Parkway. Cop cars had blocked off all traffic. The road was theirs. Three minutes until detonation.

'Faster!'

★

Cat and Scott got into the elevator. It was a construction-type elevator, more like a big basket than an office elevator. A security guard jumped aboard and took them up.

Beckeman could see the lake just ahead. The police escort peeled off and stopped. They drove onto a low bridge over the lake. It was a two-lane bridge with concrete abutments lining both sides. It was not the Golden Gate Bridge or Lake Michigan; but it would do. On the other side of the lake, police cars with lights flashing had stopped oncoming traffic. The bridge was empty. Two minutes until detonation.

'Drive to the middle then veer off the bridge,' Beckeman said.

He had fought for freedom his entire adult life. He had always thought he would give his life for his country, but all soldiers say that. He knew now that he meant it. Some things are worth dying for. Like America. He braced himself—

—but the Arab braked the truck to a stop.

'What the hell are you doing?' Beckeman said.

One minute.

The Arab turned to him and said, 'Get out.'

'No. I have to make sure this truck goes into that lake.'

'I did this. Now I will stop this. Get out.'

Forty-five seconds until detonation. Beckeman opened the door and jumped to the ground. The Arab shifted the truck into gear and hit the accelerator hard.

Saadi Khalid got the truck going as fast as he could. When the detonator showed fifteen seconds until detonation, he veered and plowed through the abutment. The truck flew off the bridge; he felt as if he were suspended in time for a brief moment. He wished he were.

'Forgive me, Father.'

★

Beckeman watched the truck disappear into the water. Then the bridge shook beneath him, and he heard a muffled explosion. The middle of the bridge buckled and fell into the lake just as the big black cab blew out of the lake, hung in midair a moment, then fell back into the lake and disappeared.

Abdul put a DVD into the player. The fans expected Beyoncé. They would get death.

Cat and Scott rode the elevator up to the screen. Halfway up, the elevator stopped.

Abdul smiled at the judge and the FBI agent swinging in the air. Did they think he had not anticipated this? The FBI was always a step behind Abdul Khalid.

'We're climbing,' Cat said.

She opened the screen door and climbed up the side. Scott followed. The security guard said, 'Hell, no.'

The main lights inside the stadium went off for a brief moment then the video screen came alive. One hundred thousand fans were expecting to see Beyoncé. They did not.

Ehan Jamal had emigrated to the U.S. from Afghanistan five years before. He brought his wife and son. They had a good life in America. A safe life. Not like in Afghanistan. No daily suicide bombings, shootings, and murders. America was peaceful. But he could never forget what he had left. Consequently, when he saw the black ISIS flag appear on the big screen above the field, he did not scream or panic or run for the exits as the fans around them did. He knew it would be of no use. So he

449

simply held his wife's hand and his son's hand and waited to die. They were all going to die.

On the big screen and thirty-five hundred screens in the stadium Abdul Khalid's voice said, 'Fear not, Americans. You are all going to die today. In the name of Allah. The end of days is upon us. Upon you. You are the infidels, the unbelievers, the *kuffars*. Do not bother to run. You cannot escape your fate. America has waged war on Islam for thirteen years. Now Islam strikes back at America. Allahu Akbar!'

'Cut the live feed!' the FBI director yelled into the phone. The president buried his face in his hands.

There was a moment of silence as the video registered with the spectators. Then there was sheer panic. Parents grabbed their children and ran for the exits. Abdul smiled as Americans ran for their lives. Look how they fight each other to get out, to stay alive, to run from death. Oh, how they love life, just as we love death. He had brought death upon them. He had put terror into the hearts of the unbelievers. Now he would join them in death. He removed his shirt, grabbed his gun, and walked out of the screen room. A fist hit him square in the nose. He stumbled back and dropped the gun. The fist hit him again and again.

'You tried to rape my daughter!'

How did the judge get up?

Scott punched Abdul down the catwalk. With each punch his anger rose.

'You fucked with the wrong father!'

450

Scott hit this man he hated as hard as he possibly could. He fell over the railing, but held on with one hand. Scott reared back to hit him again, to send him ninety feet to his death—

'No, Scott!'

Cat's voice stopped him. He pulled back. Abdul swung one leg over the railing. He smiled.

'There's nowhere for you to go, Abdul,' Cat said.

'Yes, there is. To heaven.'

'It's over,' Scott said.

Abdul smiled. 'Do you not understand, Judge? It will never be over.'

'It's over for today.'

'No, it is not. Judge, do you think I do not have a Plan B?'

'We know about the sarin. Hard to execute Plan B hanging on this catwalk.'

'It is already executed. And you are too late. See you in heaven soon, Judge. Unless you can hold your breath for a very long time. Allahu Akbar!'

He let go of the railing and fell backwards to the stadium field below. He lay sprawled on the white star on the fifty-yard line.

FBI agents gathered on the playing field next to Abdul's body. They were down in a hole. Literally. The playing field sat fifty feet below the ground level. The fans were in full panic, running to the exits above. But one hundred thousand people could not get out that fast.

'This is the perfect venue for a sarin attack,' Cat said. 'The roof is closed, and sarin is heavier than air, so it'll sink down to that hole. To the fans in the stands.'

She looked up to the closed roof then grabbed her handheld radio.

'All FBI agents. The terrorists deployed sarin in the ventilation system. Whoever is closest to the HVAC system center, get there and find it before it detonates.'

A voice came back.

'Ace here. I'm on it, Cat.'

'Hurry! But be careful.'

'We're way past careful now.'

Special Agent Ace Smith ran up the flight of stairs to the HVAC control center. A security guard stood sentry at the door. Ace flashed his badge.

'Open up.'

The guard unlocked the door. They went inside.

'What's up?' the guard asked.

'We're looking for sarin.'

'What's it look like?'

'Liquid. Until it hits the environment. Then it turns to gas.'

'Where should we look?'

'Near the intake for the AC.'

'Over here.'

They searched the area around the AC intake but found nothing. They turned to leave—

'What's this?' the guard said.

He pointed at a black box the size of an equipment locker.

'It doesn't belong here?' Ace said.

'No. I've never seen it before.'

Ace put his handheld to his mouth. 'Cat, we found it.'

'It?' the guard said.

Cat came back. 'Ace, you've got to disarm it before it detonates.'

'Detonates?' the guard said.

'I know,' Ace said into the radio.

Ace knelt before the box. He tried the top, but it was locked.

'Get some tools,' he said.

The guard returned in a few minutes with a tool kit. Ace took a screwdriver and jammed it into the keyhole. He took a hammer and rapped the handle of the screwdriver. The lock popped; the top opened.

'Shit,' the guard said.

Inside the box were ten containers, perhaps two gallons each, and a detonator. Ace rummaged in the toolkit for wire cutters. He found a pair. He took a deep breath and reached into the box.

It was the last deep breath Ace Smith would ever take.

The detonator blew. The containers exploded. The liquid sprayed out and evaporated. The intake unit sucked the sarin into the ventilation system. The guard fell to the floor. His body twitched, and his eyes got wide; but his pupils got tiny. Ace had to warn Cat. He put his handheld to his mouth. But he fell to the floor. Ace Smith realized that he wouldn't spend the rest of his life bass fishing. The rest of his life was now.

'Cat, the sarin is out.'

'Ace!'

His radio went dead. They were riding in the elevator down to the playing field; the security guard found the override. She looked up to the large metal ventilation tubes wrapping around the top of the stadium. She could see the vents but not the sarin. But it was flowing out. Sarin is heavier than air so it would fall the three hundred feet to the stands below. It would kill everyone in the stadium.

Unless—

She thought. She was in the box. She needed to think outside the box. She needed to get out of the box. Out of the stadium. Inside was air saturated with sarin. Outside was fresh air where the sarin would disperse quickly. When they hit the ground, she grabbed the security guard.

'Take to me to the control center for the roof. Fast!'

They ran up the stairs from the field and to the control room. A technician sat behind a desk.

'Open the roof!' Cat said.

'I can't just open the roof.'

'Why not?'

'First thing is, it has to open very slowly or the change in pressure inside the stadium will shatter the glass panels at each end.'

'Good.'

'Why is that good?'

'Sarin is heavier than air. It's sinking from the ventilation ducts along the roof down to the people in the stands. The change in air pressure should suck the sarin out of the stadium.'

'You sure?' Scott said.

'No. But it's our only hope.'

'How will we know?

'If we don't die.'

'Did you say sarin?' the tech asked.

'Open the roof.'

'I need authorization.'

Cat pulled her gun and put it to his head. 'You're author-ized. Open the fucking roof. Fast!'

He pushed a lever slightly. The monitor showed the two roof doors slowly part. Cat rammed the lever open full.

'What are you doing?'

'Saving your life.'

They went back outside and watched the roof open. The two doors in the roof retracted quickly, one to the east, the other to the west. She could feel the air pressure change. She looked to the door panels above each end zone. They suddenly shattered; the glass blew inwards and onto the playing field below. Balloons and trash and papers and Cowboys banners were sucked out through the roof.

With the sarin.

An hour later, Scott and Cat, Louis and Carlos, and the girls wore sweat suits and dried their hair with towels. The girls were shivering in the cold. First responders in Hazmat suits had set up decontamination stations to be on the safe side. No one had displayed symptoms of sarin poisoning. They had been stripped of their clothes and washed down behind plastic cubicles.

'You were right, Peña.' Agent Beckeman had walked up. 'It was a diversion.'

'You're not dead.'

'Not today.'

'Ace is. Dead.'

'I heard. He was a soldier. He honored his oath. He died defending his country.'

Chapter 29

Monday, 8 February
The day after the Super Bowl

'A federal judge does not seek these cases; they come to him. He does not seek controversy; it comes to him. That is the nature of the job. The two cases on which I rule today came to me; both rulings will be controversial. When I accepted this job, no one said it would make me popular. No one was right. As a federal judge, you learn to live with a harsh fact of life: someone will always be mad at you. Because in every case, someone must lose. It is a lifetime of letting someone down. And so I shall today.'

United States District Judge A. Scott Fenney sat behind the bench in his courtroom on the fifteenth floor of the Earle Cabell Federal Building in downtown Dallas. Every available seat and space along the walls was occupied by interested parties, spectators, and members of the press. FBI Special Agent Catalina Peña occupied one such seat.

'In the matter of *The State of Texas, et al. versus The President of the United States of America, et al.*, some people will think my

456

ruling unfair. But it is not my job to determine what is fair, only what is legal. Fairness is a political matter; legality is a judicial matter. My ruling isn't about the president, politics, the election, immigration, or fairness.

'It's about the law.

'We live under the law. A judge enforces the law. Against murderers, drug traffickers, Islamic terrorists, and presidents. No one is above the law or exempt from the law or better than the law.

'No one.

'This case is about one thing: the president's authority under the Constitution. This Court does not pretend to know what is good social policy and what is bad social policy when it comes to immigration. Fortunately, that job is not my job. That job belongs to the Congress and the president. The president issued an executive order that the states contend changes the law unilaterally. The states sued the president in federal court. They asked the judicial branch to decide if the president exceeded his constitutional authority. That is my job.

'The Court's ruling will outrage some and encourage others. Some will cheer, others will jeer. Some will love it, some will hate it. And the people who love this ruling will hate the next one, and vice-versa. But public opinion has no relevance to the resolution of a judicial matter. The Constitution does not blow with the wind. It stands strong against all winds. It is the rock in the storm. It is the solid foundation of a solid nation. There is a reason why America is the land of the free and home of the brave, why America is the leader of the free world, why America is the most powerful, the richest, and the freest nation on God's earth.

'That reason is the Constitution.

'My duty is to the Constitution. My job is to defend the Constitution against the Congress and the president, because politics will always push the constitutional envelope. Our Founding Fathers were smart men who knew that establishing lifetime appointments for federal judges would remove politics from the bench. They knew that this was the best insurance to keep the people free from their government. Some people agree with the immigration law, some disagree. Some agree with the president's order, some disagree. But we all must – we *must* – agree with the Constitution. The Constitution created this country, and the Constitution preserves this country. Without our agreement, belief, obedience, respect, and honor of the Constitution, America would not be the nation it is today.

'The president's executive order does not agree with the Constitution. It violates the separation of powers doctrine and exceeds his authority under Article Two. The president does not like the law and cannot convince the Congress to change the law, so he changed the law himself. Perhaps the president's desires are correct social policy; but they are not the law. The president's executive order does not enforce the law; it contradicts the law. The president's executive order is not an exercise of prosecutorial discretion; it is an exercise of legislative power. The president cannot, under the guise of exercising enforcement discretion, rewrite the laws to accord with his political views. The president himself said his executive order changes the law. That he cannot do.

'If the president possessed the power to make the law as well as to enforce the law, that power would make him a king. Our Founding Fathers decided America would not have a king. The president is the most powerful person on the planet, but he is not a king. He is subject to the law. To the Constitution.

'Therefore, the Court rules that the president's executive order exceeded the authority granted to the office of the president in Article Two of the Constitution. The order is hereby declared null and void. All Executive Branch agencies and officers thereof are hereby enjoined from implementing the president's executive order.'

Half of the spectators stood and applauded; half booed and stormed out. Half had won; half had lost. Or so they seemed to think. Scott removed his glasses and looked for Cat; he saw only her backside as she walked out of the courtroom.

'Judge, you ready for the defendants?' Louis whispered.

Scott nodded. Louis went to the door leading to the holding cell and returned with the imam and his co-defendants. They remained handcuffed, but not shackled; they no longer wore jail jumpsuits, but their Muslim attire. Street clothes. Where they would soon be. Scott gave them time to find their seats and the spectators to settle again. He put on his glasses.

'In the matter of *The United States of America versus Omar al Mustafa et al.*, I address Omar al Mustafa, also known as Omar Mansour, born in America and blessed to live in America. Mr. Mustafa, you should hit your knees and thank God every day of your life to have been born in America. To be an American citizen. To enjoy the freedoms the Constitution granted to us and protects for us. To live in safety and security that so many people in this world do not enjoy.

'But you don't.

'You hit your knees and pray for the destruction of America. And in America, you are free to do so. You are free to speak against America.

'As a federal judge, I must protect you from prosecution for exercising your right of free speech and freedom of religion. So I must release you from custody today.'

'Allahu Akbar!' the imam shouted.

'Mr. Mustafa, you're not guilty, but you're not innocent. The legal definition of innocence is the absence of guilt. You are innocent of the crimes for which you were indicted, so this court dismisses those charges against you. But you are guilty of crimes against humanity. You feel no guilt, but you are not absent of guilt. You walk free today, but life will not dismiss those charges against you. Life has its own system of justice. One day, Mr. Mustafa, life will convict you and punish you for your crimes. And the punishment will be severe.

'You hate this country. I wish you would just leave. But you won't. I wish I could throw you out of this country. But I can't. But I can throw you out of this courtroom. Omar al Mustafa, get the hell out of my courtroom.'

Omar al Mustafa stood and held his handcuffed hands out to the federal marshal. He could not restrain a grin. The marshal unlocked the cuffs and freed him; other marshals freed the others. He turned to his disciples.

'Come.'

Omar led them down the center aisle of the courtroom like the Prophet leading the people to Mecca. He pushed the double doors open, rode the elevator down, and marched through the foyer of the courthouse and out the front doors. On the steps the media had gathered *en masse*. He stood triumphantly before the cameras and microphones.

'Allahu Akbar! Praise Allah!'

I defeated America!

I won!

Now I will show my power to America!

Now I will bring America to its knees!

Now I will—

'Omar al Mustafa, you're under arrest.'

He looked down as handcuffs were slapped around his left wrist and up to Agent Beckeman's face. The agent pulled his left arm behind his back and cuffed his right wrist.

★

460

'You have the right to remain silent. Anything you say can and will be used against you in a court of law. You have the right to an attorney and to have him present with you while you're being questioned. If you cannot afford an attorney, one will be appointed to represent you before you are questioned.'

'Terrorism?' Mustafa said.

'Taxes,' Beckeman said. 'Your heart might be in Syria with your Muslim brothers, but you live in America. You've got to pay your taxes, Omar.'

Al Capone had failed to pay income taxes on his bootlegging income. The FBI could never nail him on the bootlegging, but he died of syphilis in prison for evading taxes. FBI Special Agent Eric Beckeman could only hope the same fate awaited Omar al Mustafa.

'Allahu Akbar, motherfucker.'

Farooq Zaman, twenty-four, aka Abdul jabbar Khalid aka Sam Taylor, and Farique Zaman, twenty-two, aka Saadi Khalid aka Al A. Hu, were born in Pakistan to Ghamid Zaman, a doctor, and Dara Zaman, a nurse. By all accounts they were happy, non-radicalized Muslim boys. Ghamid was killed in an errant drone strike in their village. The U.S. government relocated the Zaman family to Minneapolis where there was an established Muslim community. They became naturalized citizens. Farooq and Farique enrolled in the University of Minnesota. Farooq earned a degree in structural engineering; Farique had finished his second year when the brothers moved to Dallas to blow up Cowboys Stadium. They assumed false identities and got jobs, Farooq as a video technician at the stadium and Farique as a driver with the beer distributor. They infiltrated the mosque, the perfect place to meet patsies for their plot – the Siddiqui brothers. They bought ammonium nitrate all across the Farm Belt with ISIS money, just a click away on the

Internet. With the expertise of Zaheed, ISIS's chief bomb maker, Abdul built a bomb and devised a brilliant plot. It almost worked. Farooq's body was returned to his mother in Minnesota. There was nothing left of Farique to return. Their mother was devastated. She knew nothing of the plot. She loved America.

Lone wolves are the hardest terrorists to stop. By the grace of God, we stopped them. This time. But maybe not next time. And Special Agent Eric Beckeman knew the harsh truth.

There will always be a next time.

Epilogue

Friday, 12 February
5 days after the Super Bowl

'Judge Fenney is an extremist judge who clearly has an anti-immigrant and more particularly, an anti-Latino judicial agenda. Mexicans are angry. The president is angry. He intends to appeal his hateful ruling to the court of appeals, and if necessary, to the Supreme Court.'

The Dallas newspaper lay open to the presidential spokesperson's quote. This time, it made the front page. Monday he was a hero; by Friday he was an extremist. Scott had the landline phone to his ear.

'You ruled against my parents,' Cat said.

'I ruled against the president.'

'You sentenced them to a life in fear. A life lived in the shadows. I let you inside me, and this is what you do to me?'

'I didn't do it to you.'

'You did it to them. They haven't stopped crying since you ruled.'

463

'I'm sorry.'

'Are you? You know what my mother said? "Why did he do this to us? I thought he liked us."'

'I do like your parents. But this isn't about them. It's about the law. The law isn't about politics. It's about process. About following the Constitution. About—'

'I don't give a damn about politics or process, only about my parents.'

'All I did was rule on the president's authority.'

'All you did was sign my parents' deportation order.'

'Cat, you've got to separate what your parents want from what the law allows.'

'I can't. Not when it comes to my parents. They love America. Mustafa and his men hate America. My parents want to *be* Americans. They want to *kill* Americans. But they get to stay, and my parents have to leave. That's not fair.'

'No, it's not. But it's the law.'

'Fuck the law.'

At ten, the chief law enforcement officer in America called.

'I'm glad you're not dead, Scott.'

'Thanks, Mac.'

'Your daughter is a hero.'

'She is.'

'I owe you, Scott. I won't forget it.'

'Mac, don't deport Agent Peña's parents.'

'What? Oh, I'm over that case. We'll win at appeals. Or at the Supreme Court. Roberts is a pushover, worried about what history will think of him. It won't. It won't think of any of us. This time will go down in history as the age of terror and evil.' He exhaled into the phone. 'Hell, maybe it is the end of days.'

★

464

At noon, Scott addressed a convicted felon in open court.

'Dennis Macklin, your sentence is hereby probated for good time and good deeds. You're a good man, Dennis. And you did good. Thank you.'

'Thank you, Judge. I'm very sorry for what I did. I will pay those ten thousand employees every penny they lost because of me. I will make things right. For my father. For me. And for you.'

At four, Bobby said, 'Guess what?'

'The imam beheaded himself.'

'No such luck. The NFL decided that the second half of the Super Bowl will be played in two weeks at an undisclosed stadium before no spectators and no media except for television cameras.'

'The world we live in.'

'Sid Greenberg produced the damning document. They settled.'

'Good.'

'And I'm pregnant . . . we're pregnant . . . Karen's pregnant.'

'Hey, congratulations.'

Everyone hugged Bobby and Karen.

'You'll work from home?' Scott said.

'Of course.'

They had gathered for a staff meeting. Once they settled back into their places, Scott said, 'So, what do we have on the docket next week?'

'I hope it's a patent case,' Carlos said. 'I love patent cases.'

'Something really boring,' Karen said.

'Amen,' Louis said.

'Oh, well . . .' Bobby said.

At four-thirty, Cat Peña sat in her cubicle at FBI headquarters. Her cell phone rang; she knew who it was without looking, but she looked anyway: *Scott.* She started to answer, but froze.

465

Her thumb hovered over the phone for three more rings, then she set the phone down. It was over.

Scott started to leave a message but decided against it. He hung up the phone and removed his glasses. He knew it was over. He would live his life alone. He would never again have a wife. He had been given a lifetime appointment to the federal bench and to a life lived alone. To a lifetime of letting people down.

At five, Scott sat in the stands in the Highland Park Middle School gymnasium with one daughter while his other daughter waited to be introduced with the starting lineup. He held Boo's hand. He might never let it go. The public address system crackled to life. The announcer introduced the team with great enthusiasm.

'Now, introducing your Highland Park Middle School Raiders. At five feet seven, starting at center, number two, Madison Richley!'

The crowd applauded politely.

'At five feet three, starting at forward, number eight, Emily Hunt!'

More polite applause.

'At five feet four, starting at forward, number thirty-three, Abigail Jacobson!'

Less polite applause.

'At five feet two, starting at guard, number sixteen, Claire Wexler!'

Barely enough applause to be polite.

'And now, at five feet five, starting at point guard, number twenty-three, our very own American hero, Pajamae Jones-Fenney!'

The crowd exploded from their seats. Thunderous applause filled the gym. Scott and Boo glanced around then stood among other white people standing and applauding a black girl. His girl. Her sister. Pajamae stood on the court and cried. Her teammates hugged her and cried. The principal hugged

466

her and cried. Boo cried. Scott cried. A tall bald black man in a sharp suit walked onto the court holding a basketball with one hand. He looked familiar. He went to Pajamae and held the basketball and a pen out to her. Pajamae stared at the man and looked as if she might faint. She signed the basketball and gave it back to him. He held it high in the air. The applause grew louder. And Scott recognized the man: Michael Jordan.

Pajamae Jones-Fenney would never again be ignored off the court.

'We're very sad,' Boo said.

Pajamae nodded. They were tucked into bed. Scott had told them about his immigration ruling, its effect on Cat's parents, and her reaction.

'We understand,' Boo said. 'You did your job as a judge. But it still hurts.'

'It does.'

But he had his girls home. They were no longer innocent. Their innocence had been taken when they were taken. They would never be the same. Neither would he.

'We'll never leave you, A. Scott.'

'Yes, you will. You will and you must. One day you will leave for college. One day you will live your life with a man you love. You will marry and have children. I want you to. I want you to be happy. Because I love you.'

'But you'll be alone.'

'That's my life, Boo. The day I married your mother, I made it my life to be alone. I will never be free of her, even if she's not with me. I took a vow. Till death do us part.'

Hector Calderon had not heard back from José and Gilberto. He knew their fate. The Arabs had killed them, and the Americans had killed the Arabs. Life involved so much death.

467

And there would be more death.

He lay in bed holding his woman. They had just had sex. Never had he enjoyed sex so much. Never had he enjoyed a woman so much. Never had he had such a beautiful woman in his life. Never had he killed a woman in his bed.

'I am very sorry, Rebecca.'

'For what, Hector?'

'For this.'

He pushed the dagger through her skin and under her ribcage and deep into her heart. Her body clenched and then relaxed. She accepted her fate. We all must accept our fate. It broke his heart to kill her. But she knew too much.

'Hold me, Hector.'

'Of course.'

Rebecca Fenney felt life leaving her. She was thirty-seven years old and still remarkably beautiful. She had sold her beauty for a Highland Park mansion then a Galveston beach house and finally this Cancun villa. She sold her beauty to men, men who gave her the life she wanted. Now this man would take her life.

She knew this day would come.

She had ruined one man's life and taken another's. Sooner or later, life would turn on her. Life would take its revenge. Life would have its way with Rebecca Fenney. Today was that day.

So she did not fight death. She accepted death just as she had lived life. With no guilt. She had left Scott for Trey and killed Trey when he threatened to leave her; she was innocent on both counts. But she would be punished just the same. Life had its own justice system. Life had given her a death sentence. It was her destiny from the day she won her first beauty pageant. When she learned what men would do to hold her beauty in their arms. She always knew her life would end this way. In the arms of a man and at the hands of a man.

468

About the Author

Born and educated in Texas, Mark Gimenez attended law school at Notre Dame, Indiana, and practised with a large Dallas law firm. He has two sons.